Taking a deep breath t̶ ̶ ̶ ̶ ̶ ̶ ̶ her nerves, Suz̶ ̶ ̶ ̶ ̶ ̶ ̶ ̶ ̶ ̶en, braced he̶ ̶ ̶ ̶ ̶ ̶ ̶ ̶ ̶in.

The smell of du̶ ̶ ̶ ̶ ̶ ̶ ̶ ̶ ̶ ̶ ̶ ̶ ̶ the second she enter̶ ̶ ̶ ̶ ̶ ̶oor close behind her as she looke̶ ̶ ̶und.

"Hello? Is anyone here?" Suzy called out.

Only the echo of her own voice answered her.

Had she gotten the address wrong? Was the kidnapper jerking her around, sending her to the wrong place to show her that he was holding all the cards and that she had none?

But she *did* hold a card, Suzy silently insisted. She dug in, holding her ground and giving it one more try.

"Look, I came here just like you told me to. Now stop playing games and show yourself, damn it!" she demanded.

There was still no answer, but she couldn't shake the feeling that she was being watched. What was this creep's game?

A WIDOW'S GUILTY SECRET

BY
MARIE FERRARELLA

MILLS & BOON

First published in Great Britain 2013
by Mills & Boon, an imprint of Harlequin (UK) Limited,
Eton House, 18-24 Paradise Road, Richmond, Surrey TW9 1SR

© Harlequin Books S.A. 2013

Special thanks and acknowledgement to Marie Ferrarella for her contribution to the VENGEANCE IN TEXAS miniseries.

ISBN: 978 0 263 90354 6
ebook ISBN: 978 1 472 00710 0

46-0413

n: is made from wood grown in sustainable forests. The ... enewable and ... nable forests. The ... l environmental

Marie Ferrarella, a *USA TODAY* bestselling and RITA® Award-winning author, has written more than two hundred books for Mills & Boon, some under the name Marie Nicole. Her romances are beloved by fans worldwide. Visit her website, www.marieferrarella.com.

To Patience Bloom,
For constantly making this fun, not work.

Prologue

Mabel Smith knew something was wrong the moment she walked into the house.

She could *feel* it.

Feel it despite the fact that there were no signs of a struggle and nothing out of place.

The longer she stayed, the more convinced she became that she was right.

As was her custom, the petite, pleasantly plump housekeeper had let herself into Professor Melinda Grayson's modern, two-story house with her own key. It was a copy of the master key, awarded to her amid much fanfare. She viewed the key as a status symbol, a testimony to her character.

Her employer, Melinda Grayson, did not trust easily, holding the people she dealt with suspect until they proved themselves worthy in her eyes. As someone who cleaned the woman's house and perforce was given access to every corner of it, she'd been watched with an eagle eye for the better part of two years.

At the beginning of Mabel's third year of service, the renowned, somewhat controversial and eccentric sociology professor dramatically bestowed her with a copy of the house key, making Mabel literally *swear* that she would never allow anyone else even to hold it, much less use it. It was a well-known fact that Professor Grayson guarded her own privacy as zealously as she delved into everyone else's when she was doing research for one of her highly contentious books.

Entering the house that she'd cleaned from top to bottom once a week, Mabel had expected to find the professor somewhere on the premises. The woman's car, a sky-blue vintage 1957 Chevy Impala, one of her few extravagances, was parked in the driveway. Since that was her only mode of transportation to and from Darby, the college where Dr. Grayson taught, Mabel had assumed that the woman was in the house somewhere, possibly working on a paper or getting lectures ready for the new, upcoming academic year.

But when she called out her greeting, the housekeeper received no answer.

That in itself was no cause for concern. More often than not, the professor was either lost in thought or uncommunicative. However, she always made an appearance within a few minutes of Mabel's entry, just to make certain that the woman had come alone and hadn't brought someone with her to help with the work.

Not that she ever did. Dr. Grayson had made it abundantly clear that she did not care to have any uninvited strangers walking across her floors, nor would she tolerate it.

"Something is wrong," Mabel said to herself, speaking loudly enough for someone else to hear—had there *been* someone else in the room to hear, which apparently there was not.

Feeling progressively ill at ease with the situation and possessing an extremely healthy and active imagination, Mabel still forced herself to clean the house, hoping she was just being unduly concerned.

When there still appeared to be no sign of the professor, she felt she had no choice but to place a call to the local police.

Private creature or not, she knew the professor would have wanted her to call them.

He didn't hear the phone ring at first.

Didn't realize the next few minutes would upend his life.

Oil baron Gabe Dawson was in Malaysia on important business, far away from Vengeance, Texas. He finally picked up the hotel phone.

"Gabe. You need to come home. Now. It's Melinda," his assistant said.

It was only when he heard his ex's name that he froze. Gabe stopped and sat on the bed, braced for the news.

"She was kidnapped." His assistant gave him some details, but there was little information. Just that someone had made her disappear.

Along with the shock, a wave of nostalgia came over him and he allowed himself to drift back and remember. Remember how things used to be with Melinda. In the beginning. Back when they had been just two overachieving graduate students, wildly in love and bound and determined to leave their marks on the world.

Melinda had been even more focused on that than he'd been. She'd been resolute about making a name for herself—her *own* name—as if she wanted everyone she had ever known from birth to know that this was what Melinda Grayson had become. It was important to her, to the exclusion of everything else.

Eventually, even he had found himself excluded, standing on the outside of her world.

In hindsight, he supposed they began growing apart almost from the very moment they took their vows before a justice of the peace ten years ago. Melinda started pointing her finger at what she perceived were social injustices, while he, with his well-honed business acumen, became a recognized leader in his field, and exceedingly wealthy to boot.

With his bank accounts totaling in the billions, he, in effect, found himself becoming the enemy against whom Melinda was so profoundly railing.

Looking back, he accepted that their divorce was inevitable.

But in the beginning, ah, the beginning, there had been some really good times. Excellent times.

"What else can you tell me?" Gabe asked.

"It is suspected that the professor was kidnapped from her home. You're the closest to immediate family that can be located. The Dean of Darby College has put in a plea that the kidnappers get in contact with him and make their demands known."

"Get me on the next flight," Gabe said. *"I'm her family,"* he emphasized. He was aware that Melinda had siblings, but she never talked about them and he never prodded her. The estrangement, he'd gathered, went way back.

Melinda had been his first love. Though they became as different as fire and ice, he'd never loved anyone as much as he had loved her. Most likely, he never would.

If something had happened to Melinda, then he wanted to help get her back. God knew, if money was the issue, it wouldn't be for long. He had more money than he could possibly spend in a lifetime. *Two* lifetimes.

Gabe started toward the winding staircase. He needed to pack.

Wouldn't it be ironic if the very money that Melinda had once turned her nose up at would come to her rescue?

He didn't know if that would come under the heading of poetic justice or not but it would certainly point to the fact that God had an incredibly sardonic sense of humor.

Chapter 1

Where *was* he?

Frustrated, Suzy Burris dropped the curtain she'd pushed back from the living room window and sighed loudly. Of all the evenings for Peter to be late getting home, he had to pick this one.

Probably seeing one of his women, she thought angrily.

And if she asked him about it, he'd look at her with that engaging smile of his and tell her he was busy with official business. "County sheriff business," he'd clarify, and then he'd tell her that he wasn't at liberty to share that "business" with her. Because she had "no need to know."

Bull.

That's all it was. Pure and simple *bull.* Like all the other times.

And she was tired of it.

Tired of the lies, tired of going through the motions and pretending that everything was all right, when it wasn't.

And it hadn't been for a long, long time.

Suzy could feel her whole body vibrating with impatience. She'd finally, *finally* made up her mind that despite the beautiful two-month-old baby boy mercifully asleep now in the nursery, her marriage to Peter was not about to recover. It had been on life support for a long time now and it was currently in its very last death throes. And while it really bothered her that she'd never loved him the way a wife was supposed to love a husband, there was nothing she could do to change the situation.

Like an epiphany, it had suddenly become crystal clear to her this morning that they, she and Peter, *both* needed to move on.

Suzy wanted a divorce and although he'd mentioned nothing along those lines himself, she was fairly convinced that her husband wanted it, too.

Why else had Peter been tomcatting around like that, turning to other women when she was right there, at home?

It had been hard for her, with her emotional state less than rock solid thanks to what having given birth had done to her hormones. But she'd had to admit to herself that there was no hope for them. No light at the end of the tunnel.

Just more tunnel.

The baby was supposed to have been that light, and his conception and subsequent birth clearly was a tactic that had misfired.

The baby had been a mistake.

Not that she didn't love Andy more than she'd ever thought humanly possible, but as far as his being the miracle that would heal and save their marriage, well, that just wasn't going to happen.

Suzy realized that she was back at the living room window, lifting the curtain and staring off into the darkness.

She wanted this to be over with, wanted it behind her.

Breaking her own rule, she'd even tried to call Peter a couple of times, to no avail. The phone had gone to voice mail immediately each time.

He had to be with a woman.

When Peter was on the job as the county's sheriff, he never shut off his phone. He'd told her that was because he never knew who might be trying to reach him. So if he *wasn't* with a woman, why was it off now?

Her frustration mounted as she continued to scan the darkness for some sign that he was finally approaching the driveway.

What was all this drama and mystery about? Or was she reading into things because her impatience insisted on steadily rising with each passing minute?

Given a choice, she wanted to avoid scenes like this morning at breakfast. Despite getting very little sleep the night before because Andy kept fussing, she'd done her best to give patching things up between Peter and her one more try this morning. She'd made Peter breakfast—waffles with eggs and sausages, his favorite—and tried to get some sort of a conversation going.

But she might as well have been trying to program a robot. The words she all but wound up pulling out of her husband had been stilted, cold, as if they were two strangers who'd just met and *hadn't* clicked, the way they had at that glitzy Dallas nightclub where she'd first met him.

She had come to socialize that night and Peter had been working private security at the club. The second their eyes met, the attraction had been instant and intense.

The trouble was, that strong physical attraction had never deepened, at least, not for her. At the time, she'd thought that it had for him, that Peter loved her. When he'd asked her to marry him, she'd accepted because she'd hoped that her own feelings would grow somewhere along the line and turn into the kind of love that was the foundation of every strong marriage.

She'd said "I do" praying that would somehow trigger the everlasting love she'd secretly always dreamed about.

She'd wanted the perfect fairy tale, happily-ever-after marriage.

But it never happened.

Although Pete seemed to love her, and he'd never laid a hand on her or physically mistreated her, Suzy knew deep down in her heart that she needed more to lay the foundations for a lasting relationship.

She also felt as if Peter was keeping things from her. Not work-related things but just *things*. He seemed to lead a secret life apart from the one he shared with her. It got to the point where she felt as if she were dealing with a photograph of a man and the actual three-dimensional man was out of reach.

On the surface, Peter was friendly, outgoing, gregarious, but after several years of marriage, she still knew very little about him. And *no* details about his childhood.

What husband keeps his past from his wife? What was it that Peter was hiding?

Or was she just being completely paranoid?

Just because you're paranoid doesn't mean that there isn't someone after you.

She supposed that she'd been hoping for some sort of last-minute breakthrough with this baby, and that was why, when Peter, completely out of the blue, had suggested having a baby, she'd agreed.

It had been an irresponsible way to go about patching up their relationship. *First* you had a stable home with two people who loved each other, and *then* you brought a baby into the equation. You didn't do it the other way around. You didn't just make a baby, and then hope everything turned out for the best.

Suzy admitted to herself that she'd been trying to create the exact opposite of what she'd grown up with: two alcoholic parents who were either drunk and passed out on any available flat or semi-flat surface, or going at one another with anything they could get their hands on when they were sober.

And whatever verbal and physical blows they threw that *didn't* land on each other, found their target in her—or her younger sister, Lori.

All she'd ever wanted was to be loved and to have someone to lean on. Someone who could be her protector if the occasion arose.

Or at least, that was what she thought she wanted when she'd married Peter. Only recently she realized she wanted more. She wanted someone to talk to. Someone who *really* talked to her as well. In essence, she wanted someone to share a life with.

That wasn't Peter.

"Come on, Peter. Come home. I need to get this over with before I lose my nerve," she pleaded.

Only the darkness heard her.

At thirty-eight, Nick Jeffries felt he'd seen it all—and for the most part, he'd left it behind him. As a former fifteen-year veteran detective on the Houston police force, he'd accepted a position on Vengeance's police force thinking that it would be a walk in the park and that chilling, stomach-turning homicides were a thing of the past. Vengeance, Texas, was one of those sleepy, picturesque little towns people dreamed about while trapped in a rat race, struggling to stay abreast of the bills, the tax man and soul-numbing, time-sapping boredom.

Apparently that wasn't the case anymore, Nick thought, looking down at the gruesome discovery made earlier that day by some enterprising geology graduate students. The students had initially been assigned to dig up and catalog several mineral specimens on the private land just on the outskirts of Darby College.

Instead, what they'd found were three male bodies buried in shallow graves and located fairly close to one another.

"Three for the price of one, huh?" Nick murmured sardonically.

The flippant comment was intended for the young man he'd been partnered with but when he looked up, he saw that the tall, baby-faced detective had done a quick about-face and was currently—and miserably—throwing up his breakfast behind the nearest tree.

"That's okay, Juarez," Nick assured the younger

man, raising his voice so that it carried. "I did the same thing when I saw my first dead body."

It actually wasn't true. For the most part, Nick Jeffries had practically been born unshakeable, but he thought it might give the young detective a measure of comfort to know that he wasn't alone or unique in his misery.

Shaking his head, Nick looked down at the three dead bodies that had been lifted from their graves.

Three separate, shallow graves—not one. Did that mean there were three separate killers, or just one with an odd reverence for the sanctity of death that had made him dig the multiple graves rather than just toss the bodies one on top of another?

And why these particular three people? Was it just convenience? The luck of the draw?

He highly doubted it.

What did these three have in common with each other, other than being buried out here just off the college campus? Did they all die at the same time, or did they meet their respective ends at different times by the same hand?

He supposed at least part of the latter question would be answered by the medical examiner after the autopsies were performed.

He wondered how long *that* would take and if

they even *had* a medical examiner around here. If not, they were going to have to find one, fast.

There were times when he really missed being in a city like Houston.

"So much for this being a sleepy little college town," Nick said, talking to Juarez as if the man had rejoined him instead of still heaving up his by now meager stomach contents behind a tree. "And let me tell you, if you thought that the media seemed frenzied and out of control when they converged here, asking questions about that Grayson woman's kidnapping, wait'll you see what happens when they get wind of this triple homicide," he predicted.

With a handkerchief held close to his mouth in case he wasn't quite finished throwing up what was left of his insides, Jason Juarez, his eyes watering, made his way back to his partner.

When he looked at Nick, his eyes appeared to be bloodshot, definitely the worse for wear.

Nick was tempted to tell him to go home, but that wouldn't solve anything. The kid needed to tough it out, Nick thought. Still, he couldn't help feeling sorry for him.

"You think that this is a triple homicide?" Juarez asked him.

It was obvious that the young detective was deliberately avoiding looking down at the uncovered bodies, which had already been on their way to becoming lunch a la carte for all the local rodents, wild animals and insects in the area.

Had he *ever* been this naive? Nick wondered. Somehow, he didn't think so.

"Well, there are three bodies buried pretty close to one another," he said to Juarez, doing his best not to let his impatience show, "and they're definitely dead, so, logically speaking, I'd say yes, there's a pretty good possibility that we're looking at a triple homicide. But if you're asking me if I think that the same person killed all three victims, that's something we're going to have to find—"

Nick abruptly stopped talking and he suddenly squatted down beside the body that was nearest to him. With an unreadable expression on his face, he gave the body a very slow once-over.

The face was not so destroyed that it prevented him from making an identification. "Correct me if I'm wrong, but isn't this the county sheriff, Peter Burris?" If that were the case, then this just took on a whole new spectrum of ramifications.

Juarez paled slightly beneath his peaked complexion. "Are you asking me to look closer?" he asked warily.

Nick rolled his eyes. "That might be helpful, yeah," he retorted.

One of the uniformed policemen, older by a couple of decades than the queasy detective, took pity on Juarez—who looked as if he wanted to bolt for the trees again—and made his way over to the body in question.

Looking at what was left of the man on the ground, the officer nodded, confirming Nick's query.

"It's the sheriff all right." Somewhat intrigued rather than repulsed, the policeman squinted and took a closer look at the other two bodies that had been unearthed at the same time. Genuine surprise registered on his leathery face. "And that looks like Senator Merris. Saw him at a fund-raiser once. I was part of the security detail." His own words seemed to hit him and he appeared properly stunned. "Holy cow, this is a real live senator."

"Not quite," Nick pointed out.

"Yeah," the policeman agreed. "There's that." He looked up at Nick, the magnitude of the situation finally hitting him. "This is big."

Rather than comment on what seemed to be

very obvious—and since Juarez was still struggling even to *glance* down, Nick directed the officer's attention to the third body. "You know him?"

The older man shuffled closer and looked at the last dead man intently for several seconds. He frowned, frustrated.

"He seems familiar, but—" he shook his head helplessly. "Sorry, can't place him."

Striking out, Nick looked pointedly at Juarez. "How about you?"

Unable to get around his duty any longer, Juarez was forced to take a look. Actually, it was more like taking a fleeting glance in the body's direction. Exhaling the breath he'd been holding, Juarez shook his dark head adamantly.

"No, I don't know him," he confirmed with relief.

But the policeman wasn't through as he continued to study the only unidentified man. Circling the body, he looked at the face from every angle.

Finally, he said, "I think he used to live around here before he went off to California—or maybe it was some other place out West." He glanced up at Nick. "He had family here if it's the guy I'm thinking of. I can ask around," he offered.

"You do that," Nick turned the offer into an instruction.

Then he turned to his boy partner. Juarez's face still lacked color. He made up his mind that come tomorrow, if things didn't change, he was working this case solo. Juarez's wife was due soon with their first child. Maybe the younger detective could take some time off and be of some use to her.

But that still left today. "You up to doing a little traveling?" he asked.

Rather than immediately answering, Juarez asked uneasily, "To where?"

"I think we need to inform the sheriff's wife that she just became his widow."

In his experience, approximately 50 percent of the men and women who were killed died at the hands of their spouse. Whether this was the case in Burris's murder remained to be seen. The sooner he ruled out the sheriff's other half, the sooner he could move on and maybe even find out exactly who was responsible for this modern-day bloodbath in a sleepy town.

He scanned what might or might not have been the actual crime scene. Things would never be the same.

Not for a lot of people.

* * *

"Did you forget your key?" Suzy called out as she yanked open the front door in response to the ringing doorbell.

It wouldn't have been the first time that Peter had forgotten his house key. But if everything went right, it would be one of the last, she thought.

Suzy did her best to contain the nervous anticipation that all but vibrated through her. She'd been up for most of the night, not because of the baby, but because she kept hearing Peter come through the door.

Each and every time it just turned out to be her imagination, hard at work. What that meant, she decided, was that she *really* wanted to get this divorce matter out and on its way.

Throwing open the front door, she found herself on the receiving end of a surprise. And not the pleasant kind, she couldn't help thinking.

Suzy instinctively took a step back.

Her hand on the doorknob, she started to close the door again, intent on locking out the strangers on her doorstep.

The sheriff's wife was quick, but Nick was quicker. He blocked her motion with his hand, at the same time putting his foot over the sill to keep the door from closing.

"We need to talk with you, Mrs. Burris," Nick said as his tongue-tied partner appeared somewhat startled by her behavior and all too ready to retreat.

Nick watched as suspicion came and then went from the pretty blonde's cornflower-blue eyes. She appeared to regard them both in silence for a moment, then said in a hushed tone, "You know my name. Why is it you know my name?"

She had a bad feeling about this—and it was escalating by the moment as she waited for an answer. She looked from one man to the other, then back at the older detective. Waiting.

"Would you mind if we stepped inside, Mrs. Burris?" Nick suggested, gesturing into her house. He was surprised when she remained planted before him. "This isn't the kind of thing a person likes to hear while standing in the doorway of her house."

Suzy raised her chin, thinking herself already prepared for the worst. "Sitting on the sofa isn't going to change whatever it is that you have to say to me, Detective…" She deliberately let her voice trail off, waiting for the tall, strikingly handsome dark-haired man to fill in the blank.

"Jeffries," he told her, then nodded toward Juarez. "And this is Detective Juarez," he added before going back to what she'd said. "No, it won't," Nick readily agreed. "But it just might help you to cushion the shock—no pun intended," he interjected when his own words played themselves back in his head. He didn't want her to think he was being flip at her expense.

Cushion the shock. Just how great a shock, she wondered. Suzy felt oddly numb, yet still somehow in control. Or so she told herself.

"Is he hurt?" she asked in a voice so quiet, it was almost a whisper. "Is my husband hurt?" she amended when neither man standing on her doorstep answered her.

"It's worse than that, ma'am," Nick told her, trying to be as gentle as possible.

Suzy felt her stomach lurch, then turn over. She struggled to pull herself together. She could handle this, she told herself. Whatever the somber-looking detective in the dark suit had to tell her, she could handle it. She could handle anything. She *had* to. She had practically a newborn depending on her. She had to remember that.

"May I see some identification, please?" she requested, holding whatever the older detective was about to say to her at bay.

Juarez fumbled for his wallet, searching his pockets, while Nick took his out and flipped it open to display his badge and ID.

Suzy could feel panic well up inside her. She barely glanced at the man's wallet, but his image registered.

"Worse than hurt," she heard herself repeating as she raised her eyes to the man's face. That could only mean one thing. Her lips felt frozen as she asked, "Is my husband dead, Detective Jeffries?"

Nick felt a wave of pity stirring. "I'm sorry to have to tell you that, Mrs. Burris, but yes, I'm afraid he is."

Every inch of skin on her body alternated between extreme heat and extreme cold.

Dead.

Peter's dead.

She waited for the wave of sorrow, of devastation to hit. But it didn't. In its place, instead, was guilt. Guilt that she didn't feel grief over his death, other than the kind of grief she might have experienced after hearing of a neighbor's death.

What kind of a person *was* she? Suzy silently demanded.

"You were right," Suzy said to the older detective, her voice sounding rather tinny to her ears as the words seemed to echo in her head.

"Right about what?" Nick asked, puzzled as he looked at her.

It was getting hard for her to breathe. "About this being easier to take on a sofa."

It was the last thing Suzy remembered saying before the bright, sunny world filtering in through her doorway went completely black.

Chapter 2

Nick prided himself on the fact that his reflexes had always been quick. This time was no exception.

One minute he was talking to the unfortunate, freshly minted widow. The next he was stretching out to catch her and keep her head—as well as the rest of her—from hitting the floor.

Beside him, Juarez stood frozen, almost in as much shock, in his own way, as the sheriff's widow. His partner was definitely in need of a crash course that would teach him exactly how to be a useful member of the police force. Right now, the man was undoubtedly well meaning, but also rather useless. The man had a great deal to learn before he could be considered a good detective.

Nick was fairly convinced that Jason Juarez had found himself in his present position only because he was related to someone either on the force, or someone who was embedded within Vengeance's less-than-dynamic town counsel. Whichever it was, the so-called guardian angel might be trying to be kind to the young man, but in the interim, he or she was setting the course of detective work back by half a century.

Juarez, he knew, was relieved when the FBI special agents had descended on the town and, specifically, the "dig" where the bodies had been found. They'd been summoned by the town fathers because one of the victims was Senator Merris. The special agents had been set to take over the entire crime scene, but he had managed to get them to agree that this would be worked as a team effort. That meant that information would be shared—supposedly.

Nick turned his attention to the woman he'd just caught. When he'd made his initial assessment of her, he'd judged that she weighed under a hundred pounds. If he wasn't right on target, he was close. Suzy Burris felt as if she weighed next to nothing at all.

Striding into the house ahead of the flustered Juarez, his arms full of unconscious damsel in distress, Nick headed straight for the sofa.

"Get the door, Juarez," he tossed over his shoulder at his partner.

It took the detective a second to process the order, and another second for embarrassment to creep up his lanky torso, reaching his cheeks and turning them a faint shade of pink.

"You want it closed?" he asked.

"No, I want you to take it off the hinges and take it with us when we leave," Nick bit off sarcastically as he lay the woman down on the sofa. "Yeah, I want it closed," he snapped quickly before the befuddled, wet-behind-the-ears detective took him at his word and started removing the door from its hinges. He wouldn't have put it past him.

The door shut and then he heard Juarez hurrying over to the sofa.

"Is she—is she all right?" the younger man asked nervously. He shifted slightly from foot to foot as he hovered about like a confused hummingbird, searching for a destination where he could alight.

"She just found out that her husband's dead, what do you think?" Nick asked, trying not to let his irritation break through. Part of that irritation had to do with the fact that he had yet to tell the woman the worst part: that her husband had been murdered.

No doubt feeling foolish, Juarez looked down at the unconscious woman. "I guess she's not all right."

There was sympathy in the younger man's voice.

At least he had the right emotional response, Nick thought. That was a start, although being *too* sympathetic wasn't a good thing, either. Nick was convinced of that. It wasn't exactly recommended for someone in their line of work. Getting too involved could get in the way, clouding their judgment and hindering them from doing their job right.

At least, that had been the case back in Houston.

Out here, when he'd accepted the job, he'd just assumed that police work involved tracking down lost dogs and occasionally finding a child who had wandered off from his or her parents. Solving homicides like the ones they were faced with came as a complete and utter surprise to him. While it was, sadly, right up his alley, Nick had come to Vengeance to take an extended break from that sort of thing.

Still, he had to admit that part of him felt suddenly alive again. He hadn't missed the nonstop pressure of the life he'd led as a detective in Houston, but he did find that he missed the challenges that sort of life had perpetually thrown at him.

At least occasionally.

"Make yourself useful," he instructed Juarez. "Get me a compress for her head."

The younger detective looked a little lost as he glanced about the room, as if searching for something to use to make this happen.

Nick sighed. This partnership was going to test his patience. If Juarez got in the way, the feds were going to want them both off the case—and as far as he was concerned, Vengeance was now his town and that made the murdered men *his* case.

"Kitchen, towel." Nick snapped out the words in staccato fashion, firing them at Juarez as if they were bullets. "Make it wet. *Cold* water," he emphasized as Juarez headed toward the section of the house where he assumed the kitchen was located. "Don't forget to wring it out," Nick added, raising his voice so that the other man could hear him.

Otherwise, Juarez would probably be bringing him a towel that left a trail of dripping water in its wake.

A beat later, Juarez cheerfully called back, "Got it!"

Nick shook his head, mentally telling himself to be patient.

When he glanced back down at the sheriff's widow, her eyes were open and she looked up at him, appearing somewhat dazed.

"Welcome back," he said, then placed his hands on her shoulders in gentle restraint as Suzy tried to sit up. "I'd hold off on that for a couple of minutes or so if I were you," he counseled, then added with a marginally amused smile, "Remember what happened the last time you ignored my advice."

Suzy sighed and remained where she was, even though it made her tense to lie down in a stranger's presence. For a second, she closed her eyes again, trying to regain her bearings.

"This isn't some cruel joke, is it?"

He heard the hopeful note in her voice and caught himself feeling sorry for her. The next moment, he banked down that emotion. He knew from experience that that was only asking for trouble.

"I'm afraid not."

She opened her eyes to look up at the man who had unwittingly thrown her world into such turmoil. "Peter's really dead?"

"He's really dead," Nick confirmed. "His body was found in a shallow grave by a group of geology grad students." After that, all hell had broken loose. It was going to be hard keeping a lid on the investigation, what with the news media already poking around.

Suzy was having trouble thinking, trouble processing this. She'd been so focused on telling Peter she wanted a divorce that this had completely thrown her for a loop.

And unleashed a great deal of guilt.

"How did he die? Was it a car accident?" she asked hoarsely.

"No." His voice was emotionless, giving nothing away. "The sheriff appeared to have been choked to death."

Her eyes widened in astonishment. "Someone *killed* him?"

Nick nodded, thinking that, all things considered, she was handling this rather well. "It certainly looks that way."

"Who?" she whispered, hardly able to force the word out.

"That's what we're currently trying to find out," Nick told her honestly.

Out of the corner of his eye, he saw the other detective approaching. Contrary to instructions, Juarez had brought back a dripping towel. He held it out to Nick like a peace offering.

Nick made no attempt to take it from him. "Mrs. Burris is conscious again, Juarez. We won't be needing that now." Then, because the detective appeared to be at loose ends as to what to do with the now unnecessary towel, Nick ordered, "Take the towel back to the kitchen, Juarez."

Happy to be given instructions to follow, the younger man quickly retraced his steps and eagerly did as he was told.

"You're very patient with him," Suzy observed.

It struck her as odd, even as she said the words, that she would notice something so insignificant, given what she'd just been told. Was she going crazy? Or was she just being insensitive to Peter's fate? Neither answer seemed like the right one.

Nick shrugged off the comment and the implied compliment behind it. "He reminds me of my kid brother," he told her. He hadn't realized that until just now, he thought, but now that he'd said it out loud, he realized that Juarez and Eddie had the same lost puppy appeal, the same eagerness to please.

It took him a second to realize that the sheriff's widow was asking him something.

"Excuse me?"

"I said, can I sit up now?" she repeated. She didn't feel up to being restrained again. She wasn't even certain just how she'd react to that.

Right now, all sorts of emotions collided within her as disbelief, anger, guilt and a sliver of relief all vied for practically the same space.

The last reaction made her ashamed. Peter had been, after all, her husband and the father of her child, relief over his death, even the barest hint of it, shouldn't be entering into the equation, she upbraided herself.

Even worse was what was missing.

What she realized was conspicuously missing was grief. *Where is the grief?* she silently demanded. Shouldn't she be feeling that predominately instead of all these other emotions that were racing through her?

What was *wrong* with her?

"Slowly," the detective was saying to her.

She blinked, confused. Had she missed something? "What?"

"You can sit up," Nick repeated. "But do it slowly," he cautioned. "You *really* don't want to get dizzy and pass out again."

She didn't like the frailty his warning implied. It wasn't as if she was made out of spun glass. If she had been, she would have shattered long before now.

"That was the first time I ever passed out," Suzy informed him with a touch of annoyance in her voice.

"First time you had a husband who was murdered, I suspect," Nick speculated.

Suzy flushed. She could feel the color rising to her cheeks, making them hot.

"Yes," she answered hoarsely, waiting to see where he was going with this.

"Drastic news brings out drastic results," he told her matter-of-factly. "Want some water?" Without waiting for an answer, he glanced at Juarez. His partner was just coming back into the room. "Juarez, get Mrs. Burris a glass of water."

Without a word, the other detective turned on his heel and went back to the kitchen.

"Makes him feel useful," Nick said in response

to the protest he saw hovering on the widow's perfectly formed lips.

"You always anticipate everything?" she couldn't help asking.

He flashed her another amused smile. Amid the vulnerability, he detected a feisty streak. He found it rather appealing.

"Saves time," he told her. "But no, I don't always anticipate everything, just the obvious things."

"Like my fainting," she assumed.

"Being told that a spouse was murdered usually comes as a shock to the person doing the listening," he said, never taking his eyes off hers.

Suzy heard the detective's emphasis on the telltale word: *usually.* Did that mean he thought that she was innocent, or did he actually think she had something to do with Peter's murder? If the latter, she knew she should be outraged at the very idea, but she still felt too drained, too devastated by the news, to summon that sort of a response.

"It did," she told him as firmly as she could, the look in her eyes challenging him to say something different.

Juarez had returned with a tall glass filled to the very brim with water. Nick put his hand out for it, then offered it to the widow.

Suzy took the glass with both hands to hold it steady and drank deeply. Strange as it seemed, the cold water helped her pull herself together and focus.

She couldn't allow herself to go to pieces. There was no one around to help her put those pieces back together again. No one to really rely on, except herself.

Just like the old days.

"Thank you," she said to Juarez, offering him the near-empty glass. Her words elicited a shy smile from the young detective as he took the glass from her.

"My pleasure, ma'am."

Ma'am. She was way too young to be a *ma'am.* Or maybe she wasn't. After all, she was someone's mother now.

"You up to some questions?" the other detective asked her. She nodded, wanting to get this over with. "When did you last see your husband?"

"Yesterday morning at breakfast." That seemed like a hundred years ago now, she thought. Had it only been a mere twenty-four hours?

"Did he seem particularly preoccupied or troubled to you?" the detective asked.

She looked at this stranger for a long moment,

wondering how to answer his question. Did she tell him that she and Peter had grown apart? That they hardly spoke to one another these last few days, except to talk about the baby? Or did she keep her secret and pretend that everything had been just fine?

Pressing her lips together, Suzy paused for a moment as she searched for some plausible middle ground. "If you're asking me if he seemed different than usual yesterday, the answer is no, he didn't."

Her words, Nick noted, were carefully orchestrated. He read between the lines.

"How long have you and your husband been having marital problems?" he asked gently.

The question surprised not only Suzy, but the other detective as well. Juarez stared at him, openmouthed. "You didn't tell me you knew the sheriff and his wife, Nick," Juarez said, sounding slightly irritated at being shut out this way.

"I don't, do I, Mrs. Burris?" Nick asked, looking at the woman.

She didn't bother addressing his last question as she focused on the one that not only caught her off guard, but upset her, as well. She didn't want any dirty laundry to mar Peter's memory. As far as the people in the county were concerned, he was an exemplary sheriff.

"What makes you think we were having problems?" she asked.

The question told him all he asked. He was right. Had there been no problems, she might have issued an indignant denial, or at the very least, stared at him as if he was being boorish. But she didn't. She was defensive. Because there was something to be defensive about.

"Let's just say I've been there," he answered evasively.

This wasn't about him, and Nick had no intentions of revisiting his own failed attempt at marital bliss. He'd married far too young and it had all fallen apart on them not that long after the vows. In keeping with his marriage, he'd been divorced young as well. He'd learned a lesson along the way: He was no good at marriage.

"Were you two talking?" he asked, trying to sound as kind as he could under the circumstances.

"Yes," she snapped back, then shrugged helplessly as she amended, "But just barely." She paused again, searching for a way to phrase what she wanted to say. "We've just had a baby—"

"Congratulations," Juarez said with enthusiasm. "Me, too. I mean, my wife, too—except not yet. I mean—"

"He means his wife's due anytime now," Nick interjected. He'd heard about nothing else this entire last week. "Go on," he coaxed Suzy, "you were saying…?" He trailed off, waiting for her to fill in the blanks.

"Despite that, Peter's been rather distant lately," she admitted.

The next moment, she regretted the words. Why was she baring her soul to these men? What did any of this have to do with whoever had killed Peter?

"Some men feel threatened by a baby," Nick told her, recalling what he'd once heard. "They think that they're being replaced in their wives' affections."

Suzy shook her head. She wanted to stop any further conjecture before it got too out of hand.

"Having the baby was Peter's idea," she told him, then added, "he thought that the baby would bring us closer together."

He noticed she didn't say "again," which meant that they probably hadn't been all that close to begin with. Nick decided to press a little further. "How bad did it get?"

Enough was enough. Suzy's own protective instincts, the same one that had her protecting her sister from their parents' inebriated wrath, kicked in.

She glared at this intruding detective. "What does any of this have to do with my husband's murder?" she demanded.

"Just trying to establish the sheriff's frame of mind the last few days before he was killed," he replied matter-of-factly.

She really didn't like exposing her private life like this to strangers, but then, what did it matter, anyway? Peter was dead and that meant her world would have to go through some pretty drastic changes—even faster than she'd initially anticipated. After all, she *had* been planning to divorce Peter. All in all, a divorce was rather a drastic life change in itself.

She blew out a breath and plunged in. "I was going to ask Peter for a divorce when he got home last night." She addressed her words to her shoes, not feeling up to making eye contact with the detective who was doing all the questioning right about now.

But then, he'd probably take that as some sort of a silent admission of guilt, she realized. Blowing out another breath, she forced herself to look up at the man.

"Except that he didn't," she said quietly once she'd reestablished eye contact.

Something sharp pricked at his insides the moment their eyes met. Nick tried to shrug it off. It didn't budge.

"I see," he said without a shred of emotion evident in his voice, successfully masking his feelings.

It was at that moment that Detective Nick Jeffries made a stunning and rather uncomfortable discovery. He realized that he was attracted to this woman, *deeply* attracted. Moreover, it wasn't just her delicate looks that had hooked and reeled him in, it was her underlying vulnerability, which he could see she tried to cover up at all costs.

But the very existence of that vulnerability had awakened his dormant protective streak, a streak he had thought he'd successfully laid to rest more than a few years ago.

Apparently, he'd thought wrong.

Chapter 3

As Nick tried to bury this unsettling and somewhat annoying realization, Juarez's cellphone rang.

Juarez snapped to attention and seemed to go on high alert even *before* he pulled his phone out of his pocket. He blinked, clearing his vision, and then looked at the screen to identify the caller.

Rather than just answer it, the young detective continued to stare at the name, as if he couldn't believe what he was seeing.

Finally, he glanced up at Nick and said numbly, "It's my wife." The next moment, he shivered as a sudden attack of nerves seized him. His mouth choked out, "This could be it."

"It?" Nick repeated. Completely focused on the sheriff's widow, he had no idea what his partner was talking about.

Juarez nodded, still staring at the phone. "The baby's due anytime now," he said, repeating what he'd said earlier—and the day before, and the day before that. "She could be calling to tell me that she's in labor." His voice took on a panicked note as it went up two octaves, then cracked.

"Don't you think you should answer it, then?" Nick coaxed, utterly mystified at the way his partner's mind seemed to work—*if* indeed it actually *was* working at all, which he was beginning to doubt.

"Yeah, right," Juarez cried.

He fumbled with the cellphone, managing to almost disconnect himself from the incoming call before he finally hit the right key to answer it.

Juarez's hands visibly shook as he put the cellphone to his ear. "Tina? Is it time?" His eyes grew huge as he listened to his wife's answer. Literally stunned, his eyes shifted over to look at Nick. "It's time," he announced breathlessly.

He gave every indication that he was about to hyperventilate.

"Then I suggest you start breathing evenly, get in your car and go," Nick responded, uttering each word slowly, as if he were speaking to someone who was mentally challenged.

"Right. Go." As if someone had fired a starter pistol, Juarez scrambled for the door. But when he reached it, he suddenly came to a skidding stop. The rest of his brain—the part that knew it was on duty—kicked in. "What about you?" the younger detective asked. "If I take the car, you'll be stranded. How are you going to get back to the squad room?"

Nick waved away his concern. "Don't worry about me. I'll call someone," he told the other man, his tone confident. And then he ordered, "Go. Your wife needs you. And try not to hit anything on your way there," he called after the swiftly departing detective.

"Okay," Juarez yelled back.

When Nick looked back at the sheriff's widow, she had an odd expression on her face. He couldn't begin to interpret it.

"Something wrong?" he asked her.

Suzy shook her head. "I just envy his wife,

that's all," she said wistfully. "He looked really excited about becoming a father."

"He looked really clueless," Nick corrected. "And so far, that seems to be pretty much his natural state," he added in what turned out to be a completely unguarded moment. It was out of character for him. As a rule, he didn't usually let on what he thought of the people he worked with—or the ones he questioned for that matter.

"Still, he loves her." And love had a way of making up for a host of failings, she thought. "You can see it in his eyes."

Nick took his cue from her wording, following it through. "And what did you see when you looked into your husband's eyes?" he asked, curious as to what her answer would be.

Suzy shrugged in a careless manner that seemed a little too precise to him—and possibly practiced. "Barriers. Walls. Someone I didn't know."

And that, she knew, had been the true reason for the death of their marriage. Because she'd realized that after all this time, Peter was more of a stranger to her now than he had been when they'd first gotten married.

Was the woman saying that because it was how she'd actually felt, or was she laying the groundwork to distance herself from whatever the investigation would turn up about the sheriff?

She wasn't as easy to read as he'd first thought. Nick felt himself being reeled in a little further, despite his resistance to the idea. He knew he was on slippery footing.

"Did your husband have any enemies?" Nick asked her.

Suzy thought for a moment, but it really didn't matter how long she took, she decided. She would arrive at the same conclusion: she didn't think so, but she didn't know for sure.

With a sigh, Suzy shook her head. "Not that he ever mentioned, but to be honest, I really don't know. I know that Peter was away at night more and more. When I asked him about it a couple of times, he said that he was working late on a case." It had sounded like an excuse to her at the time, but maybe she was doing Peter a disservice. "Maybe he was," she said out loud. "But at the time, I thought that there was another woman in the picture—or six."

How had she arrived at that number, Nick wondered. Most women would have said one or two. "Six?"

When he said the number, it sounded foolish.

Suzy shrugged. "Sorry, that was flippant. I really don't know how many he was seeing—or *if* he actually was seeing someone else. My pregnancy had me pretty miserable and looking back, maybe I took it out on him."

Added to that, she'd worked until a little more than a week before she delivered. What that translated to, Suzy thought, was that she and Peter hardly saw each other toward the end.

Nick wasn't quite ready to allow this line of questioning to drop just yet. "Did you ever find anything concrete to back up these suspicions, something that might have got you thinking he was seeing someone else?"

"I didn't look," she admitted, unconsciously raising her chin again defensively. "I didn't want to be one of those snooping, bitter women." Besides, she thought, as long as she didn't find anything, there was always the hope that she was wrong. Other times, she was fairly sure she *wasn't* wrong. "To be honest," she continued in a distant, quiet voice, "I was a little relieved when I thought that Peter was seeing someone else."

Nick came to his own conclusions: a guilty conscience might welcome a level playing field.

"Because you were seeing someone, as well?" he guessed, watching her face intently.

Stunned, she stared at him. Despite the growing chasm between Peter and her, she'd never once thought of seeking solace in someone else's arms. She might not have been in love with Peter, but she was definitely loyal to the institution of marriage.

"What?" she cried, thinking she'd heard wrong. But the expression on the detective's face told her that she hadn't. "No, of course not. Why would you say something like that?" she asked.

"Just a natural assumption," he answered mildly. "If your husband was seeing someone, that made you feel less guilty about you seeing someone."

"You have it all wrong," she informed him with more than a touch of indignation.

"Then enlighten me."

Suzy took a breath. She really didn't like baring her soul this way, but she knew she had no choice. If she kept things back from this man, she was certain that he would think the worst.

"If Peter *was* seeing someone else, that would have made me feel less guilty about not having feelings for him."

Now, there was a novel approach to marital

discord, Nick couldn't help thinking. "I see. And when did you stop having feelings for him?"

Suzy shrugged again, her slender shoulders rising and falling beneath the light blue cotton blouse she had on. She thought of telling the detective that was none of his business, but he'd probably counter that protest by telling her that right now it was. She might as well avoid a verbal squabble with him and just answer the question.

"I don't think I ever started to have feelings for Peter, not the deep, everlasting kind. Don't get me wrong," she cautioned quickly, not wanting the detective to come away with the wrong impression. "There was a really intense attraction between us from the very first moment we met, but there turned out to be nothing behind it, nothing substantial. At least, not for me," she told him sadly. With all her heart she wished that there could have been. But this was a case where wishing just didn't make it so.

"But there was for him?" Nick questioned, watching her closely.

To him, half of police work was getting a feeling for the person you were dealing with, looking beneath their layers, their complexities. He was fairly certain that he would be able to tell if this woman was lying to him.

The answer to the last question was yes, but how did she get that across without sounding conceited?

"Well, Peter *said* he loved me, that he wanted to take care of me for the rest of my life," Suzy said. A rueful smile curved her mouth as she remembered the first stages of their relationship, before the wedding ring, the disappointments and the baby. "You have no idea how good that sounded to me at the time."

She raised her eyes to Nick and he saw a defensiveness entering the bright blue orbs, as if the woman *dared* him to find fault in her words.

"I had less than an ideal childhood," Suzy added by way of an explanation, "and just wanted someone to care whether I lived or died. Peter said he did." At the time, that seemed to be enough of a basis for marriage. "So I married him, hoping that I'd eventually feel the same way about him."

"But you didn't." It wasn't really a guess at this point but a conclusion drawn from what she'd already told him.

"Well, I didn't want him dead." And then she relented slightly, adding, "But I didn't particularly want him living with me. Especially when he was growing so distant—not that I really blamed him for that." This was all coming out really badly. To her ear, it sounded as if she was digging herself into a hole. "I began to think that the whole thing—marrying Peter—was a mistake.

"The baby wasn't a mistake," Suzy quickly added in the next breath, anticipating what the detective was probably thinking. "But on the other hand, no baby should be used as a way to keep a marriage together. It's not fair to the baby or to the two people involved."

That all sounded very noble. Maybe *too* noble, Nick thought. "Do you know how much insurance your husband was carrying?"

Suzy frowned, confused for a moment. "Life insurance?"

"Yes, life insurance," he repeated, a trace of impatience in his voice. "How much was your husband carrying?"

She was still reeling from news of Peter's murder. Practical questions like the one the detective had just posed hadn't even occurred to her yet.

"I have no idea," she told him. "As far as I know, he wasn't carrying any." And then, although she didn't want to believe anyone would even remotely think this horrible way about her, that she would kill someone, especially her husband, for money, Suzy demanded, "Why? Do you think I had him killed so I could get the insurance money?"

The whole thing was too ludicrous to believe—yet the detective obviously saw it as a possibility. Suzy didn't know whether to be angry—or afraid. Was she going to need a lawyer on top of everything else?

Nick deliberately didn't answer her directly. "It's been known to happen."

"Well, not as far as I'm concerned," she retorted angrily. Stress and overworked hormones had her fairly shouting at him. "I'm an accountant. I have a good job and I don't need extra money from some stupid life insurance policy."

"Everyone needs extra money," Nick told her matter-of-factly. And women had killed their husbands for reasons other than money.

Her eyes flashed. Okay, she was getting really tired of this verbal sparring match. If he thought she'd killed Peter for the money, she wanted him to come out and just *say* it.

"Are you trying to accuse me of something, Detective?"

Just then, before he could respond, they heard

the baby begin to cry, Andy's wails clearly audible over the baby monitor she'd placed on the coffee table. There were two more monitors scattered throughout the first floor, one in the kitchen, one in the bedroom.

But Suzy remained where she was. Waiting for an answer.

"No," Nick told her, "I'm trying to rule you *out* of something, Mrs. Burris. Where were you yesterday?"

She walked away from him and went up to the nursery. Her son needed her. "Here. At home."

Nick was right behind her, following the woman up the stairs. Walking behind her was eventful, he caught himself thinking as he watched the gentle, rhythmic sway of her hips as she went up the stairs.

"Can someone verify that?"

Stopping at the landing, Suzy looked back at him, a cynical expression on her face. It was her mask, allowing her to hide from certain people.

"The baby," she answered flatly.

He laughed shortly. The kid was a bit too young to take on the role of witness. "Can anyone older verify that?"

She thought for a moment as she went into the baby's room. It was everything that her own room—hers and her sister Lori's—was not. The space was cheerfully decorated in bright yellows and greens since she'd opted not to know the baby's gender until after he was born. It proclaimed to the world that a child was happy here—also not like her childhood bedroom.

The second she entered the nursery, Suzy did her best to shift gears. She smiled brightly at the fussing baby in the crib. At two months old, Andy was the picture of perpetual motion, his little arms and legs all going at once.

"Hi, little man. Miss me?" she murmured.

Picking up the baby, Suzy turned to look back at the detective. She expected him to be out in the hallway and was surprised to see that he had followed her into the room.

Just what did he expect to find in her son's room?

"The mailman saw me," she finally told him. "He came early and I had a bill I wanted to mail, so I hurried out before he pulled away."

That helped, but a mailman could easily be dissuaded from remembering certain facts, especially if a class act like Suzy Burris was doing the "dissuading."

"Anyone else?" Nick asked.

Suzy resented this, resented all the questions, even though she knew that it was necessary and, most likely, routine.

"My sister called me at around four o'clock yesterday to see how I was doing. Does that count?"

He nodded, couching his words carefully. "If it checks out on your phone bill, it does."

"Not a very trusting soul, are you?" she tossed over her shoulder.

From the ripe smell that was coming from Andy's lower half, she knew that the first order of business was to change him. She took him over to the changing table. Both ends of the table were buffered with the latest, most absorbent diapers on the market. Never having so much as *looked* at a diaper until two months ago, she'd gotten very proficient at changing them in the past eight weeks.

"It's not a very trusting line of business," Nick answered. "You should know that," he added, "seeing as how your husband was the county sheriff."

Was. Not *is.* It was really hard to absorb that, she thought.

"Like I said," Suzy said out loud with emphasis, "I wasn't privy to my husband's professional life. Or his private one, it's beginning to seem," she added under her breath. She spared Nick another glance as she deftly went about the task of getting rid of the soiled diaper and putting a brand-new one on the baby. "And as far as alibis go—that's what this is about, right?—*this* is my alibi," she informed him, nodding at the baby on the changing table. "Andy kept me busy all day. He hardly slept at all. That didn't leave me any time to—how was my husband killed?" she asked, suddenly realizing that she couldn't remember if the detective had told her that or not. If he had, she'd blocked it out. But now she wanted to know.

Had Peter been shot, stabbed, strangled or mowed down by some vehicle? The very thought of each method made her want to shiver.

"You really don't want to know," Nick told her quietly.

"Yes, I do," she said emphatically. In a strange way, she felt she owed it to Peter to know all the details regarding his death. She could at least do that much for him.

"All right—just remember, you asked to hear this. Your husband was strangled," Nick told her crisply. "The medical examiner will give the official verdict, but from the looks of it, I'd say someone put a plastic bag over the sheriff's head and held it tight against his face until he suffocated."

Now she did shiver, visualizing the scenario in her mind. Peter might not have been the husband she'd always dreamed of, but he didn't deserve to die like that.

He didn't deserve to die at all, but to live a long life, being there for his son even if they weren't going to be there for each other much longer. She hoped he hadn't suffered.

"How do you know it was a plastic bag?" she asked. "Maybe someone just strangled him with their bare hands—or hung him." Each method she suggested just made it that much worse for her. But now that the detective was talking about it, she wanted all the details—and then she'd lock this subject away forever. She never wanted to revisit it for *any* reason.

"Well, for one thing, there were no dark ligature marks around his neck. If he was hung or manually strangled, there would have been telltale marks left around his neck."

Nick paused a moment, thinking of the card that had been found on the sheriff's person. Specifically, in his pocket. Similar cards, with something different written on each, were found on the other two men who had been dug up.

He considered withholding this from her, then

decided that it might be better out in the open. You never knew where something might lead.

"He had a card on him."

"A card?" she repeated, puzzled. "You mean like a playing card or a business card?"

"More like the kind that's used to print business cards, except that there was nothing printed on it except for just one word, and that was handwritten."

She didn't know why she instinctively braced herself, but she did. "What was the word?"

"Liar."

Suzy blinked and stared at him. Had he just accused her of lying? About what? "Excuse me?" she cried.

"That was the word written on the card—*liar,*" he explained. "Would you know anyone who would accuse your husband of being a liar?"

She shook her head, painfully aware that she was no help in finding Peter's killer. The detective was probably tired of hearing her negative answers. But she couldn't exactly tell him what she didn't know.

"Can't think of a single person. As far as I know, Peter was regarded as a pillar of the community, a real good guy. I don't know of anyone who would accuse him of being a liar. Unless it was one of the women he was seeing," she amended. Now that she said it out loud, his "good guy" status was on shaky ground.

Suzy shrugged her shoulders again in a hapless gesture. "And, like I already told you, I don't even have any proof that he *was* seeing other women. It wasn't as if I'd found any love notes in his pockets, or any lipstick smeared on his collar. It was just a feeling I had," she admitted, "because things were so strained between us lately."

"Maybe that wasn't your fault," Nick suggested. When she glanced in his direction, confusion written on her features, he added, "Maybe the sheriff was acting that way because of whatever got him killed."

She supposed it was possible. But then, why hadn't Peter said something? Why had he shouldered this burden on his own?

A ragged sigh broke free as she finished changing the baby.

She looked at the detective, her eyes meeting his. Hers were guilt ridden. "He should have talked to me, told me what was going on."

"Maybe he just didn't want to burden you—or get you involved," Nick told her.

But she was already involved. She was his wife and this was where the words *for better or for worse* came into play.

Had she failed Peter?

She couldn't think about that now. If she let herself get mired in guilt, she wouldn't be of any use to Andy and right now, he was her top priority.

Replaying the detective's words in her head, Suzy suddenly realized something. With a now fresher-smelling Andy in her arms, she turned to look at the man who'd forced her into all this introspection.

"I take it that by saying that, you no longer find me to be a—how do they put it?" she asked, searching for the right terms. "A person of interest?" she recalled.

He wouldn't exactly say that, Nick thought. Not by a long shot. But since he didn't mean the phrase the same way she meant it, he refrained from making a direct comment on her question.

Even if he *did* find her person to be of interest.

Chapter 4

After a beat, Nick realized that the sheriff's widow was still waiting for an answer. "For now," he told her, "we're moving on."

"For now," she repeated.

Did that mean that he really *did* suspect her? The idea was utterly insane to her, but obviously not to him. The last thing she needed or wanted was to have that hanging over her head like some sword of Damocles. If nothing else, she wanted this absurd notion to be cleared up and gotten out of the way.

Now.

"Does that mean you're planning on revisiting your assumption that I had something to do with my husband's—" She couldn't even bring herself to say the word *murder,* much less contemplate the horrid act. How in heaven's name could this solemn detective possibly think she caused Peter's death? "Just for the record, Detective Jeffries, I draw the line at killing anything larger than a swarm of ants."

"Ants," he echoed, nodding. The barest hint of a smile threatened to curve his lips. "Can't stand them myself," he told her by way of agreement.

For a moment Nick watched her as she stood holding her baby, swaying to and fro ever so slightly to soothe him and keep him quiet. Unless he missed his guess, those were tears causing her eyes to glisten like that. He had a gut feeling that they were genuine, which in turn made him feel guilty for his questioning.

"Do you have anyone you'd like me to call?" Nick asked, his voice a great deal less stern than it had just been.

Her mind in turmoil, Suzy tried to make sense of the question. "You mean so you could question them about my marriage?"

Maybe he *had* been a bit too harsh on her. But

damn it, it was his job. He had to eliminate potential suspects, take in motives, opportunity and all the rest of it. Spouses killed their other halves more often than not.

Even so, he could feel guilt weighing heavily on him. And that was new. Cases—and the people involved in them—didn't, as a rule, get to him.

This woman was different. He'd sensed that even before he'd carried her into her house.

"No," he explained. "As in getting someone to come and stay here with you, maybe help you out with the baby while you try to pull yourself together."

She tossed her head, her long blond hair flying over the shoulder that wasn't currently occupied by her son. "Newsflash, Detective Jeffries, I *am* together."

Detective Jeffries sounded so formal, and although he usually liked maintaining that wall between a potential suspect and himself, he didn't this time.

"Call me Nick," he told her.

"Doesn't matter what I call you, 'Nick,' my answer's still going to be the same," she informed him.

He knew he should just back off. That any more

interaction with this woman would get him in deeper. He didn't want that. But somehow, he just couldn't make himself walk away yet, not when she looked as if the whole world had just exploded in on her—and he'd been the cause of her pain.

"Look, I meant no disrespect, but you are dealing with an emotional situation and taking care of a newborn isn't exactly a walk in the park, especially not when it's your first baby and you find yourself questioning every move you make, every thought you have." At this point, there was nothing but sympathetic understanding in Nick's voice. "I just asked if there is a friend or a relative I could call for you. Somebody for you to lean on if you needed to."

And this way, he thought, *I won't have to volunteer for the position.*

Suzy flushed. The man was trying to be nice to her, and she had all but bitten his head off. Maybe she really *was* going to pieces over this and didn't even realize it.

"Yes, there's someone," she admitted quietly. "My sister, Lori."

He waited a moment, thinking she would give him her sister's phone number. When she didn't, Nick prodded, "Can I have her number?"

"That's okay, I can call her," Suzy told him.

Maybe that wasn't such a bad idea, getting Lori to come, she thought. She could always count on Lori, just as Lori could always count on her. They were each other's support system. They always had been, going all the way back to the days when they had thought that all children had parents who fell asleep, fully clothed, on any flat surface that was handy, clutching a bottle of whiskey.

A little more than a year apart in age—with her being the older one—she and Lori were in tune to each other's feelings. It was Lori who had first sensed that she wasn't as happy in her marriage as she'd hoped to be. And it was Lori who'd made her promise that she would come to her if there was ever a problem.

This certainly qualified as a problem.

Since the woman wasn't making an attempt to walk over to the phone and pick it up, Nick made another offer. "I can hold the baby for you while you make your call."

She hadn't made a move yet because she was trying to find the right words to apologize to him. She supposed that saying "I'm sorry" was a one-size-fits-all catchall. It felt insufficient, but she used it anyway.

"I'm sorry." When she saw him raise a quizzical eyebrow, she added, "I know you were just trying to be nice and I just about bit your head off. I really didn't mean to—"

He smiled at her for the first time since she'd opened the door to him and his partner. Really smiled. Suzy caught herself thinking that he had a nice smile, one of those terrific boyish ones that utterly captivated the beholder and transformed his face.

Rather than an austere representative of the law, Nick Jeffries suddenly became human, someone she could relate to and even talk to.

"Don't worry about it," he told her. "My skin's a lot tougher than you think, Mrs. Burris."

"Suzy," she corrected. "Call me Suzy. Being called Mrs. Burris makes me feel like a gray-haired grandmother in sensible shoes."

He glanced down at her feet, noticing for the first time that she wasn't barefoot, the way his own wife used to be the minute she walked in through the front door. And rather than wearing something like comfortable slippers, Suzy had on high heels. Three-and-a-half or four-inch heels if he didn't miss his guess. She moved around so effortlessly in them, he'd just naturally *assumed* that the woman was barefoot.

But now that he'd looked—and, he had to admit, admired—he could see how very wrong he'd been. The shoes made her legs look sexy.

"Nothing sensible about *those* shoes," Nick commented with an appreciative grin. "Don't they bother your feet?" he asked.

She shook her head. "I don't even know I have them on."

The shoes had been one of her ways of coping with her situation. She gravitated toward pretty things, toward things that *made* her feel pretty and took her attention away—for however short a time—from whatever was bothering her.

When she'd been a teenager, she sought distractions to make her forget about her abusive parents, now she'd looked for distractions to make her momentarily forget about the husband who was pulling away from her. The husband who had never really made the "magic" happen for her, even in the beginning.

"They're my guilty pleasure," she explained.

"If you say so." Nick looked at the baby in her arms who was growing more and more vocal about his mounting unhappiness. "My offer still stands.

I can hold him for you while you call your sister. You might find it a little hard to talk with him crying like that."

The detective had a point, she thought. Pressing her lips together, she glanced from her son to Nick—and hesitated.

Nick could almost read her thoughts. "I do know how to hold a newborn."

There was no missing the confidence in his voice. "You have children, Detective—Nick?" she corrected herself at the last moment.

He thought of his ex-wife and the baby she'd chosen to erase from their lives without giving him the opportunity to voice his opinion, or even say a word in its defense. Just like that. It was gone before he even knew of its existence.

He'd found out quite by accident—looking for their bankbook, he'd come across the notification from a test that her gynecologist had run that Julie was pregnant. That was the afternoon he'd gone through a huge potpourri of emotions, all jumbled up and overlapping one another. But ultimately, the biggest emotion he experienced, was pure joy.

Elated at the news, he'd stopped off at his local bookstore during his lunch break and loaded up on every parenting book he could find, as well as a huge book singularly devoted to the selection of a name for the baby.

His head crammed full of plans for the baby-to-be, he came home only to discover that there was no need for plans at all. Julie had "gotten rid of the problem," to use her phraseology when he'd started talking about needing to move to a larger home in a better school district. Without a word to him, she'd swept away their unborn child as if it was some annoying, trivial inconvenience.

The discovery of what she'd done—leaving him out the way she had—left him reeling and destroyed the last drop of love that still existed. In effect it sounded the death knell of a marriage that was already staggering on its last legs.

"No," he answered Suzy quietly, "I don't have any children." Then, in case she had any further questions about his lack of family, he added, "I'm not married. But that doesn't mean I don't know how to hold a baby."

Then, as if to make his point, he gently took her son from her arms.

Nervous about surrendering Andy to this man, she was about to warn Nick not to let the baby's head drop back—or forward, But before she could get the words out, she saw that she had no need to coach him. The detective was holding her son far better and more comfortably than Peter had the handful of times that he'd made an attempt to act like a parent.

Suzy looked on in admiration and gave the detective his due. "You're a natural."

Nick blocked the bittersweet feeling unexpectedly filtering through him as he held this tiny miracle in his arms. Even so, he couldn't help wondering what it would have been like had he learned about his baby in time to talk his ex into having it. Who knew the kind of turn his life might have taken?

He glanced away from the baby for an instant. "You sound surprised."

Andy had settled down. The infant seemed to be fascinated by this new person holding him. "I don't really think of police detectives as having nurturing instincts," Suzy confessed.

Nick smiled down at the infant who was staring at him and seemed to be all eyes at the moment. "Maybe you should think about changing your opinion about members of the police force," he suggested.

She thought he was serious until she saw the amused glint in his eyes.

"Maybe," she agreed. Rousing herself—his eyes had a definite hypnotic effect—she said, "I won't be long," and walked out of the living room.

There was a phone in the kitchen and she made her way toward it. There was another extension in the living room, where she had just been with Andy and Nick, but she wanted a little privacy. It wasn't that she had anything secretive to share with Lori. She just wanted to be able to break down if it came to that.

Lori would understand.

This detective would just think of her as being weak, and she didn't feel like being judged right now. Her last shred of bravado and defensiveness had been used up. She had nothing to shield herself with, no weapons close at hand to help her deflect any unwanted criticism—or pity for that matter.

She might not have been in love with Peter, but his totally unexpected, sudden death, had left her shaken and confused about the immediate future.

She didn't like feeling this way, didn't like the vulnerability, and until she could get herself under control—until she could feel that she was *back* in control of her life—she wanted to be able to talk to her sister without anyone overhearing her.

Because they were so in tune to one another

due to the bond they'd shared growing up in their less-than-idyllic nurturing household, Lori knew something was wrong the instant she heard Suzy utter her name.

It was the *way* she said it. "Lori?"

"Suzy? What's wrong? Why are you calling?" Lori asked. The next second she'd jumped to her own conclusion. "Is it the baby, Suzy? Is there something wrong with Andy?"

It was hard to keep her voice from shaking. Somehow, she managed, although she wouldn't have been able to say just how. "No, it's not Andy."

"You? Do you need to go back to the hospital? I told you that you checked yourself out too soon. Another day or two with nurses close by to help wouldn't have killed you," her sister protested.

It took a couple of seconds before Suzy could get a word in edgewise. "I'm fine, Lori." But that wasn't strictly true, she upbraided herself silently. "That is, there's nothing wrong with me. At least, nothing physical." God, this was coming out all wrong, she thought in despair.

Her words led her sister to the only remaining option. "Is it Peter?"

Suzy closed her eyes. She could feel an emptiness forming within her. But, if she were being honest with herself, that emptiness had been there before Peter's death. She'd just worked hard at ignoring it.

But that wasn't possible anymore.

"Yes," she answered, the word all but sticking in her throat.

Suzy heard her sister sigh on the other end of the line. Lori, as loyal as the day was long, reacted to Peter according to the information she gleaned from her, and at present, because she *had* shared her feelings that Peter had been growing more and more distant with her, Lori was not too keen on her brother-in-law.

"All right, Suzy, out with it. What's the almighty sheriff of the county done now?" Lori asked.

She felt disloyal to Peter because of the image Lori had of him, thanks to her, and hypocritical at the same time because she just couldn't pretend that she actually loved the man. That had ended way *before* the baby had been born.

"He died," she told Lori, her voice flat and devoid of any emotion.

There was a pause on the other end. Finally, her sister said, "Suzy, I think there's something wrong with the connection we have. I thought I just heard you say that Peter—"

"He died," Suzy repeated in the same flat, disembodied voice. The words sounded so strange, so stilted, to her ear. Swallowing, she forced more words out of her mouth. "Peter's dead, Lori."

"How? When?" Lori cried in utter disbelief.

"The police detectives who came to the house said that someone suffocated Peter yesterday." Guilt shot through her with sharp, fresh arrows, piercing her conscience if not her heart. "Oh, Lori, I was waiting up all night for him—"

"Because you were worried," her sister ended her sentence for her. They'd always been able to do that with each other, second-guess what the other was going to say. Except for this time.

"No, Lori. Because I was going to ask him for a divorce. That's what makes this so much worse. Peter might have been fighting for his life at the very moment that I was sitting here, trying to figure out just how to finally tell him that I was leaving him, that I wanted a divorce."

Lori heard the pain, the heavy sting of guilt in her sister's voice and she ached for Suzy.

"It's not your fault, you know, Suz," she told her. "Not your fault he's dead."

Suzy blew out an unsteady breath. "I know. But I still feel guilty."

"Don't," her sister ordered, then added, "I'll be there as soon as I can. Hang in there, Suzy. Everything's going to be all right," Lori promised just before she hung up.

Suzy stared at the phone receiver in her hand. "Everything wasn't all right before this happened," Suzy said quietly, more to herself than to the sister who was no longer there.

She didn't remember hanging up the phone. It was in her hand one minute, then back in the cradle the next. She stared at it in surprise.

Get a grip! she ordered herself.

Taking a deep breath, Suzy squared her shoulders, turned around and walked back into the living room, placing one foot in front of the other numbly. It was all that she could do.

She was just in time to see Andy spit up on the detective's jacket.

Rushing over, she scooped up the baby, taking Andy from him with one arm while offering Nick a cloth wipe that she had left draped on the arm of the sofa.

"I'm so sorry," she apologized with feeling. "If you take that off, I can clean it for you so that the stain doesn't set."

Though being christened with recycled milk

didn't particularly upset him—he'd had worse things hurled at his clothing—Nick regarded her offer to clean his jacket rather dubiously.

"You have a dry cleaner out back?" he quipped.

She placed Andy into the playpen she had set up in the living room. The infant fussed for a moment, then began playing with his feet, which were still a source of utter fascination for him.

"No," she replied to Nick as she held her hand out for his jacket, "but I got pretty good at getting all sorts of stubborn stains out of clothes when I was growing up."

Nick came to the only logical conclusion he could with the information he'd been given. "You were a tomboy?" he asked. He shrugged out of the jacket and folded it so that the stain was on top before he handed it over to Suzy.

"No, I had parents who made falling down in a drunken stupor wherever they might happen to be into pretty much of a way of life."

She said it so matter-of-factly, he thought she was just being flippant. But one look into her eyes told him she was serious.

The woman had led one hell of a life in her relatively short time on earth.

For the second time within an hour, he felt the

very definite, strong stirrings of protectiveness
rising to the surface.

He did what he could to block them.

Chapter 5

"There you go," Suzy said, emerging from the laundry room roughly fifteen minutes later. She presented Nick with his jacket. "I did manage to get the stain out, and once that section dries—" she pointed it out to him "—there shouldn't be any telltale evidence that my son decided to use your jacket as his napkin. If you still want to take it to the cleaners anyway, I'll be more than happy to pay the bill."

Nick looked the jacket over carefully, clearly impressed. He couldn't detect even a trace of the milky substance that had decorated his shoulder a short while ago.

At this point, all that remained was just the faintest hint of a damp spot, and that looked as if it was disappearing, as well.

"How did you do that?" he marveled. He had a razor-sharp mind when it came to solving crimes. Common everyday things, though, like cooking or doing laundry, turned out to be far more of a challenge for him than he was happy about.

Suzy looked at him with an utterly serious expression. "I don't usually give away my secrets."

Maybe the woman was trying to get a patent on the process. It certainly had performed a minor miracle on his jacket. "Oh, well then—"

The serious expression was instantly gone, replaced by a suppressed laugh. Suzy put her hand on his arm to keep him from withdrawing. She'd always been a toucher when she spoke to people. It was one of the things that had attracted Peter to her in the first place—and one of the first things he'd objected to once they were married. He didn't like her touching other people. And by "other people" he'd meant men.

"I was just kidding," she said quickly. "The secret is just getting to the stain fast, before it sets, and then soaking the area with lemon juice."

He had to have heard her wrong. Was she talking about cleaning something or cooking it? "Lemon juice?"

She nodded. "Lemon juice. You'd be surprised at how good it is at getting out all sorts of stains— including blood."

"Blood," he repeated, wondering just how she'd found that out. "I'll have to remember that the next time someone shoots me," he said drolly.

Nick slipped on his jacket again. As he did so, he glanced down at his watch. He'd been here far longer than he'd intended for an initial interview, but even so, he was rather reluctant to leave the woman alone like this. And then he suddenly remembered that he had to call the precinct to have a car sent for him since Juarez took off in the one they normally shared.

"Excuse me a minute," he said to Suzy as he took his cellphone out of his pocket and turned away from her to make the call.

The moment he pressed the last number, someone immediately came on, needlessly identifying themselves as "Dispatch."

"Dispatch, this is Detective Jeffries. I need a

car sent to Sheriff Burris's house." Pausing to listen to the question being asked of him, he replied, "Because Juarez's wife went into early labor, and I let him have the car so he could get to the hospital, that's why. Now I need to requisition another car so that I can get back to the station house and start digging through some paperwork."

The detective, Suzy thought, didn't sound very happy about having to explain himself. He struck her as someone who was accustomed to following his own rules, going his own way, without being subjected to questions.

"How long?" she heard him ask sharply. From the impatient noise he made, she took it to mean that "how long?" had suddenly translated into "too long."

Suzy thought for a moment, made up her mind quickly and then planted herself directly in front of the detective to get his attention. He looked at her quizzically.

"I can drive you there," she mouthed to him, not wanting her voice to interfere with the voice that he was listening to on his cellphone.

"Hold on a minute, Gus," Nick told dispatch. Covering the lower portion of his phone, he addressed his question to Suzy. "What?"

Because her throat suddenly felt hoarse out of the blue, she cleared it before she spoke up. "I can take you to the station."

He'd just told the woman her husband was murdered, and then all but accused her of being behind the crime before he'd decided that she could be ruled out. That was more than enough for anyone to handle in one day. He had no intention of imposing on Suzy Burris any further—at least not unless he had absolutely no other choice.

Nick waved away her offer. "That's all right, I can have—"

"No, really, I insist," she said a little more forcefully, although she made sure that she maintained a friendly expression on her face. "The fresh air might do me some good. I've been in the house for going on two days straight and I'm coming down with cabin fever."

Nick looked over toward the playpen where Andy was still finding his extremities to be utterly fascinating entities. "What about your son?"

"He's too young for cabin fever," she told him matter-of-factly.

Nick completely missed the humor in her eyes. "No, I mean what are you going to do with him while you're driving me?"

"Andy has a car seat," she assured Nick. "And I've already taken him on road trips, so yours won't be the first. He's very accommodating." Thank God she had Andy, she thought. He made everything worthwhile, even if he had wreaked havoc on her hormones. "Of course," she speculated, looking over toward her son, "he doesn't talk yet, so that might change once he thinks he has a say in matters."

Her banter didn't distract him from his concerns. "Are you sure you're up to it?"

"Up to it?" she echoed with a small laugh that wasn't altogether laced with humor. "I'd say I pretty much *need* it." She paused for a moment, taking a breath before continuing to try to convince the detective. "A little fresh air might help me clear my head. And this way, I'll have a direction instead of driving around aimlessly, so you'll actually be doing me a favor."

He watched Suzy for a long moment, debating whether or not to believe her. Finally, he inclined his head. "If you put it that way, I guess I can't turn the offer down." Removing his hand from his cellphone's mouthpiece, he changed his instructions to dispatch. "Cancel the car, Gus. I've just managed to hitch a ride." Terminating the call, he closed his phone, looked at her and smiled. "Whenever you're ready," he told her, letting his voice trail off.

She nodded. "Just let me get a coat and an extra blanket for Andy." For the beginning of February, it was unseasonably warm, but this was still winter and she wasn't about to take any chances on her son catching a chill if the temperature suddenly dropped.

She'd crossed to the stairs to get the items when the doorbell chimed and stopped her in her tracks. Backtracking, she went to the front door. But as she was about to open it, she heard Nick shout out a warning, "Suzy, don't!" then suddenly found herself being physically blocked from the door because Nick had put himself in between her and it.

"Have you lost your mind?" she demanded. She nearly stumbled and fell backward because of the body block, and most likely would have, had Nick not grabbed her arm to steady her. "What the hell was that all about?" she cried, utterly stunned.

Was he trying to keep her sister out, after telling her to call Lori over?

Nick realized that it was a woman standing on the doorstep, a petite blonde who resembled the sheriff's widow.

This had to be the sister, he thought, feeling

somewhat relieved. Lowering his guard, he allowed himself to relax a little.

"You have to be more careful about answering the door," he told her.

"Any particular reason why?" Suzy asked, a hint of sarcasm in her voice.

He didn't want to frighten her or add to her burden, but it was better for her to be cautious than sorry.

"Your husband wasn't the only one killed yesterday. He was one of three. Now if his death was a random killing, or one that was carefully planned with the other two murders thrown in to throw people off the trail, I don't know. But until we sort it all out, I'd say it was better to ask the person to identify themselves before opening your door."

Oh, Peter, what have you done? "Then you think that my son and I might be in danger?" she asked before Lori could ask the same question.

"There's a possibility," he allowed. "Until I start getting some straight answers, I really can't tell you what it is you might be up against."

Worried about what she had inadvertently dragged her sister into, Suzy told her, "Then maybe you shouldn't stay here with me."

Lori was cut out of the same fabric as she was.

"My place is here with you and my nephew. Just *try* to get me to stay away," Lori dared her. Turning, she gave the man her sister had been talking to a thorough once-over. "Hi, I'm Lori, Suzy's sister."

Nick took the hand she offered, closing his over it. The women more than just looked alike. They obviously had the same temperament.

"I kind of figured that out," he told her warmly. He looked back at Suzy. "Forget about driving me," he said. "Stay here with your sister, try to get a decent night's sleep if you can. I'll be back tomorrow—or the day after," he qualified. He had no idea how the rest of the investigations were going and always wanted to leave space for adjustment in case the feds had other leads that were more pressing. When he saw the confused expression in Suzy's eyes, he explained, "I have more questions I need to ask you."

Although Peter's death was still very much of a shock to her, she was beginning to regain control over herself, beginning to find her way back to even ground. But the last thing she needed right now was to be left wondering what else would be unearthed about her husband. If the detective had more questions, she wanted to hear them now, not spend the next twelve or so hours anticipating them.

"I doubt if I'm going to be able to fall asleep at all tonight, much less get a decent night's sleep, so unless you have to be somewhere else right now, you might as well get started asking those other questions, Detective. Although," she reminded him, "I'm really not sure how much of a help I'm going to be. Like I said earlier, Peter didn't exactly bring his work home with him."

"Literally?" he asked.

She had no idea what Nick actually meant by that. "Excuse me?"

"Literally," he repeated. Seeing that she was still puzzled, he elaborated on the question. "Did the sheriff bring home any files, a briefcase he might have carried back and forth with him. A laptop computer he kept locked up somewhere?"

The answer to all but the last question was yes. "Peter turned the guest bedroom into his office," she volunteered. "Anything he brought home I guess would be there. He never left any of that anywhere else in the house."

A home office. Maybe now they were finally getting somewhere. "Do I have your permission to go through it?" Nick asked.

Peter was gone, there was no longer a need to protect his things, she thought.

"Sure, if it'll help you find out who killed Peter. But first," she cautioned, "you're going to have to get into it."

It was Nick's turn to be confused and say, "Excuse me?"

Before she could explain, the baby began fussing again. Suzy looked toward the playpen, torn.

"Go, I've got this," Lori told her, waving her sister off as she went to get her nephew out of the playpen.

"Thanks," Suzy said to her sister, then beckoned for the detective to come with her. "It's this way," she told him, leading the way to the room in question. "Peter keeps—kept—" she corrected herself "—his office locked up. When I asked him about it once, he said that it was to make sure that if anyone ever broke into the house, they wouldn't be able to get into what he called 'sensitive' material."

Nick wondered if that was just a term the sheriff had bandied about to make himself seem important, or if it actually stood for something.

"Any idea what that was?" he asked her.

Suzy stopped before the closed door and shook her head. "Not a clue."

Nick regarded the door for a long moment. It didn't look particularly reinforced. Why the drama?

"You realize that anyone who could break into the house could easily break into this room, as well," he pointed out.

The weary smile that curved the corners of her mouth told Nick that the sheriff's widow was well aware of that.

"The way I saw it," she told Nick, "whatever Peter had in there was something he didn't want me to see. Can't say I wasn't curious," she admitted, then shrugged indifferently, "but then I thought that maybe it was like Pandora's box— once it was opened, the things that I'd find there could never be put back and life might never be the same again. I decided not to risk it.

"But I can't say I liked him having secrets like that. It really bothered me. A lot." She looked at Nick. "It's one of the reasons I decided to divorce him," she confessed with a sigh. "There were just too many secrets."

Whatever she could tell him might just make his job that much easier. "What were some of the others?"

"The usual things." When he looked at her,

waiting, she elaborated. "Hang-ups when I would answer the phone. More and more late nights out. Inconsistencies in the things he told me."

"Such as?" he prodded.

"Such as why he left the Dallas police force." That was the biggest inconsistency—she didn't want to call it a lie, but in her heart, she knew it had to be. Or at least, that one of the reasons—if not more—that he'd given her was a lie. "When he first told me about it, Peter just shrugged it off, said he felt it was just time for him to make a move, to try something different.

"Another time he said that he left because he felt there were just too many corrupt cops on the force and rather than turn on them—and risk getting killed himself—he just resigned.

"And then there was the time he ran into someone he knew from Dallas," she continued. She wasn't aware that her expression hardened somewhat—but Nick was. "I overheard the other man saying something about Peter having to disappear quickly because of some kind of scandal he was involved in."

Nick made a note to look up the sheriff's record with the Dallas Police Department. "Do you know who the other man was?"

She shook her head. "Never saw him before—or after. When I asked Peter if his friend was coming back, he cut me off by saying the man wasn't a friend, he was just an acquaintance from the department. He seemed pretty upset, so I didn't press the matter." Suzy shook her head. She couldn't help wondering if any of this was her fault. If she could have done something differently to keep Peter from getting killed. "Maybe I should have."

"You wouldn't have known if he was telling you the truth or not, anyway," Nick pointed out. "That's the trouble with someone who keeps changing his story."

Suzy nodded sadly. "I know." She indicated the locked door that was keeping them from looking through Peter's things. "Do you want me to call a handyman to take that off its hinges?"

He didn't view the locked door as an obstacle. "No need," he told her. "I'm kind of handy myself." But rather than taking the hinges off, Nick merely took out his wallet and extracted two very thin looking metal tools. Using both, he inserted them into door's keyhole and swiftly began working the lock.

Glancing at Suzy over his shoulder, he asked,

"I've got your permission to unlock the door, right?"

The gesture she used told him to have at it. "Be my guest."

Before she'd uttered the last word, Nick already had the door unlocked and was turning the doorknob to enter the room.

Suzy was suitably impressed at how effortlessly the detective had managed that. "They teach cat burglary at the police academy?" she asked, amused.

"No, they don't. That particular skill comes under the heading of extracurricular activity," he answered with as straight a face as he could manage. "It's something—if you're lucky—that you pick up along the way from the criminals you wind up arresting."

Once in the room, Nick looked around slowly. His first impression was that there was nothing outstanding about the room, nothing to set it apart or make it appear special. It was just another bedroom converted into a home office.

The man did have a very large desk. Was that to convey his importance, or did he just favor large writing areas? It definitely dominated the room, but the surface of the alder wood desk was completely devoid of any papers despite the fact that there was a laser printer set up right next to a computer tower. Both were turned off.

On the far side of the desk, standing next to it, was a professional-looking shredding machine. Its container, Nick noticed, was partially filled. He crossed to that first.

Removing the much heavier top portion, he found that the paper inside the container was shredded to the point that it would take a team of dedicated experts, working nonstop for several days, before they could even hope to begin to attempt to re-create the pages that had been fed through the machine's sharp teeth. And even after that, it wasn't a foregone conclusion that there could be anything gleaned from that effort.

Why would a sheriff of a county need that kind of a shredder? Just what was the man shredding and why?

Leaving that puzzle for later, Nick turned to the computer next. He hit the power button and waited for the tower to reboot. When it finished going through its paces, a picture came together on the screen.

"Interesting screen saver," Nick commented as he studied it.

Peter had never had the computer on around her. Curious, she took a look and saw that the screen saver was comprised of an army of dollar signs marching off into infinity.

She wasn't surprised. "Peter always had a weakness for money," she told the detective. "He complained more than once that he didn't feel he was getting paid what he deserved." Already the marching dollar signs were getting on her nerves. "Can you get into it?"

The computer was, as he expected, password protected. "This is a little trickier than unlocking a door," he told her. "But then again, a lot of people elect to go with things they can easily remember. What's the date that you got married?" he asked.

She sincerely doubted that Peter would use that. That would indicate that he was sentimental about the date and she knew that he wasn't.

But she gave the date to Nick anyway and he typed it in.

The second he hit Enter the words *Wiping out hard drive* appeared. Below it was a sixty second countdown.

And they already had just forty-five seconds left.

And then they had forty-four.

Chapter 6

"I can't stop it." Nick was acutely aware that the seconds were ticking away.

His fingers flew across the keyboard and he was using every trick he could think of, but nothing was working.

The countdown continued. The seconds were slipping away.

"Damn it," he muttered in frustration.

And then, with three seconds left to go, the screen suddenly went blank. There was no telltale sound, no indication that anything was being destroyed. He had no idea what had happened but it appeared that the crisis had been averted.

How?

Had this countdown been some kind of elaborate hoax? Nick knew that, with all his desperate typing, he still hadn't come up with the right combination of keys needed to save the information.

So why had the screen gone blank?

"I did it?" It was more of a question than a triumphant boast, directed at the universe in general.

As he turned toward the sheriff's widow to vocalize his confusion, it suddenly became clear.

"You did it," Nick amended, almost amused at how simple the solution had been.

Suzy stood there with a smile on her face— and the computer power plug in her hand. She had pulled it out of the wall socket, causing the computer to stop its destructive activity and just shut off.

Why hadn't he thought of that?

"Quick thinking," he complimented her.

"Basic thinking," she corrected. She looked at the plug before placing it on the table beside the tower. "Actually, it's the only kind of thinking I'm capable of—I don't know that much about computers, I just know that the ones that aren't the portable kind that run on batteries need a power source. I got caught in a blackout once and the term paper I was working on disappeared because the computer shut down the moment the power stopped flowing through it." A slight smile curved her lips. "Knew that hard-learned lesson would come in handy someday."

Had she shut off the computer's power source fast enough? Nick wondered as he regarded the dark computer screen.

"I certainly hope so," he muttered out loud.

"So now what?" she asked, nodding at the tower. "Are you going to bring it to some tech expert in the police department?"

"We don't have one of those in Vengeance." At least, none that he was aware of. "But the FBI does." The FBI had everything available to them. It was a matter of knowing who to ask. He'd never been very good at taking hat in hand and pleading his case, though.

"The FBI?" she asked incredulously. Did they even have a satellite office out here? "You can do that? Just walk in and bring a computer to them?"

"Probably not under normal circumstances," he conceded, but God knew this case didn't fit under that heading. "But right now, there's a local police/FBI joint task force working on the murders."

"Murders," she echoed. For a moment, she'd forgotten that Peter's death was not an isolated incident. She really didn't know if that made it better or worse. "If other people were killed, maybe Peter's death was just collateral damage. You know, wrong place, wrong time, that sort of thing. Maybe the killer didn't want to leave a witness behind."

"You're forgetting about the card that was found in your husband's pocket." He looked at her, wishing that for her sake, he could say that her theory was right. But it wasn't. Burris had been singled out, just the way the other two men had been. "This was personal."

A thought occurred to her. A horrible, crushing thought. "Could Peter have gotten the other two people killed?" she asked. "Could they have been unwilling witnesses to *his* death, and then the killer eliminated them, too, to keep them from talking?"

There was only one thing wrong with her theory. "The other men had cards on them, too."

Suzy steepled her hands before her lips, covering them, holding back the sound of anguished distress that had risen to them and was still hovering there.

"Then it *is* a serial killer," she cried. How many more people were going to have to die before this monster was caught?

"We're not ready to say that yet," Nick cautioned, fervently hoping that wasn't the case. "The last thing we need is having the public panic on us. We want to keep them in the dark as long as possible—in case we're wrong and this is just part of some elaborate vendetta."

She ran her hands up and down her arms, feeling a definite chill though the temperature inside the house hadn't changed. She could feel her nerves go on high alert.

"Are my son and I in any danger?" she asked.

Nick gave it to her straight and was as honest with her as he could. "I don't think so. The killer seemed exclusively focused on the three people he killed."

But maybe the killing would be extended to the victims' families.

Get a grip, Suzy. You can't let yourself think that way.

She was struck by something Nick had just said.

"Then you know it was a man who killed Peter and the others?"

"Actually, no, I don't," he admitted. "It's just an assumption. Most multiple killers tend to be men," he told her. "And given the people who were murdered, it would have had to have been a fairly strong woman to get them all out there and bury them. Process of elimination says it's most likely a man," he concluded.

Suzy kept going back to the other two men in her mind. She needed answers. Were they friends of Peter's? People he dealt with?

"Can you tell me who else was killed, or are their identities something that's being kept from the public for the time being?" she asked.

"You'll know soon enough. We have to make sure all the families are contacted first." The FBI was handling that part of it, the part that involved handling the media and releasing information. The names were going to be released sooner than later, because of the media that had converged on Vengeance, thanks to the Grayson disappearance and probable kidnapping. The reporters were everywhere, digging into everything. Suzy was going to hear about the other two men soon enough, but he could talk to her later about the details.

"I understand, Detective."

"Did the sheriff ever talk about anyone in particular? Did he discuss his personal affairs with you?" Nick asked.

There was no humor in the small laugh that escaped her lips. "Peter actually talked less and less to me in the last six months or so. I think he'd started to have real regrets about talking me into getting pregnant and having a baby."

"If you don't mind my asking, why did you?" She didn't strike him as the type who would blindly do anything her husband asked her to— unless she wanted to. "Let him talk you into having a baby?" he explained when she seemed confused.

Her initial reaction had been to say no, but then she'd changed her mind.

"Because I felt I owed it to the marriage to give it another try," she told him honestly. "And I thought that maybe a baby would help us find that spark. The one I never seemed to have felt," she confessed, then pressed her lips together as her words replayed themselves in her head.

"I guess that's a little too much information." Suzy laughed ruefully, embarrassed over what she'd just admitted to a total stranger. He had a sympathetic look in his eyes, but she didn't want his sympathy. There was no reason to have allowed that slip out. It was much too personal. "That's certainly not going to help you solve the crime. Any of them," she tacked on.

"Technically, I'm only working your husband's murder," he told her. "We have the other two murders assigned to other people and we're sharing information—if there's any to share," he qualified. It was still early in the investigation and so far nothing was being shared. "Do you know if your husband kept any files or extraneous information around somewhere? You know, things that weren't on the computer, but he still didn't want anyone else to see?"

As he spoke, he started to conduct a search himself. He pulled at the middle drawer, only to find that it wouldn't budge. He looked down, his expression registering only mild surprise. "Did he always keep his desk locked?"

"I wouldn't know. Peter didn't want me in here." She knew how that had to sound, but she'd really had no interest in his work, other than it helped pay his share of the bills.

"How about when he was at work?" His guess was that most women would have taken the opportunity to poke around then. "Weren't you curious?" he prodded.

"Not really. Peter kept the office door locked. Besides, I was at work myself for most of that time." She paused a moment, then added, "I told myself that whatever he had in this room had to do with the job."

"And did you believe yourself?" Nick asked, watching her closely to get a handle on what she was really feeling.

She looked at him knowingly. "I'm not an idiot, Detective."

"No, ma'am," he agreed. "In my opinion, you're definitely not an idiot." He ended the sentence on a firm, upbeat note, waiting for her to follow it up with something, anything.

He didn't have long to wait.

"I felt that as long as I didn't ask questions and accuse him of cheating—as long as I supposedly didn't know what he was up to, we could make our way back from there, save the marriage. Maybe start over, for Andy's sake." But that hope had quickly died when Peter made himself even more scarce. He'd left her no choice but to ask for a divorce.

She blew out a long, heavy breath. "Now there's

no need to start over, at least, not with Peter." She looked up at the detective. "But I certainly will be starting over, won't I?"

He felt her discomfort. The woman had been through the wringer today. Nick made a quick decision. "I think I have enough here for now." He nodded at the computer tower. "I can come back tomorrow. And I am sorry for your loss, Mrs. Burris."

A bittersweet smile curved her mouth. "My loss, Detective, happened long before today—or yesterday." She watched as he took the various plugs and cables off, uncoupling the computer tower from the monitor and all the other peripheral bells and whistles that comprised its accessories. "You need any help with that?" she asked, indicating the tower.

He picked it up from the desk and tucked it under his arm. Nick couldn't help grinning at the offer. He was a good six feet tall with a solid athletic build while she was—what?—five-two, five-three and slight? The thought of her offering to help him carry *anything* amused him.

"Thanks," he told her, "but I think I can manage."

Of course he could, she thought wryly. "I'll walk you to the door."

He was about to say that he could find his own way out, then decided against it. Instead, he just nodded and said, "Thanks."

She was a nice woman, he thought. And, from what he was piecing together, she seemed *too* nice for the likes of the deceased sheriff.

Suzy stopped at the front door, opening it for him. "Do you have any idea when I can...pick up Peter's body?" That sounded so bizarre to her. Peter's body. A man like Peter should have had at least another forty years ahead of him, not cut down so soon. "For the funeral," she explained.

"The medical examiner has to complete his autopsy first." Because they had no medical examiner of their own, the department had requested one be brought in from Dallas. A J. D. Cameron arrived an hour ago, looking none too happy about being temporarily transplanted. "He probably won't be releasing any of the bodies for at least another day or so," he told her. "Best guess," he qualified, since he had no idea exactly how things worked in this formerly sleepy little town.

There'd never been a murder here before, at least not since it had been officially christened

"Vengeance" and incorporated. Legend had it, though, that the town's name came as a result of someone taking their revenge and killing a guilty party.

Suzy took the detective's qualification into account. She was about to say goodbye when he stopped and put the tower down on the front porch.

"Did you forget something, Detective?" she asked.

Nick dug into his pocket and took out one of the cards that he'd had made up for himself when he accepted this job—Vengeance, it turned out, didn't have "money to waste" on trivial things like business cards for its police detectives.

Maybe that should have warned him about the kind of place where he'd decided to settle down. But it had seemed like a good idea at the time. Besides, all things considered, he honestly didn't have a better place to be.

"I wanted to give you my card in case you happen to think of something before I come back tomorrow—or if you just want to talk—you can reach me at either one of these two numbers," he told her, pointing to the two phone numbers printed in the lower right-hand corner.

Accepting his card, Suzy looked at it as she nodded in response to what he had just said. "Thank you," she murmured.

Why did the sound of her voice, lowered like that, sound so incredibly sexy to him just now? Maybe, instead of jumping from one police force to another, he should have first gone on an extended vacation, somewhere peaceful where it would have been only him and several seashells?

"Yeah, well, I'll see you tomorrow," he mumbled. Turning on his heel, Nick made his way to the car one of his colleagues had dropped off for him. He noted absently that the vehicle was in desperate need of a wash.

He glanced up at the sky, wondering if it was going to rain. That would solve his problem and the countryside could certainly use a little rain these days. The land was rather parched. The summer had been a hot one and for the most part, there had been no relief except for an occasional anemic sprinkle.

He was doing it again, Nick suddenly realized as he popped the rear hood and put the computer tower inside the trunk. He was filling his mind—crowding it—with trivial information. It was a habit he'd developed years ago, a way to keep from thinking about what was *really* on his mind.

In this case, it should have been on details about the sheriff's murder. But it wasn't. Instead, his head was filled with extraneous details about the sheriff's widow. Those light blue eyes that had gotten to him.

He caught himself thinking that for a woman who'd given birth two months ago, she certainly had regained one hell of a figure. That in turn made him wonder what kind of a fool the sheriff must have been, to go tomcatting around when he had *that* waiting for him at home.

Some men didn't deserve the luck they had, he thought darkly.

He pulled himself up short. This was *not* where his head was supposed to be. What the hell was wrong with him, anyway? Nick silently demanded, upbraiding himself as he drove away from the house.

He had a murder to investigate and solve, a murder that could hold the key to the other two murders. And he certainly wasn't going to come to any definite conclusions thinking about that little blonde.

That way only led to trouble and he knew it.

"He seemed really nice," Lori said to her sister the second Suzy walked back into the living room.

"Are you going to call him?" she asked, indicating the card Suzy had in her hand.

Suzy let the card drop on the coffee table. "No. I don't have any more information to give him, other than what I already told him."

Lori sighed, shaking her head. "I wasn't thinking about you giving him *that* kind of information, Suzy," she said pointedly.

Stunned, Suzy could only stare at her sister. All right, so even if she wasn't in love with Peter, and hadn't been for a long time, there were still nice times to remember. "Lori, Peter's not even cold yet."

Lori rolled her eyes. "Honey, from what you told me, Peter's been cold for a real long time." She shrugged. "But you know me, I don't like to speak ill of the dead—"

"Then don't," Suzy said angrily.

Her tone fell on deaf ears. "—but Peter was never right for you."

Suzy didn't feel she was emotionally equipped to hear this right now. "Lori, I know you're just being loyal to me and all that, but trust me, honey, now just isn't the time for this."

Lori nibbled on her lower lip, looking very indecisive, as if she was debating with herself on whether or not to say something.

"I never told you this, Suzy, but Peter made a play for me about a month before you gave birth to the handsomest nephew in the world." Unable to continue with the topic, she'd opted for humor— except everyone wasn't laughing.

Suzy was speechless for a second. When she found her voice, it came out in a quiet whisper. "Why didn't you tell me?"

"Because I didn't want to hurt you, Suzy. Because I told him that because he was married to you and you were having his baby, I was going to pretend that he never made a move on me, but I warned him that if I ever heard that he was cheating on you, I was going to tell you that he propositioned me—and then I was going to vivisect him, cutting out one piece at a time."

"You threatened him? Oh, God," she cried, thinking of what the FBI could do with that. She knew that Lori was all talk, nothing more, but no one else did. "Lori, what were you *thinking?* He was the sheriff, for God's sake," she cried.

"Being sheriff certainly didn't make him perfect," Lori said sarcastically.

"No," Suzy agreed quietly, "it certainly didn't.

And for the record, Lori," she added in a more quiet tone, "I knew that Peter was cheating on me. I had no tangible proof," she admitted, "but I *knew*."

Chapter 7

It wasn't that Nick didn't trust the FBI, or that he'd once worked on the Dallas police force— because he hadn't.

The Houston Police Department had been the only one he'd served on before coming here, but Dallas was closer to Vengeance than Houston was—only forty miles away—and he liked being hands-on when it came to conducting an investigation. Had he had the option, he would have preferred working within his own department, but the Vengeance police department had some lamentable gaping holes when it came to being able to offer comprehensive services.

From what he'd observed recently, the officer who doubled as a tech advisor on the force knew about as much as he did about computers. Right now, Nick needed an expert. Preferably one he both knew and trusted.

And he knew and trusted someone in Dallas.

So, rather than heading back with the late sheriff's computer to the Vengeance precinct, Nick drove the extra forty miles and made his way into the crime investigation section within the Dallas police station.

He stopped long enough to sign in with the desk sergeant and requested "professional courtesy." After the stocky man had checked him out, Nick was escorted down into the bowels of the building in order to see Chester Bigelow, a tech expert he'd gotten to know when they had worked for the Houston police department at the same time that he was there.

Nick found the man in the break room, enjoying the last of what appeared to be a triple-decker Reuben sandwich, one of Bigelow's "guilty pleasures" as he liked to refer to it. Consumption of the latter was also one of the things that had earned Bigelow the nickname "Big." In appearance, he was anything but. Nick had often maintained that the man had a tapeworm. No matter what he ate, Bigelow remained as skinny as the proverbial rail.

Sensing another presence in the heretofore empty break room, the computer tech looked up from the article in the technical journal he'd been reading. A surprised smile replaced the neutral expression on his face when he recognized who was in the room with him.

"Look what the cat dragged in," Bigelow cried, grinning. "Nick Jeffries." And then his attention shifted to the computer tower that his old friend was cradling in his arms. "You know, they've got these newfangled things called laptops now. They're a hell of a lot easier to carry around. You might think about getting one."

Nick placed the tower down on the table in front of Bigelow. "I need your help, Big."

"That's what they all say," Bigelow responded with a laugh. "What's the matter, the lab tech in your department can't be browbeaten?"

Nick didn't waste any time with long explanations. "The lab tech in my department doesn't have as much computer savvy in his whole body as you do in your little finger."

Bigelow nodded, making no pretense at any false modesty. He knew he was good. Damn good. "Flattery. You must be desperate."

Nick saw no reason to deny the computer expert's assessment. He didn't waste any time getting down to the crux of the problem. "I tried to crack the password and the hard drive went into self-destruct mode."

"Amateur." Big laughed. "So I take it the drive is fried?"

"Don't know," Nick told him honestly. "The power plug was pulled out before the program reached the end of the countdown."

Bigelow nodded his head in approval. "Simple but direct. Quick thinking for a non-geek. There's hope for you yet."

Nick never took credit when it wasn't due. This time was no exception. "I wasn't the one who pulled the plug out of the socket."

Bigelow laughed to himself. "I should have known. So, what kind of a timeframe are we looking at. When do you need this by?"

Nick didn't beat about the bush, or couch his answer in niceties. "Yesterday."

This time the laugh was hearty. "Still always in a hurry, I see." Finishing his sandwich, Bigelow wiped his mouth, tossed the napkin onto his plate and leaned back in his chair. He studied the computer for several seconds before raising his eyes to his friend's. "So what's the story behind this?"

Nick filled him in, giving him all the information he had at the moment. Bigelow accepted it as his due. It had to do with respect for him as well as for his overall expertise.

"The computer tower belongs to a sheriff who was murdered sometime yesterday and then dumped in a shallow grave." For now, Nick kept the fact that Burris was one of three bodies, as well as the FBI's involvement in the case, to himself.

Bigelow regarded the tower thoughtfully before raising his eyes again. "And you think the reason he was murdered is on the computer?"

"Maybe," Nick allowed since he had no proof that he was right—although the hard drive attempting to self-destruct seemed like a dead giveaway. "Right now we're just looking into everything," Nick admitted to the other man.

"This sheriff have a name?" Bigelow asked.

"Most sheriffs do," Nick replied wryly. When his friend continued to look at him, one thick black eyebrow raised expectantly, Nick told him the man's name. "Peter Burris."

The response he got from Bigelow was not one he expected or was prepared for. "You're serious," Bigelow demanded in obvious disbelief. "Well, son of a gun, looks like Burris's sins finally caught up with him." The laugh had a hollow ring to it as he shook his head again. "How about that?"

"Back up, Big," Nick requested, trying to factor in this latest piece information he'd just been thrown. A new wave of anticipation telegraphed itself through his body. "You *know* Burris?"

"Wrong tense if he's dead," Bigelow pointed out. "But yeah, I knew *of* him," he said, emphasizing the difference. "Saw him a couple of times while he was still on the force, heard about him a lot more."

Nick wanted to be very clear on this. "Go on."

"Okay. From what I knew, Burris disappeared rather abruptly. The official story had it that he left for personal reasons, but the rumor was that there was some kind of scandal behind his now-you-see-him-now-you-don't act. He got the wrong people angry," Bigelow told him. "Heard he worked security for some kind of upscale nightclub here in Dallas after that. Then he left that to become the sheriff of Dogpatch, or some such story."

"Actually, he became a county sheriff, but I think you're referring to Vengeance," Nick corrected. "The name of the town is Vengeance." He was surprised at the prick of annoyance he felt to hear the place he lived being belittled. He'd thought himself indifferent to the town. Maybe he wasn't so indifferent to it after all. "It's a forty-mile drive from here."

"I'll put it on my list of places to see," Bigelow quipped. "Vengeance," he repeated, somewhat amused. "Sounds like a place Burris would go to. Heard he wasn't exactly a very forgiving man," he explained. And then Bigelow looked at the tower that Nick had brought in with him. This time he gave it a far more interested once-over. "So this was his, huh?"

Nick nodded. "I'd be really grateful for anything you can manage to pull off it."

"Grateful, hell," Bigelow mocked. "I get anything off this little beauty and you'll owe me your first-born."

"Not much chance of that," Nick assured the other man flatly.

Bigelow looked at him knowingly. "Still swearing off commitments, huh?"

"Let's just say I'm married to the job," Nick told him crisply.

"That'll get old eventually. Job can't keep you warm at night, or curl your toes when they need curling."

"Don't stay up nights worrying about my toes, Big. I'll manage." He nodded at the tower. "When do you think you can have something for me?"

Bigelow shook his head again. "Still as laidback as ever, I see." He regarded the tower. "It's not like I can work on this on the clock."

"Can't you pull some personal time?" Nick suggested. "I've got a hunch this is the key to Burris's murder." He looked at the other man. "I'll owe you one."

"You'll owe me twelve," Bigelow said, but it was obvious that his curiosity had definitely been aroused. "Okay, leave it with me," he instructed. "I'll give you a call if I find something."

Nick rose to his feet. "I need it sooner than later," he emphasized. He paused a second, then decided to give the tech expert another piece of information. Maybe it would motivate him. Bigelow always had a strong sense of competition. "The FBI's involved in this."

"The FBI?" Bigelow repeated incredulously. "Anything else you want to share? Like the name of some other alphabet-crazed federal bureau that's in on this, too?"

"No, as far as I know it's just the Vengeance police force and the FBI," Nick told his friend.

"FBI has its own lab techs," Bigelow pointed out. "Why bring it to me?"

The answer was simple—and one he knew would appeal to his friend. "Because you're the best, Big."

"More flattery. Cheap trick," Bigelow pointed out. And then he shrugged his thin shoulders. "Lucky for you, it works. Give me a few hours or so, I'll see what I can do." With that, Bigelow rose as well, tucking the tower under his arm.

He looked, Nick couldn't help thinking, like a kid who had just gotten what he wanted for Christmas and was about to take it apart to see what made it tick. He knew from the old days that Bigelow liked nothing better than to pit his intelligence against a computer and take the machine down.

* * *

Life Goes On.

It was a motto that John Abramowitz, the head dean of Darby College, had hanging on the wall behind his desk. His wife had needlepointed it for their first wedding anniversary. It was a simple truth that couldn't be disputed. No matter what happened, good or bad, life always went on.

And so it was at the college, even though their most celebrated professor, Melinda Grayson, had apparently been abducted.

Although, he thought nervously, as of yet, there had been no ransom demand made. Shouldn't there have been a demand by now?

As the head of the college, Abramowitz fully expected that the demand would be directed to him, since Melinda Grayson had no close family to speak of anywhere in the state.

All there was, if he remembered her application form correctly when she'd submitted her résumé to the college, was an ex-husband. Ex-husbands weren't known to step up with the proper ransom money when their ex-wives were kidnapped.

No, the note or the call regarding the amount of the ransom and where to drop it off would have come to him, and so far, there hadn't been any.

In the meantime, life had to go on. And so did Professor Grayson's classes. Someone would have to step in and temporarily take her place. The classes were all filled with students, all waiting to be taught something that would make the price of their tuition seem worthwhile, or at least bearable.

Fortunately, as if blessed with some futuristic insight, the professor had left behind lesson plans and very detailed notes for each of the upcoming classes in the semester ahead. Lesson plans and notes he intended to pass on to the assistants he was about to assign to take over her classes. The two assistants stood at attention, waiting for his direction.

"Sit down, please," Abramowitz requested, gesturing to the two chairs before his two-hundred-year-old hand-carved, hand-oiled desk. When they did, the dean got started. "As you might know, Dr. Grayson is currently missing—"

"Excuse me, Dean, but wasn't she kidnapped?" Ben Craig asked. "I thought I heard that she—"

"That is one school of thought," Abramowitz allowed, cutting the grad student off. His eyes swept over the lanky young man, and then Amanda Burns, the other graduate assistant he'd called into his office. "But until the school receives an official confirmation that she has indeed been kidnapped, the professor is just currently not on campus. Hopefully, that situation will change soon." He steepled his fingers together as he leaned back in his chair. "But, until she does return, she has classes that need to be helmed."

Dropping his hands back down, Abramowitz leaned forward over his desk, his small eyes looking at each student in turn, forming a silent bond with them—or so he assumed.

"Which is why I've asked you both to be here. I would like the two of you to split her classes between you and take them over."

"Take them over?" Amanda echoed, stunned and more than a little nervous about the very thought of having to step into the professor's shoes. "But we can't take her place."

"No one is asking you to take her place, Ms. Burns," Abramowitz pointed out patiently. "What the department needs is to have you and Mr. Craig just fill in for a little while," he instructed. "With any luck, it won't be for too long. You are both familiar with Dr. Grayson's work—"

"Familiar, yes," Craig agreed, interrupting. "But

those are really giant shoes you're asking us to fill, even temporarily." He began enumerating all the things that needed to be put into place. "We need time to prepare lesson plans for the classes, see what material needs to be covered—"

Having quickly worked up a full head of steam, Ben was forced to stop talking because the dean was holding up his hand.

"That's all been taken care of, Mr. Craig. It seems that Professor Grayson had all her lesson plans already written up for the entire semester, so all you two need to do is stick closely to it, teach what she had intended to teach, and everything will be fine." Abramowitz smiled broadly, as if what he'd just proposed were as simple as breathing.

The two graduate students, however, didn't seem that easily convinced.

"She had them all written out?" Amanda asked in disbelief. "Really?"

"Yes. Lucky, I know," the dean said, agreeing with what he thought both the students were thinking. "I found the lectures in her study after the FBI finally allowed me to have access to her home. They'd been left neatly on her desk, all labeled, in chronological order, with a separate sheet of notes tucked into each dated folder."

"Wow," Ben couldn't help murmuring under his breath, "talk about being anal."

The remark, audible enough for the dean to hear, earned him a rather annoyed, withering look. "Lucky for Darby College that the professor is such a stickler for detail," Abramowitz said, deliberately rephrasing Ben's assessment. He indicated the two stacks of papers on his desk. There was a preprinted sheet on top of each stack. "Now here are the classes, along with her notes. Sort it out between the two of you and be sure to stay on schedule so that when the professor finally returns, she'll be able to pick up just where you left off."

"You really think she's coming back, Dean?" Amanda asked him nervously.

"I most certainly do," Abramowitz assured her with alacrity.

In her short time at the college, the professor had swiftly earned near-celebrity status. That in turn had brought a great deal of attention to their little, heretofore unheard of college. The dean wouldn't allow himself to contemplate anything *less* than the woman's unharmed return. Getting her safe return was his ultimate goal and he was determined to reach it, no matter what it cost.

The phone rang, rousing Nick from a dead sleep. He had no recollection of laying down, but he must have because when he jolted into a sitting position, he realized that he had sprawled out on his sofa.

Damn, but his back hurt. He needed to invest in a new sofa, he thought grudgingly, clearing the cobwebs from his brain.

A beat later, he realized what had woken him up.

Focusing on the source of the ringing, Nick grabbed the landline receiver, put it against his ear and growled, "Jeffries," into the mouthpiece.

"You sitting down, Jeffries?"

It took him a second—because his brain was still struggling out of the haze that had surrounded it—but he managed to recognize the voice.

Bigelow.

The lab tech he'd gone out of his way to approach earlier today.

"In a manner of speaking," Nick mumbled, dragging a hand through his hair and trying to pull his thoughts together at the same time. Neither was a complete success.

"I finally cracked Burris's password and got into the computer," Bigelow announced with no small amount of triumph in his voice.

Nick might have been sleepy before, but he was wide awake now. "And?" he prodded. He knew that Bigelow liked his share of drama and, when there wasn't any, he had no problem with building it up himself.

"*And,* my friend, it seems that your town's dead sheriff was one hell of a busy little beaver while he was still alive. Burris was into all kinds of stuff—if what I just pulled off his computer was on the level." He paused for a moment, as if waiting for a drum roll. "—not the least of which was blackmail."

"Blackmail?" Nick echoed, stunned. "Who was he blackmailing? Were you able to get a name?" he asked.

"Oh, I got a name, all right," Bigelow assured him. "Seems our black-hearted sheriff was blackmailing a number of people, but I think you're really going to like his main target."

Nick waited for a second, but Bigelow was silent, drawing the moment out. "And that was?" he prodded. "C'mon, Big, it's the middle of the night. Don't make me beg."

"All right, all right, but just because we're friends. Peter Burris was blackmailing Senator John Merris."

Chapter 8

At this point in his life and career, Nick was confident that very few things could still surprise him.

What Chester Bigelow had just told him, however, definitely qualified as one of those few things.

"Are you there, Jeffries?" Bigelow asked when he received no response from the other end of the line. "Did you hear what I just said?"

"I heard you, Big," Nick answered. The case was officially messy now—if what Bigelow had just said was true. "Are you absolutely sure about this?"

Nick heard the man sigh impatiently. "I did what you said, I took some personal time and I've been working on recovering information from this damn hard drive since you brought it in. I haven't been to bed yet, so, yeah, I'm sure," Bigelow retorted waspishly. "I could email all this to you—and there's a hell of a lot of stuff—this guy documented *everything*—guess he wanted to make sure he didn't wind up being blackmailed himself." Bigelow paused, as if reconsidering what he'd just offered to do. "Tell you the truth, I'd rather not put it out there," the tech told him. "You never know who could hack into your system. How soon can you get over to my place?"

Nick looked at his watch again, trying to get his brain to engage and actually *see* the numbers. It was half past two—not that it affected his answer one way or another. He did a quick estimate involving traffic at this time of night and distance.

"I can be at the Dallas station in less than an hour."

"Don't go to the station. I'm at my house." Bigelow proceeded to rattle off his home address. "I'll be on the lookout for you. I take it you still drive with a lead foot. One hour, huh?"

With the phone receiver nestled against his

shoulder and neck, Nick was already shrugging into the shirt he'd absently discarded last night. He was still wearing the jeans he'd changed into when he came home.

"Give or take."

"I'd rather give," Bigelow told him. "Okay, see you soon." And with that, the line went dead as the call was abruptly terminated.

Nick staggered into his master bathroom, threw some water onto his face and went looking for his shoes, which weren't where they were supposed to be.

The search for his shoes made him think of Suzy Burris and the high heels she'd had on—and how sexy her legs had looked to him.

Pushing aside his intense, immediate reaction to her image—damn, he was going to have to really police himself more stringently—he focused on the problem of her late husband.

Had she really been oblivious to what Big had just uncovered? Had Burris managed to keep all this from her, or was she actually his silent partner, taking part in his blackmail scheme?

Nick vacillated between feeling protective of her and angry for being duped by the woman.

She hadn't said anything about *any* of this to

him yesterday. Was she just being secretive, or had she *really* been in the dark about this?

And just what was this information going to do to the investigation—besides blowing it sky high?

It couldn't be just a weird coincidence that the Senator had been killed, too.

Or could it?

Had Burris conducted the blackmailing on his own, or was he an instrument for yet another, unknown party? Had that "unknown party" been the one to have killed Burris? Why?

And what did the third victim, David Reed, have to do with any of this?

Damn, Nick thought in exasperation as he hurried out of his house and into his car, he had far more questions than he had answers. Certainly a hell of a lot more questions now than he'd had before.

This investigation was *not* going well.

Nick turned up the music. It was going to be a long drive.

She'd been right. Even with Lori there to take over caring for Andy during the night, she hadn't been able to sleep more than a few minutes at a time. And even those minutes were comprised of sleep that could only be termed as fitful.

Consequently, Suzy was up and sitting in the kitchen, nursing a cup of coffee when she heard the doorbell. Glancing at the watch that was only off her wrist when she showered, Suzy frowned.

She wasn't expecting anyone. Who could be on her doorstep at seven in the morning?

It had to be a reporter, she decided. Who else would be so insensitive as to bother her at this hour, especially just after her husband had been murdered?

By the time she reached the front door and yanked it open, Suzy had worked up a full head of steam. She was more than ready to give the person standing on the other side of the door a piece of her mind.

The hot words hovering on her lips died when she saw a rather rumpled-looking Nick Jeffries on her doorstep.

What was he doing here at this hour? She couldn't tell by his expression if it was good news or bad news that he was bringing her. Suzy braced herself for the worst, just in case.

"Detective, are you all right?" she asked,

quickly looking him up and down. She couldn't come to a conclusion—other than he looked tired.

Welcome to the club, she thought.

"Did you know?" Nick asked sharply.

It wasn't quite an accusation, but there would be no room for forgiveness if she'd knowingly lied to him and he made that clear by the tone of voice he used.

Suzy stared at him. She hadn't the slightest idea what the detective was talking about—but his tone made her uneasy.

"Did I know what?"

Nick strode past her into the house, pushing the door closed behind him. He was in no mood for her to play innocent.

"Did you know that your husband was black-mailing a number of people, including Senator Merris?" He swung around to look at her. "One of the two other murder victims found near your husband's grave."

Suzy turned pale.

This couldn't be happening.

Just when she thought that it couldn't get any worse, it did. Who *was* this man she'd married? When had he managed to do all this? It didn't seem possible. Could she have been so blind to this darker side of his?

"He was *what?*" she cried, staring dumbfounded, at Nick.

"Blackmailing Senator Merris." No one could fake that pale color that had just come over her face, he thought. His anger vanished as quickly as it had materialized. She wasn't in on this with the sheriff. She looked too stunned and upset. Compassion made a comeback, stirring his gut.

"You didn't know, did you?"

The detective's voice became a distant buzzing in her head. None of the words registered as Suzy somehow managed to make her way to the sofa. Clutching the armrest, she sank down.

Actually, her knees just gave way a second before she reached the sofa. But rather than go down on the floor, she'd been caught. Held.

Suzy was vaguely aware of arms closing around her. Aware of a presence beside her, a person whose touch was exceedingly gentle. It was understood that she would shatter if any sort of actual physical pressure, no matter how well meaning, was applied to her limbs.

And although she'd always thought of herself as

tough and made of sterner stuff, at this moment, she wasn't all that sure that she *wouldn't* shatter.

She heard the command "Breathe!" uttered near her ear and did as she was told, drawing in air, and then slowly releasing it again.

Once, twice—by the third lungful of air, Suzy had begun to come around, to be able to focus again.

She blinked a number of times, and then looked to see that the detective whose revelation had just torpedoed her world for a second time in two days was the one sitting beside her on the sofa, his arm protectively around her shoulders.

He'd created a haven for her.

There *was* no such thing, she told herself bitterly the next second, feeling numb and hopelessly betrayed at the same time.

"I'm okay," she told Nick.

But when she tried to get up, she found that the detective was firmly holding her in place, his hands on her shoulders.

"Sit for a little longer," he told her. It wasn't a suggestion. "I don't think you want me picking you up from the floor."

He was talking about fainting. Just like she'd

done the day before. Suzy had no intentions of embarrassing herself twice in two days.

"I wasn't going to faint," she protested.

"Whatever you say," Nick allowed philosophically. Now that he realized she'd had no part in Burris's dark actions, he was feeling bad for having detonated this newest bombshell on her like this. "But humor me for a couple of minutes."

Suzy shrugged carelessly, remaining where she was. Not so much because she was going along with the detective's veiled order, but because what he'd just said had all but paralyzed her, or at least had frozen her in place.

Where did she begin to try to untangle all she'd been hit with?

Feeling utterly helpless, she looked at Nick and clutched at a straw. "Are you sure? About Peter blackmailing people? And what did he have on them? How could he be blackmailing someone? Why would he do such a terrible thing?"

Suzy suddenly covered her mouth with her hands, as if she was attempting to physically hold back the questions until she could organize them so that they made more sense.

"God, you must think I'm a total idiot not to know about any of this." Her eyes shifted to his.

"But I didn't. I swear I didn't. When Peter didn't talk to me, I didn't realize that there was this much he wasn't talking about."

Suzy blew out a long breath, feeling completely overwhelmed.

"A lot of smart people get fooled by people they trust," Nick told her gently. "Did you ever notice the sheriff spending lavish amounts of money, buying large-ticket items he wouldn't have been able to afford on a sheriff's salary?"

She shook her head. *That* she would have noticed. "No, nothing. No fancy clothes, no vacations, no expensive cars, nothing," she insisted. "You can search the house if you like." She dragged her hand through her hair. It hung loose, like a blond storm, about her shoulders.

This all sounded like something out of a movie, not her life. "Everyone seemed to like him," she told Nick helplessly. She'd already told him that, she realized, but it was the only thing she could think of to offer as a defense.

And then, overwhelmed, she shook her head. "It's like he had this whole other life that I didn't know about." It would take her a while to wrap her head around this. To believe that Peter had done all these things. "So do you think that this—this blackmailing that Peter was doing—was what had gotten him killed?"

At the moment, that was the million-dollar question, Nick thought.

Out loud, he said honestly, "I don't know. Especially since the main person he appeared to be blackmailing was Senator Merris and like I said, Merris was buried in the grave near your husband."

"Blackmail," she repeated incredulously. It was so hard to believe. "And here I thought that Peter's affairs were the most sordid thing he was guilty of. I guess that really shows me," she laughed harshly, a trace of bitterness hovering around her words.

She suddenly looked very fragile to him. Moreover, Nick was actually feeling her pain and all the insecurity the situation generated. She was the kind of person, he sensed, who felt responsible for her husband's shortcomings. But it wasn't her fault.

"What your husband did has nothing to do with you," Nick told her firmly. Placing the crook of his finger beneath her chin, he raised her head so that her eyes met his. "The only people we are responsible for in this life are ourselves. Sometimes a spouse does evil things that you might feel reflect badly on the person they're married to but the real truth of it is, it just reflects badly on them.

Most of the time, their spouse has nothing to do with their bad behavior. They don't even know anything about it."

She looked at him for a long moment. And then she understood. Nick had gone through this himself.

"You sound like you know about that firsthand." And just like that, the tables turned. Sympathy rose like a solid wall when she saw him shrug at her words. "Are you married, Nick?"

He thought of the wife he'd once loved. And of the woman who had ultimately betrayed his trust. It seemed like a hundred years ago now.

"No," he responded, his voice distant.

She wasn't ready to let this go just yet. Nothing made her forget about her own situation faster than someone else in need of comfort. "But you were?"

He could have easily said that his marital state had no bearing on the case. But instead, he heard himself answering her question. Maybe it was because he felt he owed it to her because he'd pried into her life.

"Once."

Suzy made assumptions from the look she saw in his eyes. "And she kept secrets from you?"

"As far as I know, there was only one thing she

kept from me." Maybe there had been more than one, he didn't know. He hadn't stuck around to find out. It was the one that had ended their marriage.

Suzy backed off. She didn't want to cause him any undue pain, especially since she now knew what that felt like. "I'm sorry, I have no right to pick at your wounds."

The denial came quickly and automatically. "It's not a wound. Besides, it happened a long time ago." He supposed, if he were really over it, he could talk about it without any residual pain.

He braced himself anyway.

"She was pregnant and she didn't tell me." He looked away, not really seeing anything. It went along with distancing himself from the words he said. "She just decided not to be."

"Oh."

The full impact of his words hit her and Suzy knew that what she saw in his eyes, despite his detached, distant voice, was raw pain. Rather than offer any platitudes or say something that would just sound inane, she put her hand over his, silently offering him her condolences as well as a mute offer of support and comfort should he want either.

When she looked back on this later, Suzy realized that this was the moment when they ceased to be just polite strangers on opposite ends of a murder investigation.

This was the moment that they bonded.

Clearing his throat—as if that would somehow also clear the air and clear away the words that had just been uttered—Nick said, "I think your husband might have been blackmailing the senator for money. Did your husband handle the banking?"

"No, actually, I did. I'm a certified public accountant," she explained. "I've been on maternity leave these last couple of months," she added, "but until Andy was born, I worked full-time for a restaurant chain and took care of all our monthly bills as well. Peter hated being bothered with all those details," she told him matter-of-factly. She realized now that he was just too busy with all the other things he was into. "So I just took over."

"And you have a joint savings account?" Nick asked her.

"Yes—and a joint checking account, too."

"Which bank?" he asked.

"First National Bank of Vengeance," she told him. An ironic smile curved her lips. "I always said that it needed a better name."

He made no comment on that. In his opinion, the whole *town* needed a better name than the one they had accepted. But that was neither here nor there right now.

"Would you mind coming to the bank with me?" he asked.

"No problem," she answered. Lori would stay here with the baby, so she was free to take off and try to possibly help undo a little of the damage that her husband had been responsible for. "Mind if I ask what you're hoping to accomplish?"

"I want to find out if Peter had another account, under his own name." It wasn't the smartest thing in the whole world to have a secret account in the same bank where your joint accounts with your wife are, but then the man in question didn't strike him as being the sharpest knife in the drawer— even if he were the *only* knife in the drawer.

She might as well get everything over with at once, find out just how black the picture was, she decided. "All right."

He didn't want her to think he was rushing her. The bank still had over an hour and a half before it would open its doors.

Nick looked at his watch and did a quick calculation. "Why don't I give you a couple of hours to have breakfast and get ready? I can come back at around nine and we can go to the bank then?"

"Do you have someplace that you have to be for the next two hours?" she asked. She had a feeling she already knew the answer to that, but waited for him to tell her anyway.

"No, but—"

"Then stay here," she urged. "Once I get ready, I can make us all some breakfast—unless you already ate—"

He'd come straight from Big's Dallas apartment to her door, stopping only for some coffee in order to fuel up and keep going—preferably awake.

"No, I haven't had breakfast yet," he answered.

Her smile lit up her face he noted, almost against his will.

"Okay, give me about ten minutes to get showered and dressed, and then I'll see what I can come up with for breakfast."

"Ten minutes?" he echoed incredulously, staring at her. "Did you just say that you could get ready in ten minutes?"

"Yes." Suzy couldn't see why he would look so surprised at that. "Why?"

He laughed shortly. "Nothing, except I've never known a woman yet who could get ready for anything in under an hour. Certainly not in ten minutes," Nick scoffed.

She smiled at him, taking a tiny personal moment out of what felt like it had the makings of an absolutely awful day if the first hour was any indication.

"That's because you've never known me before, Detective," she assured him. And then she grew serious. "If you suddenly feel as if you're starving, feel free to help yourself to anything in the refrigerator while you wait," she tossed over her shoulder.

He stood where she'd left him, watching Suzy hurry up the stairs. The sway of her hips seemed almost rhythmic to him.

No, he thought, *I've never known someone quite like you before.*

Nick wasn't aware he was smiling until he caught a glimpse of his reflection in the window as he passed by.

Chapter 9

Nick wasn't one of those people who had a favorite restaurant or even a favorite dish. Ever since his divorce, he was more apt to eat whenever he was hungry rather than at a given time. He adhered to structure in his professional life. His private life, however, was a different matter. It was entirely flexible.

So when he sat at the kitchen table and the sheriff's widow placed a Spanish omelet before him, urging him to "dig in," he was surprised to discover his appetite kicking in. His taste buds came to life as a rather spicy, tantalizing taste registered when he took his first bite of the omelet.

Nick looked down at his plate as if he'd just had a whole new taste experience. That was as surprising to him as his unexpected attraction to Suzy Burris had been.

"What's in this?" he asked.

"Is it too spicy for you?" she guessed, concerned. Lori had opted to take her breakfast later and was tending to Andy so it was just the two of them in the kitchen. Suzy slid into the chair directly opposite her unexpected guest.

"No, it's not *too* spicy," he allowed, "but it is definitely spicy. And really good," he told her belatedly. He wasn't much on giving compliments so it felt rather awkward on his tongue. But he thought it only right to let her know that he was enjoying what she'd just made. "What's in this?" he asked again.

She merely smiled, pleased that she'd actually made something that the detective enjoyed eating. It had been a long time since she'd gotten positive feedback of any kind, and that included on her cooking. The only way she knew if Peter liked something or not was that if he didn't like what she'd made, he'd leave it on his plate.

"Oh, a little bit of everything. That's what's so neat about this recipe, you can use practically anything you have on hand that's edible. This time around I used ham, cheese, mushrooms, eggs, of course and one tiny, diced-up jalapeño. That's the spicy part," she told him with a grin, then nodded over toward the stove. "There's more if you're still hungry."

"Maybe later," he told her. "Right now, I have a feeling that if I get too full, I'm just going to get sleepy, and there's no time for that. The clock's ticking on this," he said with emphasis.

That had a very ominous sound to it, Suzy thought. "What aren't you telling me?" she asked.

He'd made a quick pit stop to his desk at the station and had run into one of the FBI special agents who had been assigned to the triple homicide. The special agent had yet to figure out how, but he felt that the murders were somehow tied in to Dr. Grayson's disappearance. And the longer the woman remained missing, the less likely, in the special agent's opinion, that she would be found still alive.

The information had been shared with him in confidence. It wasn't for the general public's knowledge and despite the fact that Suzy Burris wasn't exactly part of the general public in this case, he still felt that he couldn't share it with the sheriff's widow, at least not at this time.

"Nothing that I know of," he told her, his voice devoid of any emotion. "But the sooner we find out who killed your husband and the others, the sooner we can get him—or her—off the street, and that can only be a good thing."

Suzy read between the lines. This wasn't over yet. "So you think this person might kill again?"

She was watching him so intently, he could almost *feel* her eyes on him. Nick realized that it took effort for him not to react. He kept his focus on the case and *not* on the fact that something about Suzy Burris was definitely getting to him.

It had to be the vulnerability angle, he told himself the next moment. The fact that she was a petite, slender blonde with sky-blue eyes was neither here nor there. He'd interacted with his share of attractive women and hadn't experienced any feelings one way or another.

Yet feelings—dormant feelings—kept insisting on coming into play here.

"If he's a serial killer, yes," he told her, controlling his voice. "If this was done strictly for revenge or some other specific reason known only to the killer, then no. But we're not at the point when we can be sure of that one way or another," he told her. "And since that's the case right now, I'd much rather err on the side of caution than be too laid-back and face possible consequences because of that."

Suzy had eaten rather quickly while the detective talked and now rose again, taking her plate to the sink. "All right," she announced, crossing back to the table and him, "I'm all yours."

He had no idea why that simple sentence hit him the way it did, or why, for just a fraction of a moment, his imagination went to places that had nothing to do with his investigation and everything to do with him as a man—and her as a woman.

The glimmer of sexual attraction he had become aware of yesterday seemed to have been simmering on some backburner ever since, and now kept insisting on springing forward, grabbing at and demanding his full, undivided attention.

He had no time for that now—or ever, really. He'd tried marriage once, found that it was an ill fit for him and had made his peace with that years ago as the ink dried on his signature on the divorce papers.

Or so he had believed until he'd encountered

Suzy Burris. Now he seemed to have this—for lack of a better term—pervasive restlessness haunting him. It was hiding in the corners of his focus, popping out at will, unannounced and unexpected, to throw him off balance.

"Detective?" she said, looking at him curiously. When he still made no response, Suzy came closer, tilting her head as she looked at him and tried again. She used his first name this time. "Nick?"

"Sorry, just thinking," Nick said, brushing off the question he saw in her eyes.

He felt fairly confident that the woman would assume that he was thinking about the case—and not her. Although right now, she very well could figure into this scenario prominently. He needed to find out if there was anything that Suzy Burris *did* know about her husband's dealings.

"When you met your husband, was he already the county sheriff?"

When she met her husband, she couldn't help thinking, he seemed like a completely different man. Which had been the real Peter Burris? The one from those days, or the one who'd died approximately three days ago?

She shook her head in response to the question. "No, he was working a security detail at a nightclub in Dallas." She recalled that Nick had mentioned the DPD yesterday. "He never said anything about having worked as a police detective anywhere."

Well, if he had amassed the kind of record that Burris had, he wouldn't have readily admitted his connection to the police force to anyone, either. Nick thought.

"So when your husband stopped working security detail, was that your idea, or his?" Nick asked.

Your husband.

What a joke, she thought. Husbands were supposed to share things with their wives. Right now, she couldn't think of Peter as anything but a stranger.

"His," she told Nick, then admitted, "it happened rather suddenly, actually. He came home one night and said he had this big surprise—that we were leaving Dallas because he'd scored a plum position—he was going to be a county sheriff."

At the time, she welcomed a change of scenery. Things had already been getting stale and going badly between them. A change of venue could be the shot in the arm they both needed, she'd reasoned.

But she'd been wrong.

"I thought we'd be moving to Houston or San Antonio— When he said we were getting a house in Vengeance, I thought he was kidding. I'd never *heard* of Vengeance until then," she confessed.

He nodded understandingly. "It's not exactly on the list of the country's ten major cities. Did you try to talk him out of it?" he asked.

She shook her head. "I didn't have the heart. He seemed too excited about getting the job. And, to be honest, I wasn't exactly happy about where I was working, so leaving wasn't really a hardship."

From where he was sitting, Nick thought, Burris had it all—a beautiful wife and a promising career. What had he done that caused it to all go south on him?

"Did your husband happen to say what brought about this sudden change in careers?"

This keeping things to himself had its roots in those early days, she realized now. "No, only that he thought his luck was finally changing."

"So you didn't know that he was a dirty cop," he pressed, watching her face for some telltale sign that would indicate she was lying to him, or that she'd known that her husband was corrupt.

Suzy grew very still. He saw all the joy that had

been there only moments ago while they were casually talking, abruptly disappear.

"What did he do?" she asked in a voice that was completely drained of any emotion, any feeling. A voice that belonged to a shell-shocked woman.

Ordinarily, Nick didn't pull punches, but he found himself weighing his words, searching around for euphemisms.

"I think he might have been doing favors for people who were in a position to show him their gratitude. Apparently, some of the cases he handled while on the force had to be dismissed when crucial evidence would mysteriously go missing.

"When your husband moved on to work security at that nightclub he somehow got wind of the fact that Senator Merris had being siphoning off millions from his oil company, funneling it to his election campaign. He used the money to get himself elected, while other people wound up going bankrupt. Your husband found out and used this to blackmail the senator. Merris pulled some strings, got the old sheriff to suddenly retire and gave your husband the county sheriff's job in exchange for his silence."

He paused for a moment, letting his words sink in, and then told her, "From some of the things your husband had on his computer, I'd say that the blackmail didn't exactly end there."

She felt overwhelmed and struggled to find a way to rise above this quicksand of demoralizing corruption.

She asked the same question she'd put to him earlier. "And this is what ultimately got Peter killed?" It was all very hard to fathom—but she had this sinking feeling that, if anything, the detective with the kind eyes was now trying to downplay all this for her benefit.

"That would be the logical assumption—except that the senator was found dead, too," he reminded her, and went on to mention again the fly in the ointment. "And I still don't know how David Reed figures into this."

It would take her a long, long time to put this all behind her. She wasn't in love with Peter, but she'd still believed that, at bottom, he was a good man. Now that belief just mocked her and made her feel incapable of judging a person's true character. Any guilt over her lack of grief was wiped out by the fact that, apparently, she'd been married to someone she didn't know. Someone she *never* got to know.

"I *knew* there were things that Peter was keeping from me, but I had no idea it was something like *this*. I just thought his secrecy had to do with other women he was seeing." Had there been signs that she'd missed? Or had she just been oblivious to it all because she'd wanted to be?

"He had his share of those, too," Nick told her.

He would have rather not said anything about it, but he knew the media. Once they started digging, they would splash it across the TV screen. He wanted Suzy to be prepared for the firestorm rather than be taken by surprise.

She struggled not to loathe the man she'd married—the man she'd *thought* she'd married.

"It doesn't make any sense," Suzy cried, anger flaring in her voice. "Why would Peter want to have a baby with me when he had all this going on at the same time? Why would he want to stay married to me at all?"

Nick could easily see why the sheriff would have wanted to stay married to Suzy. Why *any* man would have wanted to be married to her. He had trouble seeing why Burris had so wantonly thrown it all away.

Nick approached her question from another, logical angle. "Maybe he wanted to have his cake and eat it, too. Being married with a family adds to the image of an upstanding lawman. You told me that most people liked the sheriff—"

She shrugged. "Maybe I was wrong about that, too. Seems I was wrong about everything else," she said disparagingly.

She was standing, facing the kitchen window, no longer able to make eye contact. Afraid that if she saw pity in Nick's eyes, she'd break down and cry. That was the last thing she wanted to do, fall apart in front of someone else.

Nick sensed what she was going through, what recriminations she was heaping on herself in the privacy of her own mind. He'd been there himself, except that his wife hadn't been in a place of public trust. But she'd turned out to be a fraud and a cheat in her own way just the same. He had felt just as empty, just as devastated, just as betrayed as he knew Suzy was feeling right now.

He came up behind her. Placing his hands on her shoulders, he turned Suzy slowly around to face him. "None of this is your fault."

So he'd already said before. She kept her eyes down, not wanting to meet his. Her voice was thick with emotion and tears she refused to shed.

"Maybe not, but being blind is. How could all this have been going on and I didn't have a clue?"

He'd asked himself that same question at the time. "Don't forget, the sheriff was undoubtedly very good. He managed to fool a lot of other people besides you—otherwise, he would have been up on charges and in prison a long time ago," Nick told her.

She supposed he had a point, but that didn't help her now.

"If I'd only known, I wouldn't have agreed to have Andy." Anguish filled her eyes. "How am I going to be able to tell my son, when he starts asking questions about where his father is, that his father was murdered because all the lying and cheating he'd done had finally caught up with him?"

Rather than answer her question, Nick asked her one of his own. It was short and to the point. "How do you feel about Andy?"

"Well, I love him, of course." That wasn't the issue. "He means everything to me, but—"

Nick stopped her before she could continue. She'd already said the relevant part.

"Then, don't you see, that's all that matters. You love him and you'll be there for him. He's your son and part of you. And in the end, having him will help *you* get through this."

Suzy pressed her lips together. He'd undone her with his kindness. Her emotions spilled out.

Nick saw the lone tear trickling down her cheek. The sight of it felt like a one-two punch straight to his gut. Holding himself in check, he took a breath, and then he took his thumb and very gently, wiped the tear away.

Suzy let out a very shaky breath. "You're very insightful for a police detective," she told him in a voice that was only slightly above a whisper. She was acutely aware of his closeness, his gentleness. Aware and finding herself getting incredibly warmed by it.

Maybe *too* warmed.

"It's my sensitivity training," Nick quipped, trying to be flippant, doing his damndest not to get reeled in any further by eyes the color of cornflowers in the spring or lips that he had a great deal of difficulty ignoring.

He'd brushed away her tear with his thumb and had been struck by how soft her skin felt. At the same moment, the realization of just how very long it had been since he had kissed a woman had hit him. Not just that, but also how very long it had been since he had *wanted* to kiss a woman.

And then, just like that, he was no longer thinking about how long it had been because the answer to that was not long at all. He was feeling it and he was doing it. Doing both.

Wanting and kissing.

Cupping Suzy's cheek with the palm of his hand, he'd lowered his mouth to hers.

Suzy remained very, very still, her eyes wide open and watching him. Afraid to move, afraid to take a breath, afraid that if she did either, she would break whatever spell had brought this moment about and make him back away.

When his lips touched hers, she felt the heart that had been, just a second ago, hammering double time all but sigh with pleasure.

The next second, as she leaned forward *into* the kiss, Suzy felt her pulse accelerate the way it used to when she was jogging and nearing the end of her run.

Except that this was far more exhilarating.

And almost as rewarding.

Still cupping her cheek, Nick took his other hand and framed her face, deepening the kiss he still couldn't bring himself to believe was happening.

Kissing her was definitely having its side effects. He could *swear* he was feeling somewhat lightheaded and, at the same time, incredibly and almost wildly exhilarated.

Damn it, Jeffries, get a grip! This has no place here! his brain was all but screaming at him, years of discipline warring with very strong, very basic needs and desires.

With a huge surge of regret thundering through his system, Nick pulled back. His hands were on her shoulders again as much to steady himself as to steady her.

How did he make this huge transgression right?

"I'm sorry," Nick began and was able to get no further.

He got no further because he couldn't. Couldn't form a single other word. This time, with her arms firmly linked around the back of his neck, *she* was kissing *him*.

When he'd pulled back, creating that chasmlike space between them, Suzy had looked up at him with dazed confusion, trying to process what he was saying to her and what she felt had to be his feelings behind his words. But then, instead of listening to anything further, instead of hearing something she might not want to hear, Suzy had launched herself back at him and had resumed the delicious, abruptly interrupted, kiss.

Because, at that particular moment, when Nick had kissed her without warning, she had realized that for the first time in close to a year, she felt alive.

More than that, she felt like a living, breathing *woman,* something that she hadn't felt like in the last year of what she now knew had been only a sham of a marriage.

This was what she'd wanted to feel when she was with Peter, but she hadn't—and now that she looked back, she realized that it had turned out for the best, though of course she'd never wanted him to die. Her love had been a lie, since he was a lie. Everything about Peter had been a lie. Had she truly loved him, it would have made things that much worse for her.

This kiss had been, Suzy suspected, an accident on Nick's part, a moment fueled by a temporary weakness. Whatever the reason behind it, she didn't care. Right now, all she cared about was the effect. She wanted to savor this sensation, this feeling before it was gone out of her life for good.

In a strange, roundabout way, she caught herself thinking before all thinking stopped, Peter was responsible for making this happen. It was the only decent thing he'd done for her in a long time, she thought, other than giving her Andy.

Chapter 10

Nick discovered, much to his surprise, that it was harder pulling away the second time around—because this kiss was even more enjoyable and arousing than the first kiss.

Somehow, he managed to draw away from the woman who'd stirred him to the point that he found himself ditching his principles, his training and his natural tendency to be cautious.

Had there been no investigation, no case that could possibly involve Suzy directly or indirectly, he would have been free to go with his instincts—

instincts he had been so very sure that he'd sealed away and left behind him years ago.

But then, had there been no investigation, their paths, his and Suzy's, most likely wouldn't have crossed. And even if they had, there would have still been a problem. At that point—if there'd been no murder—she would have been a married woman, he reminded himself.

It seemed that no matter how he sliced it, this— whatever *this* actually was—was just *not* supposed to be happening between them.

And yet, there was no denying that something was definitely happening between them.

It took Nick more than a couple of seconds to get his bearings—and that, too, surprised him. Until now, he'd always been able to land on his feet no matter *where* he fell from.

"I'm sorry, that shouldn't have happened," he apologized, taking the full blame for both occur- rences. "It's just that you looked so upset and I wanted to help somehow."

Nick suppressed an exasperated sigh. That hadn't come out right. Words, whether verbal or written, had never been his long suit. He'd always been better at doing, at acting rather than talking. Now was no exception.

Despite everything that was going on, Suzy couldn't help but smile at him. This tall, powerful-looking police detective was stumbling around like a newborn colt trying to stand up on his unsteady legs.

"Actually, you did help," she responded. "It's been a long time since I've felt—anything."

Suzy left it at that, a vague statement he could interpret any way he wanted to. To say more now would only scare both of them off and she had no idea if what she was feeling was born of gratitude—or something else.

"Maybe I'd better come back later—tomorrow," Nick suggested, wanting to give her some time to reassess the situation—wanting to give himself some time, as well.

As far as he was concerned, this was nothing short of conduct unbecoming in his case and no matter how attractive he found the woman, that wasn't supposed to have any bearing on his behavior. He wasn't supposed to be acting on impulses even if his intentions had been honorable to begin with—or so he'd told himself.

"No, please." Suzy caught his sleeve, holding on to it far more firmly than he would have thought her capable of doing. "I want to help you with this investigation. I *need* to help," she emphasized. "The Peter Burris I knew wasn't a monster, but if what you're telling me is true, he was far from being the honest man he pretended to be and he did things that I will always be ashamed of—"

Nick didn't want her dwelling on that. "I told you, it's not your fault," he said firmly. "*None* of this is your fault."

"Then let me help," she requested simply.

He saw the need in her eyes and relented. Not to would have been cruel.

"All right, I could use another set of eyes as well as hands," he allowed. "And you'll probably make much less of a mess than I would—although," he warned her, "this is going to have to be a thorough search."

She wasn't going to hide. If there was something damning hidden here, it had to come out. And if there wasn't, then maybe the picture wasn't as black as Nick had painted it. Either way, she wanted the truth.

Suzy nodded. "I understand."

They spent the next several hours going over the three-bedroom home with a fine-tooth comb, emptying closets, clearing drawers, climbing up ladders and examining places that were normally inaccessible to anything but dust accumulation, such as the tops of kitchen cabinets. The search took twice as long as initially projected because they painstakingly disassembled then reassembled each room.

And for their trouble, they found a few things that Suzy had long thought lost. As far as discovering why Peter Burris had been murdered, along with the man who'd been his mark, or why there'd been a third victim thrown into those shallow graves, they got no further in their investigation.

Somewhat drained by the search and the subsequent disappointment, Nick suggested they take a break. They'd just finished going over the master bedroom and, crossing into the hallway, they sank down onto the floor, their backs resting against the wall.

Seeing her sister and the detective looking so weary, Lori must have taken pity on them. After putting Andy down for a nap, Suzy's sister hurried downstairs and within minutes returned to present each of them with a tall, frosty glass of pink lemonade.

Suzy took hers with both hands and first applied it to her forehead and cheek, absorbing the coolness with an appreciative sigh.

"You're a saint," Suzy told her. Lori had placed a straw into hers, just the way she preferred it. It had the effect of taking her back to the early days of her childhood, when life was far less complicated and demanding.

Before she became aware that her family unit was far from idyllic.

"That's not how she felt when we were growing up," Lori confided to Nick as she handed him his glass.

"You needed a lot of work back then," Suzy deadpanned. "But you let me guide you and you turned out really well."

"Guide me, ha!" Lori declared with a pseudo-haughty laugh. "I 'turned out really well' *despite* your so called guidance, dear sister, not because of it," she concluded with a triumphant note.

Nick had no idea if this was headed for a confrontation, or if it was some battle solely based on habitual banter, so he decided to divert the conversation into a different direction.

"This really hit the spot," he told Lori, holding up his glass after downing half the contents in one long gulp. He hadn't realized that he was *that* thirsty until Lori had handed him his lemonade. "Thanks."

Without turning around, Lori waved her hand over her head as a sign that she'd heard him and appreciated his comment. "My pleasure, Detective," she said just as she disappeared around the corner.

"So, is that every place?" Nick asked Suzy once he was alone with her again.

She nodded. They'd been through every room, including the nursery and all the bathrooms. "There's just Peter's car left—"

That, he thought, turned out to be another dead end. "I already had a crew go over that. They didn't find anything except that the late sheriff seemed to have a thing for chewing gum. There were a lot of discarded gum wrappers on the floor, both in the front *and* the back. Maybe he was going for a record in most accumulated gum wrappers."

She laughed shortly. "Peter tends—tended," she amended abruptly, correcting herself as she wondered how long it was going to take for her to get used to the idea that Peter was no longer among the living, "to chew gum when he was tense."

"Whatever he was doing that was making him tense, it was recent," Nick judged. "The wrappers hadn't gotten dried out from the sun shining into the vehicle," he told her. Finished with his lemonade, Nick wanted to get back to work. He rose to his feet then extended his hand to her to help her up.

Ordinarily, she would have ignored the silent offer of help and just gotten up on her own, but there was something about this man, something that made her trust him despite the way she had gotten burned in her marriage. Something that made her *want* his help. To welcome his touch.

So, placing her hand in his, she allowed Nick to help pull her up.

Taking in and releasing a long, cleansing breath, she looked up at him and asked, "Now what?"

Nick found he had to tear his eyes away from the way Suzy's chest rose and fell as she drew in that deeper breath.

That was *not* going to help him keep a clear head here, he upbraided himself silently.

Damn it, he *knew* better.

"I think I'd like to go over the sheriff's office one more time, see if we maybe we might have missed something."

She cocked her head, trying to keep things straight. "You mean Peter's office in town?"

"No, here," he corrected. "The FBI guys are

taking your husband's office in town apart piece by piece—most likely not making any points with the new, interim sheriff," he guessed. "They would have called if something had turned up."

She nodded. "All right, you go ahead." Suzy felt her stomach pinch her and she glanced at her watch. "It's getting late." As she talked, she started to lead the way downstairs. "I should start getting dinner ready." Stopping midway down, Suzy looked at him over her shoulder. "Would you like to stay? For dinner, I mean?" she clarified in case he thought she meant anything else.

Distance, you need to keep your distance. "I shouldn't—" Nick began.

"You have to eat, Nick," she insisted. She wanted him to understand that there was no need to reject her hospitality because of what had happened between them earlier. "And I promise to let you do it in peace."

There was a hint of an ironic smile curving Nick's lips. "You're not the one I'm concerned about," he told her.

Suzy stopped at the bottom of the stairs and turned around to look at him again. Amusement had crept into her eyes. "Oh?"

"Yeah, 'oh,'" was all he allowed himself to say by way of a comment on her reaction.

The truth was he didn't trust himself. It was almost as if, when he hadn't been paying attention, he'd undergone a breakdown in self-discipline.

But no matter how it came about, that would end as of this moment. Once was a fluke, not right but forgivable. Twice was the beginning of a pattern—and the end of his career as an impartial officer of law enforcement.

"So, three plates for dinner?" she asked, silently telling him that her sister would be joining them and that Lori would serve as their insurance policy that nothing remotely compromising would happen if he decided to stay for dinner.

She was a good cook and the prospect of heating up a frozen dinner or bringing something home from one of the takeout restaurants in his neighborhood didn't sound nearly as appealing, so after what amounted to an incredibly short internal debate, he nodded, accepting her invitation.

"Three," he echoed, then flashed what came across as a tight smile. "Thanks."

Suzy caught herself grinning in response. She was really pleased the detective was staying.

Maybe it was wrong of her, but she was beginning to see the light at the end of the tunnel and because of that light, she knew she would get through this ordeal intact.

And it was in large part due to the detective.

"Good—and don't mention it," she added as an afterthought.

They parted there, at the bottom of the stairs, each going their own way. She went to the kitchen while he went to give the sheriff's already carefully examined home office one last once-over.

He'd just walked into the center of the room when his cellphone rang. Nick had it out and against his ear before the second ring had a chance to complete its chimes. "Jeffries."

He instantly recognized the voice on the other end. It belonged to one of the members of the hastily formed task force, comprised of his men as well as several of the Bureau's special agents. So far, they seemed to be working rather well together.

"Hope you're having better luck over there than we are over here, Nick," Detective Robert Littleton said. "That interim sheriff they appointed, Tony Berretti, wasn't exactly all that pleased to have us ripping apart what's now his office."

"I already figured on that. Just remember, we're not in the business of pleasing small-time county sheriffs. We're after bigger things," Nick reminded Littleton.

Having come up against dead end after dead end, at this point Nick found himself dangerously short on patience. He felt as if his back was against the wall. He bit back a sigh as he dragged one hand through his dark, and at this point, unruly hair.

"Yeah, I know, which is why it would have been great if we had something to show for our efforts, but there's nothing here to give us so much as a clue that the guy was even *thinking* about black-mailing the 'honorable' senator from Dallas, much less doing it—or blackmailing anyone else."

Someone called to Littleton and he shouted back that he'd be right there before continuing with his "non-report" to Nick.

"And there's not a damn incriminating thing on his computer here. It's just lucky that you got hold of the one that Burris kept at his house," Littleton told him.

Nick could almost *hear* the relieved expression echo in the other man's voice.

"Yeah, lucky," Nick repeated. But they were going to need something more to corroborate "All right, Littleton, if you've got nothing to report, I'm hanging up. I'll see you later at the office."

He was about to terminate the connection when he heard Littleton call out to him.

"Um, Boss, if you don't mind, the guys and I are gonna call it a night and actually go home at six for a change." Littleton broached the idea slowly to his lead on the case. "My wife's been complaining a lot lately that I'm not spending enough time with her and the kids. She's got the kids calling me 'stranger' instead of Daddy."

Nick suppressed a laugh at this piece of information. He kept forgetting that although he had no family, the other men on his team did. He couldn't fault them for wanting to see them for more than a total of ten minutes a day.

"Fine, I'll call you if anything comes up," Nick said, then broke the connection as the man on the other end was thanking him.

He didn't need gratitude. What he needed was more evidence, something concrete. For all he knew, someone could have doctored Burris's home computer, planting damning evidence that would turn the dead man into a scapegoat. He needed something else to go on.

Preoccupied, he started to tuck the phone back into his pocket, but he wound up missing his target. The phone slipped from his fingers and fell onto the rug.

Hitting the floor at an angle, the phone bounced twice and wound up landing under Burris's desk.

All the way under.

"Great," Nick muttered, biting off a ripe curse in case either Suzy or her sister was passing by and could overhear him.

Getting down on all fours, Nick carefully crawled under the desk to retrieve his phone. The space was crammed and he had to be extra careful to keep from hitting his head.

The phone had landed at the extreme rear of the desk. Nick was forced to snake his way as far back as he was able to go.

He couldn't help thinking that as a kid, he would have really loved getting under a desk like this one, with only one side opened up the way it was. He would have spent hours playing under it, envisioning the desk to be a dozen different things, not the least of which would have been a cave.

The Bat Cave, Nick decided with an unconscious grin.

And, since he was away from any prying eyes, Nick allowed himself a momentary nostalgic respite as fragments of memories came back to him.

Memories of the little boy he'd once been before he'd become disillusioned with the world and found out that nothing ever turned out the way you expected or wanted it to.

But that time was years behind him, Nick reminded himself. Time to act like a responsible adult.

Phone in hand, he began to crawl backward out of the small spot. As he was snaking his way out, he thought he heard a landline ringing. Startled by the unexpected sound—half thinking it was coming from his own phone—he straightened abruptly and raised his head, only to smack it against the bottom of the drawer. Hard.

This time he did curse, although he managed to keep it under his breath, as pain shot through his skull and even vibrated along the bridge of his nose.

Moving carefully back one small "step" at a time, Nick glanced at the underside of the offending drawer to see if he had dented it—or left any blood behind.

And stopped short.

Unless he was hallucinating from the swiftly growing bump that was forming, there was something, a small padded envelope from what he could see, taped to the underside of the drawer.

Holding his breath, Nick began to work at peeling back the strips of tape and separating the envelope from the underside of the drawer.

The clear packing tape that held it in place was strong, which told him it was still relatively new. The weather in the area tended to be humid in the summer. The humidity was strong enough to leave its mark, corroding things like plastic shower curtains and plastic packing tape.

After finally freeing the envelope, Nick resumed backing out from the desk. He made sure not to lift his aching head until he was well clear of the desk. The top of his head was still throbbing from the sudden contact.

"Okay," he said to the envelope once he was clear and out in the open. "Let's hope you're worth this trouble and not just another so-called lead that's going to go nowhere."

Ripping the envelope open, he turned it upside down and shook it.

A single, thin, silver key fell at his feet. The

paper tag attached to it had a four digit number clearly typed on it.

The kind of number that was used to denote a bank safety deposit box.

Chapter 11

Nick studied the key thoughtfully for a moment, turning it over to see if the name of the bank had been embossed on either side.

He found nothing.

Still, he felt it safe to assume that it *was* a safety deposit key. He was just going to have to find out which bank housed the box.

Looking at it, he wondered if Suzy knew about the key. Its existence may have slipped her mind in the face of all this turmoil. Or she was deliberately holding back information. All things considered, he was rather a good judge of character, but he wasn't infallible.

Nick found the sheriff's widow in the kitchen, whipping up something that smelled incredibly tempting on three of the burners.

Almost as tempting as she was.

He *had* to get hold of himself. Otherwise, his thoughts would wear him down and there was no telling how he'd wind up acting on these feelings, which kept blindsiding him when he was least prepared.

Suzy looked up from the green peppers she was chopping into fine slivers. "What did you find?" she asked.

Habit made him feel her out warily. "What makes you think I found something?"

"You've got that look on your face, that look that says you came across another possible piece of the puzzle." She paused, waiting for him to disprove her assumption—or agree with it. When he didn't, she pressed, "Well, did you? Find something?" she specified, her eyes never leaving his face.

"Did your husband ever mention having a safety deposit box?"

Suzy thought for a moment. "He said something once about getting one," she recalled. "He said he thought we could keep life insurance policies and the deed to the house in it. But as far as I know, it was just talk." She saw what looked like a flash of interest flicker in Nick's eyes and second guessed what he was probably thinking: that maybe she'd had Peter killed to collect on the life insurance policy she'd just mentioned. "And, as far as I know," she said, reiterating a point she'd made when he'd first asked her about the life insurance policy, "there are no life insurance policies. That was just more talk on Peter's part."

Picking up the chopping block she'd been using, she tilted it and poured its finely chopped contents into the pot where she already had chicken breasts, parsley and mushrooms simmering in chicken broth.

"Maybe there were no life insurance policies, but it looks like there *is* a safety deposit box," he told her, holding up the key.

She stopped working and crossed to him. Wiping her hands on the apron she had carelessly tied around her waist, Suzy took the key from him and swiftly examined it, then handed it back to Nick.

"Never saw it before," she told him with a puzzled frown. "What do you think is in the box?"

Something that might have gotten Burris killed, but he kept that thought to himself for now, saying instead, "We're going to have to open it to find that out—and in order to open it, we're going to have to locate it."

"Well, I'm going out on a limb here, but seeing as how Vengeance isn't exactly a thriving metropolis, I don't think that's going to be overly difficult."

Her droll comment made him grin wryly. He wouldn't have thought she was capable of sarcasm. That she was amused him.

"Vengeance has two banks within the town limits. A lot of people are creatures of habit, so I'd start with the one where you have your checking accounts," he suggested. "Unless," he reconsidered for a second, "the sheriff was the type to try to hide his money in an offshore account somewhere, like in the Cayman Islands."

That *really* didn't sound like Peter, but then, this person who was emerging didn't sound like Peter, either, she thought, shaking her head.

"As far as I know," she told Nick, going back to the meal she was making on the stove, "he liked to keep things close by. I once told Peter I half expected him to keep our money under the mattress—for easy access. It wasn't that he really didn't trust banks," Suzy explained, "he just wanted to be able to get his hands on what he needed quickly, night or day."

Nick closed his hand over the key and tucked it into his pocket. "Nearby bank it is," he told her.

With a course laid out for them, Suzy was all set to take her apron off and drive to her bank, but one glance at the overhead floral kitchen clock on the opposite wall told her that going to the bank was not exactly an option right now.

It was seven o'clock, an hour after the bank had shut its doors. "It's closed," she realized with disappointment.

He nodded. "Nothing we can do until morning."

Suzy regrouped. "Well, we can eat dinner," she pointed out.

"There is that," Nick readily agreed, drawn closer to the stove by the aroma that was wafting over to him.

He recalled that he hadn't really been near a stove—other than in passing—since his divorce. He made coffee for himself in the morning, using a coffee machine he'd brought along with him on his move from Houston. If he wanted more, there was always a takeout restaurant in the area to call or drive to. The only items he purchased in the supermarket were coffee filters and coffee. The largest cans of coffee the market had to sell so that he could keep his trips there to a minimum.

He inhaled deeply—and appreciatively. "Smells good," he told her, nodding toward the pots on the stove.

Suzy smiled at the compliment. "I'm hoping it tastes better."

Hard as it was to believe, it did, Nick thought approximately forty-five minutes later. The meal Suzy had made tasted so incredibly good that he'd done something he rarely did. He overate.

He ate so much that if he consumed one forkful more, he wouldn't have been able to get up from the table and walk anywhere, much less to the front door.

He liked to think of himself as fighting trim. At this point though, he was more like pacifist fat. Or at least he felt that way, stuffed to the gills.

Suzy saw his empty plate and began to ask if he wanted another serving. "More—"

She didn't get a chance to finish her question because Nick held up his hand to halt the oncoming flow of words.

"No more," he told her. "Otherwise, I'm going

to burst at the seams right where I'm sitting. That was probably one of the best meals I've ever had," he told her honestly.

His words surprised her and pleased her more than she could begin to say. "Thank you," she said when she found her voice. "You really didn't strike me as the type to hand out compliments like that."

Nick caught himself thinking that he liked the way that her eyes crinkled at the corners when she smiled broadly.

"I'm not," he told her. "I guess this just brought it out of me. It changed the rules," he added, trying to explain things to himself more than to her.

She was definitely a game changer for him. Being with her made him look at the world a little differently—made him feel more the way he assumed a normal person felt.

Made him think about and want things a normal man might want, instead of being the emotionless machine he had become in these last years.

You're waxing poetic, Jeffries. Time to go.

Taking a deep breath, Nick placed his hands against the table and pushed himself back. Abruptly, he said, "Bank opens at nine. I can be back here at a quarter to the hour if that's all right with you."

She nodded. "A quarter to nine is fine with me," she assured him. "I want to find out what Peter had in that safety deposit box as much as you do."

He'd only been looking at it from his own point of view, as a cop. What was this like for her, finding out over and over again that she was married to a virtual stranger? He was surprised that Suzy wasn't becoming increasingly bitter with every new discovery. He had felt bitter when Julie had been guilty of only one secret, not a score, like Burris seemed to be.

In her own way, Suzy Burris was made of sterner stuff than he was, Nick thought in admiration. He almost said as much to her, then caught himself at the last moment. He had to remember to keep this on a professional level.

"A quarter to nine tomorrow, then," he confirmed formally.

"I'll be ready," she promised.

But she wasn't.

When Nick arrived at her door the next morning, he found Suzy trembling, fighting to keep back tears. This was so different from the woman he'd left last night, he was instantly on the alert.

His hand went to his gun as he quickly scanned the immediate area, looking for an intruder.

"What's wrong?" he asked her sharply.

For a second, it was still all too fresh, too unnerving, and Suzy couldn't talk, couldn't organize what had just happened into coherent words.

Her heart was hammering hard in her chest, so hard that she thought it would literally break through her ribs.

Since there appeared to be no clear and present danger in the house, Nick removed his hand from his weapon and looked at the woman he had begun to think of as cool under fire.

This was definitely *not* cool under fire.

He saw the anguish in Suzy's eyes and he felt it twisting his heart. Before he could stop himself, Nick took her into his arms, his gruff voice transformed into a softer, infinitely more soothing one.

"Suzy, what's wrong?" he asked again, then coaxed, "Talk to me."

She willed herself to calm down as she took in a deep cleansing breath, and then let it out slowly. She had to do it a second time before she could even begin to answer him.

"I just had a phone call." She pressed her lips together to keep the sob that was hovering in her throat from coming out. "Someone just threatened Andy. He threatened my baby," she cried, her voice hitching. "He said that if I didn't hand over what Peter had on Senator Merris, what Peter had been holding on to as his 'insurance policy,' he was going to kill Andy."

Her voice shook now. "And he told me if I called the police, or told anyone at all about this, he was going to slit both our throats."

The senator again, Nick thought in exasperation. But the man was dead. Who the hell was calling if the senator was dead? Who was left to gain anything by getting their hands on whatever it was that Burris had stashed away? And what *was* it that Burris had had on the man? Compromising pictures? An incriminating tape?

Whatever it was, Nick had a hunch it was in that safety deposit box. The sooner they located it and opened it, the better.

Nick's arms tightened around her, as if to silently tell her that he was going to keep her safe, no matter what.

Because he was.

"No one's going to hurt you or your son," he told her fiercely. "I'm going to protect you. I swear I will." He needed her to try to remember everything she could about the call. "Suzy, this person who called you, did you recognize his voice? Did it sound familiar?"

Ashamed of her tears, she buried her face in his chest and moved her head from side to side in response to his question. A sense of hopelessness echoed in her voice.

"No, it was distorted." She raised her head to look up at him, her cheeks stained with tears as she struggled to regain control. "I can't even tell you for sure if it was a man or a woman. It was like being threatened by some mad, futuristic robot."

It sounded insane, but he knew what she was trying to say.

"For the time being, let's just assume it was a man. We need to find out what that key that your husband kept taped to the underside of his desk unlocks and what's inside. I have a feeling that it's going to be whatever this guy is looking for."

He knew what she was thinking, that the second they left for the bank, the person who called her would break into the house, harm her baby and her sister. "I'll have a patrolman keep an eye on things here while we're at the bank," he told her, taking out his phone.

Suzy let out a sigh and nodded her head. The

promise of a police officer on the premises didn't calm her down completely, but it was a start. If anything ever happened to Andy—or her sister—because of this, she wouldn't be able to live with herself.

Frank Kellerman smiled to himself. It was the kind of smile whose full impact sent chills through brave men's hearts and caused casual strangers to cross the street in order to avoid him and pretend he didn't exist.

The cold expression had served him well in his dealings as the late Senator Merris's head aide. Due to his dedication—and his less-than-upstanding dealings on his boss's behalf—he had clearly been on the rise. The senator saw him as an asset. Who knew how far he would have gone?

But then, according to new reports, someone had placed a plastic bag over the senator's face, suffocating him—and simultaneously sent all his well-orchestrated plans crumbling into the dust. He'd been filled with rage at the unfairness of it all, ready to lash out at the world and everyone in it.

And then, out of the blue, he'd been contacted by party or parties unknown. No names had been used, but the caller had known an unnerving amount of information about him. He'd been given specific instructions: retrieve the damning evidence that the late Sheriff Burris had had on the senator any way he could.

The disembodied voice on the other end of that fateful call had told him that if he served well, he'd go much further than he could possibly have ever dreamed.

Failure, the caller made it very clear, was not an option.

Kellerman wasn't planning on failing. Failure was for men without ambition or backbone. He had both—in spades—and he intended on going places.

He'd thought he'd get there after hitching his wagon to Merris's star, but obviously he'd been wrong there. The senator had gotten himself killed. For all his cunning, John Merris had ultimately turned into a loser.

Well, that wasn't going to be him, Kellerman thought fiercely.

As if to underscore that, out of the blue, he'd been given a second chance and he was going to make the most of it. Lightning had struck twice, it wasn't about to strike a third time.

Whoever had initially called and pressed him

into service was not going to be disappointed with his performance. He would get results. Hell, he'd had the sheriff's widow in tears, he could hear it in her voice. She wasn't about to risk her son's life and cross him.

Whatever it was that his mysterious caller was after, he'd be able to get it from the woman, despite her protests that she had no idea what he was talking about.

"Then *get* an idea," he had ordered in no uncertain terms, seeing through her innocent act. "Or your son dies. Your choice."

And with that, he'd hung up, confident that he had left her nerves in tatters. She'd be afraid not to comply with his order, it was as simple as that.

Satisfaction permeated all through him.

His feet were firmly back on the ladder of success and this time, he thought, shoving his hands into his pockets, he intended to climb up all the way.

About to leave the study where he'd gone to place the call, Kellerman stopped abruptly when his fingers came in contact with a folded piece of paper.

That hadn't been there the last time he'd worn

this jacket. As far as he could recall, the paper hadn't been there when he'd *put on* the jacket.

Puzzled, he pulled the paper out. It was folded over in a square and his first name was written across the top. Who the hell had put that into his pocket?

He looked around even though the room was empty. He half expected someone to pop out from behind the drapes, but no one did.

How did the note get into his pocket?

More curious than ever, he unfolded the paper. Printed inside were four words: "I'm proud of you."

An eerie feeling came over him. Someone was watching him.

But who? And where were they?

And exactly why were they proud of him?

He stared at the words for a very long time. The longer he stared, the less sense it all made.

Chapter 12

"Really, Andy and I will be fine," Lori assured her sister for a second time. "There's a patrolman on his way," she reminded Suzy, nodding at Nick for backup, since he'd been the one who'd placed the call. "You don't have to hold my hand until he gets here. Go, see what's in that mysterious safety deposit box," she urged. "You know I'm dying to find out myself."

But Suzy refused to budge. She stood by the window, looking out and waiting for some sign of an approaching police car. "The safety deposit box'll still be there if we leave fifteen minutes from now. I'm not going *anywhere* until I know you're safe."

"Can't you *make* her go?" Lori asked, appealing to Nick. "She's been overprotective and stubborn like this all her life."

"Well, if that's the case, nothing I say to her is going to change her mind and frankly, I'm afraid I agree with Suzy." Suzy flashed him a smile for his support. "That's why I called for a patrolman in the first place. It's better to be safe than sorry."

"He's here," Suzy announced, dropping the curtain back into place. "See," she said to Lori. "That wasn't so long, and now I don't have to worry about you."

"Ha," Lori jeered. "That'll be the day. You'd worry about me even if I had a ring of superheroes surrounding me."

"Shut up and take care of my son," Suzy said fondly, kissing her sister's cheek before she grabbed her jacket and purse.

The patrolman came in and, after a quick introduction to Lori, was briefed on his assignment. He was to park his vehicle in the driveway and make sure no one came anywhere *near* the house until they'd been officially cleared. The

FBI's temporary satellite office had been placed on speed dial.

"Feel better?" Nick asked her as they got into his car.

"Yes." Suzy was not oblivious to the fact that Nick hadn't pressured her either to give him back the safety deposit key, or leave the house before the patrolman arrived. She was grateful to him for that. "Thank you."

He made his way to the main road. "For what?" he asked her.

These past couple of days had taught her not to take *anything* for granted. "For not trying to get me to leave before your patrolman arrived."

Nick laughed shortly. "He's more your patrolman than mine." When he felt Suzy looking at him quizzically, he elaborated by making reference to the pledge each law enforcement officer took upon being sworn in. "Citizens are the ones the patrolman is supposed to 'serve and protect.' That's something we in the department take pretty seriously."

She thought of Peter and all the different ways she was discovering that he had failed to live up to that simple code.

"Too bad everyone doesn't," she murmured. For the sake of privacy, Nick pretended not to hear.

* * *

The bank manager at First National Bank of Vengeance appeared surprised when Suzy requested to see him. Other than when she had come in with her husband to sign the necessary papers when they had initially opened their checking and savings accounts, she hadn't been in. If there were any transactions to be handled, it was the sheriff who came in, not his wife.

Parker Stephens looked at her a little skeptically when she'd asked to be taken to the safety deposit box. "Would you happen to have your driver's license with you, Mrs. Burris? Protocol," he explained, flashing a shallow smile.

Suzy refrained from asking the bank manager why he'd think she wouldn't and instead just held it up for his examination.

He nodded, apparently satisfied, and flashed another forced smile. "Can't take people's word for things anymore, I'm sorry to say."

"No, you can't," Nick agreed crisply. "Can we hurry things along, please? Mrs. Burris would like to open her safety deposit box before Christmas."

The manager hesitated, seeming grossly uncomfortable about the situation.

"Something wrong, Mr. Stephens?" Nick asked him.

"Well, technically," the man hedged, "the safety deposit box belongs to the sheriff."

Nick's eyes narrowed. By now, everyone in town knew what had happened to the sheriff and the two other men. Did he expect the man to come back from the dead?

"Well, 'technically,'" Nick countered, his tone stern, his eyes steely as they pinned the bank manager in place, "the sheriff is dead. As his next of kin, not to mention his widow and cosigner on both accounts, Mrs. Burris is now entitled to have access to the safety deposit box in question."

For a moment, the bank manager appeared likely to contest Nick's statement, but then he seemed to visibly wilt and backed down. "Yes, of course. Come this way, please."

With that, Stephens led the way to the vault in the rear of the bank where the safety deposit boxes were housed. The sheriff's deposit box was Number 1094.

Although there was an entire wall devoted to safety deposit boxes, Suzy noticed that many of those doors were left wide open. Those were the boxes that were waiting for someone to put them to some use. Apparently most of First National's patrons had nothing they wanted to store or keep safe.

Turning to face her, the bank manager said, "I trust you have the key with you, Mrs. Burris."

She produced it and held it up before the man. "Right here."

With a nod, Stephens took hold of the key he wore on a long chain around his neck and inserted it into the larger of the two locks guarding the safety deposit box in question.

"Now you," he instructed. Once she inserted her key Stephens said, "Turn it, please."

He turned the bank's key at the same time and the lock gave. Dropping his key back to its place under his shirt, Stephens opened the door, slid the small box out and walked toward a booth off to one side that was actually three walls enclosed around a counter. He set the box on the counter and stepped back.

"Please call when you're done." And with that, Stephens retreated, leaving them alone in the vault.

The moment the bank manager was gone, Nick opened the safety deposit box. Inside he found a passport with the sheriff's picture, but not his name. It was issued to an alias. The passport was sitting on top of a white envelope.

Suzy took the passport from his hand and looked at it. It wasn't hard to put two and two together, even though she would have never thought it of him.

"I guess he was planning on a quick getaway without me," she murmured.

Suzy was surprised that the discovery bothered her, but it was more the idea of the deception rather than the thought of being abandoned by Peter that wounded her pride, she realized. No one liked the thought of being duped by someone.

It wasn't hard to guess what she was thinking. "The man was a fool in more ways than one," Nick told her flatly.

The comment had her looking at him sharply. Was that a compliment, or just a casual observation about the types of people Peter had most likely been dealing with? The fake passport indicated that he thought he had to be ready to pick up and run at a moment's notice.

Leaving her and the baby to fend for themselves. Since he had no other family, disappearing would have been easy.

Bastard, she thought.

Again she couldn't help wondering what was going on and just *who* Peter Burris—if that *was* his real name—actually was.

But she had no time to ponder the question any

longer because Nick had just opened the envelope and taken out its contents.

The envelope was filled with photographs. A great many photographs. Most of them were rather unfocused, some were even so blurred that it was hard to make out just what or who was supposed to be in them.

But others were definitely clear enough to make out.

And clear enough for the photographer and his or her subject to have them both convicted of treason against the United States.

Suzy's eyes narrowed as she looked at the top photograph. She recognized one of the men in it. "Is that—?"

He anticipated the name she was about to use and nodded. "Sure as hell looks like him," he confirmed. "He is one of the top known arms dealers in the world." To his way of thinking, it wasn't a ranking to be proud of.

The man he'd just mentioned had recently been implicated in a weapons trade with a country that didn't exactly make the U.S.'s top one hundred friends list. On the contrary, the country had been on the brink of war with the U.S. not once but several times.

Each time, the people in question had backed off because of a lack of sufficient firepower. But apparently the country was getting closer and closer to the point where that would no longer be a problem.

Suzy's eyes widened as she looked at another photograph. This time, there wasn't even a hesitation. "That's Senator Merris," she breathed.

"Not his best side," Nick commented dryly. "But this one's clearer," he said of another photograph he produced from in the stack.

She raised her eyes from the pile and looked at Nick. "Do you think Peter took these pictures?"

There were only two possibilities. "Either he did or he stole them from someone who did," Nick answered.

The photographs appeared to have been taken from a certain angle. Had the sheriff worn a spy cam on his person and let it roll automatically? Obviously, since the person who'd called Suzy had referred to them as "insurance," that was the way the sheriff had viewed them. They were something to use as leverage in case things went south.

Also just as obviously, Burris had never gotten a chance to use the photographs. Or maybe they were what had gotten him killed in the first place.

Suzy looked at Nick after they'd reviewed all the photographs. Many lives would be forever changed if these photographs saw the light of day. "What do we do with them?"

"I'm going to have to figure that out," he told her honestly. In their present situation, he wasn't sure just whom they could trust. He needed to do a little investigating before he came to any decisions. "For now, let's just leave them here. As long as you have the only key, they'll be safer here than in your house—or at the police station," he told her.

She nodded, feeling somewhat stunned at this latest discovery. Once again she couldn't help thinking how completely in the dark she'd been for most of her relationship with Peter. She would have never dreamed that he was involved in something like this.

What other secrets were waiting for her? she wondered uneasily.

Suzy fervently hoped that this was the last of the surprises. Right now it was just shock on top of shock and she wasn't sure just how much more she could actually take.

As they left the bank, Nick noticed how pale she appeared. All this was really rough on her. Sympathy stirred within him.

"Let's get you back home," he told her gently. "Give us both a chance to process this latest little development," he said wryly.

"Nothing to process," she told him, struggling not to sound exceedingly bitter. "I was married to a monster, a man who thought nothing of being a traitor to his own country." She raised her eyes to Nick's, daring him to contradict her. "Otherwise, he would have tried to stop what was going on in those photographs. At the very least, he would have sent them to a major newspaper or a national news channel, exposing the senator and those other people who're involved in those awful dealings." The moment the words were out, Suzy realized what her next course of action had to be. "That's what we have to do," she told Nick abruptly. "Get those photographs to the news media."

He understood where she was going with this and why. But things weren't that simple.

"Not yet," Nick cautioned. "This is just another piece of the huge puzzle and we have to see how it all comes together first. We can't afford to jump the gun," he warned, then promised her, "the pictures will definitely see the light of day. But not until we find out who killed your husband and the others."

She was convinced that it would be too late by then. With each breath she took, the feeling of impending doom continued to grow. And no matter what she did, Suzy just couldn't shake it.

The feeling grew even stronger when she and Nick arrived at her home. She noticed that the patrol car was still parked in front of her house.

But at first glance, the police officer who was supposed to be on duty appeared to be AWOL.

Nick pulled up his vehicle right beside the squad car and looked in. The patrolman wasn't AWOL, he was dead. One shot to the head at relatively close range. The killer was either cocky, or stupid. His money, Nick thought in frustrated anger, was on stupid.

Panic ripped through Suzy as she stifled the involuntary cry that rose to her lips. She was out of the car before Nick could stop her and she ran to the house.

The door wasn't locked.

"Suzy, wait!" Nick called after her angrily, his gun already drawn. "Damn it, listen to me," he shouted at her, fear getting the better of him.

He sprinted from the car to the house. Catching up to her, he grabbed Suzy by the arm and stopped her in her tracks before she could cross the threshold. There was no telling if the killer was inside, waiting for her.

"Getting yourself killed isn't going to help anyone," Nick snapped.

She didn't care about her own safety. It was her baby and her sister she was worried about.

"Lori!" Suzy shouted. "Lori, are you there? Answer me!"

The only answer was the echo of silence.

It was terrifying. This meant that her baby and her sister were gone—or worse.

"Stay here!" Nick ordered. His weapon poised, he moved into the house methodically, making sure each area was clear before going on to the next one.

"The hell I will," she retorted, shadowing his every movement.

He had no choice but to let her. There was no one to keep her back.

The scene that met them in the living room said it all.

A shattered lamp was on the floor, its pieces scattered, a side table was overturned and the playpen was glaringly empty.

Lori had obviously tried to fight off whoever had gained access to the house. Because the door hadn't been broken down or jimmied, the killer had probably posed as the police officer he'd killed. By the time Lori realized what was going on, it was too late. The killer was already in the house.

He'd kidnapped her sister and her baby.

"You said they'd be safe," Suzy cried, finally breaking down. "You promised, you promised," she sobbed, struggling not to crumble to her knees. The feeling of helplessness overwhelmed her.

Nick took her into his arms. She fought him, struggling to get free and then, suddenly utterly drained, she limply collapsed against him.

"We'll find them," Nick swore to her. "We'll find them."

She had no choice but to believe him. If she didn't, the hopelessness she felt vibrating within her would swallow her up whole, burying her.

What the hell is wrong with me? a voice inside her head demanded.

Since when did she fall to pieces like some fragile China doll? Lori and Andy *needed* her. There was no time for self-pity or sobbing. Crying and recriminations weren't going to save them. Getting her act together and looking for leads, for clues, so that she could come after them, *that* was going to save them.

Nick felt her suddenly straightening in his arms. He could almost *feel* Suzy rising to the occasion like some fictional super heroine rather than just falling to pieces.

What surprised him even more than this unexpected show of spirit and strength was his reaction to it. Not only did he admire this stronger side of Suzy, but he was turned on by the subtle display, as well.

It made him want her even more intensely than he had before.

"This is my family," she told him as she drew away and stood her ground. "It's up to me to find them." She lifted her chin defiantly. "This isn't your fight."

"The hell it's not," he countered. "We're in this thing together, and I intend to help find them and bring your sister and your baby back home whether you want my help or not."

There was a place for independence and for operating alone, but only a fool turned down knowledgeable help and she knew she could definitely use all the help she could get.

"Of course I want you," she responded with

feeling, then realized that a crucial word was missing and corrected herself. "I mean, of course I
want your *help*." And then she tried to salvage the
moment—and disarm it as well—by saying, "For
one thing, your gun's bigger."

But it was too late. Both of them were aware
of her slip of the tongue and what it meant: she'd
told him she wanted him.

Just as he wanted her.

This, Nick realized, would be one tricky high-
wire act to negotiate.

"Let me call this in," he told her, taking out
his cell phone, "and get some of the FBI's crime
scene investigators out here. Maybe whoever did
this obligingly left a print somewhere." He began
pressing numbers on the keypad. He was going to
have to call for an M.E., as well. Luckily—if that
word could be applied to this case—the one sent
in from Dallas was still here. "And then I'm getting you out of here."

She wanted nothing more than to get away, but
she couldn't think about herself right now. There
was just too much at stake. "What if they call? I
don't want to miss it," she emphasized.

"They want what you have," he reminded her.
It had to be the photographs in the safety deposit

box. A lot of people were implicated in those photographs. A lot of careers would be ruined and a lot of people going to prison. "They'll call back. Right now, you need some time to pull yourself together. Some time to get in front of all this," he added.

So far, he judged, she was doing remarkably well, but that didn't mean she'd keep on going this way. Like someone who'd been shot and was still walking about, she hadn't felt the full impact yet and when she did, there was a possibility of complete collapse—far greater than what had almost transpired here.

Suzy fought back angry tears as she looked around the chaotic room. She should have been here to fight off the intruder. If she had been here, she could have kept Lori and the baby safe. For God's sake, she was stronger than Lori, she thought, upbraiding herself.

Get in front of all this. That was what Nick had just said.

If they didn't get Lori and Andy back, safe and unharmed, Suzy didn't think she would be able to get in front of all this.

Ever.

Chapter 13

As much as she wanted to go out and clear her head, feeling that any second now she would start climbing the walls, waiting for the kidnapper to call, she just couldn't make herself leave.

She stopped short of the threshold. When Nick looked at her, she shook her head and said, "I can't."

Knowing that to prod her might just push her over the edge emotionally, Nick nodded. "All right, I'll go get us some dinner," he told her.

She exhaled a breath. "Thank you."

"Nothing to thank me for," he answered. Calling in a patrolman to stay with Suzy, he left, promising to be back within the half hour.

The moment she saw Nick coming up the front walk, a little of her anxiety receded. It was as if only good things could happen as long as he was around. She knew it was a completely unrealistic attitude, but comforting nonetheless.

Nick came bearing several packages and was pleased that everything inside was still hot. He'd driven from the diner as if the very forces of hell were after him.

"Eat it while it's hot," he urged, depositing the various containers on the kitchen table and then opening them.

"You really didn't have to go to all this trouble," she protested. "I don't think I can keep anything down."

"But you'll give it a good try," he said in a voice that told her she really had no choice in the matter.

Suzy dutifully sat down once the plates and silverware were out. Nick had ordered two servings of baked ham, mashed potatoes and baby carrots drizzled with brown sugar and honey.

Taking first one bite, then another, Suzy was surprised to discover that not only *could* she eat, she was actually very hungry. One bite followed the other until suddenly there was nothing left on her plate.

Finished, she looked up at Nick with a touch of chagrin. He'd been right. Which meant he knew her better than she knew herself.

"I guess you called it."

Amused, Nick pretended not to know what she was talking about. "How's that again?"

He'd read her better than she'd read herself, Suzy thought. He deserved an apology, but she couldn't bring herself to muster one at the moment. Consequently, this was as close to one as he was going to get.

"When you said I was hungry." A rueful smile curved her mouth. "I guess I really was."

Nick had no need to hear an apology—he was just glad he could get her to finally eat something. "Just stands to reason that if you're going to keep pushing yourself so hard, you'll need to keep up your strength. Fastest way to do that that I know of is to remember to refuel. Eat," he told her, reducing the solution to one word.

And she had certainly done that, he thought. There wasn't so much as a crumb left on her plate. "Want anything else?" he asked. "Dessert? Coffee?" And then he shifted gears by asking, "Or would you like to have a drink?"

Suzy shook her head in response to each suggestion, although she hesitated for a moment when he mentioned the last item.

Part of her wanted to throw back a drink, or three, in order to numb the fear and pain that were so very close to the surface. She was so very afraid for her son's and sister's safety. But she knew that aside from it being only a temporary "fix" that actually fixed nothing, a drink, depending on its strength, could render her incapable of thinking clearly. And she needed to remain clearheaded just in case the kidnapper called back tonight—or Nick's team called with a lead for them.

"No, no drink," she finally said. "We'll have one together to celebrate once Lori and Andy are safe again."

"Sounds good," he responded, and she believed he meant it.

To her surprise, he helped her clear the plates and load them into the dishwasher. When they went back out into the living room, she couldn't help looking around, part of her expecting to see Lori there holding her son.

When she didn't, the pang that rose up within her was all but paralyzing. Tears rose in her eyes.

Nick saw the tears and knew what she was thinking. "We'll have them home before you know it." Promises like that were not typical for him, but he sensed she needed to hear the words.

"Home," Suzy echoed. The word sounded so empty to her. *Felt* so empty, she thought, looking around. "Right now it doesn't seem very much like home," she confessed freely. "Not after all that's happened."

Nick nodded. "I understand how you feel."

The words cut across her heart, drawing blood. She looked at Nick sharply as her temper suddenly flashed. Suzy couldn't keep the words back. "How could you possibly understand?" she asked, struggling not to lash out, not to shout at him for being so condescending as to assume he knew what she was suffering through. She wasn't being fair to him, but she didn't want this police detective patting her on the head as if she was a child, giving her platitudes. "My cheating, *dead* husband turns out to be a possible traitor, betraying not just me but his whole country as well and because of him, my sister and my son were kidnapped and who *knows* what else? Are you trying to tell me that happened to you, too?" she demanded hotly.

"No," Nick replied in a voice that was completely stripped of any emotion. He debated leaving it at that. He was, after all, a private person. But in the face of her pain, he decided to make the ultimate sacrifice and share his experience with her.

"I found out my wife was pregnant a week *after* she'd terminated her pregnancy. She'd swept that little life away without so much as passing thought, despite the fact that she knew I really wanted to have a family. When I called her on it, she told me that if I wanted to have something looking up at me adoringly, I should get a dog." He paused for a moment to purge the bitterness that always came along with the memory of that confrontation, then said, "I got a divorce instead."

Once the words were finally out, he realized that they—and the anger that propelled them— had been bottled up inside him all these long years, ever since he'd walked away from Julie that same afternoon he'd found out about what had happened to his unborn child. He'd never looked back. But the anger had lingered. And festered.

He felt almost liberated.

And just like that, her heart ached for him. "I'm sorry," Suzy whispered, emotion threatening to all but choke her windpipe.

It started to rain outside. The raindrops hitting against the living-room window made for a mournful sound, separating the two of them from the rest of the world.

"I didn't tell you that to get your sympathy—I told you to let you know that you're not the only person who's ever been blindsided by someone they thought they could trust. And if you ever repeat *any* of this," he warned her, "I'll deny it."

So he'd confided something to her that wasn't common knowledge. She found that comforting somehow, to be sharing a secret with him.

"I won't," she promised, then said in a slightly clearer voice, "And I'm still sorry. Sorry you didn't get a chance to find out what it feels like to hold your baby in your arms. But most of all, I'm sorry that I yelled at you just now. You're only trying to help me."

She dragged her hand through her hair, wishing she could organize her thoughts as easily. "I feel like my nerves have been peeled down to the very core, but that's still no excuse to take out my frustrations on you. You've been nothing but good and kind to me and I shouldn't be repaying you for that by going ballistic on you just like some kind of shrewish harpy—"

Nick held up his right hand for a second, calling a halt to Suzy's torrent of words. "Don't go painting wings and a halo on me just yet," he told her.

Suzy smiled at him, waiting for a second, just until the tears in her throat left so that she could talk. "Too late," she whispered.

But he heard her, even though he chose to say nothing, and just shook his head. On his *best* day no one would have *ever* accused him of being an angel.

"Well, I guess I'd better be going," he told her.

Her eyes widened. "You're leaving?"

"I'm not going very far," he answered. "If you need anything, I'll be right outside." He nodded in the general direction of his car. He intended on keeping vigil a few steps from her front door.

She shook her head, vetoing the idea. "The last policeman who stayed right outside my house didn't fare too well," she reminded him. "He wound up dead."

Her concern touched him even though he tried not to let it.

"I've pulled protective duty before," Nick assured her. "And I obviously lived to tell about it. Now, once I go out, I want you to lock up," he instructed. "I'll wait right outside the door until I hear you flip the locks and put the chain on."

She caught his hand as he turned to leave. He looked at her quizzically. Her eyes held his for a long moment. When she spoke, it was to make a request. "Come inside. Stay the night with me."

The way she said it, and the plea he saw in her eyes, left him no choice.

"Wait right here," he told her. Crossing to the door, he flipped first one lock, then the other, testing each individually before finally putting on the chain.

"I'll camp out on the couch," he began as he turned around to face her.

He supposed that he wasn't surprised by what came next. If he was honest with himself, on a subconscious level he'd seen it coming.

Because, on that same level, he'd been aware not just of Suzy's overwhelming vulnerability, but of his own, as well.

Something about the look in her eyes, the pain she was feeling not only *spoke* to him but also evoked memories of his own pain—the pain he'd thought buried along with all his unspoken hopes and plans for the future and for a family life.

Julie's heartless, thoughtless betrayal and the callous way she had erased all traces of their unborn child, not even pausing to think of the promise she was also erasing, had wounded his heart. To save himself and to stem the hemorrhaging flow, he'd literally denied his pain and sealed off that area of himself.

Sealed off all possibility of his feeling *anything* except a sense of duty and dedication to keep the citizens he served safe.

That was supposed to be enough.

It *had* been enough.

Until Suzy sealed her mouth to his.

Nick had no weapon at his disposal to try to hold her off. And rather than hold her off, he did the exact opposite. He eagerly sought the comfort, the warmth that she silently offered.

The flicker of momentarily unguarded pain she had seen in Nick's eyes reached out and touched her, communicated with her own pain and went so much further than merely letting her know that he'd endured hurt the same as she had.

It assured her that she wasn't alone. That he wasn't just there for her but he had *been* there—

where she was—as well. Reaching out to comfort him temporarily silenced her own pain.

Her own fears.

She desperately wanted something to blot out the overwhelming fear for her baby and her sister that made it hard for her to even breathe.

And then it was no longer about pain, about fear, about the waves of anxiety. It was stripped raw of all its layers and, at bottom, it was about the solace she discovered there, in Nick's arms, in his touch. In his kiss.

And she was ravenous for it.

Peter hadn't been a husband to her from the moment he'd learned that she had conceived. In withdrawing not just his attention and sexual contact, but any displays of affection as well, he'd made her feel like half a person, completely undesirable. She'd found herself adrift in loneliness.

More than anything, she now admitted, she'd craved a gentle touch, craved quiet, reassuring affection. Craved knowing that she mattered.

All these needs, wants, desires had seemed to burst to the surface the moment she and Nick walked into the house and closed the door. Unable to cope, to be alone with all these burdens she'd been carrying a second longer, Suzy threw her arms around the only lifeline she had.

Nick.

Every logical bone in his body told him this was wrong. That he couldn't go through with this. That he needed to separate himself from this woman he was so completely attracted to before he compromised not only her and himself, but his principles.

Nick knew he would regret this—for her sake—but he didn't care. He'd had regrets before. Better to regret a deed that was done than to regret never having done it at all.

He wanted to feel whole again, for however brief a time. Though it made no sense to him, for some reason, Suzy Burris made him feel whole. He'd sensed it almost from the moment he'd first laid eyes on her.

As was the case with everything in his life that didn't go by the book, he'd tried to bury it.

But it just wouldn't stay buried, not when she presented herself to him like this, all warm and willing, supple and wanting.

Nick was no match for that.

Nick was no match for her.

He kissed her over and over again, even as his brain ordered him to stop. He couldn't stop. It was beyond his control, beyond the spectrum of his power.

He needed what she had, what she gave, and a part of him tried to assuage his conscience by telling himself that she needed what he had to offer, as well. Comfort, affection and reaffirmation.

It wasn't a slow, languid dance the way he would have wanted it to be if it had been in his power to bestow on her. Instead, what was happening between them resembled a charged frenzy, underscored by articles of clothing now littering the floor, marking a path that went from the front door to the sofa several feet away.

And in the interim, as clothes continued to rain down, he kissed, caressed, touched and worshipped every square inch of her that he came in contact with, every single part of her body.

Firm and taut, her skin still felt like cream against his palms. He lost himself in that sensation. His heart raced as every kiss, every pass of his hand and hers bred a desire for more of the same.

No matter what he did, he couldn't seem to get enough of her. He found himself desperately wanting that final thrill yet just as desperately wanting this momentum they'd created to continue forever.

Or at the very least, awhile longer.

She didn't know what had come over her.

Maybe it was the abject loneliness. Maybe she just wanted to feel desirable again, to feel *something* other than pain, anger and weariness again. Peter had had her doubting herself, doubting her womanhood and even, these past few days, doubting her sanity and her ability to think clearly and make solid judgments. By his very actions— staying out late, hardly saying a word to her when he was home—he'd made her feel like a victim, unworthy of attention or affection or even the smallest kindness.

He'd begun to make her withdraw from life, which was when she'd decided she needed to save herself and divorce Peter.

But now, seeing herself in Nick's eyes, she saw a different image, a different person. Moreover, in Nick, she both saw and sensed a kindred spirit. He spoke to her soul, made her transcend the rubble she'd found all around her.

She'd never thrown herself at anyone before, never wanted anyone before the way she'd wanted Nick the moment they'd closed the door and sealed off the world.

Suddenly there had been nothing and no one, just him, just her. And the hurt that thrived within both of them grew smaller with each step she'd taken toward Nick, each kiss they'd shared so wildly.

It was almost an out-of-body experience for her. She was in awe of her own actions, of the liberties that she was taking. She'd always been faithful to the man she was with, and as Peter's wife, she'd been faithful to her vows. But Peter was dead and for the first time in a long time, she was not.

Nick brought out a wildness in her, and yet, there was this overpowering need for a connection. *He* was her connection.

To life, to love, to herself.

Every kiss seemed to flower into another one, creating equal partners of them even as she and Nick both tottered back and forth between being master and slave, captor and captive, each taking a turn at assuming all four roles.

When she felt she couldn't hold back anymore, couldn't wait a fraction of a second longer, Nick gathered her to him and, sealing his mouth to hers, he entered her, forming their union, making them one, a heartbeat before the rhythm of the act throbbed through both their bodies.

The tempo quickened with each passing second, each increasingly more zealous thrust.

Gasping and holding on to each other tightly, they leaped off the edge of the world and were suspended in space for an eternal moment. The euphoria surrounded them even as it pulled them back down to the earth.

And as they fell, she could feel his heart racing against hers.

She clung to that sensation, aware that all too soon, she would be at the mercy of her fears again, fears for her family's safety. But for this singular moment, she took comfort in the thought that she was with someone who cared about her as much as she cared about him.

Chapter 14

Slowly Nick's heart rate returned to normal, as did his ability to think.

And to own his actions.

Nick turned his head to look at the woman he was supposed to be protecting, not compromising. "You know, this *wasn't* what I had in mind when I agreed to spend the night in your house."

Her eyes met his. The euphoria had settled down to a comfortable glow within her. She knew she should be feeling guilty about this, but she couldn't. Peter had been dead only a few days, but he hadn't been her husband in close to a year.

There were no ties there, no promises that she'd broken by making love with Nick.

She smiled at him now. "I know."

As far as Suzy was concerned, she knew that she had made the first move. It truly *was* a first move on her part because she'd never done anything like that before, never literally thrown herself at a man before. But there had been something, a bond, a kindred spirit she'd sensed between the detective and herself that had removed the barriers.

But while there was no guilt for making love with Nick so soon after Peter's death, something else hit her hard, broadsiding her when she least expected it.

He saw the tears in her eyes. "What's wrong?" he asked, concerned. "Did I hurt you?"

She shook her head, afraid to speak, afraid that she would sob if she did.

"Tell me," he coaxed softly.

It took her a moment more to gain control over herself. "What kind of monster *am* I?" she cried. "My son and my sister were kidnapped. Right now they're at the mercy of some deranged lunatic—or worse," she sobbed angrily. "And what am I doing? I'm throwing myself at the police detective who's investigating my husband's murder."

Nick drew her into his arms, holding her as she struggled against him. Suzy finally just crumbled, her tears flowing freely.

"You're not a monster," he told her. "You're a human being. And human beings need comforting when they're in the middle of a stressful situation, the way you are. Suzy, you did nothing wrong," he assured her, his voice low, reasonable. Comforting. He wiped away her tears with his thumb. "It's going to be all right, Suzy. I promise. We'll find them and get them back."

She knew he couldn't really guarantee that, but just as before, she clung to his words, to the idea that somehow, some way, they were going to find Lori and her baby.

She'd made love with him in order to stop thinking, but there was more to it than that. She'd made love with Nick because he made her feel that she wasn't alone.

And she was grateful to him for that. But she didn't want him to think she was some sort of a clinging vine.

Taking a breath to steady her nerves, she told him quietly, "This isn't going to develop into a pattern."

The remark seemed to come out of the blue,

catching Nick off guard. Was she warning him off, or saying that for his benefit? How did he tell her that he wouldn't mind if it did become a pattern? That making love with her had opened doors and windows inside him and had allowed the sun to come in for the first time in years?

He didn't want Suzy to feel he was crowding her, as if he expected anything more from her, even though he would have welcomed it.

He didn't want to scare her.

Going on instinct, he just continued holding her.

"You talk too much," he told her quietly.

Maybe she did, Suzy thought. "Makes up for you hardly talking at all."

Amused, Nick laughed quietly and brushed what was intended to be nothing more than a fleeting, chaste kiss against her lips. But he discovered the second that contact was reestablished, when it came to this woman, there was no such thing as fleeting, no such thing as chaste. He'd opened up the floodgates again and gotten himself swept away.

He had no choice but to swim for his life.

He did it with pleasure.

She woke up alone.

The moment Suzy opened her eyes, the languid feeling had vanished.

Startled by the silence that all but smothered her, she bolted upright.

She was still in bed.

Her bed.

Last night came back to her in fits and starts, accompanied by a wave of heat. They'd made their way to her bedroom where they must have fallen asleep after making love again. Twice.

But where was Nick?

She listened intently—and heard nothing but more silence.

Tumbling out of bed, Suzy grabbed the robe that must have fallen to the floor sometime during last night's very passionate activities. As she shrugged into the robe, slipping it over her nude body, she saw the folded paper on the bureau.

Knotting the sash at her waist, she crossed to the bureau and quickly skimmed the note.

"Went to follow up a lead. There are two detectives posted in a utility van across the street. They'll keep you safe. I'll call you soon. Nick."

How could he have left without her?

"What lead?" she asked the note, exceedingly frustrated as she slipped the paper into her robe's pocket. "And when's 'soon'?"

He hadn't marked down a time on the note,

hadn't indicated when he'd written it, so she had no way of gauging just what he meant by "soon."

Why hadn't he woken her up? She would have gone with him instead of staying behind, to spend the next excruciatingly endless hours perched on the sharp ends of pins and needles, waiting to hear something, *anything*.

From him.

From the kidnapper.

Waiting to learn if her baby and her sister were safe, or if something had happened to them because she had made an unforgivably horrible mistake and gotten involved with the wrong man.

And, by everything she'd come to discover, Peter Burris was definitely the wrong man.

Forcing herself to go through the motions of living, of actually being able to function, Suzy took the fastest shower of her life. As a precaution, she'd brought both her cell phone and a portable phone connected to her landline into the bathroom so she'd be able to hear either one if they rang.

They didn't.

Feeling increasingly more helpless and frustrated, Suzy got dressed and went downstairs. Her intent was to get some coffee and hope that it would somehow jump-start her energy and push the anxiety she was experiencing into the background.

When she came to the bottom of the stairs, she saw what looked like another note in the foyer on the floor. It had obviously been slipped under the front door.

Had Nick written her a second note before leaving?

The moment she picked up the note and looked at it, she knew this wasn't from Nick. Moreover, it had to have been slipped under her door after he'd already left, otherwise, she was certain that at the very least, he would have put it with the other note.

There were only four words on this one written in a flowing, flowery script:

He loved me more.

The person—most likely a woman—who had written this note had to be talking about Peter.

Suzy clenched her hand into a fist. Angry, feeling as if she was about to lose her mind, Suzy started to crumple up the note, then stopped herself. Nick would want to see this and have it analyzed for possible prints. Any satisfaction she might have gotten from tearing the note into tiny bits would have to be put on hold. Evidence took precedence over everything else.

"Damn you, Peter. And damn me for not seeing any of this," she cried, suddenly feeling very close to tears.

He's not worth it.

No, he wasn't. But Andy and Lori were.

Suzy let out a shaky breath. Without knowing where Nick had gone, she had no choice. She was forced to remain exactly where she was and hope that the kidnapper would get in contact with her. She needed him to call with instructions, telling her what she had to do in order to get Andy and Lori back.

Suzy went into the kitchen to make coffee. She definitely needed the distraction—and the caffeine.

She was surprised to discover that the coffee was already made. Nick had obviously left it brewing for her. She found this fact immensely comforting even though she wouldn't have been able to explain to anyone exactly why.

"Think he killed them?" Juarez asked Nick.

It was his first day back. He'd brought cigars with him to hand out to everyone, following an age-old tradition passed on to him by his fore-bearers. In addition, Juarez had brought a stack of photographs of his newborn son with him and was proudly showing them to anyone and everyone who came within fifteen feet of his desk.

He'd arrived just as Frank Kellerman, the late senator's chief aide, was brought in and placed in the interrogation room.

Nick had done the interview, and then had come out, leaving Kellerman sitting in the room by him-self.

For the time being, Nick just wanted to study the man through the one-way glass, wanted Keller-man to wait and wonder if there was more coming.

In a lot of the cases he'd dealt with in Hous-ton, the suspects did a far more effective job on themselves, anticipating the worse and working themselves up.

"I don't think he actually killed any of them," Nick answered. "But I'd bet a month's pay that he's guilty of *something*. Innocent men just don't fidget like that. He could hardly sit still throughout the whole interview."

As he and Juarez looked on, the aide on the other side of the glass was all but tap-dancing at the table. His feet and legs seemed to be moving almost independently of his upper torso. The rest of him shifted nervously in his seat, first over to one side, then to the other—and back again.

Juarez readily agreed, pointing out, "Look at the way he's fidgeting."

"That's way more than fidgeting," Nick agreed. "If he were a rocket, he'd be set to launch any second now."

Too bad there was no concrete evidence right now enabling them to hold the aide. They would have to let him go soon, he thought grimly, searching for a way he could use that to his advantage.

"Guilty conscience?" Juarez guessed.

"He sure as hell is guilty of something," Nick responded. The trouble was, guilty of what? "And scared."

"Of us?" Juarez smirked.

Nick shook his head. "Not us. He's afraid of whoever he's working for," was his guess. Glancing at his watch, Nick knew they'd run out of time and they had nothing on the man to hold him any longer. "I'm going to go get a coffee out of the vending machine. You let Kellerman go."

That wasn't what the younger detective had expected to hear. "Just like that?" Juarez asked, stunned.

"No, not just like that," Nick amended. "I plan to tail the S.O.B. and see if he winds up incriminating himself somehow." He glanced back into the interrogation room. "He knows more than he's telling, and I intend to find out just what, even if I have to follow him to hell and back," he told Juarez as he walked away to the vending machine.

Suzy nearly jumped out of her skin when her landline finally rang.

Her heart hammering wildly, she picked up the receiver with both hands to keep from dropping it, then placed it to her ear. "Hello?"

"One ring." The sound of harsh laughter met her ear. "You must be anxious."

It was him.

The kidnapper.

The man with the metallic-sounding voice.

Suzy ordered herself to hold it together. She knew she needed to sound as if she were calm and in control, if not of the situation, of at least herself. Otherwise the man on the other end of the call would know he was holding all the cards and that could prove fatal for Andy and Lori.

But her voice almost broke as she demanded,

"Let my sister and my baby go. They're not part of it."

"Oh, but they are, Mrs. Burris, they are. They're my leverage. Otherwise, you won't do as I say and you'll think that boyfriend of yours can keep you safe. By the way, did you have a nice night together?" he asked her knowingly. "I see it's true what they say about still waters." The laughter unnerved her, getting under her skin. "My, my, but you really are a wildcat."

Her heart all but stopped as embarrassment flooded her cheeks. This monster who was talking as if he'd witnessed everything that had happened here last night. But how could he?

"How did you—"

"I have eyes everywhere, Mrs. Burris, which is why I'll know if you try to get in contact with your detective boyfriend after we hang up." His voice turned malevolent as he went on to warn her, "Things will go very badly for your little family if you do. You won't want them to wind up like your husband now, do you?"

Fear ripped right through her heart. "No, no, I don't. I'll do anything you want," she cried, "just please, please don't hurt them."

"All right, I'm not a monster, Mrs. Burris. I

can be reasoned with." The man on the other end paused, shifting gears. " Now listen very carefully. I want you to slip out of the house without alerting those detectives in the van. Once you're clear of them, I want you to go get that envelope you found in the bank's safety deposit box—don't stop to make any copies. I'll know if you do," he said ominously.

"I won't make any copies," she promised. "Just tell me where you want me to bring the envelope."

But rather than tell her, he laughed again, no doubt enjoying himself and this torturous game he was playing.

"One step at a time, Mrs. Burris. One step at a time. And remember," he underscored darkly, "if you tell your boyfriend—or anyone else about this—they die. You make copies of a single photograph—they die. You don't follow all my instructions to the letter, they—well, I think you get the picture by now." He laughed at his own little joke. "Get it? The picture."

She let out a long, shaky breath, loathing the person on the other end with every fiber of her being. But for Lori's and Andy's sakes, she was forced to play along, to feign admiration.

"I get it," she said between clenched teeth. "Very clever."

"Yes, I am," he agreed. "Glad you realize that." And then he seemed to shift gears, for the moment tiring of the cat-and-mouse routine. "All right. You have an hour before the bank opens. Have yourself a nice breakfast, *then go get the envelope,*" he ordered gruffly. "And wait for my call."

The line went dead.

Have yourself a nice breakfast.

As if she could keep anything down, Suzy thought angrily. Her stomach was so knotted up, she was amazed she could still breathe.

Suzy looked at her watch. It was only ten to eight. Early. But she might as well drive over to the bank and wait in the parking lot for it to open its doors. This way, if Nick came back before nine, she wouldn't have to come up with any excuses about where she was going or why she didn't want him with her.

If he knew the truth, there was no way he'd let her go alone—besides, she had no doubts that the kidnapper *was* watching her every move. There had to be cameras planted in her house.

In her house she thought angrily, feeling horribly violated. Who had done that? And when?

Could Peter have put the cameras up? Why? Was it to keep them safe, or to spy on her? She'd never given him any reason for the latter, but she was beginning to think there didn't have to be a reason for some people to do criminal things.

Her head *really* began to ache. It felt as if her skull were being cracked in two.

Running on adrenaline, she decided to make her escape from the house via the side yard. There was a gate that opened behind some garbage pails. The detectives in the van were watching for someone breaking in, not sneaking out. It was her only hope, and with a little bit of luck she could get away. From there, she could call a cab to take her to the bank.

Just as she was about to leave, the phone rang again.

It took effort to stifle the involuntary scream. Bracing herself, Suzy picked up the receiver. Was it him again? Had he changed his mind about making her pick up the envelope for some reason? It was too soon for the call naming the drop-off point. He knew she hadn't gone to the bank yet.

Suzy could feel herself trembling inside as she said, "Hello?"

"Hi."

Her shoulders tensed for another reason entirely when she realized it was Nick calling and
not the kidnapper. Her mind scurried about, trying to come up with something she could say to
make the kidnapper think she was warding Nick
off while still leaving him a clue.

Nothing was coming to her.

"I know I left rather abruptly," Nick said, "but
one of the men on the joint task force found some
evidence that might have implicated one of the
late senator's aides and we brought them all in for
questioning." He paused as if to let all this sink in.
"I'm not sure when I can be there, but the minute
I wrap this up, I'll be over and—"

"Don't bother," she snapped. "I don't need you
coming over." Her voice rose with each word she
uttered. "I don't need you hounding me every minute. Why don't you do something productive, like
find my husband's killer and put him in jail?"

This sounded nothing like the woman he'd been
with last night. Had the kidnapper called her? If he
had, wouldn't she have told him that immediately?
Why was she responding like that?

"Suzy, is something wrong?"

"Wrong?" she jeered. "What could possibly be
wrong? Everything's just ginger-peachy—as long

as you leave me alone," she added, adding a nasty edge to her tone. "Go do your job, and I'll do mine, understand? Go do your job!" she shouted and with that, she banged down the receiver, terminating the call and praying that Nick would realize what she was really trying to tell him instead of just think that she had gone off the deep end. That, she hoped, was the way she meant for the kidnapper to interpret what had just gone down.

Hopefully, Nick was smarter than the kidnapper.

"Wow, I could hear her yelling all the way over here," Juarez commented, looking at his partner as he came forward. "You really must have done something to tick her off."

Nick didn't answer Juarez. He felt like a man who had just been handed the ultimate puzzle. He stared at the phone thoughtfully, trying to make sense out of what had just happened. He had an uneasy feeling that if he was slow in figuring it out, it would be too late.

His cell beeped. Flipping it open, he saw the text. The man he had following Kellerman just alerted him that the senator's right-hand man was on the move.

Nick frowned. He knew what he had to do. For the time being, no matter how much he wanted to go see her and find out what was going on, Suzy's puzzle would have to wait.

Nick had gotten into his car and had just turned the ignition when his cell phone beeped again.

Now what? he wondered impatiently.

Pausing, he took his phone out again and looked at the text message. One of the detectives he'd instructed to keep an eye out on Suzy had sent his own message. Suzy had just been seen sneaking out of the side yard and getting into a cab down the block.

Chapter 15

Janice Maxwell was considered by one and all to be the perfect administrative assistant. She came in early, left late and in between handled both daily routines and emergencies with the same aplomb and maximum efficiency. No one at Darby College could remember ever seeing the stately, fortysomething woman acting as if she was even the least bit ruffled or upset.

She was the eye of the storm, the one everyone, including her employer, Dean Abramowitz, turned to when they needed the opinion of someone who was calm and levelheaded.

Which was why, when Janice Maxwell suddenly burst into the dean's office, looking white as a sheet and clearly seven degrees beyond upset, the dean fully expected that, at the very least, the devil himself was on her heels.

But she was alone, as well as breathless and apparently speechless.

"Ms. Maxwell, what is it? What happened?" he demanded. Never in their long history together had the woman *ever* burst into his office without first knocking, and then waiting for permission to enter.

His nerves were already fairly shot, what with Melinda Grayson's undeclared kidnapping and then those grad students finding the three murder victims just outside of the school grounds.

Dean Abramowitz was afraid even to hazard a guess as to what had brought on Ms. Maxwell's highly unusual break with decorum.

"Answer me!" he instructed. "What the devil is going on here?"

Rather than say a word, the tall, thin woman who appeared to be all angles, quickly came around to the dean's side of the computer and proceeded to elbow him out of the way despite his protests. The moment she did, she took control of his keyboard, her fingers flying over the keys.

"What the hell's gotten into you, woman?" Abramowitz indignantly shouted. He was strongly debating calling Campus Security and having her taken away.

"Look!" She choked out the single word, turning the monitor so that he could get a better view of the video she'd just pulled up. A video that, according to the number of hits indicated in the corner, had gone insanely viral.

The dean didn't have to ask her, "At what?" The video Janice Maxwell had just pulled up commanded his complete, undivided and utterly horrified attention.

Abramowitz stared, openmouthed, as a terrified Melinda Grayson, her hands and feet tied securely to a chair, pleaded with someone just off camera not to kill her. She was sobbing almost uncontrollably.

The dean's body was as tense as a fireplace poker as he watched someone's hand suddenly dart out to strike the professor across the face.

Just as contact was about to be made, the screen went black.

The whole video lasted a total of thirty seconds.

It felt as if time had stopped while he watched.

His eyes huge, Abramowitz looked at his administrative assistant. The woman who ordinarily brought order to chaos had succeeded in doing just the opposite to his life.

"Where's the rest of it?" he asked, waiting for the video to start up where it had left off.

Ms. Maxwell shook her head. Her voice, when she spoke, was hardly above a choked whisper. "That's all there is, Dean."

His hands shaking, Abramowitz took a card out of his jacket pocket and began to dial Detective Nick Jeffries's number.

Nick looked at the caller's name on his cellphone screen as it rang.

It was Dean Abramowitz.

Again.

Undoubtedly calling to find out if he'd discovered anything new. The dean had been calling him on the average of four, five times a day since he'd questioned him about both the professor's disappearance and the three murder victims. As per his habit, he'd left his card with the educator, asking him to call if he happened to remember something else about either case. Instead, the dean would call to quiz *him,* wanting to know if any progress had been made in the investigation into the professor's disappearance.

After the first few calls, Nick had told Abramowitz that he would be able to spend his time more wisely *investigating* the case rather than updating him on it. For a dean, the man was rather thick. He hadn't taken the hint.

Right now, Nick didn't have time to hold the dean's hand or reassure him that they'd find the professor as well as whoever had killed those three men. In his book, actions spoke louder than words.

He let the call go to voice mail.

Please let them be all right, please let them be all right.

The single sentence kept repeating itself in Suzy's head over and over like an endless loop as she drove, first to the bank to retrieve the envelope in the safety deposit box, then to the address she'd been given. The metallic voice on the phone had called with the drop location approximately five minutes after she had gotten the envelope with its photographs out of the safety deposit box.

Was he watching her somehow? Had he planted a camera in her car? Suzy wondered uneasily, looking around the interior of her vehicle. The thought that this man was spying on her sent chills down her spine and all but cut off her air supply.

She forced herself to get her mind back on the only thing that mattered: saving Andy and Lori. She'd find a way to deal with the man who was torturing her this way later.

The address she'd been given turned out to belong to an abandoned storefront in the more run-down section of town. It had once served as a satellite campaign office when Senator Merris was aggressively running for reelection. An old campaign poster, faded from the sun and hanging at half-mast, the tape in the upper corners no longer able to support it, was still in the window, forgotten by whoever had been charged with cleaning up that particular go-round.

Getting out of the car, Suzy approached the empty looking storefront and tried the door. She expected it to be locked, but it easily gave beneath her hand.

Suzy took a deep breath to at least *partially* steady her nerves. She pulled the door open, braced herself and then walked in.

The smell of dust and mold assaulted her nose the second she walked in. She let the door close behind her as she looked around.

"Hello? Is anyone here?" Suzy called out.

Only the echo of her own voice as it bounced off the emptiness answered her.

Had she gotten the address wrong? Was the kidnapper jerking her around, sending her to the wrong place to show her that he was holding all the cards and that she had none?

But she *did* hold a card, Suzy silently insisted. She had the photographs. The ones he apparently was so desperate to get his hands on. That had to be worth something.

She dug in, holding her ground and giving it one more try.

"Look, I came here just like you told me to. I have the photographs. Now stop playing games and show yourself, damn it!" she demanded.

There was still no answer, but she couldn't shake the feeling that she was being watched. What was this creep's game?

"Okay, have it your way," she declared, retracing her steps to the door. "I'm taking these photographs straight to the newspaper office. I'm sure they can find a place for some of them somewhere on their front page."

She willed herself to turn around and start to go out the front door.

"Stay where you are!"

But rather than freeze, the way the man clearly wanted her to, Suzy swung around to face whoever had called out the order.

She didn't recognize the man standing there.

He was the kind of man, Suzy realized, who easily faded into the woodwork and could, just as easily, fade from memory five minutes after he left a room. It didn't seem possible that someone so nondescript could have taken her sister and her child, but then, she was discovering as more things about Peter's dual life came to the surface, that *anything* was possible.

Especially that which seemed to be impossible.

With quick, angry steps, the man crossed to her. "Give me the photographs!" he demanded.

She'd stuffed the whole thing into her oversize shoulder bag just before she'd left the bank and now angled her purse so that it hung behind her, out of his initial reach.

"First let me see my sister and my baby," she countered.

"You're in no position to dictate terms," he growled malevolently at her.

Rather than shrink away, Suzy raised her chin defiantly and retorted, "We've got a difference of opinion here, because I think I am. Now, you're not getting your hands on *anything* until I see my son and my sister with my own eyes."

Agitated—this was *not* going according to plan—Frank Kellerman cursed at her, and then grudgingly said, "All right, they're in the back room."

Tying Lori up like a Thanksgiving turkey, he'd left her and the baby in what had once been the senator's office whenever the man had swung by his smaller campaign headquarters.

Kellerman meant for her to follow him, but Suzy remained exactly where she was. She was not about to allow this man to get behind her for any reason. If she did, she thought, she'd deserve just what she got. The man had *psychotic* written all over him.

"Bring them out," Suzy told him. "I'll be right here. Waiting."

Kellerman's eyes narrowed, all but shooting lightning bolts. "Don't dictate terms to me," he shouted.

"Take it as a request, then," she retorted. There wasn't even so much as a hint of friendliness in her voice. She placed her cards on the table. "When I see with my own eyes that they're all right, *then* I'll let you have the photographs," she promised.

He said nothing for a moment, his eyes raking up and down her body. "You've got guts," he told her with what amounted to the thinnest trace of admiration.

She supposed that in his world, he was flattering her. Maybe even flirting with her. But in her world, he was a stomach-turning lowlife who couldn't be trusted and she wasn't about to let her guard down.

The man was a psychopath, she thought.

"I've got the photographs," she pointed out, knowing that to him, that was all that mattered.

"Stay here," he ordered.

She'd gotten her way. But there was no time to savor the victory. It was on to the next battle, the next confrontation. But for now, she promised, "I won't move a muscle."

"Yeah, you will," he smirked as he whirled around, a gun in his hand. He raised it quickly, his intention clear. He would kill her and take the photographs.

And then, just like that, he was aiming his gun at her. There was no place to run, no place to hide. This crazy person was going to kill her.

The thought that she had less than a minute to live galloped through her head.

But just as she braced to be killed, she heard the kidnapper scream. It was a pain-riddled cry, not a triumphant battle charge.

The man who would be her killer crumpled to the floor right in front of her, the blood flowing from his shoulder hitting the floor at the same time that he did. When his knees made contact with the floor, they immediately began to absorb the blood, discoloring his very expensive suit.

Stunned, not knowing what to think, Suzy turned around to see where the life-saving shot had originated. It seemed to be from directly behind her, but there was no one there, only the empty storefront window and the curling poster.

That was when she saw him.

Nick, sprinting toward her, a rifle held tightly in his hand. Throwing the door open so hard it banged on the opposite wall, he demanded, "Are you all right?" in a tough, no-nonsense voice.

"I'll let you know when I stop shaking inside," she answered. A hundred different questions popped up in her mind, all simultaneously piling on top of one another. "Did you just shoot him?" she asked, amazed at the accuracy of the shot he'd taken.

When Nick nodded in response, she still couldn't make sense of it. That seemed like an impossible shot.

"But how?" she demanded. "There was no one out there when I walked in." She scrutinized him, completely stunned by what he'd just managed to do. "Just what kind of superpowers do you have, anyway?" As far as she was concerned, it would have taken someone with exceptional vision to nail that shot. Why hadn't he mentioned being a sharp-shooter to her?

Because the man doesn't like to call attention to himself, that's why. Don't you know anything about the man? Apparently not, but she was willing to learn.

The aide was conscious and groaning pitifully, in between emitting squeals, complaining of almost being killed. He let loose a string of profanity, declaring that he was at death's door.

"You killed me," he sobbed angrily. "I'm thirty years old and you killed me!"

Jerking the man up to his feet none too gently, Nick answered Suzy's question simply, "I was a sniper in the marines."

She had more questions for him, a lot more, such as how he knew she was there, but they could all wait until she got the answer to one question out of the man Nick had taken prisoner.

"Where are they?" she demanded angrily. "Where're my baby and my sister?"

Kellerman countered by demanding, "Get me to a hospital. I'm bleeding to death here."

Nick grabbed Kellerman by his shoulder, sending a fresh wave of pain shooting right through the man down to his very core.

"Haven't you heard?" Nick asked sarcastically. "Only the good die young. Which means you're not going anywhere but to jail."

"I need a doctor!" Kellerman sobbed, his knees buckling.

Nick was unmoved, his eyes ominous as he regarded the babbling aide. "Tell us where her sister and baby are, and I'll see what I can do about that hospital."

It was obvious that under different circumstances, Kellerman would have loved nothing better than to keep that piece of information from either of them, but he was growing weaker and he could see the blood oozing from his wound. He was afraid that the detective would just leave him handcuffed here to die.

"All right, all right, I already told you where they are," he grumbled, jerking one thumb toward the rear of the building. "They're in the back room."

Suzy didn't even wait for Nick.

She flew to the back office of the defunct campaign center. Scanning the area, she saw a single closed door and made for it. The door was locked. Infuriated, frightened, she didn't even wait for Nick. Instead, she managed to kick it hard enough to get the door off its hinges.

Tears sprang to her eyes as she found herself looking at her only family. Lori was bound and gagged and tied to a chair. Andy was on the floor, his eyes shut.

Terror instantly shot through her as Suzy dropped to her knees and gathered her son to her. The next moment, the terror abated when she saw the infant stir and open his eyes.

"Oh, Andy, you're alive. You're alive," she cried as tears of relief and joy filled her eyes, and then spilled out.

With Andy nestled against her, she turned toward her sister to free her. But by then Nick had come in and he quickly made short work of the ropes holding Lori bound to the chair and the duct tape over her mouth.

The second the gag was off her mouth, Lori cried, "Where's that horrible man?"

Apprehension vibrating in every fiber of her being, Lori was looking past Nick, searching for Kellerman. At this point, she was afraid that he would burst into the room and kill them all, just as he'd threatened her he'd do, once her sister came for them.

"On his way to the jail soon. The man I asked to tail Kellerman called for backup. They just got here. Don't worry. Kellerman's not going to be a threat to any of you anymore," Nick assured her as he removed the last of the rope from her wrist, doing it as gently as he could. He still heard her suck in her breath, stifling a cry. "Sorry about that," he apologized.

"You just freed my nephew and me, trust me, you have nothing to be sorry about, Detective," Lori told him as she rubbed her wrists and tried to get the blood flowing through them again.

"How did you know I would be here?" Suzy asked Nick as she continued to hug Andy to her.

The way she felt right at this moment, she didn't think she would ever be able to let her son go.

"I didn't know," he told her. "I followed you here. After that tongue-lashing you gave me," he explained, "I knew something had to be up." Since Lori was within earshot, he refrained from adding that he thought her behavior particularly suspect after the night they'd just shared.

Suzy blew out a breath, happy that Nick had managed to catch on quickly instead of thinking she was just some nut job with a screw loose.

"I don't know how I'll ever be able to thank you," she told him sincerely.

He grinned at her, more relieved that she was unharmed than he could ever begin to put into words. "Oh, I'll think of something," he promised her.

A warm feeling began to mingle with the one of utter relief. Her eyes crinkled as she smiled at her lover and the protector of her family.

"If you don't, I will," she promised.

Chapter 16

Suzy moved to one side, getting out of the way as the EMTs Nick summoned wheeled the unconscious Kellerman out of the abandoned campaign headquarters. The ambulance, its lights momentarily dormant, was waiting just outside the front door.

As a precautionary measure, one of the paramedics had also checked out Lori and Andy, pronouncing them to be none the worse for their harrowing ordeal. Andy had even fallen asleep right after the paramedic had finished.

Lori had taken the sleeping infant and was es-

corted to one of the squad cars, where she was
content to stay out of the way and wait for Suzy
and Nick.

Suzy watched as the man who'd almost killed
her disappeared into the ambulance. "Who *is* he?"
she asked Nick. "I still don't know."

"His name is Frank Kellerman. According to
the information we have, he was Senator Merris's
top aide," he told her.

That was the only thing that Nick could answer. He knew the man's identity. That had been
checked into and verified after he'd been brought
into the police station.

As for the rest of the questions surrounding this
investigation, they still resided in the realm of the
unknown. That included who the aide was currently working for and exactly what, if anything,
Kellerman had to do with the three murder victims the graduate students had discovered during
their dig.

Had Kellerman killed the three men? Or, if he
hadn't, did he know who had? And what did any
of this have to do with Melinda Grayson's apparent kidnapping?

Juarez had filled him in on the video that the
dean had tried to call him about. That, too, an-

swered only one question—that her disappearance was due to a kidnapping. But it raised so many more questions in its wake. If the professor *was* the victim of a kidnapping, why hadn't there been a ransom demand made, the way there had when Suzy's sister and baby were kidnapped?

What sort of game were the kidnappers playing?

Suzy nodded toward the departing ambulance. "He was the one who'd been calling me." It was a statement, but there was a question wrapped up in it. "What did he want with those photographs that Peter took? The man Peter wanted to blackmail is dead."

There was more than one person in those photographs. Which meant that there could be more than one vulnerable target—or not, Nick thought.

"Either Kellerman wanted to blackmail someone—or eliminate the possibility of that person being blackmailed by getting rid of the evidence." He sighed, running his hand through his unruly hair. He was still having trouble getting his heart rate down to a respectable rhythm. "Right now, your guess is as good as mine," he confessed to her.

He wasn't exactly feeling triumphant as a police detective, but at the moment, that all took a backseat to what he *was* feeling good about—the fact that he had arrived just in time to save the woman he'd fallen in love with from becoming one of Kellerman's victims.

This last event, he realized, had helped him put his life back into perspective. He was a cop and he loved being a cop, but being one—even a good one—hadn't made him feel whole. Loving Suzy, being part of her life, *that* was what had finally made him whole again.

And, he'd almost lost it all practically at the very moment that he'd found it.

"That was a very brave thing you did, going out on your own like that, trying to rescue your son and your sister."

She was about to demur, denying his praise, but she didn't get the chance just yet because he continued talking.

"—and if you *ever* do anything like that again, put me through anything like that again, I'll have you locked up for your own good faster than I can say 'I love you, Suzy,' do I make myself clear?" he demanded.

He had a smile on his face, but she had a feeling that he was dead serious.

"You can't threaten me like that for trying to save—wait," she cried, coming to a verbal, skidding halt as her brain replayed Nick's last words in her head. "What?" she demanded, grabbing hold of Nick's shirt to anchor him in place in case he had any plans on walking away from her without answering her question. "What did you just say to me?"

His expression never changed. "That I'd have you locked up—"

"No, no, not that part," she said impatiently, waving away his words. "The other part."

"You mean about loving you?" he asked innocently.

"Yes!" Suzy practically shouted the word at him. "That part."

He continued looking at her innocently. "What about it?"

"Do you?" she cried incredulously. Then, just to make it completely clear, she added, "Do you love me?"

This was a potentially fragile limb he was climbing out on and he knew it, especially since Suzy hadn't said anything even remotely in kind to him. But nothing ventured, nothing gained and he was growing extremely tired of spending his time gaining nothing.

"I wouldn't have said it if I didn't," he answered her simply. Then, because he didn't want her to feel obligated to reciprocate—he only wanted to hear her say it if she did so from the heart—he switched to a lighter tone and said, "Seems to me that you're going to need someone to keep an eye on you for a while, just to make sure that everything's all right." His smile was from the heart—and intended for hers. "I can't think of an assignment I'd welcome more."

She wasn't certain if Nick was teasing her—or on the level in this case. "So you don't think Andy and I are out of danger?" she asked uneasily.

"I'm not sure anyone is until all the pieces are put together and we find out exactly who killed your husband and just who's behind all the killings. Not to mention what this has to do with Professor Grayson's kidnapping, or who ordered Kellerman to take Lori and Andy."

"So you don't think Kellerman was acting on his own?" she asked. That would have at least made things a lot simpler for her. Because, if that were true, with Kellerman out of the picture, she could breathe more easily.

"Kellerman doesn't strike me as the type for independent thinking. He's more the lackey type, which means that he's trying to ingratiate himself to someone who he thinks is holding all the cards."

She thought of the senator, Kellerman's late boss. With him dead, that meant that Kellerman was now dancing to someone else's tune. "You mean 'the king is dead, long live the king'?"

Nick nodded. "Exactly." ·

She brushed her hand along her forehead. This was definitely making her brain ache. "My head hurts."

Suzy saw the look of concern that flashed through Nick's eyes. She hadn't meant to make him think something was wrong, but on the other hand, she found it comforting that someone cared about her, about her welfare and even how she physically felt. It had been a long, long time since someone—other than her sister—had.

"It's just a headache," she told him, waving it away. To prove that she was really all right, she said, "I guess you have to take my official statement now, right?"

Rather than leave now that everyone else was gone from the premises, Nick paused for a moment longer and brushed her hair away from her face. He laced his other hand through hers.

She thought to herself that she had never felt such a gentle, loving touch before.

"Tomorrow," Nick told her. "There's time enough for that tomorrow."

Suzy took in a long, shaky breath, then gave him her bravest smile. "I'd like to get it over with today if you don't mind." She knew that Lori would want to put the entire ordeal behind her as quickly as possible, too. He could take both their statements.

He nodded. At this point, he wasn't about to try to talk her out of anything. "Whatever you want."

She liked the sound of that.

The whole thing took longer than he'd expected.

When it was over, Nick took all of them home, acutely aware of the bullet they had all dodged today—literally.

Once at her house, which he insisted on thoroughly checking out just in case, he helped Suzy feed her son and get the infant ready for bed. Lori had murmured something about going to her apartment, but it was obvious that she would have felt more at ease spending the night with someone.

Suzy was quick to sense that. "You can stay here as long as you want, Lori. I owe you more than I can ever repay for what you went through. For what it's worth, my home is your home—you know that."

"Thanks," Lori said sincerely. "But it's not your fault there was a psycho on the loose." And then she smiled at her sister and Nick. "Now, if you don't mind, I really need to soak in the tub for a long time—maybe even a week," she speculated glibly. "So I'll just say good night now."

"Good night," Suzy called after her. "And thanks again!"

Lori raised her hand over her head, wiggling her fingers to show she'd heard but continued to make her way up the stairs.

"You know I'm not leaving tonight," Nick said to Suzy the moment her sister was out of sight.

"I was counting on it," Suzy told him as she laced her arms around his neck. "As a matter for fact, I'm not sure if I'm ever letting you go again."

"Works for me." He smiled into her eyes, then made her a solemn pledge. "I'll keep you safe, Suzy, you and Andy and your sister," he added, knowing what her family meant to her. What they had begun to mean to him. "I swear, I'll keep you safe."

"Busy," Suzy countered, brushing her lips against his as she said it. "I was hoping you'd keep me busy. I do love you, Detective Jeffries." She punctuated her statement by kissing him between every word she uttered.

She was doing it again, he thought, his pulse accelerating. She was making him crazy. Making him realize that for once in his life—and once was all it took—he'd lucked out. This time, he *knew* he'd found the right woman for him.

"That, too," he murmured agreeably just before they both lost themselves inside the fire that had just been ignited between them.

* * * * *

You're just playing a part.

Despite everything, Tate could feel his body responding to Hannah. Responding to the intoxicating, sweet taste of her skin against his lips.

Dammit, get a grip, Colton.

Satisfied that he had performed as expected for whatever camera or cameras hidden in the room, Tate whispered the same message into Hannah's ear that he'd told her yesterday.

"I'm here to rescue you," he told her.

He couldn't allow his guard to go down, not even for a moment. "You and the others," he added. "But this isn't going to be easy and I'm going to need your help to pull it off."

Hannah turned her head slowly to look at him. He could tell by the look in her eyes that he'd made a breakthrough.

She was finally beginning to believe him.

COLTON
SHOWDOWN

BY
MARIE FERRARELLA

First published in Great Britain 2013
by Mills & Boon, an imprint of Harlequin (UK) Limited,
Eton House, 18-24 Paradise Road, Richmond, Surrey TW9 1SR

© Harlequin Books S.A. 2012

Special thanks and acknowledgement to Marie Ferrarella for her contribution to THE COLTONS OF EDEN FALLS miniseries.

ISBN: 978 0 263 90354 6
ebook ISBN: 978 1 472 00711 7

46-0413

Marie Ferrarella, a *USA TODAY* bestselling and RITA® Award-winning author, has written more than two hundred books for Mills & Boon, some under the name Marie Nicole. Her romances are beloved by fans worldwide. Visit her website, www.marieferrarella.com.

To
Sebastian Burgess,
Welcome to the world,
little guy

Prologue

Her face haunted him.

Ever since he'd seen her on that DVD, the one that had been made to showcase the "selection" available for purchase by the members of the "discerning" male audience viewing it, Detective Tate Colton had been equally fascinated and sick to his stomach.

Fascinated because Hannah Troyer, one of several young women displayed on the video, was at once hypnotically beautiful and so obviously innocent. And sick to his stomach because he knew what was going to happen to Hannah. Knew what was going to happen to *all* the innocent young women who appeared on the video. Each and every one of them was destined to become the object of some depraved pervert's lechery—as long as the right price was quoted and met.

Unless he and the FBI agents on his team got to those girls first.

Someone was kidnapping Amish girls and selling them to the highest bidder because in this jaded age of too much too soon, the idea of an untouched, pure young woman still held an almost addictive allure for some men.

In this case, the "some" were exceptionally wealthy men because innocence had become a commodity that did not come cheap. Instead, it was bade and bargained for like the rare product it had become, only to be forever lost at the hands of depraved men who had no idea how to rightly value such a treasure.

Eyes on the screen, Tate went back over the DVD and played it forward again, watching the same small section he'd viewed before of the girl he'd seen while going undercover as a prospective buyer.

Watching her.

Gray-blue eyes, alabaster skin, hair like flame.

They called her Jade. But she was Hannah Troyer.

He knew her name—her *real* name, only because Hannah's brother, Caleb, was desperately searching for his younger sister. The search had created strange bedfellows because, just recently, Caleb had wound up becoming engaged to his sister, Emma, a Special Agent with the FBI. They were working together on a joint task force to find the missing girls. According to what his sister had said, she and Caleb were going to be married once this case was finally wrapped up.

That made it sound so easy, Tate thought cynically. A piece of cake—and it wasn't.

There wasn't anything at all easy about this case. Not for the two dead girls they'd already found. Not for the whole of the small Pennsylvania Amish community— ironically called Paradise Ridge—which was holding its collective breath, waiting and praying for their own to be returned to them unharmed.

Tate had an uneasy feeling that wasn't possible. Even if they found all the other missing girls and they were still alive, they were no longer unharmed. Far greater than the physical scars they might have incurred were the emotional scars that had to run across their young, tender souls.

In this sex trafficking ring, the mostly faceless bastards who were abducting the young women were systematically destroying their innocence so that the girls—all between the ages of 16 and 20—bore little to no resemblance to the sweet young women their families were frantically searching for.

"I'd like to gut each and every one of those bastards," he muttered under his breath, finally shutting off the DVD player. The large screen he'd been watching went blank.

Emma, the only other person in the room with him, laughed shortly. There was no mirth in the sound. "You're not the only one who feels that way."

As she spoke, she put her hand on Tate's broad shoulder and was surprised by how rigid it felt. Well, maybe not so surprised, she silently amended. Tate, who'd been the one to initially ask her to join his task force, took his work very seriously, but this had to be a new level of intensity, even for him.

"I think that if we ever find the people who kidnapped Hannah, Caleb would be tempted to temporarily renounce his pacifistic ways, just for the time it would take to pummel these worthless scum into the ground. But indulging in fantasies isn't going to help us rescue these girls," Emma pointed out. "And we *are* going to rescue them," she told Tate with utter conviction, not for the first time.

Failure, as the saying went, was not an option here. There were too many lives at stake, too many families waiting to get their daughters back.

Tate knew he would have felt a personal obligation to bring the girls all back to their families even if the people affected by this heinous ring were *not* technically his neighbors.

The Colton family ranch in Eden Falls, Pennsylvania, was named the Double C in honor of Charlotte Colton. Charlotte was the woman who, even though she hadn't given them biological life, had, for all intents and purposes, along with her husband, Donovan, given him and his five siblings a reason to exist, a reason to live.

The couple, whose lives were so tragically cut short along with those of so many others on 9/11, were well-known for their dedication and their generosity. Over the course of two decades, they had adopted six completely unrelated orphans, given them their name and their love and knitted them into a family. A family who never took what they had for granted. The ranch where they grew up was right outside a little village named Paradise Ridge.

Civilization, with all its technological progress, seemed to have stopped at the borders of the tiny town. The hardworking citizens of that town led what was considered an idyllic life that echoed their ancestors' existence. Until a serpent somehow found its way into Paradise Ridge and stole some of the town's young women.

Tate was determined to find those girls and the ones from Ohio.

Especially, he silently promised the face that haunted

him, Hannah. Find them and free them. Even if it was the last thing he ever did on this earth.

"C'mon, Big Brother," Emma was urging him. "You and I have a sting to plan and coordinate."

Snapping out of his mental fog, Tate rose from the chair he'd taken to view the DVD for the umpteenth time, searching for some telltale clue he might have missed before.

He looked at his sister as they got ready to meet the others involved in this undercover operation. "Tell the truth, Tomato-head, you're going to miss this once you turn in your badge for a butter churn." He still loved to use her childhood nickname, to her annoyance.

Try as he might, he just couldn't picture his driven sister in that kind of laid-back, rural setting—not for more than ten minutes.

"No, I'm not," Emma countered with feeling. Then, when Tate's eyes held hers, she shrugged. "Well, maybe just a little," she allowed as they left the office. Because he'd forced the truth out of her, Emma punched his arm.

Tate's deep laugh echoed up and down the hallway. Maybe Emma wasn't going to miss this life, but he sure as hell was going to miss Emma.

Chapter 1

He wasn't one of those people who had an obsession about cleanliness. Tate Colton had never had a problem with getting his hands—or any other part of him, for that matter—dirty, if the job required it. That kind of dirt he could put up with and ignore.

But dealing with these subhuman creatures who made their living trafficking in human flesh, in destroying young lives and thinking absolutely nothing of it, was an entirely different matter. It made him want to go back to the hotel room where he was registered under his assumed name and take a shower. A long, scalding-hot shower to wash away their stink.

Once he received the assignment from his supervisor, Hugo Villanueva, he knew that going undercover in order to find and save the Amish young women who had been kidnapped would require him to associate with, in his opinion, the absolute dregs of the earth.

Dregs in expensive suits.

You could dress a monkey up in fine clothes, but he was still a monkey, Tate thought. No amount of expensive clothing could change that, or change the fact that the people he was forced to interact with were lower than scum.

He'd think more about stepping on a beetle than he would about terminating the existence of one of these cockroaches.

To look at the man who had brought him up to this particular hotel suite—his current tour guide to this underworld—someone might have thought the man was a successful businessman or the CEO of a Fortune 500 company instead of the utterly soulless lowlife that he actually was.

Impeccably dressed in what was easily a thousand-dollar suit, his guide to this lurid world of virgins-for-sale smirked at him confidently as he opened the door leading into the suite's bedroom.

"I'm sure we can find something to pique your appetite, Mr. Conrad," he said.

Tate scowled at the shorter man. "I said no names," he snapped, mindful of the part he was playing in this surreal drama.

The other man laughed, enjoying what he considered to be the display of ignorance on the part of this new client.

"Nothing to be worried about. What are they going to do?" he asked, gesturing at the bedroom and the young women being held there. Each and every one of them were dressed in identical long, slinky white gowns. "Post it on the internet? None of them even know what the hell the internet *is*," he stressed, jeering at the young women who were virtually prisoners in this suite. "They all live in the Stone Age. Trust me." He patted Tate's arm and the latter shrugged him off as if he was flinging off an annoying bug—an act that wasn't lost on the man. "Your name—and your sterling reputation—are both safe here," he assured Tate.

"C'mon, c'mon," the man snapped at the young woman he was herding into the room for his "client's" final review. "He hasn't got all night. Or have you?" he asked, looking over his shoulder at Tate, a lecherous grin spread across his angular face. "You know, if you've changed your mind and want to make your purchase now—" He left the sentence open, looking at Tate expectantly.

"I haven't changed my mind," Tate answered formally. The deal was that he got to see the young women in person in order for him to finalize his choice, and then the negotiations regarding the pending "purchase" would go from there.

Inside, Tate was struggling to contain his fury. The woman he'd "requested," "Jade," was looking at him apprehensively like a mistreated animal afraid of being beaten.

Had she been beaten?

Tate looked her over quickly. "What's wrong with her?" he demanded, channeling his anger into the part he was playing—a man who wanted the "goods" he was considering purchasing to be perfect. He was well aware of the fact that the blue-gray eyes continued to watch his every move. Tate swung around to confront the other man. "She looks like she's been manhandled," he accused angrily.

The man shrugged indifferently. "Don't worry. Nothing happened that would have left a visible mark on her." His flat, brown eyes raked over Hannah from head

to toe, as if to reassure himself that she wasn't displaying any sign of bruising in plain sight. "That's the one
rule—other than payment up front—the boss won't
tolerate any visible marks left on the merchandise."

Out of the corner of his eye, Tate saw Hannah flinch
at the label the man had contemptuously slapped on
her. *Merchandise.*

His anger flared.

"She's a person, not merchandise," Tate retorted,
glaring at the guard.

"Hey, at the price you're going to pay, she's anything
you want her to be. You want a person? You got it, she's
a person." He turned to look at the redhead he'd led
out of the bedroom for Ted Conrad's perusal. "A soft,
sweet-smelling person, aren't you, honey?"

Smirking, he slid his hand along her cheek and down
the side of her neck.

It was obvious that the guard didn't intend on stopping there.

"I'll thank you to take your hands off her," Tate
warned darkly as the man's hand just grazed the swell
of her breasts.

Anger flashed in the other man's eyes, but just as
quickly, it subsided. The main reason he'd been told to
bring this client here was to get Conrad to make his
final decision so that the deal could proceed.

Apparently, it looked as if the deal was about to
be sealed. The bottom line was, and had always been,
money. So, much as he would have personally rather
shot out this client's kneecaps, the guard raised his
hands in the air in mock surrender.

"They're off," he declared dramatically, wiggling his
fingers in the air to underscore his point. The smirk on

his face deepened as he looked at Hannah knowingly. "So, this is the one you want, eh?"

"She's the one," Tate replied, his tone scrubbed free of any emotion.

The other man nodded his approval. "Gotta say, you've got good taste. She's a beauty." With hooded eyes, he looked her over again. It was obvious that he was putting himself in the client's place. "She also looks like she might last you awhile."

Hannah drew in a breath. They'd given them all some sort of pills, but she had managed to fool her captors into thinking she'd swallowed hers when she hadn't. Each word from the guard felt like a dagger, stabbing into her heart.

Her eyes swept over both men. "Please don't do this," Hannah pleaded.

It was impossible to know which of them she addressed her plea to.

For his part, though he took care not to show it, Tate felt terrible. He could certainly imagine what was going through Hannah's mind. What Caleb's sister was anticipating. He would have given anything to comfort her, but that wasn't what was going to save her.

In order to accomplish that, he had to be convincing in his role. Which meant that he needed to go on with this charade, continue to maintain this facade so that he could, ultimately, get her and her friends away from these men.

If he went about it the traditional way, pulling out a service weapon and threatening to shoot the other man if he got in his way, Tate knew that he might—or might not—be able to get out of the hotel with Hannah. Most likely, they'd be stopped before they ever made it to the street level.

No, this way was more effective. It just required a great deal of focus and an iron will—and the ability to block out that look in her eyes to keep it from getting to him.

"What did I tell you about opening your mouth?" the guard was demanding angrily. He pulled back his hand, ready to bring it down on her face.

Hannah's alarmed cry tore at his heart.

"If she has one mark on her, the deal's off," Tate warned him in a voice that was deadly calm, belying the turmoil that lay just beneath.

The guard stopped in midswing. The expression on his face told Tate that the guard was getting fed up with what he undoubtedly considered a high-and-mighty client. The man let his guard down for a second, the sneer on his face telling Tate that he thought he knew his type. Not just knew it, but hated it because he felt inferior to the supposedly rich client.

"You don't buy her, someone else will," the guard jeered contemptuously. But he dropped his hand to his side nonetheless. "Sit!" he ordered Hannah with less compassion than he would have directed to a pet dog. Only when she complied did the guard finally look his way. "So, I take it we've got a deal. You're interested in acquiring this tasty morsel?"

Tate's expression gave nothing away, including the fact that he could easily vivisect him without so much as a thought. "I might be," he replied after a beat had gone by.

"Might be," the man echoed with contempt. He was at the end of his patience. "Look, the man I represent doesn't like having his time wasted. We're alike that way because neither do I."

Tate slowly walked around the young woman, deliberately pausing and taking a lock of her hair between his fingers. He made a show of sniffing it. "That goes both ways."

Suspicion immediately entered the guard's eyes. "So what do you have in mind?"

There was no hesitation on Tate's part. "A man doesn't buy an expensive car without taking it on a test run, seeing how it handles," he pointed out, his voice continuing to be flat.

It killed him to see that Hannah had winced again in response to his words, and he saw real fear in her eyes as she watched him.

How did he get it across to her that he was one of the good guys without blowing his cover?

"Go on, I'm listening," the other man said.

"I'd like a private session with her, to see how we 'get along,'" Tate proposed.

"The boss doesn't deal in damaged goods," the other man snapped.

"I have no intentions of 'damaging' her. Just 'sampling' her," Tate informed him. "There are a lot of ways a man can see if he likes the goods he's getting."

He was standing in front of Hannah now, looking into her eyes, wishing there was some way to set her mind at ease. His back was to the other man and he smiled at Hannah. The smile was kind, devoid of the lust that had supposedly brought him here. Lowering his head so that his lips were right next to the young woman's ear, he whispered, "Caleb sent me," before straightening and backing off.

Her eyes widened, but she held her tongue.

Tate said a quick, silent prayer of thanksgiving to whoever it was that watched over law enforcement officers.

"What did you say to her?" the guard demanded. There was no arguing with his tone.

Tate turned to look at him, emulating the latter's previous smug look. "I told her that paradise was at hand."

As he said that, Tate slanted a look toward Hannah, hoping she would put two and two together and take some comfort in the covert message. He couldn't tell by her expression if she'd believed him—or even understood what he was trying to tell her. He wasn't even sure if she'd heard him say that Caleb had sent him.

Terror, he knew, had a way of blocking out everything else.

The man relaxed a little, then laughed. "Good one," he pronounced. "That's where she and some of those other girls come from, some backward hole-in-the-wall called Paradise Ridge."

Tate tried to sound casually uninterested. A man making small talk, involved in a meaningless conversation that would be forgotten before he walked out the door. "Is that where all the girls are from? This Paradise Ridge place you just mentioned?"

His question was met with a nod. "This batch is. They picked up others from—" He abruptly stopped his narrative. His eyebrows narrowed over small, deep-set eyes. "What's with all the questions?"

Tate shrugged. "Just trying to find out how big a selection you've got—in case things don't work out with this one," he explained.

"Oh, it'll work out," the man promised. There was no room for argument. He looked at Hannah pointedly. "She knows what'll happen to her if it doesn't. Don't you, honey?" The smile on his lips was cold enough to freeze a bucket of water in the middle of May.

This time, instead of fear rising in Hannah's eyes,

Tate thought he saw anger. Anger and frustration because, he guessed, there was nothing she could do right now about the anger she was feeling.

The other man was apparently oblivious to her reaction. It was clear that fear was all he looked for, all he valued.

"Don't want to wind up like your girlfriends now, do you?" he taunted her.

Things suddenly fell into place. The annoying little troll was referring to the two dead girls Emma and Hannah's brother had initially discovered. Solomon Miller, a so-called "repentant" Amish outcast had brought them straight to the bodies, hoping to use the fact that he was informing on his "boss" as a bargaining chip.

Initially part of the group of men involved in the sex trafficking ring, Miller had become the task force's inside man, trading information for the promise of immunity once all the pieces of this case came together and they got enough on the men running this thing to take them to court—and put them away for the next century or so.

If they didn't wait until they discovered exactly who was behind all this and bring him—or her—in, if they just grabbed up the two-bit players they were dealing with in this little drama, the operation would just fold up and relocate someplace else.

And Amish girls would continue disappearing as long as there were sick men to make their abductions a profitable business.

No, they had to catch the mastermind in order for this operation to be deemed a success.

"Don't threaten her," Tate warned. When the guard shot him a malevolent look, he told him, "I want her to be willing to be with me, not because she was threatened with harm if she wasn't."

The guard looked at him as if he wasn't dealing with a full deck. "Hey, man, don't you know? It's better when they fight you."

The world would be a much better place if he could just squash this cockroach, Tate thought, struggling to hang on to his temper. With no qualms whatsoever, Tate would have been more than willing to put everyone out of their collective misery—himself included.

But instead, he was forced to tamp down his temper and nonchalantly tell him that "We each have our preferences."

"Yeah, well, you're the man with the bankroll," the guard grumbled resentfully.

"Yes, I am."

Tate was grateful for the elaborate lengths the department had gone to in order to give him a plausible backstory. His brother, Gunnar, had funded his huge bank account.

Whoever was running this sex trafficking operation wasn't a fool, Tate concluded. He was very, very careful to get everything right. That included vetting his clients rather than just accepting them at face value, or going with hearsay.

Nothing was simple anymore, Tate thought. Not even the peddling of flesh.

"So it's settled?" Tate asked the man. The blank look he received in return forced him to elaborate. "I can have a private session with her?"

"Soon as I run it by the boss" came the reply.

"And how long is that going to take?"

He knew things had to progress at their own pace, but he hated the idea of leaving the girl alone with this thug for another moment, much less for another day or two. There was no telling what could happen in that amount of time, and he didn't want to take any more chances than he had to.

"Anxious?" the other man jeered, enjoying himself. He liked having the upper hand and, in this case, he clearly got to call the shots. "Tomorrow. Come back tomorrow. She'll be ready for you then."

Just what did that scum mean by "ready"?

A premonition had a shiver zipping down Tate's back, but there was absolutely nothing he could do about the circumstances. Tate was well aware that if he pressed, if he remotely said that she looked ready now or tried in any way to hurry this along, the whole thing could just fall apart on him. There were steps to take and he knew it.

That didn't make taking them any easier.

If this was rushed, the people they were after would smell a setup and not just back off but vanish into thin air, taking the young women with them. He'd seen it before.

Hell, he'd *been* part of it before—having an operation unravel on him that allowed a killer to be set free. The man was ultimately taken down and brought to justice, but not before he'd killed several more young women. Young women who wouldn't have died if he had done his job right in the first place, Tate thought ruefully.

That wasn't going to happen again, he vowed. This time, he was going to do things by the book. Even if that meant he had to find a way to physically restrain himself.

"What time tomorrow?" he asked the guard.

"We'll get back to you about that," the man told him, affecting a superior attitude.

Tate narrowed his eyes, looking as cold as the man he was dealing with. Colder. "I don't like being jerked around," he said in a voice that contained an unspoken warning.

"Nobody's jerking you around," the other man promised, sounding more than a little nervous that this encounter could turn physical. "I'll call you tomorrow," he said again, this time far more amiably.

"I'll look forward to it," Tate said, not bothering to tone down the note of sarcasm in his voice. He looked from Hannah to the man, wondering if she even realized how breathtakingly beautiful she was. She reminded him of a rose newly in bloom. "In the meantime, I don't want anyone touching her."

The other man began to smirk again. "She really got to you, eh?"

Tate was aware that men like the one he was dealing with directly understood only one thing: money. It was the only language they spoke. However, he hadn't been given the suitcase that was to be filled with the cash he was to trade for Hannah. That came tomorrow.

Whatever cash he had on him at the moment was his own, but it was only paper as far as Tate was concerned. Paper that was capable of buying both him and Hannah a little peace of mind.

Taking out his wallet, Tate removed a hundred-dollar bill. As the other man eagerly put his hand out, Tate tore the bill in half and handed one piece to him.

"What the hell is this?" the man demanded. "Some kind of stupid game?"

"No game," Tate assured him. "You get the other half of the hundred when I come back tomorrow and see for myself that she's all right." His eyes bored into the other man's dark ones. "We have a deal?"

The other man cursed roundly, then shoved his half of the bill into his pocket. "We have a deal," he retorted grudgingly.

"Good." Tate turned on his heel and crossed to the door.

Tate could almost feel Hannah's eyes watching him as he walked out of the suite.

Tomorrow seemed like an eternity away.

Chapter 2

"**D**id you see her? Was she there?"

Caleb Troyer fired the anxious questions at him the moment the thirty-one-year-old cabinetmaker walked into the makeshift, satellite FBI office.

Rather than the customary laid-back attitude normally associated with people who came from the Amish community, Caleb reminded him of a rocket that was ready to go off at the slightest provocation.

He couldn't say that he blamed the man, either.

"Yes, I saw her," Tate answered.

He glanced toward his sister, who'd come in with Caleb. He sincerely wished that Emma had followed protocol and persuaded Caleb to stay away and let the task force do its work.

Granted, the distraught man was Hannah's brother as well as Emma's fiancé. However, Caleb was also a civilian and, in his experience, overzealous, emotionally involved civilians had a way of causing a mission to fall apart.

They couldn't afford to have that happen. Too many young, innocent lives were at stake. And Tate had absolutely no intention of watching another mission self-destruct on him.

"How did she look?" Caleb pressed. "Have they…" At a loss, Caleb searched for a word that didn't drag a cat-o'-nine-tails across his soul, making it bleed when he considered the implication. "Have they *hurt* her in any way?" he finally asked nervously.

Beneath the cabinetmaker's apparent restlessness was anger. Tate could see it in the other man's gray eyes. Tall and muscular, Caleb Troyer, once unleashed, would be a force to be reckoned with. Not that he could honestly blame Caleb for what he was feeling. If all went well, maybe Caleb would get his chance at some payback when the operation was over.

But until then, the man had to be restrained.

"She looks tired and frightened," Tate told Hannah's brother.

His response was true—as far it went. What Tate didn't add was that when he'd initially seen Hannah in the motel room with the other two girls—before he'd been given the DVD to watch, she'd appeared to be drugged, as were the other girls. It was the easiest way to control the "inventory" and keep them from escaping.

Caleb definitely didn't need to know that. If he did, that might provide the missing ingredient that would set Hannah's brother off and God knew that Tate had more than enough to deal with without having to worry about the father of three suddenly going ballistic on him.

He could just picture Caleb storming into the motel

room, breaking down the door and subsequently getting shot for his efforts. If that happened, he'd have another body on his hands—as well as his conscience—and his sister to deal with.

Omitting certain details was the far safer way to go in this case.

"If you know where she is, then what are we waiting for?" Caleb demanded impatiently. He looked from Emma to Tate, searching for a glimmer of support. Why were they hanging back? "Let's go get Hannah and the other girls," he urged.

Turning on his heel, he was almost at the office door when Tate moved in front of him, blocking his way.

Tate completely sympathized with what the other man had to be going through, but what Caleb was proposing almost guaranteed a bloodbath.

"We can't just burst in there," he told Caleb as calmly as possible.

"Why not? Why can't we just walk into the place?" Caleb wanted to know. He didn't understand why this detective who'd promised to bring his sister and the other girls back was acting so reticent. Was he going back on his word? "You said there were just two godless thugs guarding the girls. There are three of us here—and you can get more," he pointed out.

Caleb was obviously focused only on rescuing Hannah at all costs. He didn't blame the man. But Tate was able to take several different points of view regarding the op besides the way Caleb did.

Tate did his best to make the other man understand. "Yes, I can get more manpower and maybe we could rescue Hannah and the other two without incident," he allowed, deliberately not going into how dangerous that sort of overt action could be. "But we also want to be able to rescue whatever other girls the ring has hidden away—the girls who were kidnapped for the same reason that your sister was taken. And we won't be able to do that if the guy who's the brains behind all this gets wind of what happened.

"The minute he does," Tate continued, "he'll go underground and those girls will be as good as dead. We'll never find them." Tate took a breath, searching the other man's face to see if his words had sunk in. Wondering if Caleb suspected that he was also lecturing himself as well as the victim's brother.

Lecturing himself because Tate had the exact same reaction, the exact desire as Caleb. He wanted to save Hannah and the girls with her as soon as possible. For two cents, he'd go in, guns blazing, and take down those two worthless pieces of trash guarding the girls with no more regret than he experienced stepping on a colony of ants.

Less.

The only problem was, right now there were only two henchmen visible and he knew damn well that there had to be more thugs involved than just Tweedledum and Tweedledee. An operation this big didn't function with just two flunkies.

There had to be more.

He put his hand on the Amish cabinetmaker's shoulder and looked at him compassionately.

"I know it's hard, but you're going to have to be patient," he told Caleb. "It's the only way we're going to be able to successfully rescue those girls. *All* of them," he emphasized.

Caleb nodded. It was obvious that he was struggling with himself. "You are right. We cannot just go in and rescue Hannah, not when there are other girls being held prisoner as well." And then he sighed and shook his head. "But this is hard," he complained.

Caleb would get no argument from him. "Nobody ever said it wouldn't be," Tate agreed. He looked at his watch. The handler should be getting the money right about now.

It was the handler whose job it was to pick up the funds from Gunnar that were needed for the exchange. At least that part was easy. Securing the funds would have been a great deal more difficult if he didn't have a billionaire brother who was willing to bring down this sex trafficking ring.

"So what's your next move?" Emma asked her brother as Caleb retreated to the far side of the room. There was tension in her voice.

"I've set up a private one-on-one session with Hannah," he told Emma. "Seems my credentials are so good that the man at the top is allowing me to have a private 'preview' with my future 'purchase.' I'm going to try to convince Hannah to trust me, but it's not going to be easy, given what she's been through."

Overhearing, Caleb looked up, suddenly alert. "Call her Blue Bird."

Tate exchanged quizzical looks with Emma. "What?" Tate asked.

"Call her Blue Bird," Caleb repeated, crossing back to them. "It was a nickname I gave Hannah when she was a little girl. She was always running around, fluttering about here and there, so full of life, of energy. One day when she seemed to be going like that for hours, I laughed and told her she was like one of the blue birds we saw in the spring. The comparison pleased her so I started calling her that. Blue Bird." A wave of memories assaulted him from all angles and he shook himself free, unable to deal with them right now. "If you call her that, she'll know you talked to me and she'll trust you."

Tate nodded. It was worth a shot. "Thanks. That'll help." As he switched his cell phone to vibrate, he saw the way Emma was frowning. "What's bothering you?"

There was a time she would have told him he was imagining things, that nothing was bothering her. But that was when the job was all important to her, and nothing came ahead of that. Now a lot of things did. And she was worried.

"Frankly, I don't like you walking back into the lion's den unarmed." She knew he was pushing his luck. "You made it out twice unharmed. The third time—" she began skeptically.

"Will be the charm," Tate assured her, finishing her sentence in a far different way than she'd intended to finish it.

But Emma continued to look unconvinced. "The people involved in this sex trafficking ring have already killed twice," she reminded him. "What's to stop them from killing you?"

He shrugged indifferently, as if she were worrying for no reason. "Well, for one thing, killing me off would be bad for business," he told her glibly. "They're after the money I told them I'd pay for Hannah. Word gets around that they've killed a client and their little virgins-to-the-highest-bidder scheme suffers a serious setback."

He put his hands on Emma's small shoulders. Funny, he never realized how fragile she could feel. Or how touched he could be by her concern. "Look, we've both been in law enforcement for a while now and nothing's ever happened to either of us, right?"

"That's my whole point," she insisted. She put one of her hands on top of his, silently bonding with him. "Our luck's bound to run out eventually."

"*Eventually* means someday—not today," he pointed out with conviction. "Now stop worrying—that's an order," he told her. "The sooner we get the information we need about whoever's pulling those strings, the sooner we get to wrap this up and Caleb over there gets to make an honest woman out of you."

Emma's mouth dropped open for a second, and then she shook her head. "I can't believe you just said that. Do you have any idea how incredibly old-fashioned that sounded?"

Her choice of words amused him. "You'd better get used to that, honey," Tate told her, kissing the top of his sister's head. "*Old-fashioned* goes with the bonnet and the butter churn."

Emma continued to look at him, a knowing look entering her eyes. She wasn't all that unusual, she thought. "Tell me you wouldn't give up everything for the right person if she came along."

"For the right person," he echoed, momentarily conceding the point, then quickly qualifying, "*If* she came along. But until she does, I've got work to do. And right now, I've got to pick up a suitcase full of money before those thugs get antsy and decide to turn Hannah over to another bidder."

The suitcase full of money meant he was seeing Hatfield, his handler. The thought of her brother walking around with that kind of money in a briefcase made her nervous. "I'll go with you," she volunteered.

But he had something else he felt was more important for her to do. "No, you stay here and make sure that your cabinetmaker doesn't decide to do something stupid and wind up breaking down the hotel suite door and hauling out one or both of those bozos."

Emma came to her fiancé's defense. "What would you do if someone kidnapped me?" Emma asked him pointedly, trying to make her brother see the situation from Caleb's point of view.

"Sending his next of kin a sympathy card comes to mind," Tate answered dryly. And then his smile faded for a moment as he gave her a serious answer. "I'd track the kidnapper to the ends of the earth and gut him seven ways to Sunday—" But he was trained to do that. It was different with Caleb. These were men they were talking about, not cabinets. "But we're not talking about me," he pointed out.

Emma shook her head as she laughed softly. "No, I guess we're not." She brushed a quick kiss against his cheek. She was going to worry until she saw him safe again. She couldn't help it. She was built that way.

"Watch your back, Big Brother," she told him.

"Always," he said. Crossing to the door, he opened it then paused for a moment to look at Hannah's brother. Lines of concern were etched deeply into his handsome, young face. "It's going to be all right," he promised the other man.

The expression on Caleb's face was half resigned, half hopeful.

It echoed perfectly the sentiment Tate felt within his soul.

The same two men he'd dealt with twice before were waiting for him in the hotel suite when he arrived with the briefcase of used hundred-dollar bills, arranged in nonsequential order, just as instructed.

The bald man with the goatee opened the door to

admit him before his knuckles could hit the door for a second time. Tate walked in, nodding at him and the equally bald African-American. On the latter, bald looked good. The same couldn't be said about the man with the goatee.

"It's all there," Tate told the African-American man eyeing the briefcase suspiciously as he placed it on the coffee table between the two men.

The man flipped both locks at the same time, then spared him a glance. "You don't mind if I see for myself, right?"

It was a rhetorical question. Nonetheless, Tate chose to answer it in his own way. He quickly pressed the lid back down in place before the other man could look inside. Tate met the guard's hostile gaze.

"I'd expect nothing less," Tate assured him.

"Then what the hell are you doing?" the guard demanded hotly.

Tate looked at the man with the goatee, then back at Waterford, the African-American. "I'm waiting for one of you to show me Jade."

"You've already seen her," Waterford snapped. "Twice."

"You're right," Tate agreed amicably. "And now I just want to make sure that she's actually here."

"He doesn't trust you, Nathan," the man with the goatee jeered.

"Shut up," Waterford ordered, obviously angry that his name had been used.

Tate pretended not to notice the flare-up. "Well, do I see her?" he wanted to know, still keeping the lid down. Tate could feel his biceps straining as he continued to hold the lid in place. It had turned into a contest of strength, one that Tate was determined to win.

Waterford did not take defeat easily. He looked as if he could snap a neck as easily as take in a deep breath.

"Bring her in," he instructed the other guard in the room.

The latter was angry at being ordered around like that in front of a relative stranger, but he was also obviously afraid to oppose the larger man. Muttering under his breath, the man with the mousy goatee went to the back of the suite, threw open the door leading into the bedroom and barked "Get out here" to the lone occupant in the bedroom.

A moment later, Hannah, her flame-red hair piled up high on her head, wearing a green gown that looked painted on, delicately glided into the sitting room.

Each time he saw her, Tate couldn't help thinking, she seemed even more beautiful than the last time. It almost made his soul ache to look at her, knowing what she had to have gone through. Was *still* going through, he amended.

He had a gut feeling that Hannah was tougher than she looked. He sincerely hoped so, for her sake.

"Satisfied?" the African-American barked, flinging his hand out and gesturing toward Hannah.

Tate withdrew his hand from the briefcase's lid. "Satisfied," he replied. Tate took a step back from the table. He smiled and nodded at Hannah before turning his attention to the man he'd made his bargain with the day before. Tate looked into his eyes, his gaze turning almost hypnotic. "And nobody touched her." It was both a question and a statement that waited to be confirmed.

"Nobody laid a damn finger on her—or anything else for that matter," the man with the goatee added when it was obvious that the client was waiting for more of a confirmation.

Tate looked at Hannah, who kept her gaze lowered, looking down at the rug. With the crook of his finger beneath her chin, he raised her head until she was looking directly at him.

"Is that true?" he asked her.

Surprised at being addressed directly without any curse words attached, a beat still passed before Hannah nodded her head.

"What are you asking her for?" the goatee demanded to know. "I said nobody touched her. I lived up to my half of the bargain," he declared impatiently. "Where's my money?"

"Right here," Tate said, placing the other half of the torn bill into the man's outstretched hand.

"What's that for?" Waterford wanted to know, eyeing the single torn section suspiciously.

"Insurance," was the unselfconscious reply. "Now I'd like some time alone with the girl."

"Sure, knock yourself out." The man with the goatee gestured toward the bedroom. "You paid for her, have at it," he urged, and then he leered, "Sure you don't want me to break her in for you?"

It was a crude play on words. Words that quickly faded away in the heat of the glare that had entered Tate's eyes.

"What I want," he began deliberately, "is for the two of you to make yourself scarce." Tate looked from one man to the other. Neither seemed to grasp what he was telling them, or made any attempt to leave the room. "You can stand guard in the hall outside the suite's door if it makes you happy."

"We're not leaving," the goatee growled.

"I'm not telling you to leave," Tate countered. "I'm telling you I want some privacy. There's only one way out of this suite and it's through that door." He deliberately pointed to it. "You can both stand guard in front of it, or take turns—I really don't care which you decide to do. But I don't want to feel crowded while I look over what a briefcase full of hundred-dollar bills just got me. Understand?" he demanded.

Waterford shook his head. "I don't know about this," he said skeptically.

"You're not leaving the hotel, just the room," Tate argued. "We'll still be right where you left us when you walk back in," he assured them, adding in a voice that brooked no nonsense, "Those are my terms. If you don't like them—" he made a move to reclaim the briefcase, his implication clear: he either got his way, or he would be *on* his way.

The choice was theirs.

The man with the goatee cursed roundly, adding a few disparaging words about having to put up with aggravating people.

In the end, he grudgingly said, "Okay, we'll be out in the hallway in front of the door. *Right in front* of the door," he emphasized. "So don't get any big ideas about making a break for it."

Tate deliberately looked at Hannah. "I assure you, any ideas I have have nothing remotely to do with the hotel door."

The men didn't look completely convinced, but they walked out of the suite. Once on the other side of the door, they made enough noise that just barely stopped short of waking the dead.

It was to let him know that they were right outside the door, as specified. Ready to stop him if he had any plans to escape with the girl.

Tate frowned. He didn't have time to think about those clowns right now. It was Hannah who commanded all his attention.

When he turned around to face her, he saw the fear in her eyes.

The real work, he knew, was still ahead of him.

Chapter 3

Finding herself alone with the stranger, Hannah did her best not to give in to the fear that had been her constant unwelcome companion since this terrible nightmare had begun.

It wasn't as if this man she was looking at was like the others she'd encountered in this world of outsiders. He seemed different than the two crude, insulting men who were in charge of keeping watch over her and the other girls who'd been abducted from her village and Ohio. Different even than Solomon Miller, a man who her small community had once turned out and who'd sought to avenge himself by throwing his lot in with the men who'd abducted her and the others.

This man she was with *seemed* different, Hannah silently reminded herself, but even she knew that appearances could be deceiving and she hadn't known even a moment's kindness since she'd been torn away from everything she knew and loved.

So why did she feel that this man somehow *was* different?

The tips of her fingers felt like ice. Her whole body felt as if it was alternating between hot and cold as she struggled to keep fear from rampaging through her like a runaway wild animal.

What was this man going to do to her?

And how could she stop him? He looked so much more powerful than she was.

Her brain was still foggy from whatever it was that the man with the facial hair had tried to force her to swallow earlier. Foggy, but not completely useless because she'd managed to keep the drug hidden in the corner of her mouth, between the inside of her lip and her gum. Still, some of it had leached into her system. But she'd heard enough to piece things together.

Even so, she couldn't really believe it. Didn't *want* to believe what she'd heard through the door that separated this new, fancy prison from the outer room where her jailers had sat, talking to the man who was now towering over her.

Had she actually been *sold* to him?

It didn't seem possible.

People weren't sold to other people. Things like that had taken place during a far more barbaric time, a shameful passage in the country's history that was mercifully a century and a half behind them.

People didn't *buy* people anymore. *They didn't.*

And yet…

And yet, she'd seen the briefcase before the lid had come down on it. There'd been money in that case. A great deal of money. Was that being exchanged for her? Had this man really *bought* her?

What did that *mean?*

Hannah could feel her soul seizing up within her as the fear she'd been trying so desperately to contain suddenly broke out of its confines and all but paralyzed her.

Maybe this was all just a horrible, horrible dream. A nightmare. And maybe, dear Lord, if she just closed her eyes, when she opened them again, she'd be back in her safe little house with her family around her. What she wouldn't give to hear the voices of her nieces, Katie, Ruthie and Grace—her brother Caleb's daughters—raised in some silly little inconsequential squabble.

Tears rose in Hannah's eyes and she fought to keep them back. She couldn't cry in front of this man, couldn't risk it. She'd seen the effect that tears had on these cruel beasts who'd ripped her world apart. Mary Yoder had cried and they'd beaten her for it, seeing tears as a sign of weakness.

She had no idea where Mary was now, or even if she was still alive.

These men who had become an unwanted daily part of her life had no respect for weakness, no compassion or even pity. They had nothing but contempt for its display, and if anything, when they encountered weakness, it just made them crueler.

She had to be strong, Hannah told herself. Only the strong survived and she needed to survive, needed to find a way to get back to her family again, back to Caleb, who needed her to help him take care of his motherless daughters.

Be strong, Hannah, be strong, she silently urged herself. *He knows Caleb. That has to mean something.*

Somehow, digging deep, Hannah found the strength

she was looking for. Found it and clung to it for all she was worth.

Raising her head, she forced herself to look into the tall, imposing stranger's eyes. They didn't look like the eyes of a cruel man. Perhaps she could talk him out of this shameful thing he was about to do.

"Please," she implored him. "You don't want to do this." Hannah took a deep breath, willing her nerves to remain steady. She congratulated herself on speaking without allowing a telltale tremor to emerge in her voice and betray her.

Her eyes remained fixed on the stranger's. Taking another breath, she repeated the sentence, her voice sounding a little stronger this time. "You don't want to do this."

The trouble was, God help him, he did, Tate thought. It wasn't that the undercover role he was playing had gotten to him. He found everything about this persona loathsome. Anyone who preyed on helpless girls, using money and connections to satisfy his unnatural lusts, was nothing short of despicable.

But the truth of it was, since the very first time he'd seen her face on that DVD recording that had contained a virtual catalog of innocence for would-be bidders to view, he'd found himself almost hopelessly attracted to the abducted young woman.

It didn't matter. He knew he couldn't do anything about it. Knew that to act in any way on these feelings under the pretext of playing his part was more than reprehensible. His sense of honor, or decency, wouldn't allow it.

But he couldn't be anything less than honest with himself and, the thing of it was, under different circumstances, he would have attempted to find a way to at least strike up a conversation with Hannah. Hopefully, that would lead to spending time with her and then perhaps…

Perhaps what? She was just twenty—and he wasn't. And hadn't been for a long time.

Besides, he reminded himself pointedly, *under any other circumstances, your paths wouldn't have even crossed.*

And it was true. When would a career detective have any occasion to meet a sheltered young woman who spent her whole life entrenched in the bosom of her close-knit Amish community? The answer to that was simple: never.

The tension in the room was so thick, he could almost *see* it. Somehow, he had to put Hannah at ease, make her relax a little by convincing her that he was *not* the enemy.

Tate took a step toward her and saw Hannah instinctively shrink back. The very action made him feel terrible for her.

I'm your friend, Hannah. Your friend.

But how did he get her to believe that? Especially since this room was undoubtedly bugged and probably under the ring's surveillance?

"Have they hurt you?" Tate asked her gently.

The young woman slowly moved her head from side to side, never taking her eyes off him, as if she was afraid that if she looked away, he would take the opportunity to jump her. It was painfully clear that she didn't trust him to maintain the small distance between them.

If she didn't trust him when it came to something so basic, how was he going to get her to trust him enough to tell him what he needed to know?

And then he recalled the nickname Caleb had told him to use. It was worth a try.

"You can tell me," he coaxed. "Did they hurt you, Blue Bird?" His voice deliberately dropped as he called her by the nickname.

Her gray-blue eyes widened and he heard Hannah's sharp intake of breath. She continued watching him as if she didn't know what to expect.

"Not since the last time you came," she finally replied, speaking so quietly that, had he not been looking at her lips, he wouldn't have even known that she'd answered.

So, the torn bill had worked, he thought. He didn't kid himself that the guard he'd given it to had any sense of honor, only greed, but that was all right. He wasn't above using whatever worked.

"But before then?" he pressed.

The small, perfect shoulders rose slightly and then lowered in an almost imperceptible shrug. The clinging green gown rustled a little.

"Before then," she murmured.

"Who?" he asked, moving closer to her.

Tate saw the young woman automatically shrink into herself again, but this time, she didn't step back the way she had before. This time, she remained where she was.

"The one with the scraggly hairs on his chin," she told him.

The man with the goatee, Tate thought. Of the two henchmen, he looked like the more dangerous one, the more unpredictable one.

"Did he hurt you…badly?" Tate pressed, unable to make himself ask Hannah if the scum had actually raped her.

Somehow, phrasing it that directly seemed to just

intensify the horror of the attack. He didn't want to resurrect painful memories for her, he just needed information.

To his relief, Hannah shook her head. "No, not badly." She knew what he was asking her. Uncomfortable, she pressed her lips together, testing each word cautiously as she uttered it. Her eyes were once again riveted on his face as she watched his reaction. "He tried, but the other man—" What was it that she'd heard the dark-skinned man called? "Nathan," she suddenly remembered. "Nathan pulled him off me and hit him. Nathan said that no one would pay for me if I was ruined." She raised her head, a glimmer of defiance in her eyes, as if these were odds she'd managed somehow to beat. "You paid for me."

Tate paused. He had no doubt that there was probably a camera in the suite somewhere—possibly several—watching his every move, recording his every word. Anything he wanted to convey to her would have to be almost inaudible if he wanted to have a prayer of getting out of here alive—and ever coming back to rescue the girls.

"Yes," he answered. "I paid for you. Or at least made a partial payment," he qualified. The rest he was to bring to the "party" that was being given. A party where he and other so-called pillars of society were to be coupled with their bought-and-paid-for virgins.

A party that, rumor had it, the mastermind behind this ring was also to attend.

She didn't quite follow him. A partial payment? "So do you own me?" she asked, still unable to grasp the concept, even as she heard herself ask the question.

"I will as soon as I make the second payment," he corrected her, playing to whatever audience would eventually be sitting on the other side of the camera and observing this.

Hannah paused, her head spinning. The conversation didn't seem real to her, like something in one of the books that were forbidden for her and young people like her in the village to read.

"And when you make that second payment," she finally said, "then what?"

"Then you're mine," he said as matter-of-factly as he could. He saw another glimmer of defiance in her eyes before it faded away again.

Good for you, Tate thought, pleased. They hadn't broken her spirit. This meant he had something to work with. And that, hopefully, would help her get back to normal once he brought her back to her village.

Watching him intently, Hannah was frantically searching for something to cling to, something to give her hope that there would be an end to this nightmare and that the end she was seeking wasn't tied to her demise.

There *had* to be more to this than what there was on the surface.

There had to be, she silently insisted.

"Why did you call me what you did earlier?" she wanted to know, focusing on the name the stranger had used. How could he have possibly known she'd been called that as a child?

Unless...

Unless he *had* actually spoken to Caleb. Had Caleb sent him, as the man had claimed? It didn't seem possible. Caleb wouldn't have left Paradise and walked among the outsiders—

He would. For me, she realized and knew it was true. Hannah looked at the stranger expectantly, waiting for an answer. Then, in case he'd forgotten what she'd asked, she said, "You called me Blue Bird."

"Blue Birds look pretty against the sky when they soar," he said evasively, doing his best to recall exactly how Caleb had explained the reason for the nickname to him. "It just seemed to fit you," he concluded, looking at her pointedly.

Willing her to make the connection between the nickname and what he'd whispered to her the last time he'd seen her.

Had she heard him then?

Or had she been too drugged or too despondent at the time to understand what he was saying to her?

Tate watched the young woman's face for some sort of clue. Unlike his own stoic expression—his "game" face—Tate saw a myriad of emotions wash over Hannah's heart-shaped face.

And then, he could have sworn that what looked like enlightenment entered her eyes—just before she shut down again. Shut down as if she was afraid to believe him. Afraid to get her hopes up, for fear that she was only going to have them dashed again.

"You don't have to be afraid," he said to her as gently as he dared. "I'm not going to do anything to you. I just want to talk."

"Talk?" she echoed, as if she didn't understand the word. As if it was just too much for her to hope for.

"Talk," he repeated. "I want to get to know you."

She still looked as if she didn't comprehend the word, or at least was confused by it. "They said…" The words felt as if they had gotten stuck in her throat and she tried again. "They said I should be 'nice' to you."

There was no mistaking what the euphemism actually meant, though she refused to think about it.

"Who's *they?*" Tate asked, doing his best not to put any undue emphasis on the question. He wanted it to sound like nothing more than an idle query, one of many that could crop up in the course of a conversation. "Do you mean the two men outside the door?" he asked, trying to get her to talk to him.

She shook her head. "No, another man. I'd never seen him before. He and the man with him said if I wasn't nice to you, I'd be sorry." Either way, she lost, Hannah thought.

Picking up the slender thread, Tate continued, doing his best to sound almost uninterested, just mildly curious. "This man you didn't know, did you hear anyone address him by name?"

But Hannah shook her head again. "They just called him 'Boss,'" she told him.

Jackpot!

Kind of.

Subduing his excitement, Tate lowered his voice and asked, "What did he look like?"

Instead of answering him, Tate saw apprehension return to her eyes as she looked at him nervously. "You are trying to trick me." It was half a question, half a statement.

"Trick you?" he echoed in surprise. Why would she think that?

"Yes," Hannah insisted. "You are here. He is the man who arranges these things. You must know what he looks like." Suspicion rose in her voice. Was he trying to trap her somehow? She didn't understand any of this, not the abduction, not why she had to be here, nothing. "Why are you doing this to me?"

"I'm not trying to trick you," he assured her gently. "And the only men that I've dealt with are those two gorillas outside in the hall. Them, and that man I first spoke to on the telephone," he added.

The first step in the operation had been finding the website. The one that had advertised "a cleaning service that will leave you swearing that you've never been serviced so well in your life." It had fairly *screamed* sex trafficking. Tate was almost certain that the voice he'd heard when he dialed the number had belonged to the man in charge. And that *that* man wasn't just some ingenious nobody off the street. Rumors and suspicions pointed to the head man being someone high up, not just on this food chain, but on the social food chain as well.

Someone with dark secrets and a darker soul, who satisfied perversions that made anything Tate had previously come up against seem almost docile and child-like by comparison.

Tate looked down into Hannah's face. Right now, she was the closest he'd gotten to this sex trafficking ring. She might even unknowingly hold the key to taking it down. He needed to find out what she knew. The only way to do that was to talk to her. But he needed to make certain that he wasn't overheard; otherwise, the op fell apart and the whole ring could just disappear into the night, taking the girls with it—or, if that was too much trouble, leaving behind their lifeless bodies. He had a feeling that it could go either way, and that was a risk he wasn't about to take.

Debating what to do, after a beat Tate took her hand in his and led her over to the sofa. It was obvious that she followed him reluctantly, but he could work with that, he told himself.

When he turned to look at her, the apprehensive expression he saw on Hannah's face almost tore him apart. He'd always thought of himself as a protector, a man women felt safe with. To see himself reflected as a potential monster in Hannah's eyes was a startling revelation. But there was no other way he could interpret what he saw. Hannah looked as if she was holding her breath, waiting for something terrible to happen to her.

Tate forced himself to continue. He was her only chance at survival—he had to remember that. Sitting down, Tate tugged lightly on her hand. When she looked at him quizzically, he coaxed, "Come sit on my lap."

Her mouth went completely dry.

Was this how it was to begin? The destruction of her virginity—was it going to start with a softly spoken invitation, only to escalate to unspeakable behavior?

She wanted to run.

And yet, she knew she had no choice. Nathan and the other man were just outside the door. She wouldn't make it past the threshold. And she didn't want to die the way her friends had. She wanted to live. To live and someday find a way to escape.

So, when the man who had paid for her tugged on her hand again, Hannah willed her knees to bend and did what he bade her to.

She sat down on his lap.

She was trembling, Tate realized the moment she made contact with his lap. He could feel her trembling and hated the fact that she was afraid of him.

Hated this whole charade.

But he knew it was the only way to save Hannah and all the other girls who had been so viciously snatched away from their families, not to mention everything they knew. And their only sin was that they were all so innocent in a world where innocence had ceased to

be a common thing and was now a rarity, something to
be elevated and observed, like a perfectly cut diamond.

He had no choice but to continue playing this role
he had swiftly come to despise.

Tate slipped one arm around her waist, holding Hannah against him. Inclining his head, he began to slowly
kiss the nape of her neck.

He struggled to keep from immersing himself in the
scent, the feel, the taste, of her.

It's a part—you're just playing a part, he silently
insisted as he lectured himself over and over again not
to get caught up in what he was doing.

Despite everything, despite his desperate attempt to
keep a tight rein on himself, Tate could feel his body
responding to Hannah. Responding to the intoxicating,
sweet taste of her skin against his lips.

*Dammit, get a grip, Colton. You're supposed to be
here to rescue her, not ravage her or scare the poor girl
to death. She's not your private playground.*

Satisfied that he had performed as expected for
whatever camera or cameras hidden in the room for
the sole purpose of observing his every move, Tate
whispered the same message into Hannah's ear that
he'd told her yesterday.

Except that he embellished on it.

"My name is Tate. Caleb sent me. He was the one
who told me to call you Blue Bird so that you'd know
I was telling you the truth. I'm here to rescue you," he
told her, his arms tightening just a touch around her
waist to prevent any sudden moves on her part, moti-
vated by surprise.

He couldn't let his guard down, not even for a moment. "You and the others," he added. His breath feath-
ered along the side of her neck as he spoke. "But this

isn't going to be easy and I'm going to need your help to pull it off."

Hannah turned her head slowly to look at him. He could tell by the look in her eyes that he'd made a breakthrough.

She was finally beginning to believe him.

Chapter 4

Hannah continued to look at the tall stranger, doing her best not to appear as startled as she suddenly was. Startled *and affected*. His breath had rippled along her neck when he spoke to her.

Heaven help her, but she'd *felt* something then, although she wasn't sure just what.

She'd been so afraid of lowering her guard, so focused on trying to remain as alert and vigilant as possible in order to resist being abused, that she'd all but turned into a brick wall.

But this man who claimed to have been sent by her brother—he'd created the tiniest hairline crack in the wall that she'd erected around herself. And because of that crack, she'd *experienced* something.

Something other than fear.

Was that his plan?

Was he trying to trick her into lowering her guard,

even just a little? Was he trying to make her believe that she was on the cusp of being rescued only so that he could take what he wanted without going through the trouble of having to physically fight with her?

Her friends had resisted and they were dead now. But she knew that small in stature though she was, she was actually physically stronger than they had been. And she was more persuasive than they had been. She'd been listening to the conversations around her. Listening and learning.

She looked into the stranger's eyes, trying to decide if he was who he said he was—someone sent by Caleb—or if he was just being clever, piecing together information he might have been told by whoever had put her virtue up for auction.

The stranger's eyes were aqua, a distinctive shade she'd never seen before. Was that a sign of some sort, that he was special, *different* from the others who pawed her friends with heavy hands?

Or was she creating "proof" where there was none to be had?

Hannah let out a slow, shaky breath. She would risk it. She would believe him. "What can I do?" she asked quietly.

Her question could be interpreted many ways, Tate assured himself, acutely aware that she'd voiced it loudly enough to be picked up by the camera. One way to see it was to believe she had resigned herself to her fate and in order to avoid being beaten for appearing to resist, she was offering to do whatever it took to comply with this role she was forced to play.

Do whatever he wanted her to do. All he had to do was tell her.

At least that was the way he hoped the goons who were watching this would see it.

Drawing Hannah even closer to him so that his cheek was against hers, Tate whispered, "Do you know the head man's name?"

There it was again, that warmth along her skin, that corresponding ripple within the pit of her stomach—or at least the general vicinity, she amended.

Hannah looked uneasily at this man who held her body on his lap and her fate in his hands.

What *was* it that he was doing to her? Where were these strange sensations coming from? She had questions, frustrating questions, and no visible way to address any of them.

In response to his question about the man who had to be in charge of all this, she shook her head. But before she could open her mouth to testify to her ignorance, he surprised her. He took hold of her chin in his hand. Then, as she watched, her breath caught in her throat, the man who had exchanged a briefcase full of money to purchase some time with her lowered his mouth to hers and lightly brushed his lips over it.

Just before his lips made contact with hers, she thought she heard him murmur, "Whisper it into my ear."

If she was going to ask "What?" she never had the opportunity, because that was when he kissed her.

And everything changed from that moment on.

She had been kissed before. One of the boys in her school had stolen a kiss from her once, then run off, afraid of being caught. She remembered thinking, as he ran away, that it was a very strange custom, rubbing skin on skin. She'd felt curious as to why he'd done it, but couldn't remember feeling anything beyond that.

The incident wasn't repeated, possibly because the boys in her village were afraid of Caleb, who was her protector.

This, however, was different.

Very different.

Hannah knew why this man was doing what he did—at least, she knew what he'd intimated his reason for taking this route was. He wanted to exchange information with her without anyone overhearing or suspecting what was really happening.

But if that was the case, was she supposed to feel this in response?

And what *was* this that she was feeling?

She had no name for it, no frame of reference, other than that time the water had been too hot for her when she was bathing and it had created a corresponding, almost unbearable warmth all over her, both without and within.

Drawing his head back now, Tate looked at her, waiting for Hannah to comply with his barely audible instruction. Doing his best to harness the hammering of his heart, which was pounding in direct response to kissing her.

Damn, he was going to have to watch himself. It was too easy to allow the lines between his roles to blur, to throw himself into the part of a man who'd just bought himself a preview of the night of uniquely exquisite passion he was being promised.

Hannah, in her innocence, was getting to him and he couldn't allow that. Distracted cops made mistakes. Fatal mistakes.

"Go on," he coaxed out loud, acting like a teacher waiting for his student to demonstrate what she'd just learned.

She was shaking again, at least she was inside, Hannah thought as she leaned over in slow motion, her lips feathering along his skin just below his ear.

"I don't know," she whispered. "I never heard anyone call him by name."

Tate's stomach muscles tightened so hard, he would have sworn on a stack of Bibles that his gut had suddenly been tied into a huge, unworkable knot.

Cupping her face in his hands, he brought his mouth down to Hannah's again, then lightly rained gentle, tightly controlled kisses along her cheek, working his way to the other ear.

"Can you describe him?" he wanted to know. They had a name, Seth Maddox, but it never hurt to verify that their source hadn't just been selling them a bill of goods.

Her breath was growing increasingly shorter, even as she felt her pulse accelerating. And her head was beginning to spin again, just the way it had when she'd been forced to drink that awful-tasting liquid. The one that robbed her of her ability to think, to differentiate shapes and people.

Leaning in against him again, she tried to imitate what he'd just done. But when she kissed him this time, she forgot to move on.

At least, she did for a long moment.

Instead, holding his face in her hands the way he had done with hers, her lips pressing against his, Hannah realized that she was lingering. Lingering—and enjoying it.

Was that pleasure she was feeling?

How *could* it be?

What was happening—all of this—was against her will. Or at least it had begun that way when the door had closed behind those henchmen, locking her in with this man.

Again she wondered if he was just pretending to be here to save her so that she wouldn't struggle when he finally had his way with her.

But he'd used her nickname, she reminded herself. He'd called her Blue Bird.

Her thoughts felt as if they were going in two directions at the same time. Her head ached.

Only Caleb knew about that name or used it.

Only Caleb and his girls, she amended.

His daughters had heard him call her that more than once. But Ruthie, Grace and Katie had no occasion to tell anyone else, she silently argued.

She raised her eyes to the stranger. So did she trust him—or not?

Hannah felt horribly confused.

He was waiting, she realized. Waiting for her to tell him something. He was waiting for her to give him the man's description, she suddenly remembered, struggling to clear her head.

Her lips lightly brushed against his cheek. At the same time, she whispered, "Older than you. Shorter. Thinner. Silver in his black hair. Perhaps fifty, perhaps younger." She raised her eyes to his, feeling as if she'd failed him. Failed her fellow sisters being held captive as well.

"I'm sorry I'm not a help," she apologized. The words of regret almost choked her.

"Nothing to be sorry about," he assured her, measuring out each word slowly, tailoring his words to the role he was playing. It had to be in keeping with the facade he had put into place. "You did very well."

She didn't see how she could have.

Hannah searched the stranger's face and saw that he was serious. She shook her head in response, but said nothing. Not until he gently slid her off his lap and helped her back up to her feet, getting up with her.

It was time to go. Before he forgot his training, did something incredibly stupid and blew the whole mission, not to mention his cover.

"I'll be in touch," he promised.

For the second time in ten minutes, Hannah's breath stopped in her throat. But this time, it was fear that created that sensation.

Her eyes were only a shade smaller than saucers. "You're leaving?" she asked.

Tate inclined his head ever so slightly. "I have to."

Because he'd gone to so much trouble to mask both his words and hers, she emulated his actions. She could see that she had surprised him when she pulled her torso up against him.

In a barely perceptible whisper, she entreated, "Take me with you."

When she added the word *please,* Tate thought his very heart would break right then and there. He would have given ten years of his life to be able to comply, to do exactly as she asked.

But he couldn't.

He had to keep the bigger picture in mind and the bigger picture involved rescuing not just Hannah, but all the other girls who had been yanked out of their homes and their schools, dehumanized, drugged and dragged here, to be offered as tantalizing pieces of flesh to men whose souls were blacker than the bottom of an abyss.

So, though he hated himself for refusing her, for forcing her to remain here another moment, Tate took hold of her shoulders and held her in place as he told her words he knew she did *not* want to hear: "I can't."

He saw disbelief, horror and desperation play over her exquisitely formed face.

"Yes, you can," she insisted, angry tears gathering in her eyes. "You can take my hand and walk out of here with me. You said you *bought* me. You gave them all that money for me."

Had it all been a lie, after all? Had he just been toying with her, making her believe there was an end in sight when there really wasn't?

But why?

It didn't make any sense to her.

"That was to show good faith," he explained.

Anyone listening to this exchange would see this as just a confrontation between a john and the unhappy object of his obsession—nothing more, he thought. It would stand to reason that she would be desperate to escape and willing to do whatever it took to make it happen.

"So I can get invited back to the party," he added, trying to make her understand why his hands were tied at the moment. Hoping that she could forgive him.

"Party?" she echoed. The word had an ominous sound to it. "What sort of a party?"

She didn't know, he realized. They really were keeping the girls in the dark. "For the organization's prospective clients—and other girls like you," he explained carefully.

Her mouth went dry again. More men meant more of a chance that someone else would claim her.

"So they can—they can—" She stumbled, unable to make herself form the words that described the ravaging that she felt certain would take place.

Tate placed his finger over her lips, silencing her. He didn't want her saying any more, didn't want her thinking about anything except that she *would* be rescued. Just not today.

The look in her eyes was clearly conflicted, but he forced himself to meet it. If he looked away, she'd think he was lying to lull her into a false sense of security and the exact opposite would happen.

"I'll be back for you," he promised. It was an oath, a vow he meant to keep no matter what it took.

Anyone overhearing would think it was just a wealthy john telling his "escort" of choice that he wasn't through with her, Tate told himself.

But he fervently hoped that Hannah would see beyond the obvious and realize he was making a commitment to her, a promise that he was going to return and rescue her as well as the others.

Because he was.

Hannah pressed her lips together. The wariness he'd seen in her eyes earlier returned. As did the apprehensive air.

She didn't fully trust him, he thought. How could he blame her? He'd given her a catchphrase, a nickname, and then turned her down when she asked him to get her out of here because she was clearly afraid of remaining here another moment. In her place, he'd have trust issues, too.

"When?" she finally asked.

Maybe there was a part of her that *did* believe him. At least he could hope. "Soon," he told her with as much feeling as he dared. "Very soon."

Just as the words were out of his mouth the door to the suite flew open and the two guards he'd relegated to the hallway came back inside.

He'd been right to assume that there were hidden cameras in the rooms and that the duo had been watching their every movement the entire time. Better careful than sorry—and dead, he told himself.

The man with the scraggly excuse for a goatee looked as if he could be outsmarted by a semi-intelligent raccoon. But the other, more powerful-looking one, Nathan, might be a real problem to them if he was so inclined.

Tate wanted the odds to be more on his side before he risked Hannah's life in an escape attempt. The sting would be a far more favorable occasion for things to go down.

If the wait didn't kill him.

"You about done?" the goateed man asked. Deep-set, marblelike eyes slid from him to Hannah.

Tate *really* didn't like the way the scum was looking at Hannah.

"Yes, I am," Tate replied calmly, his tone once again belying the churning emotions that were swirling dangerously just beneath the surface.

He could easily envision himself smashing that smirking, annoying face dead center with his fist. He was really going to enjoy taking these people down, he thought. Enjoy it the way he hadn't enjoyed anything in a long, long time.

"When will I receive my invitation to the party?" he asked, making certain that his question was addressed to both men.

He was well aware of the danger of openly favoring one henchman over the other at this point.

Pitting them against each other had its place and its benefits, but not yet. That was a card to be played closer to the end.

"When the boss is satisfied," the Scraggly Goatee answered condescendingly.

Tate kept his hands at his sides, but he curled his fingers into fists, wishing he was free to act on impulse rather than orders and protocol. He could take both men easily, even though they had guns and he didn't. He was trained for that sort of thing, using surprise and skills to his advantage. He could even make a clean getaway with Hannah if he timed it just right—but it would be at the cost of all those other lives. The abducted girls would be forever lost to their families, swallowed up without a trace.

So he remained immobile, telling himself it was all for the greater good.

Nathan eyed Tate with more than a little contempt in his eyes before he answered. "Keep your cell handy. You'll get a call soon. Within the next few hours," he added.

Tate nodded. "Thanks."

A noise behind him made him look over his shoulder. The man with the bad goatee hustled a weary-looking Hannah back into the bedroom again. He raised his voice so that the henchman knew he was talking to him.

"The deal's off if she's hurt in any way." That was so neither of them would feel free to strike her where her injuries would be initially covered up by clothing.

Looking on, Waterford appeared to be somewhat amused.

"You really like this one, huh?" he asked. As if he'd already had his answer, Nathan shook his bald head, bemused. "Don't really see why," he confessed. "One pretty much seems like another. Cover up their faces and you can't tell the difference."

Tate paused by the door. It was a very narrow line

he was walking and he knew it. One misstep and he would go headfirst into the lion's den, to be ripped apart and devoured.

But he wanted to be sure that nothing happened to Hannah in any way between now and whenever the so-called "party" was going to take place. After that, they were going to be home free.

Because the sting was set to go down at the same time.

He looked at Waterford pointedly, his message clear. "I'm not planning on covering her face," he told the muscular man.

He was surprised to hear Waterford laugh in response. The man looked almost human as he shrugged his wide shoulders and said, "Every man's got his own thing, I guess."

Tate couldn't imagine what Waterford's "thing" was, but he was fairly certain that he didn't want to stick around to find out. The only thing he wanted was for this operation to be over—successfully over—so that he could bring Hannah back to the people who were waiting for her. Back to her family.

If, at the same time, the thought generated an odd emptiness within him, well, he didn't have any time to try to explore that or figure out why he felt that way. There was much too much to do in the next few hours. He had a sting to finalize. And more money to get from Gunnar to use as bait. Greed had a way of escalating and the price that had been agreed to at the first auction was most likely suffering from growing pains because it had been increased.

He wasn't about to lose this opportunity—or have the sting go bad—because of something as insignificant as not being able to come up with enough funds to pull it off.

He hurried down the hall to the bank of elevators and punched the down button.

The next few hours were going to be crucial. For all of them, he couldn't help thinking, looking over his shoulder down the corridor toward the hotel suite he'd just left.

And envisioning the girl inside who was waiting to be rescued.

"I'll come back for you," he whispered again under his breath.

Chapter 5

"You've earned an invitation to the party," the cold, steely voice on the other end of the line said to Tate later that same evening. The call had come in on the cell phone that was exclusively registered to his "Ted Conrad" persona.

Tired after his long day, Tate nonetheless was instantly alert. He'd been waiting for the call—and, his gut told him, to hear from this specific man—since he had walked away from that tenth-floor hotel room earlier today.

Still, there was a game to play and to win, and Tate knew that he had to play it well. He feigned confusion. "Who is this?" he asked sharply.

"Why, the facilitator of your dreams, Mr. Conrad, who else?" the cold voice replied. The laugh that followed was all but frost-coated. It was obvious that the man on the other end of the line was enjoying the cat-

and-mouse game, secure in the knowledge that he was in control. "I must say, Mr. Conrad, for a man I've never heard of until just recently, your background has turned out to be truly impressive."

The background the caller was referring to had been created and entrenched in the right places thanks to his handler and the small crew he worked with who knew how to plant detailed information in files thought to be absolutely above hacking.

Even so, suspicion was never far away and always within reach. Because of that, Tate wondered now if the man on the other end of the call was on the level or mocking him.

If it was the latter, then he would have to be alert for some kind of a setup. This party he'd just been vetted for—did attending mean that he would be walking into a trap?

Tate's natural instincts warned him to proceed with caution, but they were also short on time. He couldn't afford to be overly wary in the name of self-preservation. There was a great deal at stake and this could very well be their one and only chance to rescue the girls and catch the main players in this sex trafficking ring. He couldn't drag his feet, but that still didn't make his uneasy feeling go away.

Tate supposed that if he wasn't so suspicious, most likely he would have been dead by now. Overconfident people were careless and being careless almost always got you killed.

"Maybe I haven't heard of you, either," Tate countered loftily, curious to hear what the man would say. The caller clearly had a large ego and that could only work in the investigation's favor, Tate thought.

For a second time, he heard the man on the other

end laugh. The sound was short, oddly cruel and completely dismissive.

"If that was an attempt to get me to blurt out my name, Mr. Conrad, you'll have to do better than that—if I were inclined to keep it secret. Which I'm not," he continued after a pause, as if he were playing out a fishing line. "Not to worry, Mr. Conrad. All will be revealed Friday night," the man promised ominously.

Okay, he was right, Tate thought. The man was definitely mocking him. Moreover, the man was clearly secure in what he perceived to be his superiority.

"Why then?" Tate wanted to know.

"All these questions," the voice mocked. For a second, Tate thought the man would hang up. But instead, he went on to answer the question. "Because after Friday's party, I will have enough on you to destroy you if I wanted to. Call it insurance."

Tate could swear he felt the man's fangs going into his neck. Thanks to his sources, he had a more than reasonable idea, although still not confirmed, of the identity of the scumbag he was talking to. Most likely, the man on the other end was Seth Maddox, a high-profile millionaire in New York City who'd made his fortune thanks to his astute investment acumen. Maddox more than fit the profile that had been put together regarding the man who was running the sex trafficking ring.

"Then this is a stalemate," Tate acknowledged.

"An equal balance of power," the man corrected. "Of course, if you'd rather opt out—" he offered loftily. His very tone said he knew there wasn't a chance in hell that would happen.

If possible, Tate's contempt for the man who was pulling all the strings behind this operation increased. "Where and when?" Tate asked, curbing his impatience.

The laugh was even more irritating this time around. It literally dripped of smugness. "So, we're still on. Good. Friday at 11:30 p.m. at the old abandoned Hubbard Warehouse just outside of North Philly." There was a brief pause, then the man asked, "You're familiar with it?"

The building sounded vaguely familiar, although he couldn't place it. But even as they spoke, the location was being plotted by one of his team. "I can find it," Tate assured the caller.

The moment the words were out, Tate remembered. The warehouse had once belonged to a thriving toy manufacturer. But when the company's target audience turned its attention toward video games, the toy manufacturer closed up shop. Hubbard's Toys disappeared from toy stores and, eventually, the warehouse was stripped bare, now housing rats rather than children's dreams.

"Good. I look forward to finally meeting you. I know I don't have to tell you to come alone." The warning in the voice was enough to send chills down the spine of a hardened criminal.

"Just me and my money," Tate replied. He was rewarded with what sounded like an actual chuckle, this time devoid of frost.

The next moment, it was gone.

"All the company a man could ask for" was the mastermind's approving response. "Except, perhaps, for a young, untried innocent. Don't be late. Doors close at midnight. After that—I don't care who you are—you won't get in."

Was the man concerned about the police or was this just a ploy to sound even more exclusive? Tate had a feeling it was most likely the latter. But he had a more pressing question on his mind.

"And Jade will be there?"

He had to ask. The man he was talking to was perverse enough to sequester her somewhere else just to keep him twisting in the wind—and returning for the next go-round, whenever that might be.

There wasn't going to be another go-round, Tate thought. *Not if I can help it.*

"Heart still set on that one, eh?" the voice mocked.

In this case, there was nothing to be gained by pretending he was indifferent to who he "received" in exchange for the briefcase full of money.

"Yes, it is."

The mastermind's response surprised Tate. "I like a man who knows what he wants. Yes, Jade will be there, ready to do whatever you want her to," the man added. "She knows damn well what'll happen to her if she doesn't."

Undoubtedly that was supposed to impress him, Tate thought, disgusted. He found it hard keeping his mouth shut and refraining from telling this subhuman how he would have loved to be given an excuse to gut him the way he deserved.

But there was nothing to be gained by that—or by torturing himself with the knowledge that his hands were absolutely tied right now and would continue to be until this was all resolved the *right* way.

He was damn glad that the sting was going down soon. He wasn't sure how much of this man he was going to be able to take. His blood ran cold when he started to think of what could have happened to Hannah, as well as the others, had Solomon Miller not come to them asking to trade information for immunity.

Without him, Emma and Caleb would have never found the bodies of those poor murdered girls and he wouldn't have known about the upcoming "party," where bored or depraved wealthy men were allowed to act out fantasies best revealed on a psychiatrist's couch.

"See you tomorrow night," the man on the other end said. Even that sounded mocking. And then the connection was terminated.

The second the call was over, Emma came into the hotel room, which was far less upscale than the one where he'd met with Hannah and her guards. His sister shook her head, telling him what he already suspected. The call wasn't traceable.

"It was a disposable cell," she said. "Randall couldn't pin down a signal," she added, referring to the computer whiz attached to their team.

Tate wasn't surprised. Despite the two goons at the hotel, he was certain these weren't amateurs they were dealing with. If they had been, the ring would have been history by now, instead of the elusive threat that it was. With any luck, though, that would all change after tomorrow night.

"We got Miller to confirm what we already suspected," Emma continued, taking a seat for a moment on the edge of the bed. "You were talking to Seth Maddox."

Well, that did fit what he'd heard about the man. Maddox was a risk taker who played for high stakes because he enjoyed the rush of the risk and the thrill of winning. He also wasn't above playing dirty to reach his goal.

"Have you got a voice match to confirm yet?" he wanted to know. There was always the chance that

Miller was lying to throw them off, playing both sides against the middle.

"Randall's working on it," she told him. "Should have it any minute now." She laughed then and saw her brother raise a quizzical eyebrow. She let him in on the joke. "I think Miller's insulted that we're not taking his word for it."

They needed more than hearsay to secure the warrants that they were going to need. A voice match was going to be part of the evidence. Besides, he had a feeling they were going to need all the help they could get.

"Right now, the sensitive feelings of a confidential informant aren't exactly high on my list of concerns," Tate told his sister. In his mind, he replayed his words to the man on the phone. "I'm going to need another briefcase," he told his sister.

Emma grinned. "I suppose you're going to want money in it."

He laughed shortly. "Well, yeah, that's the general idea."

"Can't get by on your good looks?" she asked, amused.

"Maybe next time," he answered dryly. "In the meantime, I need that briefcase crammed to the locks with money."

Money to supposedly buy an entire evening of ecstasy with a virgin of his choice. From the intel they had picked up so far, he was going to be in the company of politicians, athletes, Hollywood movers and shakers, not to mention renowned Wall Street investors. All well known, all powerful men.

And all depraved.

Tate felt as if he needed to take a shower already.

"Gunnar has taken care of it," Emma assured him seriously.

The pieces were all coming together, Tate thought as he nodded.

"You up for this?" Emma asked her brother the following evening.

Tate was dressed in a designer suit that appeared to have been hand-tailored just for him. He cut a handsome figure, Emma thought proudly. But pride took a backseat to concern. Of late, she had become more and more aware of the body count and she couldn't help being worried about him.

"You're going to be all alone in a tank of piranhas," she reminded him.

He saw the concern in his sister's eyes and thought of all the times they'd fought as children. But, fighting or not, there'd always been an undercurrent of love there. Their adoptive parents had seen to that. He doubted if he and his siblings could have been closer if they *had* shared the same bloodlines.

"Yeah, but knowing there's a SWAT team, not to mention you, right outside, ready to rush the place, will make me feel bulletproof," he said, trying to get Emma to focus on the manpower that was backing him up. It was practically a squadron. That should make her feel better about this. "How about you, Tomato-head?" he asked her, deftly changing the topic. "How does it feel knowing this is your last assignment?"

She wasn't focusing on anything except the next step in the plan. "Ask me after we get them," Emma told him. She placed the suitcase in front of him on the bed and snapped the locks open.

"I'll do that." Tate lifted the lid and glanced at the

sea of green. "All there," he murmured more to himself than to Emma.

"By the way, I forgot to tell you. Randall confirmed the voice patterns," she told Tate. "You were talking to Seth Maddox, all right. Guess being a millionaire NYC investor, rolling in cash, just wasn't enough for the man."

"No satisfying some men," Tate quipped dryly, shaking his head. He took a deep breath, bracing himself. The next moment, he was surprised by Emma, who threw her arms around his neck and hugged him. "Hey, what's this?" he asked.

"For luck," she answered, then backed off self-consciously.

"Since when do we need luck?" he teased her. "We're Coltons, remember? We make our own luck." He snapped the locks back into place, then picked up the suitcase. "Okay, let's get this show on the road," he urged and led the way out of the hotel room.

The cars that were parked outside the abandoned warehouse that evening would have made an automobile enthusiast's mouth water. There had to be over twenty of them and, Tate observed, not a single economy model in the lot.

He wasn't much on cars himself. If it had four wheels and was reliable, that was good enough for him. But he had to admit that the BMWs, Mercedes and Ferraris, not to mention a host of other high-end vehicles, were an impressive sight, especially when they were all in one place, the way they were tonight. He had driven over in a Ferrari. Part of the act. He'd parked the car next to a Bentley and gotten out.

He saw no one in the shadows, but knew his people were there. They were good at being invisible.

Tate talked to them now, taking advantage of the two-way amplifier he had hidden deep in his right ear.

"You'd think people who were lucky enough to afford wheels like that without blinking would be happy with their lot instead of trolling the internet, looking to get their thrills by ruining innocent young girls," he murmured to the people he knew were listening.

"No justice," he heard Emma answer.

"Sure there is. It's us," he said just before he terminated any further exchange.

He was drawing too close to the entrance to be seen murmuring to himself. This had to go off without a hitch in order to ensure that no one would be hurt. At least, no one who mattered, he amended, thinking of Hannah and the others.

The towering hulk of a man standing guard at the warehouse entrance looked him over with eyes that gave the impression that they missed nothing. They would have easily made his blood run cold had he actually been who he claimed to be and not a carefully trained Philadelphia detective, Tate thought, approaching the man.

"Ted Conrad," he said, identifying himself as he held up the driver's license the tech department had crafted for him at the beginning of this operation. Closing the wallet, he slipped it back into his pocket. "I'm on the list."

"Indeed you are, Mr. Conrad, indeed you are."

The voice behind him belonged to the man he'd spoken to on the phone yesterday. As he turned to look at Seth Maddox for the first time, Tate felt the man's arm come around his shoulder as if he and Maddox were old friends.

Even if Randall hadn't found the voice pattern match, recognition would have been immediate once he caught a glimpse of him. It was a familiar face that habitually graced the covers of business magazines and routinely appeared on the pages of the country's business sections. Fortunes were made or lost according to the words Seth Maddox uttered.

"Mr. Seth Maddox, I presume," Tate said dryly.

Maddox eyed him for a moment before the insincere grin bloomed forth. "Right the first time." Playing the grand master and loving the role, Maddox gestured about the huge, festively decorated warehouse as they entered. "Welcome to paradise, Mr. Conrad," he declared with no small fanfare.

Tate was surprised the man didn't have a five-piece orchestra shadowing his footsteps. The place would have warranted it, he couldn't help thinking. Tate took a moment to get his bearings and try to take as much in as he could. He'd seen amusement parks that had less going on.

The warehouse that once housed innocent dolls, stuffed animals, wooden puzzles and train sets was effusively decorated to mimic an artist's conception of Shangri-La.

It looked like an old Arabian Nights movie he'd once seen as a child, Tate couldn't help thinking. Except everything had been supersized. He wasn't very big on fantasy, favoring the truth instead, but it was plain that truth had no place here.

Strategically placed fans were causing filmy pastel-colored drapes to billow out seductively. It did the same for the scanty apparel that Hannah and her friends were

forced to wear, emulating harem girls whose only option was to obey the will of their masters.

The way the curtains were positioned along the far
wall toward the rear, Tate had a feeling that was where
the makeshift "rooms" were located. Rooms where each
"buyer" got to "play" with his "merchandise" for the
night.

That was where, he thought darkly, the young
women, purchased for the night, were taken to be used
and abused, feeding lusts of men who would never be
satisfied.

"Must have cost a pretty penny to have the warehouse decorated like this," Tate commented, pretending to be impressed as he scanned the surroundings.

"Don't worry, I plan to recoup every penny," Maddox told him with an amused laugh.

"That's your right," Tate agreed. He didn't see Hannah. He could feel his uneasiness grow. Was that his
intuition or just his fear of things going wrong? "Not
to seem rude, but I'd like to see Jade now," Tate told
the man.

He wasn't going to have any peace until he finally
got Hannah out of here in one piece and back to her
family. But the first step was to locate her. Once he
was certain she was all right and all the players were
in place, he was going to give the signal for SWAT to
come bursting in and finally put an end to this.

"Of course, of course," Maddox was saying in that
same mocking voice he'd used on the phone yesterday.
"She's right here, Mr. Conrad." Turning, he called to
someone in the milling crowd. Because of the din, Tate
missed the name.

The next moment, Tate saw a humorless, tall, wiry
man bringing in a young woman.

Hannah.

She looked like every man's dream come to life, he thought.

Dressed in swirling layers of see-through, colorful nylon, Hannah looked clearly humiliated. Tate would have given anything to throw his jacket over her to lessen her shame a little. But a gesture like that would be a dead giveaway. It would have been clear that he wasn't here to try to satisfy any perverse appetite.

He needed the charade to continue a little longer. Somehow, he was going to make it up to Hannah, he silently swore.

Hannah's eyes were again filled with wariness as she regarded him.

He was back to square one with her, Tate thought, frustrated. So be it. He resigned himself to that, focusing on his goal for now. It was going to be over soon, he promised himself, slanting a quick glance toward Hannah. He offered her a quick, encouraging smile.

The next moment, a high-pitched noise had him wincing as it proved to be almost unbearable for him.

Maddox looked at him with pity that wouldn't have fooled a five-year-old. "My apologies, Mr. Conrad. Please, come with me."

The next wave of noise was even more jarring.

At the same time, he also noticed that Maddox had managed to herd both him *and* Hannah into a space well removed from the rest of the crowd.

"What *is* that noise?" he demanded as the decibel level increased, practically vibrating inside his ear. It was all he could do not to wince again.

"Why, it's jamming, Mr. Conrad," Maddox told him almost gleefully. The investment guru nodded conde-scendingly toward his pocket. "Your cell phone won't work here. There's no signal. Sorry, precautions, you understand," Maddox said, watching Tate take in his every word.

Tate was getting a really bad feeling right about now, even as he nodded, playing along. "Makes sense," he acknowledged, inwardly cursing the man.

He was completely cut off from his backup outside, unable to transmit *or* receive instructions. By now Emma and the others had to realize they'd lost the signal. Were they scrambling for another vantage point so that they could renew the connection? Or was he going to have to be the Lone Ranger in this operation after all?

"I'm so glad you agree, Mr. Conrad. Or should I say Detective Colton?" Maddox's smile was malevolent as his eyes bored into Tate. The game was over. "Which do you prefer? And please don't insult me by saying you don't know what I'm talking about. That's so very trite and beneath you, Detective Colton. Besides," he continued as he gestured for his surprise to be brought in, "Mr. Miller already gave you up. He really isn't very much for pain, are you, Solomon?" he asked, his eyes narrowing as he watched the beaten, semiconscious Solomon Miller being brought in, supported by two of Maddox's nameless henchmen.

They were going to kill him, Tate thought. More importantly, they were going to kill Hannah. Maddox would have terminated his own mother without blinking an eye if his agenda called for it. There was no two ways about it. Maddox was an out-and-out sociopath.

Tate knew he had only seconds to do something—or die. He had no weapon, no backup and, at this point, absolutely nothing to lose. Pushing Hannah directly behind him, he grabbed Maddox and bodily shoved him into the incoherent, babbling Miller.

The gun Maddox was brandishing went off.

A scream mingled with a flood of curses. Chaos broke out all at once.

"Go, go, go!" Tate ordered Hannah, grabbing her hand and breaking into a run that took them through the maze of filmy curtains, wisps of smoke and mingling bodies.

Tate had no idea where he was going, all he knew was that they had to get out of here if they wanted to live out the night.

Chapter 6

There was nothing but static coming through.

The eerie sound filled the interior of the van where Emma, Randall and another Bureau tech were currently sequestered, monitoring the transmissions and waiting for Tate to give the signal to initiate the takedown.

The SWAT team was aching to rush the warehouse. The last time she'd checked, their eagerness was puncturing the very air.

"Tate," Emma cried, urgency rising in her voice. "Tate, can you hear me?"

Nothing but more static answered her.

They'd lost him.

Emma felt an iciness spread out through her limbs as her heart all but froze in her chest. She struggled to keep her fear at bay.

This isn't happening.

"Try a different frequency," she ordered Randall,

the tech closest to her. He was already doing just that, as was his partner.

Tate would get out of this, she told herself. He was a survivor.

The static continued as if to mock their efforts.

"Nothing," Randall lamented, exasperated, his eyes focused on the monitor he was trying in vain to adjust. "They're jamming us," he declared in frustration.

Which meant someone was onto them, Emma thought. Someone had told Maddox.

It was all falling apart. Something was very, very wrong.

The door to the van opened and Abe Kormann, the head of the SWAT team, stuck his head in. One look at the faces of the van's inhabitants and he knew something was awry. No one had ordered them in yet and by his reckoning, it was past time.

He looked at Emma. "What do you want to do?" he asked.

She weighed the options. They could wait, and her brother could lose his life, if he hadn't already. Or the SWAT team could rush the warehouse and Tate could get killed in the cross fire. Either option wasn't very good, but she knew that Tate believed the same way she did: that to go down fighting was a far better way to go than to meekly accept defeat.

"Go in," she ordered, then repeated the command, her voice stronger and more confident the second time. "Go in!"

Weapons raised and at the ready, the men and women comprising the SWAT team quickly flew across the expanse that was between the van and the entrance to the warehouse.

They closed the distance in less than five seconds.

The hulking three-hundred-pound-plus bouncer guarding the door reacted automatically, producing a gun. He never got the opportunity to discharge it. The barrel was still pointed down when a marksman's bullet hit him. The bouncer dropped like a stone.

Several men on the team used a ram to break down the warehouse door. It splintered and fell to the ground, useless, as the SWAT team quickly infiltrated the former warehouse.

Screams and cries of confusion greeted their appearance.

People began running in all directions, bumping into one another, adding to the mass chaos.

More screams, gunfire and monumental panic broke out moments after the first shot inside the warehouse was fired. Having the building stormed by men and women in full black regalia with guns drawn only added to the sense of disorientation and imminent danger.

It was a classic case of every man and woman for themselves.

"What's happening?" Hannah cried as she ran alongside Tate, stretching her legs as far as she could as she desperately tried to keep up with the man who was holding on to her hand.

They'd given her drugs shortly before the event had started, but she'd managed to fool them again, pretending to swallow the pills only to hide them between her upper lip and gum. Less had dissolved this time, so she was not as affected as she had been the first time. She was aware of everything.

"You're being rescued," Tate shouted to her so she could hear him above the almost-deafening noise and gunfire.

It was only a half truth at best. The sting had obviously gone awry. But those were still his people who'd burst in, firing their weapons. If there was any justice in the world, Maddox would be captured—if he wasn't already.

But life had taught Tate not to make any assumptions—logical or emotional—until he could verify them with his own eyes.

For now, he and Hannah had to keep going. He didn't want her to stop, not even for a moment. They needed to put as much distance between them and Maddox and his people as possible before he could even remotely entertain the possibility that Hannah was safe. Only then would he stop to find out if Maddox was among the captured or, better yet, among the casualties.

At this point, he really didn't care which it was, as long as the operation could be put to an end and the girls returned to their families.

Abruptly, their path was suddenly blocked by one of Maddox's tuxedoed henchmen. Equal parts fearful and angry, the man clutched a rapid-fire weapon in his hands. Raising it quickly, he didn't warn them to stop, he just began discharging the weapon.

Tate pushed Hannah to the ground as he simultaneously lowered his head and charged into the gunman. Catching the man completely off guard, Tate knocked him down. Moving quickly, Tate had the man's gun before the criminal could recover it.

The weapon discharged once.

The henchman stopped moving.

Tate stood back up, exhaling slowly. Behind him, he heard Hannah's sharp gasp.

"He's dead," she cried in horrified wonder. It didn't seem real to her.

"He was the minute Maddox recruited him," Tate informed her crisply, his voice devoid of any feeling. He held on to the dead man's weapon. They might still need it.

Pulling Hannah to her feet, his eyes swept over her quickly, making assessments. "Are you hurt?" he asked as gently as possible.

Hannah shook her head. "No, I'm not hurt." Her eyes were wide, like someone trapped in the middle of a nightmare that wouldn't end.

"Then let's go," he ordered, taking her hand and running again.

He'd looked up a schematic of the warehouse on an official website listing building plans filed with the city. He liked knowing where he was going before he began his journey.

"I think there's a side exit we can use," he told her.

Tate was relying on what his mother had once referred to as his uncanny sense of direction, picking his way through the maze of interwoven bodies and mayhem. Getting to the exit felt as if it was taking forever, but finally, he could make it out in the distance. The end of the rainbow.

The end of the rainbow in this case was a door to the outside world. Freedom was just beyond that.

Hannah was breathing audibly by the time they finally reached the door. He looked at her over his shoulder again to assure himself that she was all right. "Hang in there." He flashed her an encouraging smile.

Unable to answer, Hannah nodded vigorously instead, offering a hint of a smile. It was all she could muster for now.

Hannah was accustomed to running. Running games among the children had been common when she was growing up, and she had always been one of the faster ones. But the stakes had never been this high and the course had never been littered with bodies before. It made a huge difference.

As they approached the exit, Tate offered up a quick one-line prayer of thanksgiving.

The door wouldn't budge.

Swallowing the curse that automatically rose to his lips in deference to the woman with him, Tate put his shoulder to the door and slammed it hard. The movement was almost imperceptible.

He tried again.

The third time, the door shuddered, then finally moved. One more full-on attack and the door abruptly gave way completely. He was still holding on to Hannah's hand and they both all but fell onto the ground on the other side.

"Success," Tate cried, relieved.

Relief dissipated immediately in the face of the frigid weather. The temperature had dropped even further and there was snow falling, sticking to the ground. Its pristine appearance provided a complete contrast to the angry red smear on the ground not two feet away from where they'd almost fallen.

Someone had escaped ahead of them. And then been killed.

Tate dropped to the ground, pulling her with him as he quickly scanned the immediate area, looking for a sniper. But whoever had killed the man on the ground was no longer there.

Taking a tentative breath, Tate cautiously rose back to his feet, momentarily blocking out the wall of noise echoing from the building behind him.

That was when he realized that Hannah was shaking.

Not from any overt display of fear—not that he would have blamed her if she had been—but from the cold. The thermometer was undoubtedly registering in the low thirties and the outfit her captors had forced her to wear was one far better suited to tropical weather.

Tate shrugged out of his jacket and quickly draped it around Hannah's shoulders, pulling it closed around her. It covered more than half her body.

"It's not much," he apologized. "But at least it's warmer than what you've got on."

Clutching the two sides of the jacket to her to trap whatever heat she could, Hannah nodded her head in thanks. "This helps a lot, thank you. But what about you?"

They were in the middle of what felt like an apocalypse and the woman was being polite. Tate could only shake his head in admiration and wonder. Hannah Troyer was one very special woman, even without taking her beauty into account. The combination was almost more than one man could bear. "I'll be fine," he assured her.

The sound of running feet approaching had Tate pushing her behind him. Hannah's back was protected by the wall while he was shielding the front of her with his body. The next moment, catching a glimmer of what turned out to be moonlight on the barrel of a gun, Tate reacted at lightning speed and fired.

An assailant transformed into a casualty, dropping to his knees and attempting to fire one last time. But the weapon slipped from his lifeless fingers before he could discharge it.

Tate heard Hannah stifle a scream.

"I know him," she cried. He turned to look at her as

she explained, "He was the one who took us, who took Mary and me prisoner and brought us to that motel."

"He won't be taking anyone anywhere anymore," Tate assured her grimly.

They needed to keep going. He couldn't afford to hang around here, waiting for the dust to settle and a body count to begin. His cover had been blown and Maddox's people knew he was a detective. If any of them got away, that made his life worth less than nothing and his death immensely desirable.

As for Hannah, she would simply be collateral damage if they killed him. He needed to get her somewhere safe—and fast. He could gather information later, once he knew she was safe. Or as safe as possible, given that she was a material witness that the state undoubtedly would want to build their whole case on.

He quickly scanned the area, looking for a means of escape. His eyes came to rest on their way out.

"My car," he declared, thinking out loud. When Hannah looked at him quizzically, he pointed to the Ferrari at the far end of the parking lot. The team had secured the vehicle to flesh out the persona he was playing in this sting-gone-wrong. "Over there."

He didn't have to add the word *run*. Hannah was already doing that.

Reaching the vehicle, he yanked open the unlocked door and pushed Hannah inside, then slid across the hood rather than rounding the short distance to the driver's side.

He got in, then threw the car into gear. Less than a second later, he was tearing out of the lot, as if the very forces of hell were right behind him.

Because they very well might have been. He wasn't sticking around to find out.

* * *

He didn't know where else to go.

With a shameful lack of contingency plans, Tate had no choice but to drive to the small apartment he maintained in the heart of Philly. He went there rather than to the hotel room he'd been staying in under his assumed name. The latter would have been the first place he knew Maddox or his men would look, provided they'd eluded capture.

He was still hoping that they hadn't.

The apartment was just a temporary stopover, he told himself. He'd regroup and get in contact with his team so he could get filled in on exactly what the hell had gone down. Equally as important, he had to stop by the place to get his backup weapon. He felt naked unless he was packing both his weapons and doubly so since he'd been forced to leave them both behind to carry off this now-failed charade.

What had tipped Maddox off? Had he been suspicious all along or had Miller slipped up and said something that had clued the man in?

He needed to get answers.

But first, he needed to get his weapons, he reminded himself. The one he'd taken off the dead man had served him well enough, but he wanted a familiar piece in his hands if he was going to have to defend Hannah, as well as himself, for who knew how long. He knew both his piece and his backup piece inside and out, knew they wouldn't fail him or jam. He took better care of the weapons than some men took care of their wives.

Because his life depended on them.

As he drove the Ferrari into the underground parking structure beneath his apartment building, Tate could feel Hannah stiffening beside him. "What's wrong?" he asked her.

"What is this place?" she asked, tilting her head slightly so that she could get a better view of the immediate area.

Tate brought the expensive vehicle to a stop in the parking spot assigned to his apartment number. Ordinarily, his vintage Mustang occupied the space. But right now, it was in the shop for its hundred-thousand-mile tune-up, leaving his parking space conveniently empty.

"This place is where I live," he told Hannah, answering her question. "My apartment's up on the third floor."

Despite recent events, she still wasn't accustomed to buildings rising above a second level. They made her nervous, as if she was waiting for the floors to buckle under the accumulated weight.

"Your family won't mind your bringing me?" she asked him uneasily.

Looking carefully around, just in case, he saw nothing suspicious or out of the ordinary. Only then did he reach in and, taking her hand, help Hannah out of the car. He remained alert as he guided her to the elevator. "My family's scattered," he told her.

The elevator arrived and they got in. He took one last look before the doors closed to make sure no one was suddenly approaching them.

Then he turned his attention to Hannah.

He knew all there was to know about her, he thought, but she didn't know the first thing about him. Maybe she'd feel a little more at ease if he clarified a few minor points for her.

"I'm not married," he told her as they rode up.

"Oh."

She pressed her lips together, feeling oddly happy over the information she was digesting. Was that wrong? In the middle of all this discord and death, she found herself relishing the knowledge that the man who had come back for her, who had rescued her, just as he'd promised, was unattached.

It gave her definite reason to smile.

Shouldn't she be feeling guilty about that instead of strangely jubilant?

When the elevator doors parted, Hannah began to step out of the car only to have him put his hand up before her, stopping her in her tracks. Keeping her in place, Tate moved ahead and looked to the left and right of the elevator, the way a child might if he were crossing the street without an adult accompanying him.

"Okay," he told her, beckoning her off the elevator car.

Tate led the way down the hall to his apartment door. Unlocking it, he went in first, making sure that she was half a step behind him.

The gun he had secured earlier was still in his hand as he scanned the remarkably neat one-bedroom apartment, looking for a telltale shadow, or something to tell him that he and Hannah were not alone in the apartment.

But they were.

He let his guard down just the slightest bit.

Meanwhile, Hannah was taking a survey of her own. "You keep a very tidy home," she told him.

He didn't tell her that he kept it that way because that made it easier to see if something had been disturbed. It was how he could tell if his living quarters had been compromised or not.

The same precautions applied to his dresser drawers. The contents of the drawers were arranged so that he could place an old volume of Shakespeare's sonnets in them without having the book touch anything else in the drawer. If it did touch something else, that meant that someone had been going through his things and had put everything back carefully—but not carefully enough.

Rather than go into any of this, Tate simply replied, "The nanny was strict."

Hannah looked at him, her interest piqued about this outsider more than she knew her brother and the others would think seemly. Secretly, she didn't care.

"You had a nanny?" she asked Tate in wonder. "Where was your mother?" She couldn't imagine one of the women in her village entrusting someone else to look after her children for anything more than a few hours. Certainly not on an ongoing basis.

"She was helping my father build a proud foundation," he answered.

Since the rooms were clear, he went about his final test—checking the volume of sonnets in the drawer—and found everything where it was supposed to be. Finally relaxing, he turned to look at the young woman he'd just brought into his world.

It occurred to him that Hannah and he could not have been more different. Her world was one of simplicity, of tranquillity and almost monasticlike dedication, while his was infused with danger and criminals, never mind the underlying social complexities he and his siblings had grown up with.

They were as different as night and day. And had just as much of a chance of coming together on any level as the sun had of swallowing up the moon.

Even so, he could finally understand what the French meant by their age-old expression, *Vive la différence.*

An image of the country mouse and the city mouse—a story one of the nannies had told him eons ago—suddenly flashed through his mind.

He'd never once thought that the country mouse could be so compellingly attractive.

Learned something new every day, he thought to himself with a broad smile.

Chapter 7

Tate flipped the three locks on his fireproof door one at a time, securing his apartment—at least for the time being.

Even so, he was aware that, as far as time went, they didn't have much of it.

Still, there was enough available to address a few basic amenities.

"Are you hungry?" he asked Hannah.

She shook her head, her long wavy red hair gently echoing the movement a fraction of a second afterwards.

"No. I am a little cold, however," she ventured shyly, as if she felt it was thoughtless and self-centered of her to complain about anything after Tate had risked his life to save hers.

"Right." And why shouldn't she be cold, he realized. The jacket he'd given her was more like a pup tent, but underneath it Hannah was only wearing what amounted to colored scarves in the dead of winter. "Follow me. Let's see what I can come up with," he told her, leading the way into his bedroom at the rear of the apartment.

Opening his closet, he paused and shook his head. There wasn't exactly much to work with. He was a good nine inches taller than she was, as well as wider. Anything of his would fit Hannah at least twice over, if not more so.

"I'm afraid I don't have anything in your size," he apologized. Feeling out of his element, Tate stepped back from his closet and gestured toward it. "Why don't you see if there's anything you can do with what you find?" He saw the uncertain look on her face, as if she didn't feel right about touching anything. The young woman was really amazingly polite, given the circumstances.

"No, I couldn't," she demurred.

They were going to have to leave soon and he knew they wouldn't get very far with her all but immobilized from the cold.

"Yes, you could," he told her firmly, adding, "Feel free to take anything you find," he urged. "I insist." He jerked his thumb back toward the front of the apartment. "I'm just going to be out in the living room, calling my team to find out if anyone knows what happened."

With that, Tate left her to make her choices in peace.

Damn, for a man who was always in control of the situation, Hannah made him feel as if he was tripping over his own tongue. So much for being a savvy police detective, he thought cryptically.

But then, he couldn't remember ever coming across anyone like Hannah Troyer before, he thought. For all intents and purposes, the young Amish woman represented another world to him. A less complicated, more honest world.

There were times, such as now, when he had to wonder if progress, which had gotten them so far away from that simple world, was ultimately worth it, despite all the perks it had to offer.

Maybe Emma had the right idea after all, turning her back on this fast-paced world.

That wasn't his to debate, Tate reminded himself. He didn't have the time. What *was* his to do, he thought, was to check in with his team and find out what the hell was going on—and just where they were supposed to go from here.

He swallowed an oath when his call didn't go through the first time. The signal was too weak. Trying again, he was rewarded with an icon that declared his signal bars were stronger.

The second he said "Hello," he thought his eardrum was going to be shattered.

"Tate?" Emma cried, shouting his name into the phone, a mix of joy and anger evident in the single utterance. "Where the hell are you?" she demanded, then, before he could say a word, she breathlessly demanded, "Do you have Hannah with you?"

Tate was glad he could give his sister *some* sort of positive news.

"Yes, she's here," he acknowledged. "Safe with me for the time being. Your turn," he declared, indicating that it was her turn to answer a question. "What happened with the sting?"

"I was going to ask you the same thing," Emma countered. "Why didn't you give the signal for the SWAT team to storm the warehouse?"

She didn't know. He would have thought that Miller

would have filled her in—unless he couldn't, Tate suddenly realized. Had Maddox killed him?

"I didn't get a chance," he admitted. "Miller blew my cover."

"What?"

He could almost envision the surprise on Emma's face. She and Caleb had been the ones to trust Miller in the first place, and urged the members of the task force to do the same.

"I don't know how, but Maddox got wind of the fact that I was a cop. I think he planned on shooting both of us." He realized how vague that must have sounded to Emma and was quick to clarify the ambiguity. "Hannah and me."

"So you shot him?"

There was no missing the hopeful note in his sister's voice. Was that because she was asking him if he was the one who killed Maddox or did she just hope that the organization's kingpin had been taken down even though he was still among the missing?

"No weapon, remember?" he reminded his sister. "I shoved Maddox into one of his henchmen and his gun went off. After that, I don't know what went down," he admitted. "Did you get Maddox?" The pause on the other end of the line turned into a lengthy silence and it wasn't because he'd lost the signal again. The bars were dark and plentiful.

Tate had his answer.

Damn!

Still, he asked, on the minuscule chance that he was wrong. "You didn't, did you?"

"No." It cost her to admit that. Emma didn't tolerate failure well, especially not her own. "From what I can gather, Maddox and a couple of his guys managed to get away." She paused a moment and Tate knew what was coming. She was trying to find a way to tell him.

They'd both found that straightforward had always been the best way.

"He'll come looking for her," she warned.

Tate knew Emma was talking about Hannah. After all, from what they were learning about the operation, it was quite possible that Hannah had been privy to everything that had happened. He had a feeling that it would only take the memory of her dead girlfriends to get her to testify against the kidnappers.

That fact made her an immense liability for Maddox and it placed her life in immediate danger.

From now on, until they caught Maddox or eliminated him, his only assignment was to keep Hannah safe. Nothing else mattered.

"Yeah, I know."

He paused for a moment, thinking. He could hear his closet door moving along the runners in the bedroom. Hannah was trying to find something to wear and most likely discovering that he had nothing she could use. But desperate times called for adjustments and so far, Hannah had been a trouper. He hoped that she would continue to be one awhile longer.

"I'm going to have to take off for a while until you and the team can find Maddox and bring him down," he finally said to his sister.

He heard Emma laugh shortly. "Tell me something I don't know."

There was a noise behind him and Tate instantly whirled around on his heel, the weapon in his hand raised and ready to fire.

He lowered it when he saw Hannah's terrified expression.

"Sorry," he apologized, then said to his sister, "Hold on for a minute, Em."

Hannah really looked like a teenager now, he couldn't help thinking as he looked at her. She was wearing one of the old blue T-shirts he used to knock around in. She'd gathered it at her waist and tied it tightly so that it didn't look as if she was wearing a potato sack. She also had on a pair of his old, worn jeans rolled up at the cuffs and securely tied at the waist with a scarf just beneath the T-shirt.

He guessed that she must have found the jeans lying discarded somewhere in the back of his closet. He'd been meaning to donate those things to the local charity. Good thing he hadn't gotten around to it.

Just looking at her made him ache.

Rousing himself, he nodded his acknowledgment of her ensemble. "Not bad."

The smile on Hannah's face was sweet as well as shy. "You're being kind," she told him. "I hope you don't mind my wearing these things. I promise to wash them when I'm done."

He shook his head. "Wasn't really worried about that," he assured her.

For someone who'd been abducted and had encountered more evil in the past couple months than she'd ever dreamed existed in the world, Hannah seemed to be holding up remarkably well, he thought.

He suddenly remembered something Hannah had said to him regarding her brother. She'd asked if he'd seen Caleb and if her brother was well. The single question encapsulated the sort of person she was: not a thought about herself, only about others.

Mumbling "Excuse me for a second," Tate turned

his back to her and took his hand off the cell phone's mouthpiece. "Emma?"

"Still here, Tate," he heard his sister answer patiently.

"Is Caleb with you?"

Officially, the man wasn't supposed to be anywhere near the now-failed sting, but knowing Emma and her soft heart, she'd probably not only allowed Caleb to come along, but was probably even now reassuring the man that his sister had been rescued.

"Yes, why?" Emma asked, lowering her voice.

Tate slanted a look toward Hannah before continuing. "I thought he might want to say a few words to his sister," Tate answered. "I know she'd really like to hear from him."

"Hold on a second," Emma responded. He could hear the excitement in her voice. It told him all he needed to know about her relationship with Caleb. Though she wouldn't say it, he now realized that Emma was simply crazy about the man.

Listening, Tate heard some kind of noise in the background, as if she was walking somewhere. And then he heard Emma calling to Hannah's brother. For his part, Tate caught Hannah's eye and beckoned the young woman over to him.

Hannah approached, her beautiful eyes filled with curiosity. Without a doubt, he could very easily spend the next hundred hours or so wading in those mesmerizing blue-gray pools.

The next moment, he upbraided himself for letting his thoughts stray so drastically from the path he needed to follow. He was supposed to be protecting Hannah, keeping her out of harm's way, not drooling over her like some lovesick pubescent idiot.

"Yes?" Hannah asked when he didn't say anything enlightening to her.

"I think there's someone on the other end of this phone who'd like to talk to you," Tate told her.

He offered her his cell phone. She took it from him uncertainly, holding the small item as if it was alive and could leap from her fingers at any moment. That was when he remembered that Hannah probably didn't have the vaguest idea what to do with a cell phone. Or a landline for that matter.

Given her lifestyle, she would have had no reason to have any experience with either one.

"You listen on this part," he told her, pointing out the cell phone's upper portion. "And talk into this." He indicated the tiny holes on the bottom of the cell.

Very gently, he placed the cell phone against her ear. She covered his hand with her own and for a second, he left it right where it was, savoring the contact and absolving himself because he hadn't initiated it.

After a moment, he slipped his hand away and let Hannah hold the phone herself.

"Hannah?"

Her face lit up like a Christmas tree as she recognized her brother's voice coming out of the strange device.

"Caleb! Oh, it's so good to hear your voice!" she cried enthusiastically. The next moment, she fell silent, earnestly listening to what her brother was saying. Tate saw her smile. "No, no, I'm fine. Really. Tate is taking good care of me." She turned her eyes toward him and her smile deepened. "He rescued me, just as he said he would. He told me you sent him, Caleb," she went on. "I confess I didn't believe him, but now I see I was wrong to doubt him. I am safe and unharmed."

She was holding the phone with both hands now, as if that could somehow anchor her brother to her. "When can I see you, Caleb?" she wanted to know.

It was time to interrupt, Tate thought, even though he hated to do it because she looked so happy to be re-united with her brother. But the longer they delayed getting out of here, the more of a risk they ran of being discovered.

"Soon," Tate promised her, gently removing the cell phone from her hands. "Very soon." Putting the phone to his ear, he made a request of the man on the other end. "Caleb, I need to have a word with my sister."

"One moment" was the restrained, polite reply. Tate heard the phone changing hands. Within seconds, he found himself on the phone with Emma again.

Before he could say anything, he heard her telling him, "That was a very nice thing you just did." Since Emma wasn't in the habit of giving compliments, Tate took her words to heart. "It meant the world to Caleb to get a chance to talk to Hannah instead of just having me reassure him that his sister was all right."

"I'm a very nice kind of guy, remember?" Tate countered wryly. "Look, we've got to get ready to take off," he said abruptly. "I'll be in touch when I figure out where we've landed." That was a lie, because he'd already figured that out. He'd just said that in case his line was being tapped or his apartment was being bugged.

He left the rest unsaid, but he didn't have to elaborate. They both knew that the less said, the less chance he ran of their being caught. Right now, Hannah's safety was paramount to him, not just because the entire case against Maddox could very well rest on her slender shoulders if the other girls wouldn't come forward as witnesses, but because he just couldn't bear the thought of any harm coming to her.

Ever.

"You be careful," Emma cautioned.

He heard the concern in her voice, heard the catch in her throat that told him she was trying hard not to let her emotions get the better of her.

It wasn't an easy life either one of them had chosen. The only difference was, Emma would be out of it soon. As for him, he usually thrived on this sort of thing. It was just every now and then that he caught himself wondering what it might be like to have a regular life like the people he saw going about their business every day.

There were times he couldn't help envying some of them. But the truth of it was, he loved what he did and wouldn't have left that world for anything.

"Always," he said belatedly, responding to Emma's order that he remain safe. With that, he ended the call.

He was using one of those disposable phones and at this point, it had served its purpose. He tossed it on the ground and deliberately stepped on it, destroying all chance of the phone's signal being traced.

The young woman beside him gasped and looked at him, a wariness entering her eyes.

She probably thought she'd witnessed a fit of temper, he guessed.

"We don't want to risk being followed," Tate told her. "And that phone would have given off a traceable signal."

"Like a telegraph?" she guessed, trying to relate what he'd just said to her to something she was remotely familiar with.

Tate did his best not to grin as he nodded. "Something like that," he said, even though what he'd actually been thinking of was a GPS.

Hurrying into the bedroom, he pulled a backpack out of the closet and quickly threw some basic items of clothing into it. Then he picked up a winter jacket and held it out to Hannah. "This might fit you a little better than my jacket did," he told her. The jacket was by no means small, but it had fit him when he was less muscular than he was now, since weight training had become a central focus in his life. It was definitely smaller than the jacket he'd draped over her shoulders earlier and she was going to need something substantial to help shield her from the cold.

Hannah took the down jacket from him and slipped it on. As expected, her hands disappeared beneath the sleeves. A quick glance in her direction would have pegged her—mistakenly—as a waif instead of the brave young woman she actually was. Hannah seemed to take all that life threw at her in stride and with a smile.

"We are leaving?" she asked him.

He nodded. "We have to. They're going to be looking for us."

She didn't ask him who *they* were. She knew. She also knew something else.

"For me," Hannah corrected.

That sounded much too isolated. She wasn't a lone wolf and, for the duration, neither was he.

"Since I'll be with you every step of the way, it's really *us*, not you," he pointed out.

For once, she dug in, maintaining her position. Having Tate risk his life for her once was hard enough on her. More than that made her feel an obligation she worried she could never be able to repay.

"But you would not be in danger if you didn't go with me," she pointed out.

He shrugged indifferently. "Makes no difference," he told her. "I *am* going with you so there's no point in talking about it."

He didn't expect her to continue trying to get him to change his mind, but he also didn't expect what happened next.

Hannah rose up on her toes and brushed the very lightest of kisses against his cheek.

On his end, it felt as if the wing of a butterfly had lightly grazed his skin.

When he looked at her quizzically, his fingers just barely brushing against his cheek, Hannah smiled at him. The smile crinkled into her vivid eyes. "You are a good man, Tate Colton."

"Just doing my job," he murmured self-consciously.

She nodded, taking that into account. "You are still a good man," she insisted quietly.

Just then, he thought he heard a commotion directly below them coming from the street level. Hurrying to a window, he looked down and saw that a sleek black Mercedes had pulled up in front of his building.

Several men came pouring out, all dressed in dark suits, as if they had come to pay respects to the dead, rather than try to add one more to Death's numbers. Even from his present vantage point, he could see they were intent on getting their job done.

He didn't have to guess what that "job" was.

He recognized one of the men from the warehouse.

Taking the fire escape to elude them was out of the question. The fire escape outside his apartment faced the front of the building and one of the men was left standing guard by the Mercedes.

But he wasn't about to stay here, waiting to be taken down. Ultimately, the fire escape was the only chance they had to get out.

Grabbing Hannah's hand in his as he slung the backpack over his other shoulder, he ordered, "Let's go."

Hannah wordlessly fell into step beside him, ready to follow him to the gates of hell and beyond, if need be, because of all that he had done for her so far. For this very reason, she felt that she owed him her allegiance and her loyalty.

Besides, she knew in her heart that Tate would keep her safe.

Chapter 8

Tate threw open the window leading out onto the fire escape. A quick glance down told him that Maddox's guard was still there. He just hoped that the man wouldn't decide to suddenly look up until they had cleared the area.

"Are we climbing out the window onto *that?*" Hannah asked, her eyes widening at the very thought.

He realized that she'd probably never encountered a fire escape before, certainly never climbed one before. "It'll hold us," he assured her. "We're going to be going up to the roof."

Rather than question him any further, she stoically said, "All right," and followed him out onto the structure.

"You go first," he instructed softly, pointing to the stairs that led up to the roof. If the guard *did* look up, the henchman would see his back first. And if the guard fired, then *he'd* be the one hit, not Hannah. "Nothing to be afraid of," Tate assured her. He tapped the hand-railing. "Everything's solid."

Hannah offered him a wan smile as she made her way up the fire escape of the forty-year-old, six-story building. She kept her eyes trained on the next rung and tried not to think about what a long, long way down it was.

Her fear of heights kept her from even climbing into the hayloft in their barn back home, but she couldn't impose her fears on Tate. It wouldn't be right. Besides, he wouldn't be asking her to do this if there was any other way to make their escape. So, with icy hands, Hannah clung to the black metal handrails and made her way up the metal steps of the fire escape, praying she wouldn't fall and embarrass herself—or possibly worse.

An eternity later, her heart pounding in her chest, she finally reached the roof. Her legs numb, she made herself move out of the way so that Tate could climb onto the roof as well.

Taking a deep breath to help steady her throbbing pulse, she looked at the man who had rescued her, utterly confused. "We are going to hide up here?"

He shook his head. "No, with any luck, we're going to go down the back fire escape."

Before Hannah could think to ask him why hadn't they just climbed down to begin with, Tate swiftly crossed the flat, gravel-paved roof. Leaning over the side of the building, he looked down to the ground below. The rear of the building was facing the alley and it was empty.

No witnesses to give them away.

So far, so good, Tate thought.

Turning toward Hannah, he waved her on. "C'mon," he urged. "Follow me."

Hannah did just that, climbing down six flights without uttering a single word, either in protest or in fear.

Even in the midst of a situation that could become explosive at any moment, Tate had to marvel how incredibly trusting Hannah was.

He'd never met anyone quite like her, he caught himself thinking again.

Focus! Tate upbraided himself sharply.

Now wasn't the time to let his mind wander, making peripheral observations about a girl who was way too young for him. And way too pure. She deserved someone who wasn't nearly as jaded as he had become.

What mattered here, he reminded himself, was for him to remain alert in case one of Maddox's men spotted them or unexpectedly showed up. If Tate slipped up and got distracted, even for a second, it would be all over for them.

All over for her.

And all the risks that had been taken would have been for nothing.

Silently indicating that she was to remain behind him, not beside him, Tate stopped dead when he got to the side of the building.

The street was just beyond that—the unprotected street that offered no shelter until they reached the other side.

Tate slowly edged out, his backup piece in his hand, loaded, cocked and ready to fire if he needed to.

The street was clear. And almost eerily empty. Hazy yellow-white light from the towering streetlamps pooled on the ground, crisscrossing and touching in several places.

"Run," he ordered, taking her hand again and lead-ing the way.

They ran for two long city blocks, passing store-fronts, pizzerias and shops that had long since closed their doors. Only the bars had glimmers of muted light emerging through their darkly tinted bay windows, but their doors remained firmly closed. Whatever patrons were left inside were far too involved with their per-sonal brand of poison to give either him or the young woman with him even a first thought, much less a sec-ond one.

It was there.

A dusty, navy blue—almost black—sedan that wouldn't have caused anyone's head to turn, either in curiosity or admiration, was parked unobtrusively, just a little beyond the crosswalk.

Tate realized after the fact that until he saw the ve-hicle parked at the curb, he'd been holding his breath. He released it now.

When he was less than ten feet away from the dusty sedan, he pressed down on the key in his pocket—the one he'd grabbed as they vacated his apartment—and it made a minor high-pitched noise.

The next second, the car's locks were all jumping to attention, opening at the same time.

"Get in," Tate ordered gruffly.

They didn't have a second to spare. Just because he didn't see them didn't mean that Maddox's men weren't closing in on them.

Hannah obeyed without question, sliding in on the passenger side and closing the door just as Tate got in behind the steering wheel.

"Whose vehicle is this?" she asked.

Since her kidnapping, she'd lost count of the cars

she'd been forced into. Because they all ran together, she hadn't been able to tell one from another.

Riding in cars was still a relatively new phenomenon for her since, up to this point, she had spent all her life around carriages and the horses that pulled them.

This vehicle seemed to look more used than the others, she thought. That made it appear different to her.

"Mine," he told her as he started up the vehicle. It came to life immediately. He paid a local teenager to keep an eye on it and to make sure that the car was started regularly when he was out of town.

This, he thought in satisfaction, was where foresight—and paranoia—paid off. He kept the car here in reserve for just this sort of an unexpected twist—to make good his escape if need be.

"You have two cars?" Hannah asked in wonder as he tore away from the curb.

Any second, he expected to see Maddox's men descending on them. Or, at the very least, the black Mercedes trying to chase them down. One thing he knew for certain. There was no way he was about to hang around and press his luck.

"It's a backup car," he explained, then realized Hannah probably didn't know what that meant. "I have it parked away from my apartment just in case I can't get to the car I usually keep in the parking structure." He didn't add that the car also had a host of emergency supplies stored in the trunk for different contingencies. There was also enough cash in the trunk to see him through whatever initially had sent him on the run. Cash rather than credit cards because it couldn't be traced.

Hannah looked duly impressed by his abbreviated explanation.

The vehicle continued eating up the road, putting distance between them and his apartment.

"You are very prepared. Like a scouting person," she concluded, pleased with her analogy.

"I think you mean Boy Scout," Tate corrected gently, taking care not to hurt her feelings. He didn't want her to think he was talking down to her.

By her expression, the thought had never even occurred to her. Instead, she looked cheerful as she nodded at the term he'd supplied that had eluded her. "Yes, like a Boy Scout."

Sitting back in her seat, Hannah watched the road as it whizzed by, merging into the darkness and disappearing behind them. It occurred to her that the world outside her village was a very large place. Did anyone get the opportunity to explore all of it?

"Where are we going?" she asked.

He couldn't risk going back to his place, since Maddox obviously knew where he lived. Turning up at some small, out-of-the-way hotel or motel didn't appeal to him. It was too isolated and too easily found.

Their best bet, he decided, was to hide in plain sight and there was no better place for that than Manhattan, the very heart of New York City.

Tate couldn't help wondering how Hannah would react to *that* news. Slanting a glance in her direction, he said simply, "We're going to New York."

"The state?" Hannah asked uncertainly.

"The city," he answered.

Tate waited, but she made no comment on the information. Instead, Hannah grew very quiet. So quiet that it began to make him uneasy. He could feel her tension.

"Something wrong?" he asked.

Hannah merely shook her head in response and continued to say nothing.

Rather than ask what was wrong again, he made the assumption that something *was* wrong and instead began to coax her to share her thoughts with him. He felt responsible for her and if he'd said anything to upset her, he needed to know so that he could make it right again.

"Hannah, you can tell me," he told her earnestly. "You can tell me anything."

Hannah looked down at her short, unadorned, rounded nails without really seeing them. She had no right to bother him with her fears. He was the leader out here in this world of outsiders. It wasn't for her to contest his judgment or challenge his choices.

Still, he was asking her to speak and to ignore his request would have been rude of her.

The tug-of-war in her head went on for only a minute. After it was over, in a very small voice she told him. "People die in New York City."

"People die everywhere, Hannah. Are you talking about someone specifically? Did someone you know die when they came to New York?" he added, hoping to prompt her to tell him the source of her fear.

Before he had gotten involved in the case, his notions about the plain-speaking people of the Amish community were admittedly preconceived and incredibly limited. He had no idea that when Amish children reached their later teens, they were allowed—even encouraged—to leave the village and live among the outsiders for a time. It was a test devised to see if they were truly meant to live out the rest of their lives in the village or if life in a large metropolis was what they really wanted.

Solomon Miller belonged to the latter group and, as Tate had come to know, there was obviously a price to pay for that choice. Being ostracized by the community was the heaviest burden. Miller had been willing to risk Maddox's wrath to get back into the good graces of the community he missed so much.

"I had a friend," Hannah began. "Her name was Eva. Eva went to New York City." Hannah turned to look at him. "She never came back."

"Maybe she liked it better there," he suggested. It was, after all, the logical conclusion.

It might have been logical to him, but not to her. Hannah shook her head. "When her mother and father went to see her, to make sure the choice was hers and not made for her by someone else, they found her dead in her small room. She had a noose around her neck."

That sounded like something Maddox might have been mixed up in. Or, if not him, than someone of his ilk, Tate thought.

"She was murdered?" he asked.

Hannah folded her delicate hands in her lap and stared straight ahead at the inky road. "We were not told. No one spoke her name again."

"Well, they'll speak yours," Tate assured her with feeling. "Because nothing's going to happen to you. I promise," he added, his eyes briefly holding hers. "And I haven't broken a promise to you yet, have I?"

"There has only been one," Hannah reminded him politely.

He grinned, knowing that she was going to say that. Predictability sometimes had a nice feel to it, he thought. Like now.

"Yes, but I kept it, didn't I?"

His answer made her smile at him. She looked back at her hands with approval. Her knuckles no longer white and tense.

"Yes, you did," she agreed. He deserved to receive better treatment at her hands. "I am sorry. I did not mean to be such a pull on you."

"Such a—?" And then the light went on in his head as the right word occurred to him. "You mean *drag,* don't you? You didn't mean to be such a drag," he reiterated, piecing together her real meaning. He laughed as what he'd just said played back in his mind. "You're not a drag, trust me."

"I do," she told him solemnly. "I trust you very much."

And that, he knew, meant a great deal to him. Perhaps even a little too much. After all, he was just protecting her the way a bodyguard might.

Nothing more.

Tate drove all night, arriving in the heart of New York City well past dawn. Specifically, he'd arrived at the Old Vic Hotel. The landmark hotel, remodeled more than a handful of times, stood guard over a section of Central Park. He was partial to it.

A valet popped up the second he pulled up before the hotel. He hurried over to the driver's side, ready to take possession of the vehicle from Tate.

But the latter shook his head. Rolling down the window on his side, he told the eager valet, "I'd rather park it myself, thanks."

The valet's disappointment quickly turned to happiness when Tate slipped the man a tip, even though no service had been rendered.

Parking the sedan himself, Tate knew where to locate the car at a moment's notice. It also enabled him to take a small packet out of the trunk before he secured it again. He tried the trunk a number of times right after that until he was certain that it was locked and no one else could access its contents.

There were a couple of passports in the trunk as well. Just in case…

Hannah watched in silence, curious, as he slid the packet open, then withdrew several crisp hundred-dollar bills and pocketed them.

"For the hotel bill," he told her.

She understood money, but she also knew that people in the world beyond her village used something she had heard referred to as "plastic." They used it for everything.

"You do not have plastic?" she asked.

The question amused him because he'd never thought that she'd be the one to ask that.

"This is simpler," he said, nodding at the cash in his hand.

That was the simple answer. The more specific one was that money couldn't be traced while credit cards—even those obtained under a different identity—could. And once they were traced, they could easily set off alarms.

He needed to buy them as much time as he could—literally.

Getting out of the vehicle, Hannah suddenly became very self-conscious. She looked down at what she was wearing. In the world she resided in, no one went visiting looking like an orphaned urchin. She didn't want to embarrass him.

"Won't someone object to the way I am dressed?"

For a long moment, Tate looked at this young, beautiful, unassuming woman he had stumbled across, then smiled.

"Don't worry. No one taking one look at you is going to object to the way you're dressed," he promised.

Hannah appeared unconvinced. "Are you certain?"

"Very certain," he replied, slipping his arm through hers. "Tell you what, after we get a little food into you, why don't we go shopping?"

"Who is *we?*" she wanted to know, thinking he was referring to a friend of his, or perhaps a lady friend he was involved with. The prospect of his bringing along another female, possibly for her input, oddly disturbed her.

He gestured to her and then himself. "You and me. *We,*" he emphasized. "Why?"

She didn't hear the question, just his definition. "No one else?"

"No one else," he told her solemnly.

Was she asking about her brother? he wondered. It wouldn't be safe, having Caleb come all the way out here. For all they knew, one of Maddox's minions was watching Caleb right now, counting on the fact that the man would be coming to see his sister.

Maddox had already demonstrated that he was desperate to eliminate Hannah. Tate was *not* about to drop breadcrumbs to make it easy for the bastard to carry out his murderous intent.

Guiding Hannah through the revolving door—which she regarded with unabashed wonder and amusement—Tate ushered her with him toward the front desk.

"My wife and I would like a suite overlooking Central Park," he told the neatly dressed man at the reservations desk when he finally reached it.

He was aware that standing beside him, Hannah's mouth had dropped open in complete wonder.

Chapter 9

"But I am not your wife," Hannah protested nervously in a hushed whisper as they walked away from the clerk at the reservations desk. Tate, she noted, had something that looked like a rectangular card in his hand. The clerk had given it to him and she couldn't help wondering why.

"I know," he replied. "But I couldn't very well register as Detective Tate Colton and the young woman he just rescued from a sex trafficking ring, now could I?" he pointed out, then grinned to put her at ease. "For one thing, there wasn't enough space. Besides, the less resemblance we bear to who we really are, the better. It's just to throw them off," Tate assured her as they reached the bank of hotel elevators. He hit the up button. It lit up.

Hannah didn't have to ask who he meant by *them*. She knew. Maddox and his men.

"You really think they will be looking for us?" she asked in an almost inaudible voice.

He didn't *think,* he *knew.* But it wouldn't help put her at ease to belabor that point. "Better to take precautions, just in case," he said, deliberately vague in his answer.

The elevator arrived and he ushered her in, then stepped into the car himself. He pressed "4." The gleaming stainless-steel doors slid shut. He noticed Hannah pressing her hand to her abdomen as they ascended, as if to keep it in place.

She wasn't used to this, he thought. It was, he mused, a little like exposing a flower grown in the shade to strong sunlight. Acclimation was going to take time and patience.

The elevator reached their floor and they got out. "But you believe that they will be looking here?" she pressed again, wanting him to give her an answer one way or another.

"They won't find you," he promised. "That's why I'm not planning on letting you out of my sight." Glancing down at the entry card the reservations clerk had given him, Tate scanned both sides of the corridor, then turned to the right, going in search of room 462.

Reaching the room, he was about to slide the key-card to unlock the door when he sensed that she was staring at him. When he looked at her, he saw her brow furrowed in confusion.

"What's wrong?" he asked.

"The man at the desk didn't give you a key," she pointed out. "How are we going to get in?"

There was precious little to smile about in his job so when the opportunity arose, Tate couldn't resist.

"Magic," he answered without cracking a smile. The

next moment, he followed up his claim by opening the door. He gestured for her to enter.

Hannah crossed the threshold, her eyes all but riveted to the door he had just opened. "You did it," she murmured in awe and wonder. "You opened the door. With that *thing*." She pointed to the keycard.

"Always keep my word," he told her.

The moment she was inside the suite, he quickly closed the door and made sure that all the locks were secured and flipped in place.

He was going to have to rig up something of his own before he felt truly protected, he thought. A rank amateur could most likely breach the hotel safety locks if he wanted to.

He'd tried twice to feed her on the way here and she'd turned down the two offers—he had a feeling that her nerves were far too tangled for her to consume anything without having it make her feel sick to her stomach. "If you're not hungry, I suggest you try to get some sleep." As if to reinforce his suggestion, he crossed over to the queen-size bed and turned down the cover for her.

Hannah made no move toward the bed. Instead, she knotted her fingers together and asked in a quiet voice, "Where are you going to sleep?"

She was concerned that he was going to take advantage of the situation, Tate thought. That perhaps he even saw it as payback for rescuing her. Her opinion of the men outside her village wasn't very high, but then, he had to admit he couldn't blame her, seeing as how she'd been forced to deal with only the dregs of the outside world so far.

"Don't worry about me," he said mildly. "I can sleep anywhere."

And he could. He'd gotten accustomed to grabbing

short catnaps whenever he could while working an assignment. But he had no intention of even doing that tonight. He wanted to remain on his guard—just in case they *had* been followed.

Turning toward Hannah, he motioned her to come forward. "Go ahead," he urged. "Get into bed."

This time, moving stiffly, Hannah did as he told her. Drawing the blanket up to her chin and holding on to it as if it was a protective shield, she watched him as intently as she could with eyes that were struggling to remain alert—and open.

Pulling a chair over to the bed—and making sure he was facing the door—Tate sank down into it.

"I could sit in the chair and you could lie down in the bed," she offered, clearly feeling guilty that he had to spend the night sitting in a chair.

Tate shook his head, staying exactly where he was. "Now what kind of a gentleman would that make me?" he wanted to know. "Hogging the bed and making you spend the night sitting up in a chair?"

He saw her brow furrow again. "Hogging?" she repeated, puzzled. The word didn't make any sense to her in its present context.

"It's just an expression," he explained, trying not to laugh at the face she'd made. "In this case, it means not sharing." He looked at her, waiting. "Anything else you want cleared up?"

She shook her head. There wasn't anything right now, but she knew that there would be again. And most likely soon. Living among the outsiders was almost like learning a new language.

"You outsiders—you do not speak plainly," she told him.

Her voice faded away with the last word. She had

lost her battle against sleep and had slipped into its confines, leaving Tate to contemplate his next move in silence.

He put making plans on hold for a moment and allowed himself to just look at the young woman whose life he'd risked everything in order to save. For everything she'd gone through, Hannah looked amazingly unscarred—not to mention incredibly beautiful.

And growing more so by the moment. Was that even possible?

He shook himself free of the thought and forced his mind back to the situation at hand.

Anyone looking at her would have speculated that the worst thing she had to contend with was selecting which ribbons to tie in her hair.

Amish girls don't wear adornments in their hair, he reminded himself. He and Hannah came from two completely different worlds—and she didn't belong in his.

Be that as it may, he couldn't seem to draw his eyes away.

What would it be like, he wondered, having someone like that to come home to every night? A woman who was warm and welcoming and cared whether or not he was happy? Up until now, he'd never thought of his life as lacking anything. Not having a wife or children was something that worked in his favor, since there was no one to consider but himself. If he was hurt, or in a dangerous situation, he wasn't burdened by guilt, worrying about how his wife and family would carry on if something happened and he was killed. None of that ever came into play or hampered him. It left him free to be a better detective, one who didn't hesitate to do whatever it took to get the job done.

That was who and what he was.

If it ain't broke, don't fix it, he told himself, falling back on the timeless adage. And his life wasn't "broke."

No, it wasn't broken by any means, but what it was, he thought, was empty. Oh, he connected with his siblings on occasion. They might not share DNA, but they shared the same values as well as love for the same pair of adoptive parents. And up until a few days ago, that had been enough.

But it didn't feel like enough anymore, he thought ruefully, watching Hannah's blanket rise and fall as she breathed.

You're getting philosophical in your old age, Colton. Focus on the assignment, don't get all sensitive about what you think is missing in your life. Thinking that way is liable to get you both killed.

It was sound advice. Now all he had to do, Tate thought, was take it.

He stopped looking at Hannah and fixed his attention on the door instead.

Hannah's eyes flew open with a start.

Heart pounding, she quickly looked around, her eyes delving into every corner, every space, trying to understand what she was seeing and what her brain was telling her was true.

She more than half expected to be back in that awful, awful hotel room, huddled three to a bed and chained to some part of it because her kidnappers were taking no chances that she and the other girls might try to escape somehow.

But when her panic eased and she began to actually grasp what she was seeing, Hannah realized that she was still in the same grand-looking suite Tate had brought her to in the wee hours of the morning, before the sun had had a chance to rise—right after they'd escaped from his apartment.

Was all of this really happening to her?

The moment she thought of Tate, she sat up, every fiber of her body acutely alert even before she managed to focus on him.

She looked at him in surprise. He was just where he'd been when she'd closed her eyes. Sitting in an upholstered chair beside the bed.

Had he spent the entire night—or what had been left of it—sitting in what had to be an uncomfortable position, guarding her? Her own body ached in sympathy just *looking* at him.

Scrambling up to her knees, she moved closer to Tate, peering at his face. His eyes were closed.

When they suddenly opened, she was caught off guard and, losing her balance, tumbled backward onto the bed. "I thought you were asleep."

"I wasn't," he told her. "I was just resting my eyes."

She sat up, swinging her legs over the side of the bed. Hannah scooted over, closer to him in case they had to whisper because someone might be listening. Habits learned during her harrowing imprisonment were hard to break.

"You really spent the night in that chair," she marveled. "Isn't it hard to sleep that way?"

"I wasn't trying to sleep," he answered.

So he'd said when she'd offered to switch places with him, she thought. "You were standing—sitting guard," she recalled, amending her words to fit the situation. "But aren't you tired now?" she wanted to know. Then, before he could answer, she made him an offer. "I could stand guard now if you like, wake you if someone tries to come in," she added.

The sweetly selfless offer made him smile. Did she have any idea how adorable that sounded? Most likely not, he decided.

"Thanks for the offer," he told her, "but I'm fine. I don't need a lot of sleep."

"But you need some," she insisted, determined to pay him back somehow. "Everyone needs some."

"And I got what I needed." There'd been a moment or two during the night when he had caught a few winks. He'd learned how to sleep with one eye open at all times. And how to stretch a few winks into making do. The job had trained him to get by on very little. And, conversely, how to make a little go a long way.

Right now, he had something far more important than sleep to attend to. He was hungry and he had a feeling that so was she. There was finally color in her face, and a tiny bit of sparkle in her eyes. He had no doubt that Hannah had a strong personality and was already working at putting what happened to her earlier—the kidnapping, the brutish behavior—behind her.

"Tell you what," he proposed, "why don't you and I get some breakfast and then go shopping?"

"Shopping?" she echoed. Why would he want to go shopping with her? And exactly what sort of shopping was he referring to? "You mean like buying some food for later?"

"No," he corrected, puzzled why she would even think that. "Like buying clothes—for now," Tate emphasized.

She still wasn't completely clear on what he was saying he wanted. "You wish to purchase clothing for yourself?"

He grinned. He knew half a dozen women, his sisters included, who would have instantly jumped at the chance to go shopping before he could have even finished saying the word. This dewy-faced young woman was certainly in a class by herself.

"No," he corrected patiently, "I 'wish to purchase' clothing for you. Not that the waif look you're currently wearing isn't very appealing in its own way..." His voice trailed off deliberately.

It was meant as a teasing remark rather than a revealing one. But the truth was that despite the fact that his clothes—even the smallest ones he had outgrown—were way too big for her, there was something incredibly stirring and enormously appealing about the way Hannah looked when she put them on.

Tate cleared his throat and forced himself to focus on what he was trying to convey to her. So far, he wasn't having much luck—in either focusing or in making himself clear. "Anyway, I thought you might be more comfortable wearing something that actually fit you and belonged to you."

Hannah flushed. She was already in his debt. This would just increase that debt by heaven only knew how much.

"I don't wish to be any trouble," she told him, demurring the offer. "And I have no money to spend on clothing." The fact of it was, she didn't have a penny to her name.

"Let me worry about the money," he told her, then added firmly, "And it won't be any trouble. Besides," he continued with a whimsical smile, "it might be fun." When he said that, he was thinking of her. As far as he was concerned, just being with her, observing how she took everything in—as if she had crossed the threshold into Wonderland—was definitely fun for him. "The store windows are all decorated for the holidays and the city is at its best this time of year."

He wasn't all that partial to New York City, frankly preferring several other cities to the Big Apple. But he had to admit that when it came to celebrating the holidays, the citizens of Manhattan took second place to no one. Store merchants went all out decorating their windows both in tribute to the holidays and in a not-so-subtle attempt to attract customers to shop in their stores.

"We can even stop to look at the Christmas tree in Rockefeller Center." The suggestion drew a blank look from Hannah and he quickly made his assumptions from that. "You've never seen the Christmas tree at Rockefeller Center, have you?"

Her eyes on his, Hannah slowly moved her head from side to side.

This, Tate thought, promised to be a great deal of fun. "Then you have a real treat in store for you," he told her. "Why don't you freshen up and we'll get started?" When she looked at him blankly for a second time, he nodded toward the opened door that was in the rear of the suite. "The bathroom's right in there," he told her. "There are fresh towels and everything else you might need in there. You can take a shower—or a bath if you prefer," he added, thinking that she might not have showers where she came from. He really should have studied up on the basic elements that comprised her Amish lifestyle, he thought. But then, he hadn't known he was going to have this sort of up-close-and-personal contact with the woman he rescued.

"And you will be where while I am in there, 'freshening up'?" she asked him haltingly, a bit of color creeping up her cheeks.

"Right where I am now," he told her. "Out here.

Waiting." He smiled at her. "You can lock the door from the inside, you know."

The expression of surprise on her face told him that she *didn't* know. And then that expression softened into a smile of gratitude.

Hannah rose to her feet. "I'll hurry," she promised, already striding toward the rear of the suite.

"You can take your time," he called after her. "I'm not going anywhere without you."

Hannah looked over her shoulder and smiled at him. She wouldn't have been able to explain to her brother, or to anyone else for that matter who might ask her why, but Tate's assurance was immensely comforting to her. More than she would have thought it should be.

"I will still hurry," she told him. She had been taught never to take advantage of someone's kindness to her, and there was no reason in the world for her to change her behavior now.

Tate couldn't truthfully say that he didn't allow his mind to wander, or that he tried to restrain it from conjuring up fantasies of Hannah slowly easing her nude, firm young body into the tub filled with warm water and soapy bubbles, as he listened to the sound of running water.

His fantasies increased threefold when he realized that the melodic sound coming from the bathroom was *not* someone singing on the radio.

There *was* no radio in the bathroom and Hannah certainly didn't have one with her. Things like that were forbidden in her simple community. No radios, no TVs. What he was listening to was Hannah, singing softly to herself.

Or maybe she was singing to him.

Heaven knew it certainly felt that way as the melody corkscrewed itself into his belly, causing one hell of an earthquake in his gut.

Her singing just added fuel to the daydream that insisted on blooming in his head, taking over all his thoughts.

If she didn't stop singing soon, he was going to need a cold shower himself.

He closed his eyes, which only made things worse. Because then he could vividly envision Hannah, her sleek, supple body submerged in the suds-filled tub of warm water, each movement making the suds recede a little more...

The very image wreaked havoc on his already twisted gut, not to mention on adjoining parts of his body as well.

His job left no time for extracurricular activity, no time for him to remember that he was still human, still a man with a man's needs. He kept that part of himself tightly under wraps because he'd told himself that gratifying those needs wasn't nearly as important as the assignment he undertook.

But being this close to Hannah, to her innocence, her purity, not to mention her exceedingly appealing face and body, unearthed all those thoughts, feelings and reactions he thought he had kept buried so well. Unleashed them in spades.

He wondered if the department gave out awards for sainthood.

It should, he couldn't help thinking, as the volume of her voice swelled and the sheer beauty of it completely encompassed him.

It really, really should.

Chapter 10

When Hannah came out of the bathroom fifteen minutes later, fully dressed, her skin glowing as she was towel-drying her hair, Tate had already made a few decisions as to what their next move had to be.

He was well aware that he was going to have to be at his most persuasive to convince Hannah to go along with something that, although less than an order, had to be more than just a polite suggestion.

However, at the moment, Hannah embodied such an entrancing picture of innocence, he just had to pause and take it all in. How could someone who appeared to look so simple be so stirring at the same time?

Hannah was quick to pick up on her rescuer's ambiguity. Utterly without vanity, she stopped drying her hair, letting it begin to air-dry instead. Given the thickness of her hair, the process would take a long time.

"Is something wrong?" she wanted to know.

"No—well, maybe." He wasn't accustomed to stumbling over his words. It was almost as if he was unsure of himself and he couldn't remember the last time *that* had happened. As a matter of fact, he couldn't recall a single time—which made what he was experiencing all the more irritatingly puzzling. Finally, he said, "It depends on your point of view."

All he had managed to do was make his explanation more confusing, not less. Hannah flashed a shy smile at him as she shook her head. Then, to his surprise, she placed the blame on her inability to comprehend rather than on his inability to communicate.

"I'm sorry, but I still don't understand."

He'd never had trouble making himself understood or getting his point across before. He had a very organized, practical mind that approached everything in a logical fashion. More than once, he'd been accused of being *born* old. But what was going on here, the way his feelings kept scrambling and retreating, would definitely *not* stand up to any close scrutiny. The young woman whose safety he was assigned to ensure was getting to him. Getting under his skin. Big-time.

Tate took a breath and forced himself to be blunt, rather than tiptoeing around the subject. "I think, in order for you to stay safe while the Bureau and the Philly P.D. try to locate Maddox, you're going to have to change your appearance a little." This was one time he couldn't allow himself to soften the blow. It would ultimately be a disservice to her. "Actually, more than a little," he amended.

She was still wearing his jeans and shirt with the cuffs both rolled up as much as possible. Even so, she was all but literally swimming inside the clothing. Hannah looked down at herself, as if trying to home in on what he was referring to. What she was wearing was legions away from her normal garb.

"I thought I had already changed my appearance— more than a little," she underscored.

Tate laughed. There was no getting away from the fact that she looked like an adorable waif. And that, right now, was working against them, rather than in their favor.

"That'll only attract attention. We need you to blend in, not stand out." Without meaning to, he scrutinized her hair as he spoke. "But still look different than you do now."

The shift was not lost on Hannah. She saw the way he was looking at her hair. Instinctively, her hand went up, covering the length that was draped down over her shoulder. But even as she did it, she sensed that the protective gesture was futile.

"You want to cut my hair." It wasn't a question.

But Tate pretended to take it as such. "Do I want to? No," he told her honestly. "But I'm afraid that I think we should. Maddox can afford to have the best men working for him, that means he's going to have professionals looking for you. Looking for a twenty-year-old young woman with long red hair. The less you look like that, the better your chances are of eluding them until my team finally takes him into custody."

For a moment, she focused on the promise of his words. "Do you really think they will?"

He could hear hope fairly throbbing in Hannah's voice. He was glad he didn't have to lie to her, that he believed in what he had to say to her.

"I do. My team is the best of the best," he assured her.

"Then perhaps I don't have to cut it..." Hannah's

voice trailed off for a moment. But before he could tell her that, although he really regretted it, she was going to have to surrender her hair—better for her hair to be cut than for her to be cut down—Hannah took a deep breath, as if resigning herself to what she was about to say next. "It is only hair. It will grow back." Her words were stoic. "Do what you must."

There was more and he wasn't happy about having to say it, but this, too, was necessary. "Hannah, we need to dye your hair as well."

Her eyes widened. No women in her world would have even *considered* adding color to their hair, much less changing that color.

"Dye my hair?" she asked, uttering the words as if each tasted sour on her tongue.

He nodded. "Redheads stand out. Having your hair cut shorter will change your appearance somewhat, but not enough. Making your hair a different color might very well save your life."

Hannah pressed her lips together, suppressing a very real desire to argue with him, to try to save her hair. But despite her desire to keep her hair just the way it was, something inside her sensed that he was right.

"I understand," she replied quietly, squaring her shoulders the way a soldier facing a firing squad might. "Do whatever you need to," she said, giving him blanket permission.

The first thing he needed to do, Tate thought, was to get a hair-dyeing product. There were a variety of shops on the hotel's ground floor, not to mention a slew of stores outside the hotel, all located in the immediate vicinity. He had his pick of where to shop.

For a second he debated leaving Hannah in the hotel room with a strict warning not to open the door to anyone. After all, it would only take him a few minutes to go and purchase the necessary item. Fifteen minutes from start to finish, most likely. But, like a parent with a child who had yet to cross her first street alone, he felt uneasy about the prospect of leaving Hannah alone right now, even for such a short time.

There was another way.

Getting on the phone, Tate called down to the front desk and asked the clerk to connect him to the nearest drugstore.

"Are you ill, sir?" the clerk asked with polite concern.

"No, nothing like that," Tate said quickly. "It's just that my wife thinks her roots are starting to show and she's insisted that I go buy her some of that hair-coloring product she seems to swear by," Tate explained with the air of a long-suffering husband who'd been this route before.

"Would you happen to know what type and color your lovely wife prefers?" the clerk asked dutifully. The man seemed genuinely surprised—as was Hannah—when Tate rattled off the name brand and the exact color number of the hair dye he was requesting. The clerk recovered in the next beat and told him, "As it happens, I believe the pharmacy around the corner just might stock that. I'm dispatching a bellman to purchase a box of the aforementioned product right now. Once he has it, he'll bring it up to your suite—if that's all right with you, sir."

Tate turned to look at Hannah. She appeared somewhat bemused. The sooner they got this over with, the better. "That'll be perfect with me," he replied, then hung up. Hannah, he saw, was still looking at him strangely. "What?" he asked her.

"You know these things?" she marveled, unabashedly surprised. "Do all men in your world know about hair coloring and such?" she asked, curious.

"The ones who worked in beauty salons to earn spending money while in high school do," he quipped. His parents had been decidedly well-off, but they went out of their way to teach all their children that money was not something to be taken for granted, that it had to be *earned* in order to be enjoyed.

So, to that end, he and all his siblings each had jobs—menial jobs—to teach them what it felt like to work hard to earn a dollar. Though he'd grumbled about it at the time, he had since learned to see the wisdom in that approach and was very grateful that his parents cared enough about him to give him such a solid foundation to fall back on.

"A beauty salon, like the one in Eden Falls?" Hannah repeated, clearly intrigued by the concept of his working around women focused on outer beauty instead of inner beauty.

"Yes, just like it."

"Why would a woman waste so much time on her hair?" Hannah asked. In her world, brushing for a hundred strokes was all the time and consideration a woman's hair was allotted. Who had the time to spend so much of it playing with hair and rendering it into unnatural states?

"Not wasted," he corrected amiably. "Hair is referred to as a woman's crowning glory for a reason." He moved closer to her, then lightly brushed his hand over her hair. Sifting it through his fingers, he was hard-pressed to remember ever touching anything that felt so incredibly soft. "You're lucky, it feels naturally silky. A lot of women would love to have your hair."

She looked down at the lock still resting halfway down her breast. "Soon, I will not have it, either."

Tate felt bad for her. He hated having to do this, but the way he saw it, they really had no choice. "I'm not going to shave your head," he pointed out.

She regarded him with those eyes that delved right to his core, picking up on something that hadn't been clear to her before. "Then you are going to be the one to do this?"

Tate nodded. He'd thought this out as well. "It's better that way. The fewer people we encounter while you still have that long red hair, the better. Unless you'd rather have someone more professional do it," he offered. He could see how allowing him to cut and color her hair might make her uneasy.

Despite his training and his protest that he'd do an incredible job, his teenage sister Piper wouldn't let him near her hair. Emma wouldn't either. If Emma needed her hair cut, she went to the same beautician she'd been going to for years.

Well, if she becomes Amish, that's *going to have to change,* he mused.

"No, I trust you," Hannah was saying. The next moment she stifled an exclamation when someone knocked on their suite door.

Fear immediately entered her eyes as they darted from him to the door.

Instantly alert, his hand hovered over the hilt of the weapon he had tucked into his belt at the back of his trousers. It was all hidden from sight beneath his jacket. Tate crossed to the door.

"Who is it?" he wanted to know.

"The hotel bellman, sir." The tenor voice cracked ever so slightly as he identified himself. Tate judged that the bellman was only recently out of his teens. "I have the hair product that your wife requested."

Tate opened the door a crack, just enough to afford him a view of the hallway.

Satisfied that only the bellman was standing outside his door, Tate opened it a little farther—just enough to trade merchandise for cash.

"Thanks," he told the bellman as he attempted to hand the latter a twenty.

The bellman looked at the denomination a little longingly. "Oh, no, sir. The cost of the hair dye will be on the hotel bill," the bellman replied.

Tate nodded. The bellman wasn't telling him anything he didn't already know. "I know. This is for your trouble."

Now that was a whole different story. The bellman thanked him twice before retreating down the hallway, the twenty clutched in his hand.

Closing the door, Tate turned around to find Hannah quietly observing him. He didn't have long to wait to find out why.

"That was a very nice thing you did, giving him that money." While she was not devoted to tracking her own money—or lack of it—she had a healthy respect for all the good money could do if spent the right way.

"It's called a tip," he explained.

Her brow furrowed as she tried to integrate what he'd just said with what she knew already. It didn't quite fit together.

"Isn't a tip something that is said, like advice about something?" she asked.

She was a treasure, she really was, Tate couldn't help thinking, charmed again by her uncomplicated innocence.

"That's another kind of tip," he said out loud.

Hannah shook her head. This was not the first time she'd discovered that the same word could mean two very different, unrelated things. How did these outsiders keep everything straight?

"You *Englischers* have a very strange language," she pronounced with another shake of her head. "So complicated."

He laughed, thinking of several examples of words that would undoubtedly prove Hannah's assessment to be correct. "I guess it is at that."

It was time to get serious, he thought, opening the package of hair dye that the bellman had brought him. He double-checked the color. It was marked light golden brown, just as he'd requested. That should do the trick, he reasoned.

He flashed an encouraging smile at Hannah and said, "C'mon, let's get this over with."

Dutifully, she bobbed her head up and down. She looked around the suite, undecided where to go. "Where do you want me?"

Home, safe, he silently declared.

"Let's go back into the bathroom," he suggested, nodding toward it.

Hannah walked ahead of him, stoic and resigned, a prisoner making her way slowly to her own execution. As she crossed the tiled threshold, he stopped to drag in a chair. He pulled it as close up to the sink as he could and she sat down stiffly without a word. He noticed that she deliberately avoided looking into the mirror.

Probably afraid I'm going to do a hatchet job, he thought. He knew the shorter hair was going to be a shock to her—not to mention when she saw it once it was dyed—but at least he knew that he wasn't going to make a botched job of it.

He cut her hair first.

Hannah sat very still. She kept her eyes closed as if bracing herself to feel each painful snip of the scissors. He noticed her wincing a couple of times, her eyes still squeezed shut. Had to be the anticipation of pain. Either that or she was wincing from the sound of scissors shortening her hair.

When he was finished, he inspected his handiwork with a critical eye. Her long flowing hair had been converted to an appealing bob, with her hair now framing her face and ending somewhere around the bottom of her chin.

Not bad, even if I do say so myself, he congratulated himself silently. *She might even learn to like it.* Granted, it seemed to erase her Amish identity, but the beautiful woman who'd emerged was definitely an unwitting heartbreaker, he couldn't help feeling.

Rousing himself, Tate donned the pair of rubber gloves that came in the box and mixed together the two components that formed the hair dye. He draped a towel around her neck and shoulders as an afterthought, then proceeded to apply the dye mix in long, even streaks, moving methodically until he'd used up every last drop of the solution in the plastic bottle.

Done, he tossed the emptied bottle as well as the box and the rubber gloves into the bag the bellman had brought. Closing the top of the bag he folded it over twice before throwing the bag into the wastebasket.

Sensing he was finished, Hannah asked, "And now?" She still avoided looking at herself in the mirror because she wasn't certain she was up to dealing with what she saw.

"Now we wait for twenty minutes," he told her. Then, because she'd looked at him sharply, waiting for an explanation as to why they had to wait for that particular length of time, he added, "The color has to set."

Even as he said it, he set a timer on his watch for twenty minutes.

When it went off twenty minutes later, as a series of chimes, he motioned her to the sink. "I've got to wash that out now."

Asking no questions, Hannah dutifully sat down in the chair and ducked her head under the faucet. Tate first rinsed the dye out, then worked the conditioner through her hair before thoroughly rinsing that out as well.

Wielding the hotel hair dryer like a pro, he not only expertly dried Hannah's new golden-brown hair, but he styled it as well.

As he worked, it brought back memories and he smiled to himself. "I got to be pretty good at this before I quit," he told her, talking to her reflection in the mirror. The words seemed to come out more easily for him that way.

"Why did you quit?" Hannah wanted to know. Still without actually looking at herself, she managed to engage his eyes in the mirror.

"College," he answered simply. "I was accepted out of state and I went." Tate looked over his handiwork, reviewing what he'd done with an eye that was far more critical than the average man might be.

He'd done a damn fine job, he thought.

"I haven't cut or styled hair since then, but I guess it's like riding a bike."

The blank look in her eyes told him that Hannah probably wasn't familiar with what was to him a very old cliché. "It means that there are some things you just don't forget how to do once you learn how, no matter how much time goes by," he explained.

"Oh, I see," she said.

Finished, he removed the towel from around her neck. He couldn't take his eyes off what was at least partially his creation. "I still have it," he murmured, pleased with himself.

"It?" she questioned. She had no idea what he was referring to.

"It," he repeated, then added a definition for her benefit. "A knack." Tate could see that the explanation *still* didn't clarify anything for Hannah. She appeared to be more in the dark than ever. "In this case, the ability to cut and style hair."

She still wasn't looking at herself, he noted. That had to change.

"Go ahead," he coaxed, indicating the mirror. "Take a look. Tell me what you think."

Rather than wait for her to look up, he gently turned her head, raising it up so that it was impossible for her not to look into the mirror. Impossible for her to avoid looking at herself any longer.

Chapter 11

Bracing herself for her first look, Hannah was prepared to say something nice no matter how she felt about the image she saw looking back at her in the bathroom mirror. She was not about to hurt this man's feelings for the world and he *was* only thinking of her safety when he told her that she had to have her hair color changed, as well as cut.

What she actually wasn't prepared for was to like what she saw.

But she did.

She blinked, more than a little surprised by the appearance of the woman she saw in the mirror. It took her a few moments to take in the change, to reconcile it with what she knew she'd looked like before this extreme shift in her life.

For a minute, she couldn't take her eyes off the image looking back at her.

"Is that truly me?" she asked in a hushed whisper, as if afraid that if she spoke any louder, the image she was looking at would dissolve and just fade away.

She wasn't freaked out. Thank God, Tate thought with more than a little relief.

He stood behind her, his hands resting lightly on her shoulders, the smile on his lips spreading to his eyes and crinkling them.

"It's you, all right," he assured her. "So you don't mind what I did?" To ask her if she *liked* what he'd done might have been pushing it a little, and he didn't want her to feel he was pressuring her in any way to voice her approval. It was enough that she wasn't upset or disappointed.

"I'm pretty," Hannah said, as if she was stunned at the discovery.

Could she *really* be this free of any trace of vanity? He would have found it hard to believe—except for the fact that this was Hannah and he'd already come to know her.

"You were always pretty, Hannah," he told her. "I just gave you a different look, but your being pretty was something I had absolutely nothing to do with. It was just something I worked with."

She raised her eyes from her new reflection and looked at his instead. There was something exceedingly comforting about seeing him standing there, literally having her back—that was the correct phrase for watching over her, wasn't it? Having her back? She recalled hearing it before he'd rescued her from that terrible place. One of those awful men who was guarding them had complained that the other man "didn't have his back."

Her mouth curved in a shy smile then bloomed into

one that displayed a shade more confidence—and more than a little additional happiness.

"You are very kind, Tate."

Tate was never very comfortable about accepting gratitude. He shrugged away the words. "Just doing my job, that's all."

"It is your job to say nice things to me?" she asked as she turned around to face him. With the sink at her back and Tate standing less than a full breath away, there was precious little space for her as she turned. So she wound up brushing against him as she did so.

Tiny shock waves shot through her at all the points where her body made contact with his. Hannah drew her breath in sharply, even as her heart began to beat a little faster.

The urge to kiss her shot straight out of no-man's-land, infiltrating his system with a vengeance and making Tate acutely aware of just how attracted he was to her. It wasn't the kind of attraction a man could easily walk away from, even when common sense demanded it.

Or at least demanded that he not act on that attraction.

For one long, drawn-out moment, Tate struggled against the attraction that only seemed to send him further into this impossible situation. And then he forced himself to take a step back, even though everything in him begged him to do otherwise.

"Let's see about getting you something decent to wear," he said suddenly.

She held out the bottom of the shirt—she could just faintly catch the scent of his cologne on it and she liked that.

"I like this shirt," she told him in defense of her attire. "It feels comfortable. Roomy," she tacked on—as if she really had to.

He laughed. "It's roomy, all right. You could probably take in a family of five and hide them in that shirt," he quipped, exaggerating—but, in his opinion, not by much. And then he grinned. "I never knew a woman who didn't like to go shopping." But then, he added silently, he'd never known a woman quite like Hannah before and that made all the difference in the world. "C'mon," he beckoned, heading for the door. "Let's go."

"As you wish," she said agreeably, donning the oversize jacket he'd given her to ward off the cold when they'd escaped from his apartment.

"Give me a minute," Tate said to her once they were downstairs and about to walk past the clerk at the front desk.

Hannah nodded and wordlessly stepped off to the side as Tate exchanged a few words with the reservations clerk. The latter in turn nodded and smiled broadly.

"Thank you, sir," he said with feeling as Tate pressed something into the bald man's hand just before he rejoined her.

"Okay, let's go," Tate urged her, taking hold of her arm and guiding her across the lobby.

"Another tip?" she asked. When he looked at her quizzically, she indicated the desk clerk just before they went through the revolving door that led out to the sidewalk. "You put something in his hand and he looked very happy. I was just wondering if you gave him a tip like you did the man who brought those things to you from the store."

Tate smiled. "You're very observant," he commented, neither agreeing with nor denying her assessment of the situation.

It hadn't been a tip that he'd pressed into the man's palm. It was a cash payment for the hotel suite for another two full days. That way, it looked as if they intended to return—something he was not about to do at the end of this little impromptu shopping spree.

But he decided that now wasn't the time to go into detail about that—in case the conversation wound up being caught on camera. Although the surveillance camera might not capture sound, getting someone to watch it who had the ability to read lips was not out of the question. The Philadelphia P.D. had just such a person and there was no reason to believe that Maddox couldn't avail himself of someone with similar skills.

The whole purpose of making it look as if they were returning to the hotel was a deliberate precaution to throw Maddox and his henchmen off their trail should they have succeeded in following them this far.

Hannah said nothing in response. She might be very observant, as he said, but she was equally intuitive and her intuition told her that something was afoot again. She was just going to have to remain patient in order to determine what that "something" was.

Besides, Tate had been nothing but kind to her and she had no reason not to trust him now.

Rather than a high-end department store, like Saks or Bloomingdale's, or another shop that only carried incredibly expensive designer clothing, Tate went with his instincts and took her to Macy's on 34th Street.

He might as well have decided to take Hannah to a magic kingdom. She was utterly enchanted, not to mention somewhat overwhelmed, by the wealth of shoes, coats, dresses and other items of clothing she saw at every turn. She was accustomed to a single store commonly thought of as a general store or an emporium. For her, shopping for clothes was an endeavor that involved practicality. It wasn't undertaken to buy something "pretty." At least, not until today.

What she discovered, holding tightly on to Tate's arm as he took her from one floor to another, was such an abundance of different things to look at that she was completely mystified as to where to look first—or second or third. Her head was fairly spinning and she had to admit that part of her was convinced she was dreaming.

This was a whole new world to her. An enchanting, colorful, lovely world.

"And all this is for sale?" she asked him, finding it difficult to comprehend how there could be so many choices available. Everything came in an array of colors, styles and sizes. How did the sales personnel keep track of everything? From her point of view, it seemed like a Herculean task.

The wonder in her eyes delighted him. He could all but read her mind. "Yes, everything's for sale."

She regarded the merchandise with unabashed awe. How could she make a decision as to what to choose when each thing she picked up was even lovelier than the last? It seemed almost impossible.

"All this," she breathed almost worshipfully.

He found it difficult to suppress his grin—so he didn't.

"All this," he echoed. "C'mon," he urged her. "Let's stop looking and let's start buying you some things."

Her arm still linked through Tate's, Hannah followed

him through the maze of clothing racks and beautifully dressed mannequins that were on display.

Eventually, Tate helped her select several outfits, making sure she had more than just a couple changes of clothing. It took a while, but they amassed a wardrobe for her. After having bought her two pairs of shoes, a pair of jeans that gracefully fit her curves—unlike the jeans he'd lent her—as well as tops to go with it, plus a few skirts and dresses, he noticed Hannah fingering an ankle-length, baby-blue nightgown spun out of a light, frothy material that seemed utterly inappropriate for surviving a cold night.

But then, he mused, it was the kind of nightgown that easily created its own heat.

"Like it?" he asked her. Hannah seemed startled that he'd even noticed her looking at it. She nodded her head shyly. The next thing she knew, he gently moved her out of the way. "All right, we'll add that to the pile," he told her, removing the nightgown from its hanger. Turning around, he handed it to the saleswoman who had been discreetly hovering close by, patiently waiting for him to give some sort of sign that her services were needed.

"Oh, no," Hannah protested, a light pink color beginning to climb up her cheeks. "I couldn't let you buy that for me. It's much too…" She couldn't find the right word to explain why she couldn't accept this from him.

Watching her, Tate couldn't help getting a kick out of the fact that, after all she'd been subjected to and been through, Hannah could still blush.

He found it refreshing, compelling and—if he was being honest with himself—very sexy and alluring at the same time.

"Every woman should have something soft and feminine in her arsenal," the saleswoman told her with a confidential wink.

Somehow the wink only made her blush that much more. Flustered, Hannah looked to him, waiting for his final say in the matter. Despite the way she'd been made to dress when those men had held her and her friends captive, she thought that the nightgown was incredibly lovely, not provocative.

Did that make her a terrible person? Something inside her said no, but there were still mixed feelings warring inside of her.

Tate merely nodded at her. "It's okay," he assured her before turning toward the saleswoman. "Just pack it all up in shopping bags."

Leading the way back to the register where she'd rung up the other sales for him, the woman suggested something more convenient.

"We could have all of this delivered to your home," she told him.

For that to happen, the saleswoman was going to need an address and that was something he wasn't about to divulge. The woman was pleasant-enough looking and most likely completely innocent as well, but he was not about to take a chance. Hannah's very life was at stake. He couldn't afford to be lax or trusting. That was a luxury for another time.

"That's all right," he assured her, taking out a wad of cash to pay for the items he'd just bought, "we'll just take all of it with us."

The saleswoman nodded. "Of course," she agreed, then cheerfully invoked the classic, age-old cliché. "The customer's always right."

Hannah regarded all the things Tate had bought for her as the woman was folding the items and dividing them up between a number of shopping bags. "This is too much," Hannah protested.

"It's what you need," he countered. He picked up three shopping bags in each hand while she quickly took two more. He led the way to the down escalator. "How do you feel about walking?" he asked as they got on.

She wasn't sure what he was asking her. "I should have feelings about walking?" To her, that was just a natural part of life.

No doubt about it, Hannah was adorably charming and uncomplicated. "Let me put it another way. Are you up to walking for a while?"

She was surprised he felt the need to ask. "Yes, of course." Walking from one place to another was nothing new for her. Getting around by any other means, such as in a car, was what she wasn't accustomed to, although, she had to secretly admit, she was becoming fond of that mode of transportation.

They had reached the ground floor and he forged a path out for them. The city, always packed with people, was even more crowded with holiday shoppers trying to complete their lists.

"Good," he acknowledged. "Then we'd better get a move on. We have a bit of a trek before us."

Hannah was not quite sure what a *trek* was, but she knew that her heart told her she could follow this man anywhere and still be safe. So she nodded and walked beside him. When he tried to take her two shopping bags from her to carry himself, she refused to allow it.

"I can at least carry some of my things," she told him. After all, the shopping bags were all filled with things he'd bought for her. Not a single item in any of them was for him.

* * *

The journey through the long city blocks to their destination was slow and at times became even slower. That was because Hannah's attention would suddenly be sidetracked by the various window displays that had been deliberately decorated with an eye toward celebrating the holiday season—and to snare passing customers' attention. All the major department stores— Saks, Macy's, Bloomingdale's—were vying for sales and doing their creative best to draw people to *their* store.

Time and again Tate would realize that Hannah had suddenly stopped walking beside him and was now staring, delighted, into yet another artfully decorated window displaying another imaginative holiday scene.

Rather than being annoyed that she was throwing them off schedule, Tate found himself utterly charmed. At thirty-two, he was being granted the gift of seeing everything during the busiest time of the year for the first time because he was seeing it through Hannah's eyes. And suddenly, just like that, the cold, impersonal city had been transformed into a place of warmth and magic, because Hannah saw it that way.

It didn't mean that he lowered his guard or ceased to be alert. Tate was first and foremost a cop and thus was still very vigilant. But Hannah's joy over the different displays, each depicting some part of the holidays, was infectious and, for once, he gave no thought to resisting. She made him remember a happier time, when his parents were still alive and Christmas was spent with people who had come to mean so much to him.

"Come," Hannah coaxed as she beckoned him over

to yet another window. The shopping bags looped over her wrists, she grabbed one of his hands and pulled him to the display that had caught her attention this time.

"It's snowing inside," she marveled, then turned to him as if he could unravel all the mysteries of the world for her. She regarded him as being extremely intelligent. "How are they doing that?" she wanted to know, pointing at the snow that was gently falling to the floor behind the glass that separated her from the person inside.

There was a machine high above the display that was responsible for the light "snowfall," but to point it out to Hannah seemed a bit harsh, not to mention that the explanation came across as very mundane. Tate tapped into his imagination and said, "They squeezed a little snow cloud into the store window."

For the tiniest second, she was tempted to believe him. But she didn't. Instead, Hannah gave him a tolerant look. "You are yanking my leg."

"Pulling," he corrected, trying hard not to laugh at her phrasing. "You're pulling my leg."

Her brow furrowed as she tried to reconcile what he was saying to what he'd already done. "No, you are pulling mine."

Tickled, he began to laugh. And then he discovered he couldn't help himself. Still laughing, Tate dropped the shopping bags, leaving them huddled on either side of him as he abruptly bracketed Hannah's shoulders with his hands, leaned down and kissed her.

It was meant to be only a fleeting kiss, the most innocent of contacts. Hardly any at all. Just two pairs of lips briefly touching, simply grazing one another in quick passing.

That was all it was intended to be.

But that wasn't the way it turned out.

The kiss rocked Tate's world without warning and rocked it right down to its very core.

Chapter 12

Someone from within the crowded streets called out, "Get a room!" A high-pitched, gleeful laugh accompanied the jeer.

It was enough to jar Tate back to his senses. Annoyed, he upbraided himself for being lax enough to temporarily let his guard down.

Pulling back, he picked up the shopping bags again and murmured, "I'm sorry," to Hannah. Turning, he resumed walking toward his destination.

Stunned at the abrupt, sudden change in Tate, Hannah quickly fell into step beside him, though it was somewhat difficult, given how very crowded the streets were.

Where were all these people coming from? she couldn't help wondering. Or, for that matter, where were they going? It felt as if they belonged to some sort of a parade—except that she didn't see one underway in either direction.

"I'm not," she told him with more assertive confidence than she had displayed up to this point.

Her voice had partially been swallowed up by the din around them. He wasn't sure what she'd said. Tate glanced at her for a second. "What?"

"I'm not," she repeated, raising her voice. They stopped at the corner, waiting for the light to change. Then, just in case he didn't understand what she was referring to, Hannah raised her voice and said, "I'm not sorry that you kissed me."

"That *shouldn't* have happened," he told her with feeling.

The light turned green and the sea of people on both sides of the crosswalk moved to navigate their way to the opposite side.

"Why not?" she wanted to know.

He was impatient, but with himself, not her. He knew the rules and he was supposed to abide by them, not give in to unexpected surges of emotion. Granted, he was attracted to her, but that was *his* problem to deal with, not hers.

"Because I'm supposed to be protecting you."

She was fairly trotting beside him now, determined to keep up. And trying very hard to make sense of his reasoning.

"And you can't protect me if you kiss me?"

She wasn't making this any easier, she really wasn't, he thought. "I'm supposed to protect you, not take advantage of you."

"But you didn't take advantage of me," Hannah insisted, not understanding why he was being so hard on

himself. "You are a good man, Tate. And I *like* you."
She didn't know how to put it any better than that.

That was to be expected, given the unique circumstances. "I rescued you from a horrible situation," he said. "It's only natural for you to think you have feelings for me. But that's just gratitude, Hannah—nothing more."

The next moment, he breathed a sigh of relief. They'd gotten to their new destination without any incident. Well, without any *further* incident, he amended ruefully. He was going to have to be more careful, he warned himself.

Tate stopped for a second. Hannah had fallen half a step behind him. When she reached the canopied entrance to the high-rise building, she looked at him quizzically. Before he could say anything, a doorman dressed in navy blue livery quickly approached from the other side of the building's ornate glass door and opened it for them.

"Mr. Colton, welcome back. It's been a long time," the man said warmly, all but beaming at Tate. "Will you be staying with us long?"

"That remains to be seen, Langdon," Tate told the jovial-looking man. He wasn't about to comment on something so specific where he could be overheard by anyone. He trusted the doorman—Albert Langdon had been a fixture at the high-rise for more than the past fifteen years—but they were out in the open and any passerby could be listening to their conversation.

The doorman followed them into the marble-tiled lobby and politely relieved Hannah of the two shopping bags she was carrying.

She glanced at Tate before surrendering them and only did so after he nodded.

"I could take a few of yours, too, sir," Langdon offered. The man looked capable of easily carrying all eight of the shopping bags, as well as a couple of suitcases at the same time.

Tate crossed to the elevator. The moment he pressed the up button, the doors slid open. "That's all right, Langdon," he said, getting on. Hannah was beside him instantly. "We'll manage from here. Take the bags back, Hannah," he instructed.

She did so quickly.

Relieved of the shopping bags, the doorman retreated, tipping the brim of his hat to them as he stepped back into the lobby.

"As you wish, sir. Miss," Langdon added, nodding at Hannah.

She offered the man a shy smile, then looked at Tate the second the elevator doors closed. "This isn't the hotel."

A teasing comment about her powers of observation was on the tip of his tongue, but he had a feeling that she might think he was laughing at her. So he refrained, and responded to her statement seriously.

"No, it's not. My parents had an apartment here that they used whenever they were in New York. They left it to my brothers and sisters and me," he told her. "Now we use it when we're in town," he explained. "I thought this would be a safer place to stay than the hotel."

The elevator arrived on the twelfth floor—their floor. She had seen the button he'd pressed when they got on and knew this was the floor he wanted so when the doors opened, Hannah stepped out. She tried to ignore the queasy way her stomach felt—she didn't think she would ever get used to riding in an elevator.

She looked around for a moment, trying to get her

bearings. The walls were all carefully textured, adding a dignified richness to the surroundings.

People actually *lived* like this?

It just seemed far too grand to her for an everyday existence. But it did appeal to the artist in her.

"This is not another hotel?" she asked, unable to fathom that it might not be. She'd never seen walls quite like these.

"No, it's a high-rise apartment building."

She nodded, as if she was absorbing what he was saying, along with her surroundings. She could come to only one conclusion. "Is everyone in New York rich?" she wanted to know.

He stifled a laugh at the last minute. "No, not by a long shot," he assured her. Where had she heard that? "What makes you ask?"

"The hotel, this place, the stores—they all look so beautiful and have so much in them. I've never seen anything like this before," she confided.

She'd found herself longing for her sketchbook back home, the one she secretly kept beneath her bed and took out whenever she had a free moment to daydream. The book was filled with sketches, both drawings of nature and drawings of clothing. The latter were a product of things she'd conjured up in her head.

"This is the *real* paradise," not her village, she added silently, despite its name.

Waiting for Tate to unlock the door to the apartment he'd brought her to, Hannah set down one of the shopping bags and lightly ran her fingertips along the swirls of the textured walls.

"Beautiful," she repeated under her breath, clearly impressed by everything around her.

Tate shrugged as he pushed the door farther open

with his shoulder. He had nothing to do with either the apartment's selection or the way the hallway was decorated. Even what was inside had been decided on by his parents, or, more specifically, his mother, who had a knack for that sort of thing.

"The maid used to complain that it was a dust catcher."

Hannah's mouth curved almost wistfully as she ran her fingers along the wall again. "Still beautiful," she insisted.

Her opinion didn't change when she walked in. If anything, it just became stronger. The apartment had high ceilings and arched doorways and appeared to be completely spotless.

That kind of thing didn't just happen. Someone had been cleaning.

"Who else lives here?" she asked Tate, wondering if that person would mind her coming here unannounced like this.

For a second, he shed the bags, slipping the loops from around his wrists. He leaned the shopping bags against the wall. "No one at the moment. We all crash here when we need a place for a few days," he explained.

Hannah's expression turned to one of concern. "Crash?"

It was hard for him not to laugh. Hannah was so adorably literal-minded. He tried to put himself in her place. Tate supposed, to someone unaccustomed to slang, what he'd just said might sound confusing.

"It's an expression," he told her, then elaborated, "*Crashing* means someone coming in and staying somewhere for a few days."

Hannah was doing her best to follow what he was saying. "Ah, like a visit."

"Something like that," he allowed, then recalled a so-called friend who'd overstayed his welcome. "Except not always very pleasant."

"Not all visits are," she agreed. She remembered when Solomon Miller had attempted to return to Paradise Ridge, only to have his family turn their backs on him because he'd forsaken them for life with the *Englischers*. Solomon had been shunned. Helping those awful men kidnap her and her friends had been his way of taking revenge on his former people.

She was remembering something, Tate thought. Something disturbing. Trying to get her mind off it, he said, "C'mon, I'll show you your room."

Hannah looked at him in surprise. "I have a room here?"

He picked up the shopping bags again. All of them this time, taking four in each hand.

"Technically," he admitted, "it's one of the guest bedrooms—my parents did a lot of entertaining and they liked having people stay over."

There was warmth in his voice when he mentioned his parents, she thought. "They sound like lovely people."

"They were." And, after eleven years, he still missed them terribly.

Sympathy, as well as empathy, flooded through her. "And they are both gone now?" They had that in common, she thought.

Tate nodded. "They were in the second tower when it went down on 9/11." It occurred to him that this, too, might be conspicuously missing from her education. "Nine-Eleven, that was when—"

She stopped him by raising her hand, as if to physically halt the terrible words. "I am aware of what nine-eleven is. Paradise Ridge is not *that* isolated," she told him.

His mouth curved in a rueful smile. "Didn't mean to insult you."

"You didn't," she answered cheerfully, then, looking at him, her own mouth curved in a shy smile. "You couldn't."

He laughed then as he led the way down the hall to the bedrooms. "You're giving me entirely too much credit, Hannah."

"I think you do not give yourself enough," Hannah countered. And then she gasped as Tate pushed open the door to the room where she would be staying. "I am to stay in this room?" she asked in a hushed, almost reverent voice.

The room was most definitely decorated with a woman in mind—an exceedingly feminine woman who had a weakness for frills and throw pillows. The queen-size bed was a four-poster, complete with a white canopy and a white eyelet comforter whose edge had a pink ribbon woven through it.

It was like standing in the middle of a fairy tale, she couldn't help thinking.

Her face was the very picture of awe. He found it hard to look away. "I take it you like it."

"Like it?" she echoed. The small word didn't begin to describe how she felt. "If it were possible to be in love with something that did not breathe, then I would be in love with this room," she admitted.

Tate had absolutely no idea how to respond to that without running the risk of making her think he was making fun of her, so he directed the conversation in another, more practical direction.

"I'll just put all your things here," he told her, setting all eight shopping bags down in the corner.

She turned abruptly to face him, afraid that he was leaving. "Where will you be staying?"

"Just next door." He pointed to the bedroom next to hers. She was still afraid, he thought. And who could blame her? She'd be lucky if she didn't have nightmares about being abducted for the rest of her life. "You don't have to worry," he assured her. "I'll be right here if you need me."

Actually, he was the one who was worried, he thought. But for a completely different reason than the one he assumed she had. The proximity to Hannah's room—and Hannah—was much too close for him to be able to get a decent night's sleep and he knew it.

But again, that was his problem, not hers.

Well, he thought philosophically, he hadn't joined the Philadelphia P.D. because he'd been in search of a decent night's sleep. He had joined to make a difference and keeping Hannah safe until they caught Maddox and she testified against him was definitely going to be making a difference.

Hannah stared at the wall that separated her room from his. Envisioning Tate on the other side. Without realizing it, she ran her fingers along the outline of her lips, reliving the unexpected kiss they had shared. A kiss that made everything inside of her feel as if…as if it was waking from a deep sleep. As if she was suddenly alive in ways she couldn't have even imagined before he had kissed her.

Would he sleep peacefully? she wondered. Or would

he yearn for her? Would he stare at the wall just the way she was staring at it now?

Would he kiss her again, now that they were alone here?

Her whole body tingled from the very thought of his lips touching hers again.

And what about after? he caught himself wondering several hours later as he lay—true to his premonition—sleepless in his bed. What about after Maddox was captured, brought to trial and then put away in state prison where he belonged? Was Hannah going to be safe, going back to her own little world? Or would she need protection, just in case a member of Maddox's inner circle was still out, scot-free and biding his time until he could exact revenge on Hannah?

Would there be anyone in that village who could protect her? *Could* they even protect her, given their sheltered way of life and their feelings about violence?

One step at a time, Colton, Tate counseled himself. He needed to take this just one step at a time. If he jumped ahead of himself, he would just be needlessly driving himself crazy.

He *was* driving himself crazy.

There was no other way to describe it. Three days had passed and Seth Maddox was still out there somewhere, still at large and capable of moving in for the kill at any time.

So that meant he had to continue being Hannah's bodyguard a little longer.

And, God help him, he really liked the role. Really liked that his days and evenings were filled with Hannah and revolved entirely around her and nothing else—except for perhaps the occasional phone call he had to make, calling his supervisor, Hugo Villanueva, on a paid burner phone to find out the latest intel. He'd picked up several burner phones for just this purpose during his drive from Philadelphia to New York City.

This, as it turned out, was the closest thing he'd had to a vacation since before he began working as a detective.

Moreover, being with Hannah, day in and day out like this, forced him to view the world in softer shades and, incredibly enough, he found the more positive outlook to his liking.

He also liked that he was getting to know her better, that she was sharing things with him, such as her flair for fashion design, something that really surprised him. She did a few sketches from memory for him, showing him things she'd created "just for the fun of it." In her way of life, fashion design had no place. But her face had lit up when he'd encouraged her to keep it up.

The light in her eyes had stirred his soul long after she'd gone to bed.

He had to force himself to focus on his prime—his *only*—directive.

But being anything but constantly alert was definitely in direct conflict with the scope of his duties as her bodyguard.

She was most assuredly having an effect on him, he thought—and he liked it.

It was wrong to feel this way and he knew it. There was no denying that she was affecting his work, but there was no getting around it, he enjoyed being with her.

What he didn't enjoy were the nights when he lay on his bed, alone with his thoughts, and they tormented him. Like thinking about what his life was going to be like once she was home again.

How quickly everything had changed for him, he couldn't help but marvel. Rather than Tate making Hannah more jaded—or, in her case, just jaded—in her outlook of the world and her own future, Hannah was turning him into an optimist—and all in an astounding record three days.

Now he caught himself looking for the upside in situations rather than the downside because down situations did not generate positive outcomes.

And more than anything, Tate knew he needed a positive outcome.

Was that why he found himself wishing, fervently, that he was free, just for a little while, to act on all these incredibly urgent demands that were forever eating away at him?

Well, he couldn't act on them, he told himself sternly. He couldn't compromise her—or himself, for that matter. Since that one slip in front of the store window, he'd been trying to slowly brace himself for the inevitable future—thinking slow and steady might just be the ticket to actually winning this race.

Somehow, he was going to have to find a way to adjust to a world without her in it.

He knew it wouldn't be easy, especially since he'd backslide again. This morning, because he still hadn't made good on his promise, he finally took Hannah to see the tree in Rockefeller Center.

And her expression when she was finally able to look up at the enormous, gaily decorated Christmas tree was a sight to warm his heart. She appeared to be so captivated by it, she became almost giddy. Once she'd recovered from her sense of awe, she bombarded him with all sorts of questions about the tree and the tradition of bringing it there. She wanted to know when it had started and looked very, very impressed when he managed to answer all her questions.

He surprised himself with the amount of information he had locked away in his mind. Somewhere along the line, he reasoned, someone must have told him about this and he'd retained it.

Too bad that same someone hadn't told him what to do in order to resist the soft, compelling—and totally unwitting—allure of someone like Hannah. She came across to him as innocence personified. He knew that her captors had placed a high price on her virginity. The bidders—himself included as his other persona, he thought ruefully—were all vying for the excitement of being her "first."

To his thinking, Hannah's first time should be memorable in a good way. That meant, first and foremost, it should be with someone she really cared about, not with some sweaty pervert who'd paid top dollar for her, and secondly, it should be with someone who was around her own age, not some old man with a ton of money to throw around.

That ruled him out as well.

Granted, he wasn't an *old* man, but he *was* twelve years older than Hannah was. As far as he was concerned, that meant that the woman whose face haunted him was *way* too young for him.

Those two reasons should have been enough to harness any and all his stray thoughts, as well as all the urges that seemed to be mercilessly and ceaselessly battering his body.

All that was more than logical and reasonable. After

all, he prided himself on being a logical and reasonable guy.

So why was it that he couldn't make himself remember any of those reasons for more than a few seconds at a time?

Chapter 13

The rustling noise barely registered on the perimeter of his consciousness.

But it was enough.

Tate sat up, instantly awake and alert, straining to make out the sound he believed he'd just heard. For a second, there was nothing.

Had it just been his imagination, or was there someone moving around in his apartment?

And then he heard it again.

Rustling.

Movement.

There was definitely someone out there.

Tate was out of bed and on his feet, the weapon he kept beneath his pillow in his hand and ready to fire before another two seconds had elapsed.

Mindful of not making any noise that would alert whoever was there, Tate slowly turned his doorknob and eased the door open in what felt like slow motion. He started to look around. The moment he did, he saw her.

Hannah.

Her body language told him that she was completely at ease and she wouldn't have been if there was someone else in the apartment with them.

She might have been at ease, but he certainly wasn't. Not from the moment he realized what she had on.

He could feel every fiber of his body come to rigid attention and hold its collective breath.

Hannah was wearing the nightgown she'd wistfully pointed out to him during the shopping spree he'd taken her on.

She was wearing the nightgown and nothing else.

The moonlight that had entered, uninvited, through the bay window and was painting everything in the room in soft, golden hues, was doing the very same thing along the outline of her body.

If Tate hadn't known that it was impossible, he would have sworn that he'd come precariously close to swallowing his own tongue at the very sight of her.

He knew that the temperature around him had gone up at least twenty degrees—if not more.

Belatedly, he lowered his gun and drew in an inordinately large breath. Only then was he able to ask her, "What are you doing up at this hour?"

Hannah almost jumped as she turned around to face him. "I'm sorry. I didn't mean to wake you," she told him. Her expression was the most sincerely apologetic one he'd ever seen on a person.

"Don't worry about it." He forced himself to look only at her face. Even so, Tate could feel his body temperature rising even more as she began to drift toward him. "I sleep with one eye open anyway—occupational habit," he added with a self-deprecating smile. "Why can't you sleep?"

"Worried, I guess." She raised her eyes to his and the part of him that wasn't overheating was absolutely mesmerized. "And restless," she added. "I feel as if I don't know what to do with myself."

"Well, given the hour, I think the logical suggestion would be to go to bed." He did his best to keep his voice steady, but it was getting more and more difficult just to concentrate on what he was saying and not on the woman he was saying it to.

Especially since she had somehow managed to get so close to him, he could feel her breathing.

"Hannah," he began, his throat closing so tight he was less than one step away from gasping out the rest of the words.

Her eyes never left his and he felt as if he was drowning in them.

"Yes?" she whispered.

He was digging his fingernails into his palms now, trying to distract himself any way he could. It wasn't working.

"Didn't we get a robe to go with that?"

"No." She thought a minute, then shook her head. "I did not see one hanging next to it. Why?" She looked down at the clinging nylon, then back up at him. "You don't like it?"

If anyone else had asked the question, he would have said it was an out-and-out calculated attempt at seduction. But this was Hannah asking, and it came out as just another innocent question.

The trouble was, he was *not* having an innocent reaction to the question, to her *or* to the nightgown. Highlighted as it was by the moonlight, it was the last word in transparent and consequently left absolutely *nothing* to the imagination.

Just as well since, in this particular case, his imagination couldn't have begun to do her the kind of justice she actually deserved.

Nothing he could have conjured up held a candle to what he saw now.

He had to tread lightly here because he was picking his way through land mines that could go off at any second at the slightest misstep.

"It's not a matter of not liking it—I do," he assured her with feeling. "It's a matter of trying to remember that I'm the one who is supposed to make sure no harm comes to you."

Hannah seemed to be able to see between the lines and hear what he *wasn't* saying. "You wouldn't harm me," she told him with the certainty that only belonged to the pure and the innocent.

"I wouldn't be so sure, if I were you," he said as he continued to struggle with himself, trying his best to ignore the very real ache as well as the breathless passion that were all but running wild throughout his entire body.

Sainthood, he thought. He was definitely a candidate for sainthood if he managed to walk away from this and leave her untouched.

"But I am," she told him. "Just as I am sure that you are a good man and that you make me feel very, very safe." Her eyes were open wide, as if her very soul was communing with his. "And I still mean what I said the other day. Except that I no longer just like you. I love you."

She reached up to touch his face and he caught her hand in his.

That, it turned out, was his first mistake.

"Hannah, you don't—"

He didn't get a chance to finish because she closed the last bit of space between them and now her body was against his, creating sharp arrows of desire that instantly shot all through him.

"Hannah, don't," he whispered, struggling against what he was feeling. Struggling not just against himself, but against her as well.

He was a man destined to fail and he knew it. Even so, he was not about to surrender his conscience without a fight.

"Don't what?" she whispered, taking his hand and placing it on her small, perfect breast. The moment she did, she drew in a long breath, igniting at the point of contact.

Her heart began to hammer wildly—he could feel it beneath his palm.

Tate tried to pull his hand back, but the light pressure from hers was enough to keep it just where it was. He was forced to fight not just his own desires, but hers as well, and he knew that he was badly outnumbered—and pretty much doomed to fail.

"Oh, Hannah," he groaned just before the last of his defenses crumbled and he capitulated. "I'm sorry," he whispered as he framed her face in his hands.

Just as when he'd kissed her for the first time, she told him, "I'm not," and meant it.

Any sliver of hope Tate might have had of rallying and pulling away from her and his own consuming desires vanished in that moment.

Tate had no choice but to bring his mouth down on

hers. The second he did, he succumbed to the very taste of her.

When she rose on her toes, lacing her arms around his neck and pressing her body against his as she kissed him back, Tate lost all ability to think, to reason, to hold himself in check. All he could possibly hope for was to be able to give her a small measure of the sheer pleasure she'd created within him with that incredibly delectable mouth of hers.

The rest all took place in a swirling haze that infiltrated his head.

Scooping Hannah up in his arms, his lips still sealed to hers, Tate carried her into his bedroom and set her down on his bed. The moment he did, he lay down beside her and proceeded—with great care—to open up a brand-new world to her.

Just as she, with her eager innocence, questing fingertips and unknowingly wicked mouth, opened up one for him.

Hannah wasn't altogether sure what made her so very bold or why she knew that, after all this time of being reserved and guarded with men, this was right, but she did.

Just as she knew in her soul that Tate was the one man she was meant to be with, meant to give herself to, and that it was all right. That what she was doing was right, even if there were no vows to sanction it, no ring on her finger. Right, despite the fact that he was not one of her own people, but an outsider.

It didn't matter. None of it mattered.

What she was feeling defied definition and was too great to be confined within such narrow things as traditions and timeless rules. She loved him and yearned for him beyond all understanding, beyond the borders of sanity.

Something had told her the first time she'd felt his hand on her arm that he was the one and that they belonged together. Together for a day, a year, for a lifetime—together for however long it was destined to be.

And should their paths be suddenly pulled apart, she knew she was going to love him until the last breath was gone from her body—and quite possibly beyond that.

So it was with something comparable to sheer abandonment that she threw herself into Tate's embrace, that she absorbed every pass of his lips along her skin, every caress of his hand along her flesh.

Abandonment yielded a euphoric ecstasy.

There were things happening to her, things a girl raised the way she had been hadn't even begun to dream about or imagine. Wonderful, delightful things that felt like intoxicating, blissful explosions all throughout her body.

She didn't know where to race within her mind in order to absorb everything, cherish everything.

It overwhelmed her.

Until he suddenly caught her hand, stopping her.

She looked at him, wide-eyed and confused. "Am I doing it wrong?" she asked.

"No, you're doing it right. Too right," he told her. He wasn't ready for the final ascent and if she'd touched him like that one more time, she would have made it begin.

The darkest, hottest and deepest spot in hell had been officially reserved for him when he died and he knew it. He was afraid he didn't have the will or the power to stop himself.

Only Hannah could do that and she wasn't stopping him.

With every twist and turn of her body, every sound that came from her lips, she was doing the exact opposite. She was urging him on.

He caught her hands a second time and she looked at him, dazed and confused.

"No, Hannah, we can't do this."

"What's wrong?" she asked in a small, puzzled voice. "Don't you want me?"

"Not want you?" he repeated. "Oh, God, I've never wanted *anything* as much as I want you."

"Then I don't understand. Why wouldn't you do this? Why won't you make love to me?"

"Because it has to happen the right way. Not here, not on the run. It should be a feast, not a snack. Your first time should be memorable—a banquet, not a sandwich snatched up in haste." He pressed a kiss to her forehead and held her to him, his own heart racing as he struggled to bank down his chaotic emotions. "You deserve the best of everything," he told her.

She raised her head, her eyes meeting his. "I have it right here," she whispered, her meaning clear. And then she smiled up at him. "You are a good man, Tate. A noble man."

"That's me, noble," he echoed, doing his best to rouse his sense of honor and use it to smother the smoldering embers of his desire.

"Would it be too much to ask you to sleep in my bed with me?"

"Hannah—" he began with a warning note.

"Just to sleep," she emphasized. "I would feel safer."

"I really don't think—"

"In my village, people who are to be married do it.

They have a bundling board between them so that each stays on his or her side of the bed."

And no one ever leaped over the board, right? he thought sarcastically. But she looked so earnest that when she followed her request with "Please," he couldn't bring himself to turn her down.

"All right," he said reluctantly, in his heart knowing that this would be the biggest challenge he had ever met.

They had no board, so they used an old broom he found shoved into the pantry, laying it between them on her bed.

Hannah fell asleep almost immediately.

Tate did not.

Instead, resigned to a sleepless night, he watched as she slept. And somewhere in the middle of the night, it occurred to him that if he actually were capable of loving anyone, Hannah would have been the one he loved.

Chapter 14

Hannah woke up slowly, by degrees, reluctant to abandon the comforting embrace of sleep. Afraid of what she might find when she was awake.

The kidnapping had done that to her, stolen her peace of mind, thrown her headlong into a world where she did not belong. Shown her the brutality of life. Robbed her of her natural bent toward pure happiness without hesitation.

When she finally opened her eyes to find Tate next to her, propped up on his elbow and just looking down at her, a bemused smile curving his mouth, a sense of relief washed over her. Last night *hadn't* been a dream and its effects burst on her mind all over again.

And once it did, the expression on her face matched his.

"Good morning," she murmured softly, stretching beneath the blanket.

Though she was covered, Tate could clearly make out the outline of her body. Make it out and feel himself responding to her all over again.

Damn, but he didn't recognize himself, not even a little. This new person he'd become was in love with a woman he hadn't even made love to. How the hell had that happened anyway? Granted, sex had never been a driving force for him. He'd always enjoyed the intimacies with women, then moved on because there was so much else going on in his life.

The prime elements in his life were, and had always been, his family and his career. Finding someone to share his bed—and, ultimately, his life—had never once been a priority with him—or even a distant third.

If he were being completely honest about the subject, had it turned out that he was never to find the right woman to spend his life with, well, he wouldn't have felt incomplete. There was so much else to occupy his time and his mind.

But one night with Hannah—just watching her sleep for God's sake—had changed his resolute position—and he couldn't even say why. He just knew that it had. *Knew* that he would do whatever it took to keep Hannah safe. And that, if he could, he would keep her in his life for as long as he feasibly could before letting her go back to her world.

Not that he wanted to keep Hannah against her will, because he cared far too much about her to do that to her. But if she seemed the least ambivalent about going back, he would do what he could to persuade her to remain in his world, rather than to return to the quaint world she'd always known.

With a slow, light movement, he brushed aside the lock of hair that had fallen into her eyes.

"Good morning, yourself." He could go on looking at her like this forever, Tate thought and for a moment, wished that circumstances were such that he could. "Did you sleep well?"

She smiled and nodded. "Very well, thank you." He noted that there was nothing shy or withdrawn about her smile anymore. It was the smile of a woman who was confident about the brand-new world she'd been initiated into.

Hannah stretched again, more languidly this time, and he felt himself losing ground fast. "You keep doing that and I'm going to forget all about getting up."

A delighted laugh escaped her lips as she deliberately stretched again, this time watching his eyes as she did so. There was mischief in her own.

Suddenly pulling her to him so that her body fit against his, Tate told her, "You have no one to blame for this but yourself."

"I'll try to remember that," she answered, doing her best to look solemn. She didn't even come close to succeeding.

The next moment, there was no more time for talking as she sank into his kiss.

It took them almost two hours before they finally were dressed and able to leave the apartment. Both hungry, Tate was taking her out for breakfast. Hannah had protested the need to go out, saying that she was more than happy—and willing—to cook for him. He stuck to his original plan, saying that he didn't want her to feel obligated to wait on him in any manner.

"You have all the time in the world to stand over a hot stove when you go back to your village," he told her. "You deserve to enjoy being spoiled a little."

She inclined her head in agreement, saying nothing.

She felt a little guilty about it, but right now, she didn't want to think about going home. She dearly loved her brother and his family and there was no denying that she missed them, but there was something wonderfully alluring about New York City and the world that Tate had opened up for her. Though she knew she didn't really belong in it, she wanted to be able to "visit" it for just a little while longer.

When they came downstairs to the foyer, Hannah nodded a greeting at the doorman on duty, but the main focus of her attention was the man whose arm she'd slid her own through.

The heavyset man offered them a cheery "Good morning, Mr. Colton. Good morning, miss," as he held the door open for them.

Hannah huddled against Tate's arm as a blast of cold December air greeted them the second they came out of the building.

"We'll take a cab," Tate decided, raising his hand to catch the attention of the next passing cabdriver.

"Oh, no. Please, let's walk," Hannah urged. She wanted to savor every moment she had with him. "I don't mind the cold."

He dropped his hand just as a cab pulled up before them. Shaking his head, he dismissed the driver. "The lady's changed her mind."

The cabbie mumbled something under his breath as he drove away.

He'd almost walked right into them, but as recognition suddenly hit him, the heavyset man managed to sidestep out of the way at the last minute.

Talk about dumb luck, Darren Sorell, the man who considered himself Maddox's right-hand man, thought.

He stared after the couple he'd almost plowed into. They were going down the block now.

He'd been looking for the woman, Jade, for the past five days, ever since that raid on the warehouse had taken place and all the high rollers had scattered like frightened mice, trying to abandon a sinking ship.

Only a handful of Maddox's men—Maddox included—had managed to escape. And Maddox didn't want to leave behind any loose ends. Jade was a loose end. A very big loose end. Unlike the other girls who'd been taken from that backward, medieval village where they lived, according to Maddox, Jade had been an unwitting witness to things that would put him away for the rest of his life.

The way around that was to find her and eliminate the threat.

Sorell had been the unlucky one to draw the assignment and he'd been combing the city ever since someone had said that the last call from the so-called high roller who had been so interested in Jade at the warehouse party had been traced back to New York City.

It looked like the tip had paid off.

Snow was beginning to fall. Sorell took shelter in the doorway of a coffee shop that had recently gone out of business. Taking out his cell phone, he immediately called Maddox to report the sighting.

The second he heard the phone stop ringing, he announced, "I found her. She chopped off her hair and dyed what's left, but it's her. There's no mistaking that face."

"Where?" Maddox bit off.

"Coming out of a fancy high-rise in the city. Building's got a doorman and—"

Maddox cut him short. "Anyone with her?"

"Yeah, that guy from the warehouse party, the one who was slobbering over her."

Maddox uttered a curse. "That wasn't a guy, that was the undercover cop, you idiot."

Used to his boss's lack of gratitude and surly temper, Sorell shrugged to himself. "Yeah, right. Now I remember. All I know was that he was sticking to her like glue."

"Plant yourself outside the high-rise," Maddox ordered. "The second he 'unglues' himself and goes somewhere without her, you know what to do."

"What if he doesn't? Unglue himself," Sorell elaborated when there was no reply on the other end.

"Then kill them both," Maddox snapped. "Do I have to do your thinking for you, too?"

Before Sorell could answer, the connection was terminated.

"Sure thing, boss," Sorell said sarcastically into the phone as if he were still talking to the other man. Frowning, he tucked his cell phone back into his pocket and stepped out of the doorway.

He was going to be out here a long time, he thought. He had no illusions about his boss. If Sorell came back before he carried out the man's orders, Maddox would have him killed.

"If I told you something, would you promise not to think badly of me?" Hannah ventured nearly two hours later as they were walking back from the restaurant where they'd had breakfast and then lingered over their second cups of coffee.

Tate laughed and shook his head. Everything about this woman was endearing. "I don't think it's possible to think badly of you."

She blushed in response and he watched her skin take on a rosy tint. He felt his heart swell again. She had that effect on him.

"I like it here," she confided in a low voice, as if what she was sharing with him was a secret. "I think I would like to stay a little longer."

No more than I'd like you to stay, he thought, silently cheering. But he managed not to give himself away as he said out loud, "Well, right now, there's not much of a choice," he answered. "Despite the number of people around us, it's easier keeping tabs on who's coming and going here in New York than if you were hiding in a small town."

"A small town like mine," she guessed.

He nodded. "Like yours."

Maybe, Tate thought, just maybe, since she seemed to be settling in for now, he could find a way to convince her to remain with him for a while longer. A *lot* longer, he amended.

He knew he shouldn't be getting his hopes up, that someone as sheltered, as pure, as Hannah should go back to her family and friends as soon as possible, but he couldn't help wishing that she wouldn't. That she'd want to stay with him.

Get a grip, Colton. You know the score, she doesn't. She's better off with her own kind.

Knowing he was right didn't make it any easier to accept.

He had no sooner walked into the apartment with Hannah than he heard his cell phone ringing.

This can't be good, he thought, though his expression gave nothing away when Hannah looked at him quizzically.

Pressing his lips together to keep from frowning, Tate took his cell phone out and looked down at the caller ID.

Nope, this isn't going to be good, he thought.

It wasn't some random call, or a call from his sister, asking for an update. Instead, the call was coming in from his supervisor.

Hugo Villanueva rarely called his people himself, preferring to delegate tasks as well as responsibility whenever he saw fit. That he was the one calling meant that something was up.

"Colton," Tate said as he took the call. Out of the corner of his eye, he saw Hannah watching him apprehensively. His body language must have given him away. He deliberately smiled at her, hoping to erase the worried furrows from her forehead.

Hoping to do the same for himself.

As with all his calls, this call was short and to the point. Villanueva was calling an impromptu meeting and wanted all hands on deck, including him. Tate looked at Hannah uncertainly as his supervisor gave him last-minute instructions.

He didn't like the idea of leaving Hannah alone— but there was no one he could leave her with while he attended this unscheduled meeting.

When he heard Villanueva pause, Tate said, "I'll do my best to be there."

"Don't 'do your best,' just be there," Villanueva ordered just before he ended the call.

The man could use a few tips on sociability, Tate thought, putting his cell phone away.

The call over, Hannah was instantly beside him. She searched his face. "Is something wrong?"

He knew better than to brush her off with a trite "No,

of course not." "That was my supervisor. He wants to have everyone who's working on this case come in for a meeting."

"Yes?" There was a question in her voice, as if she knew there was more and she was coaxing him to continue.

He sighed, tamping down his agitation. "And I can't bring you with me."

She continued looking at him, waiting for him to say something that explained the look on his face. "And?"

"And I don't like leaving you alone," he ground out. Leaving her unattended went against all his instincts.

Hannah smiled patiently, placing a gentling hand on his shoulder. For now, their roles had reversed and she was the reassuring one. "I'm not a child, Tate. I know how to lock the door. And I won't open it," she added, sensing he needed to hear her assure him of that. "Go to your meeting with your supervisor. Hear what he has to tell you. I will be fine," she stressed with a warm smile.

He wasn't convinced. This was making him extremely uneasy, as if he was going against his better judgment. "I don't know—"

Handing him his overcoat, Hannah began pushing him toward the door.

"I do," she insisted. "Go. I will be right here, waiting for you."

He supposed maybe he was overreacting and worrying too much. After all, there *was* a doorman in front of the building, and Langdon never allowed anyone in unless he either knew the person, or one of the tenants could vouch for the guy. No stranger was going to get by him.

Putting his overcoat back on, he turned to look at Hannah. If anything happened to her, he wouldn't be able to live with himself. "And you promise you won't open the door?"

She held her hand up solemnly, making a pledge. "I promise I won't even come near the door until I see you walking across the threshold."

"I guess that'll have to do," he said. His hand on the doorknob, Tate paused long enough to kiss Hannah soundly. "I'll be back as soon as I can."

"And I will be here, waiting," she promised. She closed the door behind him, then flipped the locks just the way he'd showed her.

She started to walk away, then stopped. Intuition told her that Tate was still there, on the other side of the door. She doubled back.

"Go!" she ordered through the door with a laugh.

"All right," she heard Tate say through the door. "Stay safe."

"You, too," she answered, raising her voice so that he could hear. "You, too."

Giving it to the count of ten, she waited for any further indication that Tate was still hovering in the hallway.

When there was nothing further, she smiled to herself and went into the kitchen. By the time Tate came back, he'd probably be hungry and she didn't want him to feel they had to go out to another one of the restaurants that seemed to be absolutely everywhere she looked.

There had to be *something* in this kitchen that she could use to make if not an exciting meal, at least a nourishing one.

A ten-minute search through the refrigerator and the pantry told her that she just might be wrong about that. She was still foraging through the vast cupboard space when she thought she heard the front door open-ing again.

At this rate, the man was never going to get to his meeting. With a shake of her head, she laughed. "What's your excuse for coming back this time?" she wanted to know.

"Didn't know I needed one."

She stiffened as every hair on the back of her neck stood up. The deep voice didn't belong to Tate, but she still recognized it.

She felt sick.

The voice belonged to one of the other guards who came into the motel on occasion. He was the one who made her skin crawl every time he looked at her. There was something exceedingly humiliating about the way his eyes swept over her.

They'd found her.

Frantic, Hannah looked around for some way to es-cape, or, barring that, somewhere to hide.

Hannah remembered that she and Tate had escaped from his apartment in Philadelphia by climbing up those iron stairs that ran the length of the building. She hadn't seen any of those stairs on the front of the building, but maybe they were located on the other side, like by the bedroom window.

She made a quick dash for the bedroom, but her es-cape was abruptly cut short before it could fully get underway. The husky, bald man, moving incredibly quickly for a man of his girth, grabbed her before she could make it out of the room.

Unlike when she'd been abducted from Paradise Ridge, Hannah fought back this time. Fought using her nails, her fists, her legs, anything she could. She was a whirling dervish, scratching, punching, kicking and biting.

Because she'd surprised him by resisting in this fierce manner, Hannah managed to escape from him when she kicked him where it did the most painful good.

Sorell cursed at her roundly as he howled in pain. Hannah darted out of the room, heading for the bedroom.

Knowing he couldn't come back without her, Sorell managed to rally and he caught her by her hair, yanking her back.

The movement was so abrupt, it was all she could do not to scream as pain shot first through her scalp and then through every inch of her. Turning her around, he punched her in the face.

Battered, with her head spinning badly, Hannah fought back like a tiger. It was then, just as she thought she could get free, that she felt the sharp prick of a needle going into the side of her neck.

Instantly, her limbs felt as if they had turned into tree trunks, completely weighing her down. She couldn't move and she was struggling to keep her eyes open, to remain conscious.

It was a battle she was destined to lose.

She thought she heard the bald man talking to someone, but she couldn't turn her head to see who.

The next moment, her surroundings faded to black and then completely disappeared.

Chapter 15

Well, those were two hours of his life he was never going to get back again, Tate thought as he made his way back to the building where he was staying. The meeting, in his opinion, hadn't really been necessary. No new information had surfaced, only a rehashing of what he already knew and suspected that Villanueva *knew* that he knew.

All right, he amended, turning down the next block and narrowly avoiding a dog walker and his Doberman, that wasn't entirely true. No new *helpful* information had surfaced. What had come to light was that several more bodies of abducted young women had been found.

Tate suppressed a sigh. This was going to upset Hannah. He knew she identified with them.

He dreaded telling her, but he didn't see a way around that. He wasn't going to lie to her or keep anything from her. If he did, he risked losing her trust, which he was *not* about to do. He just needed to pick the right time to tell her, he thought, and that wasn't going to be easy.

The distant sound of a siren splintered his thoughts.

The sound grew closer and he looked over his shoulder in time to see an ambulance, its lights flashing wildly, coming down the block.

There was no reason in the world that seeing it should make him suddenly grow apprehensive. It wasn't as if an ambulance, flying by traffic, was an uncommon sight in Manhattan. At any given moment, there were eight million people in the city with a great many of those people stuffed into every square block. The ambulance could have been summoned by any one of them for reasons that had nothing to do with Hannah.

He pulled over, parked the car and broke into a run anyway, heading straight for the high-rise building where he'd left her.

The feeling of dread and anxiety tripled the moment he saw the ambulance double-park right in front of his building.

The next moment, as he came closer to the building, he saw that Langdon was missing from his post.

Did that mean the doorman was inside, tending to whoever the ambulance had come for?

Oh, God, don't let it be Hannah.

Still running, Tate finally reached the front door. The paramedics were already inside. Yanking the door open, he could see one of them kneeling over someone.

Fear all but strangled him.

I should have never left her, Tate silently upbraided himself. *Why the hell didn't I go with my instincts and take her with me?*

"Is she—?" The question died abruptly on his lips

as he came to a halt directly behind the kneeling paramedic. The body on the ground wasn't Hannah.

It was the doorman.

Langdon lay unconscious in a pool of his own blood. There was so much blood, it outlined the upper part of his torso. The paramedic was feeling for a pulse.

"It's thin, but it's there," he told his partner. And then he saw Tate. "Move back, buddy, and let us do our job," he ordered impatiently. "You can look on from the sidelines."

Tate didn't bother mentioning that he was a cop. He was moving too fast. There was only one reason anyone would try to eliminate Langdon: they didn't want a witness.

The lobby began to fill with tenants. Tate raced past all of them. The elevator was in use. Rather than wait, he took the stairs.

Tate didn't remember running up all those flights to his floor. He was only aware of praying.

By the time he finally reached his floor, his legs felt like rubber—disembodied rubber. He couldn't feel his feet and he wasn't sure just how he did it, but he managed to cross the hallway to his apartment.

There wasn't even an attempt to hide his tracks. The gunman had left the apartment door wide open.

The living room was a shambles. With its overturned table, scattered books and broken figurines—the figurines he'd given her as souvenirs of their night on the town—giving clear testimony that a fight had taken place here just within the two hours he'd been gone.

Hannah hadn't gone quietly with her abductor.

Had to have been one hell of a surprise to whoever had been sent to get her. She'd gone from a docile, meek young woman who gave herself less rights than her shadow to a woman of spirit who couldn't be easily overcome.

He took comfort in the fact that Hannah had to be still alive. If Maddox had merely wanted her dead, Tate knew he would have been looking down at her body right now, not the aftermath of a battle.

Okay, *they'd* taken her—but taken her where?

Looking around his apartment, he hadn't a clue.

It had to be a place where Maddox felt he had the advantage over whoever might come looking for him—or for Hannah.

Tate tried to think if there was anyone who would have been privy to that kind of information. But fear for Hannah's safety was undermining his ability to think clearly.

He took a deep breath, ordering himself to calm down, to look at this as if it was just another case to be solved and resolved with optimal results.

But it *wasn't* just another case, dammit. Hannah's life was at stake and he couldn't afford to be wrong, couldn't afford to fail.

Hurrying out of the apartment, he didn't even bother to close the door. Instead, he pulled his cell phone out and called the only person he trusted right now.

Emma answered on the third ring. "Colton."

"Emma, they took her."

She'd attended the meeting with Villanueva as well and hadn't expected to hear from her brother so soon. As it was, she could barely make out his voice.

"Tate? Is that you? Where are you, you're breaking up."

He raised his voice, exasperated at the reception and far more exasperated with himself. He should have never left Hannah alone.

"I'm in the stairwell at the high-rise. That meeting with Villanueva, Maddox used the opportunity to have Hannah kidnapped again. The apartment's in shambles."

Emma took that as a good sign. "That means she tried to fight them off. She's still alive, Tate."

But for how long? "She knows too much," he said, taking the next flight down. "Maddox is going to kill her."

Emma searched for slivers of hope to offer her brother, as well as Caleb when she told him about this newest development. "Maybe not. If that's all he wants, then he would have done it already."

"And maybe he wants to make an example of her to the others," Tate countered. Even as he said it, he felt sick to his stomach. Maddox was going to torture Hannah, *then* kill her—he was sure of it. "I've got to find her before that happens, Emma."

"*We'll* find her, Tate," his sister told him with as much confidence as she could muster. He didn't need to hear the actual odds against that right now. Besides, miracles happened every day—they just needed one. And this was the season for them, she told herself.

Reaching the ground floor, he pushed open the door leading from the stairwell. "Who would have any idea where Maddox would take her?"

Emma tried to think. "Anyone who'd know is already dead. The people we arrested at the raid are just grunt-level henchmen—"

Before him, in the lobby, Tate saw that the paramedics had just finished strapping Langdon to the gurney. Pale and bleeding, the wounded doorman had apparently regained consciousness, which was a good sign,

Tate thought. The paramedics were going to be taking the man to the hospital—

"Hospital," Tate suddenly said out loud as an idea hit him.

"What about a hospital?" Emma asked, confused.

"What hospital did they take Miller to after the raid?" He knew that the informant had been shot, but lucky for him, the bullet had gone straight through and, despite a large loss of blood, the formerly disgraced member of the Amish community was going to make it.

"Let me think." Emma paused, then said, "Philadelphia General was the closest one to the warehouse. They'd have taken him there."

"He still there?" he asked eagerly. Miller was the only one he knew to question. The man had known all the ins and outs of Maddox's operation from the first kidnapping. Maybe he'd have an idea where the man would take Hannah.

"As far as I know," Emma qualified before saying, "yes."

"Then that's where I'm heading. Call the hospital, have them double the guard. Maddox might have gotten it into his head to clean house."

It was an educated guess, but Tate was reasonably certain he was right. A man like Maddox, who saw himself above the people he dealt with, would easily kill Miller without so much as a passing qualm.

It was ninety-seven miles from the heart of New York City to Philadelphia, a trip that, on a good day with traffic permitting, could be made in just a little under two hours.

Calling in favors, he managed to get his hands on a NYPD detective's car, complete with portable flashing lights, and Tate made the trip in a little over an hour. He spent the entire ride trying his best to calm down, but it was no use. He was highly agitated, highly wired and praying he wasn't already too late.

Hannah had trusted him to protect her and he'd failed in his assignment.

He'd failed *her*.

If anything happened to her, he'd never forgive himself. If that madman so much as—

Tate stopped. He couldn't let himself think about anything except getting her back. It had to be his entire focus. Otherwise, he'd be no good to anyone, least of all to Hannah.

Reaching the hospital, he made his way upstairs then hurried down the surgical unit hallway to ICU, the area where Miller was being kept. While the man technically was not under arrest, he was still a prisoner in his room. There was an armed guard posted right outside his door, cautiously watching the movements of every approaching person with a wary eye.

Tate took out his badge and held it up for the guard to check. "Detective Tate Colton. I need to talk to Miller," he told the man.

Nodding, the guard stepped to the side to allow him access to the room.

The moment Tate walked in, the listless look on Miller's face vanished. "You here to spring me?" the man asked hopefully.

Tate didn't bother answering the question. Every second counted and he had an anxious feeling that there weren't very many left.

He led with his reason for being there. "Maddox's got Hannah Troyer."

Miller looked at him, confused. "I thought you rescued her—"

"I did. He kidnapped her again," Tate bit off. His tone left no room for a discussion. "Where would he take her? We've got people watching all his known hangouts." Emma had taken care of that for him, sending out extra agents to cover Maddox's former haunts. "And he hasn't shown up at any of them. Is there any place, some secret hideout maybe, or a place that means something to him, that he'd go to?"

Miller thought for a second, then bobbed his head up and down like one of those annoying big-headed dolls people kept insisting on putting in the rear of their vehicles.

"He's got this place where he'd take the girls whenever he was getting ready to get rid of them. He called it the Kill House." Miller raised his eyes to Tate's face. "It's this abandoned boathouse just off the Allegheny River." Miller's voice grew quiet. "That was where he took those girls whose bodies I led your sister and Hannah's brother to. He killed them himself. He got off on the life-and-death power trip," Miller added with an involuntary shiver.

The boathouse.

That had to be it.

It was a gamble, Tate admitted, but it was one hand he was going to have to play until the end. "Tell me how to get there," he ordered Miller.

With Miller's directions freshly embedded in his mind—as well as into the GPS in the car he was using, Tate drove on the expressway as if the very devil were behind him in hot pursuit.

But the devil wasn't after him, he thought wryly.

He was actually on his way *to* the devil. And fervently praying that he would get there in time. Because if Maddox had killed her—hell, if he'd harmed a single hair on Hannah's head, Tate couldn't be held responsible for what he'd do to the black-hearted bastard.

He *had* to be on time, Tate prayed over and over again, he just *had to be.*

"What is this place?" Hannah asked, looking around, doing her very best not to sound as frightened as she really was.

"The last place you'll ever see," Maddox told her nastily. "Gotten real chatty since the last time, haven't you?" he mocked. "That undercover cop do that for you? Teach you how to run off at the mouth? What else did he do? Make you a lot of promises that if you testify against me, wonderful things were going to happen to you? Bet you didn't count on this being one of those 'things,'" he jeered. "Did you?"

His laugh sent a chill zigzagging down her spine, forming icicles along its way. Somehow, Hannah still continued to hold her head up.

"You're an evil man and you have to be stopped," she told him hotly. He was responsible for her friends being killed. She remembered now, remembered it clear as day, and her anger rose to a dangerous level.

He laughed shortly. "Maybe so, but not today, sweetheart. And not by the likes of you, that's for damn sure." His eyes narrowed as he looked at her. "Dead men tell no tales—it's a trite saying, but it's accurate. And it applies to dead whores, too."

The moment they came to the dilapidated building, she braced her hands on either side of the doorway, refusing to enter. Cursing, he pushed her hard through the open doorway. Hannah found herself stumbling into the old, abandoned single-story structure. Inches away from her foot, a rat scurried away.

Hannah swung around to face him. "Why are you doing this?" she cried.

The condescending sneer on his face deepened and he laughed. The sound made her skin crawl. "Because I can, my dear. Because I can."

Hannah knew that her ways were completely different from this man's, but she still couldn't understand his reasoning. Why would he risk everything he'd worked for to kill her, not to mention her friends and the other Amish girls? "But you have so much to lose."

"Leaving you alive isn't going to change that," he told her. "But it will teach that bastard, Colton, that he can't mess with me and not suffer consequences for his actions." His eyes seemed to bore right into her, pinning her in place. "The same goes for you. Now," he took a deep breath as he stepped toward her, "not that this hasn't been interesting, but I really have somewhere else to be so—let me take care of this loose end and I can be on my way."

The next moment, moving so quickly that had she blinked, she would have missed it, Maddox had his hands around her throat.

Startled, Hannah tried to back away as she pushed her hands hard against his chest. But she couldn't budge him. There was no way.

His hands were tightening around her throat, cutting off her air supply.

Frantic now, knowing she only had seconds left, Hannah started to claw at Maddox's face. She raked her nails down his cheeks, then tried to stick her finger into his eye, hoping to create enough sudden pain to make him drop his hands from her throat.

Rather than push her hands away, he just continued doing what he was doing. Squeezing harder.

Hannah felt her strength quickly being sapped away. She didn't know how much longer she could last, how much longer she could keep trying to resist.

It couldn't end like this, she thought, flashes of heat exploding through her brain so that holding on to thoughts was proving to be very difficult.

She didn't want to die. Not when she was just on the brink of this wonderful new world that Tate had shown her. She wanted to live, to be with him. To make him happy that he'd saved her.

To make him happy…

The pain was awful and her grasp on the world was beginning to swiftly fade away.

She thought she heard a loud noise, like something breaking, falling to the floor, but she couldn't begin to identify the sound.

Or even know if she'd actually heard it or just imagined it.

Everything was spinning out of control and she could swear she was leaving her body, separating from this heavy, heavy flesh that was anchoring her, holding her down.

The last thing she remembered before the darkness came was falling and hitting something hard.

Chapter 16

He'd called Emma the moment he'd gotten back into the car and started following the directions that Miller had given him. He gave her the same directions to the abandoned boathouse and knew she would be coming with backup. Given the circumstances and knowing how fast Emma operated, he was fairly certain that she was no more than five minutes behind him.

She might as well have been an hour behind him.

Tate couldn't shake the sense of urgency that was consuming him. Something in his gut told him that he didn't *have* five minutes. In this situation, even *one second* could mean the difference between life and death. *Hannah's* life or death.

So when Tate pulled up to the boathouse a few minutes later and saw Maddox's custom-made sedan parked some distance away, he bolted out of the car, barely stopping to pull up the hand brake.

The door was locked from the inside.

Abandoned buildings didn't have doors that were locked from the inside. If anything, there would have been a padlock on the outside.

Maddox was inside with Hannah—he'd bet his life on it.

Tate didn't bother to use his skeleton key tools to jimmy the lock. Instead, he put his shoulder to the door, slamming against it with all his might.

The door, weakened by weather and termites, splintered in its frame and cracked open.

The first thing Tate saw was Maddox with his hands around Hannah's throat. The next second, she was sinking, apparently lifelessly, to the floor.

Tate felt as if a broadsword had just slashed through his heart.

He was too late.

"No!" Tate cried, wildly enraged.

He didn't remember flying across the floor, didn't remember launching himself at Maddox, but he must have because he suddenly found himself pounding on the man.

The fury inside him flared out, coloring everything in hues of red. His fists made contact, over and over again, with Maddox's face and body. The skin on his knuckles tore and bled.

He kept on punching.

Tate heard a high-pitched buzz and realized a beat later that it was the sound of shrieking. It was coming from the sex ring mastermind beneath him. The man was begging him for mercy.

The irony of that was mind-boggling.

Damning Maddox's soul to hell, Tate promised, "I'll give you the same kind of mercy you doled out to those girls, to Hannah! How's it feel?" Every word was punctuated with another jarring punch.

He had Maddox's blood on his hands and he just kept swinging—until he heard it. A soft little plea, so soft that he *didn't* hear it at first.

It came again.

"No, Tate, don't."

Holding Maddox up with one hand, his doubled-up fist pulled back to deliver yet another reeling punch, Tate stopped. His heart hammering, he looked at Hannah. Her eyes were open, looking at him, and she was trying—in vain—to sit up.

Instantly, Tate released Maddox. The man fell to the floor, a crumpled, bloodied, sobbing heap, as Tate ran to Hannah's side.

Falling to his knees, Tate gathered her to him. "Hannah? Hannah?" Her eyes were closed again. Panic filled him as he begged, "Stay with me, Hannah. Please, stay with me. Oh, God, Hannah, I can't make it without you. You *have to* stay with me."

Hannah felt as limp as a rag doll and if she had indeed been awake a second before, she wasn't now. But he could detect just the faintest of pulses and he clung to that.

"It's going to be all right, Hannah, it's going to be all right," he promised her as he rocked her body against him. He held on to her tightly, as if the very action was the only thing tethering her to life.

Behind him, he could hear the pounding sound of approaching feet. Emma had arrived with the SWAT team.

"My God," Emma cried, looking at the unconscious,

bloodied heap that was Seth Maddox. She barely recognized the man. "What happened to him?"

Tate didn't even bother glancing in the man's direction. He was afraid he'd become enraged all over again and this time kill the bastard.

But that would have made him just as bad as Maddox. He had a feeling that Hannah felt the same way about it. That was why she'd rallied and called to him. To stop him from doing something he would eventually regret.

"He ran into a wall," he told his sister stonily.

Emma looked from her brother to the unconscious sex trafficker and nodded. "Works for me." And then she took her first real look at her brother—and the girl in his arms. Tate looked like hell. A very pale hell. "Oh, Tate, is she—?"

"Barely alive," he whispered numbly. "But there's a pulse and she's a fighter," he said, more to encourage himself than to give his sister an update.

Paramedics entered the old building, pushing a gurney before them. They were about to attend to Maddox, but Emma called them over to Tate and directed their attention to Hannah.

"Call a second bus to collect the trash," she instructed one of the agents who'd come in with her, nodding at Maddox. Turning toward the paramedics, she indicated the girl in her brother's arms. "She goes first."

Emma saw the absolutely haunted look on Tate's face. He looked as if he wasn't about to release Hannah to the EMTs.

As if he *couldn't*.

Placing her hand on Tate's shoulder, she did her best to try to comfort him. "Let them do their job, Tate," she coaxed gently. "They know best how to take care of her. How to save her life."

He made no move for a beat, no indication that he'd even heard her. And then a sigh shuddered out of him as he finally rose and backed away.

"I wasn't there for her," he said to Emma, watching every move the paramedics made. "If I'd been there—"

He couldn't blame himself. He wasn't at fault, Emma thought fiercely. "You couldn't have known and vermin like Maddox would have found another way to get to her." Emma gently tugged Tate out of the way as the paramedics slowly transferred the unconscious victim to the gurney, then snapped the wheels back into position. "You got him, Tate. You got Maddox. A lot of girls, as well as their families, are going to be grateful to you."

He nodded, barely hearing her. He was unable to take his eyes off Hannah. As they began to guide the gurney out, Tate suddenly came to. "I'm going with you," he told the two attendants.

There was no room in his voice for an argument.

Tate couldn't remember *ever* having lived through a longer night. The seconds had just dragged by, feeding into eternity without leaving a mark.

The moment Hannah was brought into the hospital, she'd immediately been rushed into surgery. A surgery that seemed to last forever. The reports, when a nurse *did* come out of the O.R. to deliver them, were not all that encouraging in the beginning.

For the first few hours, the situation was touch and go. Tate felt as if his emotions were attached to a yo-yo string, going up and down so much and so frequently, he felt dizzy.

The prognosis, when it was finally delivered after the surgery was over, was very guarded.

"But there is some room for optimism," the surgeon told Tate. A hint of a sympathetic smile faintly curved the man's thin lips as he said, "I suggest, Mr. Colton, that if you're a praying man, this just might be the right time to call in some favors from an authority higher than mine."

Praying made him uneasy. It meant the situation was entirely out of his hands. Tate didn't like losing control. It made him feel helpless.

"When can I see her?" Tate pressed.

"She'll be in recovery for another hour, then she'll be transferred to her room. I'll have a nurse come get you after she's settled in," the doctor promised.

"I'll be right here," Tate replied, leaning against the wall again. He felt more drained than he could ever remember being.

She wasn't doing him any good, hanging around here, Emma thought. But she could deflect some of the things he was responsible for doing.

"I'll go tell Villanueva you got Maddox," Emma said abruptly. Tate nodded, but she had a feeling that he really didn't hear her. She wished she could make him feel better, but she knew that only he could do that.

She gave his shoulder a squeeze. "She's going to be all right, Tate. Hannah's tougher than she looks. And when she comes to, tell her that we found her friend Mary Yoder and that she's all right. That should make her feel better," Emma told him with a smile.

"Yeah." His voice echoed in his head, hollow. Nothing was going to make any difference to him, wasn't going to matter to him, until he could see Hannah opening her eyes again.

* * *

Restless, Tate maintained a vigil by her bed. Though he knew he could do more good back in the field, tying up the myriad of loose ends taking Maddox down had created, he couldn't make himself go anywhere, do anything other than what he was doing.

Holding up a wall.

He belonged right here, waiting for some sign that Hannah was going to be rejoining the living.

"I'll spell you for a while," Emma offered the next day, popping her head into the room to see how both Tate and Hannah were faring. One was unconscious, the other might as well have been. She didn't know who her heart ached for more.

"Go, stretch your legs," she urged. "Get something to eat. Wash your face." She felt a sense of desperation as each suggestion seemed to fall on deaf ears.

Tate shook his head, rejecting her offer. "I'm fine," he told her stoically.

No, he wasn't, but she knew she couldn't argue with him about that. She'd only lose.

Emma tried another approach, one with a little humor laced through it. "I think the department has some kind of rule against wearing the same clothes for three days in a row." She nodded at the shirt and slacks he had on. She didn't have to ask if he'd changed his clothes, she *knew* he hadn't. "You don't want to smell gamy when she wakes up."

"*If* she wakes up," Tate corrected darkly.

"*When* she wakes up," Emma insisted firmly. "Tate, you have to have faith and believe."

He nodded, too tired to get into a discussion about it. All he knew was that he'd made his deal with God and Hannah still hadn't opened her eyes. How could a man go on believing after that?

Tate shifted in the plastic chair he'd pulled over to Hannah's bed eons ago. He'd lost track of how many days he'd been sitting there, watching Hannah. Keeping vigil. Emma brought him regular updates, as well as forcing him to eat the food she'd smuggled in. Sandwiches mostly, but she refused to leave until she saw him consume at least half of what she'd brought.

Tate tried to take solace in hearing that Maddox had been charged and jailed without any possibility of bail until his trial. The date wasn't set yet.

He knew that he should be happy to hear that the girls Maddox hadn't had murdered were all safely returned to their families and homes. For all intents and purposes, the case seemed to be all over except for the trial, which, a D.A. had assured Emma, was a slam dunk.

The upshot was that Maddox was going away for several lifetimes.

"It's over, Hannah. We got him. He's not going to hurt anyone ever again."

Holding Hannah's hand as he spoke, Tate felt as if his heart was breaking. It had been breaking over and over again these past few days and he wasn't sure just how much more he could take.

"Open your eyes, Hannah, please," he pleaded. "I miss your eyes and the way you looked at me. Like I mattered. Like you loved me."

Unable to hold back any longer, Tate laid his head on the sterile white hospital blanket and cried.

At first, when he felt the light pressure of a hand on

his head, he thought that Emma had returned and was trying to comfort him.

He didn't want comfort, he wanted Hannah to wake up. But if that couldn't happen, then he wanted to be left alone. Alone to share what would probably be the last moments he had with Hannah.

"You don't have to stay here with me," he said hoarsely, thinking he was talking to Emma.

"But I want to stay with you," the small, perplexed voice replied.

The second he heard her voice, Tate jerked his head up. He was afraid that his imagination had taken off again.

But when he looked, he saw Hannah looking back at him. Was he dreaming?

No, no, this was real.

He didn't know whether to laugh or cry. He did a little bit of both.

"Welcome back, stranger. You gave us quite a scare there." Almost giddy with relief, Tate pressed his lips against her hands, first one, then the other, kissing each in turn.

Hannah started to nod, but stopped and winced a little.

"My throat hurts." The moment she said that, she remembered. Fear entered her eyes as they moved about wildly—searching.

Tate instantly knew who she was looking for—and why there was fear in her eyes. "He's not here, Hannah. Maddox is in a prison cell. He's never going to hurt you again."

She seemed not to hear. In her weakened state, she only had enough strength for one thought at a time, one person at a time. And she needed to tell that person something.

"You found me," she said, her smile widening slowly. "I knew you'd find me."

His instincts had been right all along. If he'd waited for backup, he wouldn't be having this conversation with Hannah. She would have been dead.

He nodded in response to Hannah's simple words of gratitude.

"Sometimes things work out." He slipped his hand through hers and changed the subject. "The doctor said it was going to take a while, but you're going to be all right," he assured her. "Caleb's been by to see you every day. He's really been worried about your not waking up. He told Emma that he's going to stay in the city until he can take you home."

Home.

The word had been so comforting to her only a little while ago. It had been a goal she focused on to get her through her ordeal at the hotel. But now, what he'd just told her left her feeling very cold.

She looked at Tate, her heart in her throat. She'd lost years, she wasn't about to beat around the bush and lose another second of precious time.

"Do you want me to go home?" she asked in almost a hushed whisper, afraid that if she spoke any louder, her voice would crack.

"I want you to be happy," he told her. "And safe."

"You didn't answer my question," she insisted weakly. "Do you want me to go home?"

Had he not been so tired, so completely worn-out, he would have had the presence of mind to couch his words and proceed tactfully and slowly. And lie.

But he *was* tired and worn-out and in that state, he

said the first thing that came to him in response to her question.

"No. No," he repeated more strongly, discovering that the word felt right on his tongue even though he knew he should have focused on what was good for her. But he had to tell her what was in his heart. "I don't."

"Good," she whispered. "Because I don't want to go back. It's not home anymore, not like it used to be," she said, trying to find a way to explain what she was feeling.

Her eyes held his for a long moment as she searched for the right words. And then she finally just told him what was in her heart.

"You're my home now, Tate."

Nothing, he knew, would ever make him happier than what he'd just heard her say. But along with the happiness came a measure of guilt. Guilt because he knew that Hannah was very vulnerable right now and as much as he wanted her, as much as he'd discovered he loved her, he didn't want to take advantage of her like this. It wasn't fair or right.

"Hannah, I love you, but, honey, you are in no condition to make this kind of a life-altering decision right now."

He was wrong about that, she thought. Her condition, as he called it, had nothing to do with how she felt. She'd been grappling with this decision for a few days now—or at least the few days that had come before her last kidnapping. Tate had introduced her to a brand-new, wonderful world—two of them, actually. The one within his arms and the one that existed right outside those arms, out on the streets of the city.

"I won't be feeling differently tomorrow, or the day

after that. Or the day after that," she told him in a voice that was growing more firm by the moment.

He'd heard the trite line about eyes being the windows of the soul and in this case, he thought as he looked into hers, whoever had come up with that line was right. Because looking into her eyes told him that she believed what she was saying.

Still, he needed to hear it one last time. "You're sure about that?"

She nodded ever so slightly, her head still aching fiercely. "Just as sure as I am that I love you."

He didn't want her getting gratitude confused with love. He couldn't bear it if she realized the difference years later. "Because I rescued you—"

"Because your heart has spoken to mine," she corrected.

He couldn't bring himself to argue with her any longer. When she was better, and released from the hospital, enough time would have gone by for her to carefully think through her choice one last time. And when she came to the same conclusion and told him she was staying with him, *that* was when he intended to ask her to marry him.

And, he thought as he took her into his arms, she would say "yes."

He had a good feeling about this.

Epilogue

It was, truthfully, an oddly harmonious blending of people who were, for the most part, complete polar opposites: the peaceful Amish community was mingling with special agents from the Bureau and members of the Philadelphia P.D., as well as members of his family—extended and immediate.

It should have made for a bizarre sight.

And yet, somehow, it didn't.

In a strange way, it made perfect sense. They were all coming together to celebrate the recovery of the kidnapped girls—and to honor the memory of those who would never be back.

Tate glanced at the young woman next to him. He had a lot to be grateful for himself, a lot to celebrate. Having his family here just made it that much more significant.

Hannah's recovery—once she'd finally regained

consciousness—had been so quick, the attending physician at the hospital deemed it as close to a miracle as he'd ever witnessed. He pronounced her well enough to travel, which left the way clear for her to return to Paradise Ridge—not because she'd changed her mind, but because she was eager to see all her friends back where they belonged—and trying to regain the peace they had once known.

There was no way that Tate was going to let her go alone. After what he'd gone through to find her—and the hell he'd endured waiting for her to wake up again— he was *not* about to let her out of his sight for more than a couple of hours at a clip for the foreseeable future.

Hannah more than welcomed his company, eager to show him where she had grown up. It was, after all, the place that had made her the person she was now. The place that had formed the survivor that she had turned out to be.

They arrived just in time to take part in what turned out to be a combination of new and old: an old-fashioned barn raising with the celebration of what was considered to be an outsider tradition: Christmas.

Tate looked around for the typical signs of the holiday season and found none. "Do the Amish actually celebrate Christmas?" he asked Hannah, curious.

"Oh, yes, we do," Hannah assured him with enthusiasm. "I mean, we just don't have a Christmas tree or all those shiny decorations that outsiders tend to put such importance on, but we do honor the day."

His mouth curved. "About those 'shiny decorations we outsiders tend to put such importance on,' I seem to recall a certain young Amish woman being completely mesmerized by the giant Christmas tree she saw in Rockefeller Center," he whispered against her ear, reminding her of the occasion. The memory of her transfixed expression was one he was going to cherish for the rest of his life.

Rather than blush, as he expected her to, Hannah smiled broadly. "Who would not be mesmerized? It was such a beautiful thing to behold."

The area where they were, at a newlywed couple's farm, seemed to be filling up with more and more people. Taking Hannah's hand, he stepped to the side to get out of the way of several carpenters, bringing in the already crafted sides of what was to be everyone's project for the entire day.

"Do you exchange presents?" he asked her.

Hannah nodded. "Small ones. We give them to each other." She thought of the man she'd seen in the department store dressed as Santa Claus and the endless line of children waiting to sit on the man's wide lap and make their heart's desire known. "There is no jolly fat man to distribute them."

Tate nodded, doing his best to look serious. He failed. "Cutting out the middleman. Very economical of you," he teased.

Looking around the ever-growing gathering, he spotted Emma. With the case wrapped up, his sister was free to leave the Bureau, and she had. She was talking with Caleb. Her fiancé's three little girls were surrounding them.

Funny how his sister seemed to fit right into this life. If he hadn't known better, he would have said that she was born in this community.

There would be a wedding to attend soon, he thought.

Two, he amended silently—once Hannah set a date. He'd left picking a date up to her because he didn't want Hannah to feel that he was crowding her in any way.

Although she'd immediately said yes to him, he wanted her to be sure. Very sure. Sure that she not only wanted to marry him, but to be in his world as well.

Sure that she wanted to be with him.

But he wouldn't have been human if he didn't try to tip the scales a little in his favor. To that end, he'd bought a little insurance. He had it with him now and decided to give it to her before the "festivities" officially started.

Since that could be any second now, he put his hand into his jacket pocket and took out an envelope. He held it up before her.

She eyed it quizzically, then shifted that look to take him in as well. "What is this?"

"Only one way to find out," he told her with a smile, offering the envelope to her.

Taking it, she opened the envelope slowly. Hesitating because she didn't know exactly what to expect.

As she began to open it, he set her mind at ease a little by saying, "It's an early Christmas gift—although not that early," he amended, "given that Christmas is tomorrow."

A Christmas present. That meant it couldn't be anything bad, like a pretty card saying he had to go, or that he was taking back what he'd said to her in the hospital when she first woke up.

Tearing the paper away, she found herself looking down at a form that informed her she'd been enrolled in the Parsons School of Design for the purpose of obtaining a degree in fashion design.

It was like being in the middle of a double dream. Her dream prince was granting her fondest wish—to study professional fashion design.

Speechless for a moment, Hannah raised her eyes to his.

"Classes start the second week in January," he told her, suppressing his own excitement. "I thought you needed an outlet for all that designing talent of yours."

Thrilled, overwhelmed—no one had ever been this generous to her before—joy all but bursting out of her, Hannah threw her arms around his neck.

"I love you very, very much!" she cried.

He laughed. "If I knew it would get this kind of reaction, I would have enrolled you in that school a lot sooner." But he had to be completely honest with her. "I have to admit that I got the idea indirectly from Violet Chastain. I overheard her tell Mary Yoder that she'd pay for her schooling if Mary wanted to go to college. After everything that's happened," he said, referring to the actress's near-fatal stab wound when the woman had been left for dead while Maddox's men had kidnapped Mary, "Violet felt that Mary should have something good happening in her life as a result."

Hannah nodded, understanding. "Violet is a good person—just think, when her movie comes out, I'll be able to see it." The idea was incredibly exciting to her. She'd never seen a movie before. "And your sister Emma is equally as good." The immediate past forgotten, she was fairly beaming as she spoke. "Already Caleb is happier than I remember seeing him in a long, long time. His girls love Emma," she confided, pleased to be able to tell Tate something positive.

She was trying to make this easy for him, he thought. But there was no need. He was pleased Emma had found someone she loved so much.

"I know she'll be happy here," he told her, then added, "And you, I hope you'll be happy in my world.

I know I'm going to spend the rest of my life trying to make sure you are."

"No woman could ask for more," Hannah assured him with a smile.

Tate leaned in to kiss her, then stopped abruptly as he saw the sleek black limousine pulling up in the distance.

It looked suspiciously like the one that President Joseph Colton—a distant cousin of his late father's—traveled in.

But it couldn't be—

Could it?

"What is wrong?" Hannah asked, twisting around to see what had caught Tate's attention so completely.

"Is that—the president?"

Even as he asked, he had his answer as he watched a man dressed in a dark suit get out of the vehicle and open the rear passenger door. The president—wearing casual clothing—stepped out and looked around at the gathering.

A cluster of agents immediately surrounded him.

"At ease, boys," the president said with an easygoing laugh. "I'm among friends here."

Tate, with Hannah in tow, made his way toward the man he'd met perhaps a handful of times, predominantly before Joe had been elected to the highest office in the land. The Secret Service guard allowed him access—but kept watching him just in case.

"If you don't mind my asking, sir," Tate said to the president, "what are you doing here?"

"Well, I was just in the neighborhood," he replied, tongue in cheek, "and it occurred to me that I'd never been to an old-fashioned barn raising. Heard they were having one here. Didn't want to let the opportunity slip by." He rubbed his hands together as he looked around the gathering, then glanced down on the ground. The four sides were now placed at the ready, waiting to be pulled together and hammered into place to form the new barn. "Let's get to it, shall we?" the president suggested to the man who was his host.

Several of the Amish elders came now to extend their greetings and they took President Colton—as well as his Secret Service agents—under their wing.

As Tate, Hannah and his siblings all joined in, Tate looked over toward the leader of the free world and decided that this was going to be one for the history books—from start to glorious finish.

"I love happy endings," Hannah confided, whispering the words in his ear.

"But this isn't a happy ending," Tate corrected. When she looked at him, puzzled, he explained. "This is a happy beginning."

And it was.

He could tell he was right by the way Hannah smiled at him.

* * * * *

A sneaky peek at next month...

INTRIGUE...

BREATHTAKING ROMANTIC SUSPENSE

My wish list for next month's titles...

In stores from 19th April 2013:

❑ What She Saw – Rachel Lee

& Deadly Force – Beverly Long

❑ Operation Reunion – Justine Davis

& Protecting the Pregnant Princess – Lisa Childs

❑ A Rancher's Dangerous Affair – Jennifer Morey

& The Marshal's Witness – Lena Diaz

❑ Cowboy's Texas Rescue – Beth Cornelison

Available at WHSmith, Tesco, Asda, Eason, Amazon and Apple

Just can't wait?

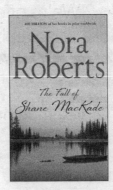

The World of Mills & Boon®

There's a Mills & Boon® series that's perfect for you. We publish ten series and, with new titles every month, you never have to wait long for your favourite to come along.

Blaze.
Scorching hot, sexy reads
4 new stories every month

By Request
Relive the romance with the best of the best
9 new stories every month

Cherish
Romance to melt the heart every time
12 new stories every month

Desire
Passionate and dramatic love stories
8 new stories every month